VOWS and VILLAINY

DARBY CUPID

VOWS & VILLAINY
Hands of Fate II

© 2022 Darby Cupid
ISBN: 978-180-068-176-7

All rights reserved.

Map Artwork © 2021 Darby Cupid
Cover Artwork © 2021 Emily Bowers Illustration
Character Artwork © 2021 @tonyviento (Instagram)
Cover Design © 2022 Tairelei

SILVER ARROW
PRESS

For the HoFST
Wings Up. Stand Tall.

Hehven

Liebe

Rakkaus

Caracy

The
Crossing

Dragoste

The Cliff

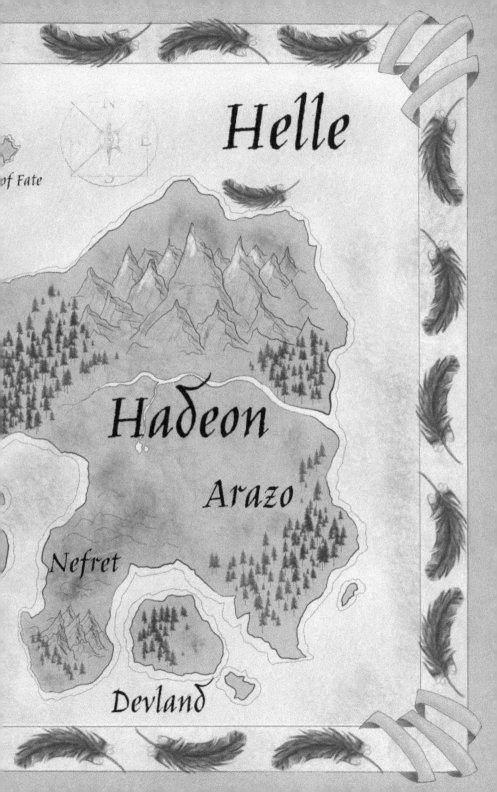

The Wendell Islands

Liridona

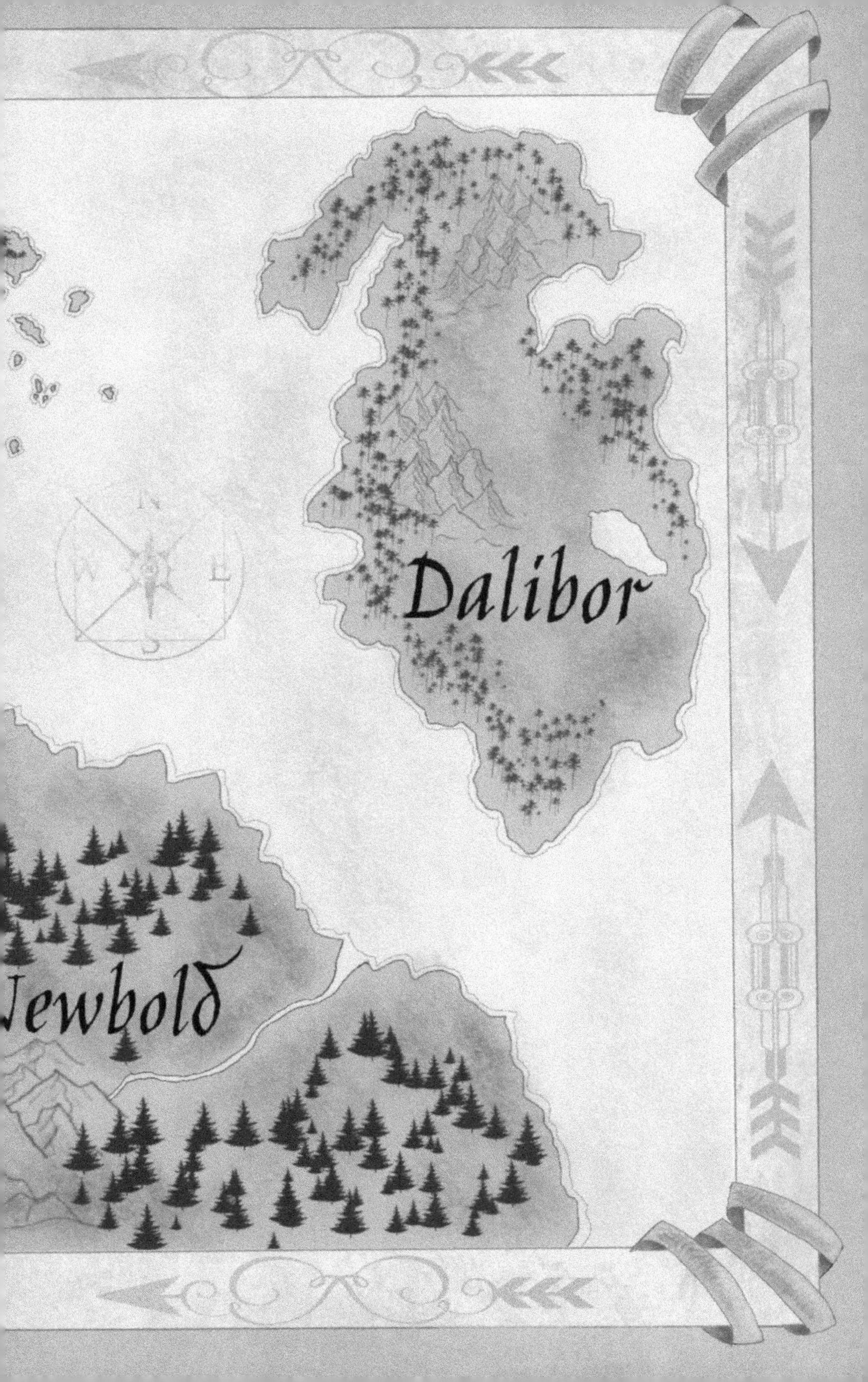

N
W
E
S
Dalibor
Jewbold

Nobody can escape destiny.

~ Plato

I
Sirain

Being officially declared the next queen of Helle had not made me any less fearful of death. Every shadow, every sudden noise, threatened a swift blade through my gut, and each meal reeked of bitter poison. I think Fin knew. His smirks and mirthful stares told me he was enjoying my fear more than anything he ever did to me himself.

Ever since my brother's whispered threat during my final Rite, I'd been waiting. Waiting to be summoned to the throne room. Waiting to be executed for being half-human. For having not a single drop of Hadeon blood running through my veins. The paranoia meant I barely slept, hardly ate. Perhaps that was how Fin planned on killing me—watching me slowly waste away to nothing. The Fates only knew there was no way I could wield a sword like I could a month ago.

I would have preferred my brother make an attempt on my life. At least then I would know. Instead, he had stepped back completely. He no longer cornered me in corridors; no longer forced his way into my rooms, his tongue slick with thinly veiled threats. Instead, he spent all his time with our father. Neither of them wasted breath acknowledging me. I'd expected more responsibilities—more work—after recovering from the blood loss of the final Rite, but both my father and brother all but ignored me.

Lifting a hand to dismiss the servant braiding my hair, I waited until the door closed before slumping forward onto the dressing table, my head on my folded arms. I was to meet the king in the throne room within the hour. My father rarely summoned me to meetings anymore, and my empty stomach slowly tied itself in knots. Would this be the day everything finally fell apart? Would today be the day I died?

Turning my head, I allowed my gaze to rest on the world outside my bedroom window. The lights of The Crossing were a mix of angry blues and purples, the white, cloud-filled sky vibrating with the reflected menace. I knew that if I walked over to the towering, arched window, I'd find the forests sweeping away to the horizon, a mix of rich golds and reds speckled with evergreens between. It was one of the reasons I didn't move closer. The sight of the pale golden leaves picked away at the barely healed scar tissue holding the battered pieces of my heart together.

The view had once filled me with such joy and wonder. How many times had I perched there, staring out at The Crossing, with excitement fizzing in my veins? How many sunsets had I waited for, before leaping from the wide, stone ledge to soar down the mountain and over the city towards . . .

I screwed my eyes shut and turned my head away. Those days were gone. Since completing the final Rite, watching my lifeblood gush from my arm in a steady, sickening stream, I could scarcely remember the last time I flew. Forcing myself to my feet, I lifted my chin, straightened my wings, and affixed a sneer to my face that rivalled my father's. Although, that was the problem. He wasn't my father. My attention flitted to the sparkling diadem of black diamonds in my hair. Everything about my life was a lie. Perhaps that would all end today.

Staring at the Chaos in the mirror, I wondered how it was possible I'd felt trapped before. I hadn't realised how much freedom I'd had until I'd been stripped of everything. My reflection looked like me. Paler. Thinner. Hardened. But still me. Just. What hurt the most was that she looked like me before. Before Pace.

Turning away from the mirror, I inwardly cursed myself for allowing his name to slip into my conscience. All it would do was bring me pain, and I had enough of that in my life already. Shaking my head, I stalked towards the door and wrenched it open. I was the next ruler of Helle. There was no time for wallowing in self-pity. Every morsel of energy I had needed to be spent on staying alert and alive.

As I stepped out into the living area of my rooms, Kwellen pushed himself off the wall and fell into step beside me. His tall, muscled frame dwarfed mine as we walked in silence, the only sound the soft clink of Kwellen's weapons. It had been a long time since I'd worn a blade between my wings or a dagger against my thigh. When we reached the bottom of the stairs, turning towards the dark corridor that would lead me to the throne room, he cleared his throat.

"Sirain, I know you said you didn't want to, but—"

"I still don't," I interrupted. "What would be the point?"

Kwellen shook his head, huffing in exasperation. "You only turn twenty once."

"Yes." I snorted. "And I already did. I was unconscious for the entirety of my birthday."

Placing his large hand on my arm, he gently pulled me to a stop. "You proved to your father and Fin—to everyone—that you have what it takes to rule. The Fates tested you and you succeeded. You won, Sirain. If you don't want to celebrate your birthday, at least celebrate that."

I stared up at him, searching his midnight-blue eyes for

some sign that he understood what he was asking of me. "I killed two people, almost lost a finger to frostbite, and nearly died from blood loss. Why in all that's Fated would I celebrate that?"

Kwellen groaned, pulling his hand over his face. "Look, I promised Odio I'd try. If you won't do it for yourself, at least do it for him."

I blinked, waiting for the punchline, and Kwellen shifted uncomfortably under my glare. After a minute, I turned and resumed my stride down the echoing corridor.

"Don't bother accompanying me," I called over my shoulder. "I'm fine."

His footsteps slowed to a halt, and a small twinge of guilt twisted in my chest. I stopped with a sigh. What if this was the last time I saw him? What if those were my final words?

My breath a solid mass in my chest, I turned. "I'll think about it, okay?"

Kwellen's answering smile was tight. With a brief nod, he turned and strode down the hallway, and I watched, my chest aching, until he was out of sight. I knew he was looking out for me, that he was trying to lift the dense fog of sadness and despair that had settled around me, but he was fighting a losing battle. It had been almost two months since the Royal Rites—since my birthday—and the Autumn Festival of the Fates was just around the corner. Just thinking about the Festival tightened my lungs. The Summer Festival seemed a lifetime ago, and it was a memory I'd locked away in an ironclad box. I couldn't let myself think about that night.

I'd considered telling Kwellen and Odio the truth so many times. That I was half human. That I wasn't a Hadeon. I knew in my heart they wouldn't turn away, that they'd help, but every time I tried, I just couldn't form the words. Especially when it came to Odio. I was certain the fact that we were no longer cousins—that I wasn't related to him by blood—would devastate him. He had so little family as it was.

"Sister!"

My head snapped up at the sound of Malin's voice. It was strange hearing the term without the usual coating of disdain. I'd kept my promise. Since recovering from the Royal Rites, I'd made the effort to spend time with my younger sister. I'd worried she wouldn't want to—that she'd be like Fin—but I'd been pleasantly surprised. The thought alone squeezed my stomach. She would turn seventeen before the end of the year and I was only just getting to know her.

"Malin," I replied, turning to greet her.

"Where are you going?" she asked, frowning at my formal attire. "Please tell me you're not going into one of those boring meetings?"

A small smile curved my lips. It was one of the only times I found myself a little lighter. Malin's blatant disinterest in politics, and her unapologetic opinion regarding anything she felt needed addressing, was refreshing, and often amusing. She was fearless, and everyone loved her for it. I was quite sure Malin had been suspicious when I first approached her, suggesting we spend time together. Not that I could fault her; I'd distanced myself from my family my entire life. Blaming Fin and my father would be easy, but I knew most of the responsibility rested on my own shoulders. Perhaps part of me had always known I was different.

"I'm afraid I am," I admitted. "Father is waiting for me."

She rolled her eyes and sighed. "I was hoping you'd accompany me into town. I ordered some new gowns from the dressmaker, and I wanted your opinion."

My smile widened. "I hardly think I'm qualified to give an opinion on dresses. I only wear what the servants force on me. I'd much rather be in my leathers."

Malin raised a dark eyebrow. "The dresses are for me. You're perfectly capable of telling me whether I look good or not."

"Are you trying to impress anyone in particular?" I asked, my lips twitching.

Malin's pale cheeks coloured, and she folded her arms across her chest. "What time will you be done?"

I shrugged. "I don't know. Father called the meeting but gave no other details."

"Fine. If you're not done by two, I'll find someone else to go with me."

I smiled and turned back towards the throne room. "I'm sure you'll have no problems replacing me, but if I'm finished, I'll find you."

"Sirain?"

Pausing, I turned around. "Yes?"

"Have you visited Mother today?"

My already knotted stomach twisted so violently, I grimaced in pain. "No. I was going to see her after Father finished with me." *If I'm still alive.* "Have you?"

Malin's smile faded, a weariness that a sixteen-year-old shouldn't have to bear settling across her shoulders. "I'm going now. I spoke to a healer this morning, though, and she said there's no change."

My teeth clamped down on the inside of my cheek as I nodded in response. There was no proof that Fin was responsible for the deep sleep our mother had fallen into since my final Rite, but I knew. Perhaps this was where I might have offered words of comfort, perhaps even an embrace. But we were Chaos, and emotions were weakness.

Instead, I gave her a brief nod and turned back towards my destination. The throne room doors were open, and I threw my shoulders back, drawing in a deep breath as I stepped through, my heart hammering in my throat. The dark space was completely and utterly silent. Was I late? Had I missed the meeting? Relief swirled with trepidation as I stood waiting in the empty throne room. The king liked spectacle. If I was to be executed, he would have been waiting on his throne, Fin at his side, and most likely, an audience gathered below. If I'd just missed the meeting, perhaps a punishment less permanent than death would be inflicted.

Bile rose in my throat as I stepped forward, my soft leather shoes making almost no sound on the polished stone. There was a meeting room to the side of the dais. Perhaps he was in there.

Making my way across the vast space, I tried, as I always did, not to look at the dais, but failed, just as I always did. The dark stone had always been marred with stains no amount of scrubbing could remove. Blood spilled from the many heads and wings my father had severed over the years. But now, one of those stains belonged to me.

I didn't remember falling. Odio had told me how Kwellen had dived forward with a cloth to stem the bleeding, while he'd stopped my head from smashing against the rock. The king had stood, watching, doing nothing. My hand had reached, trying to find something to halt my fall, and found the bowl filled with my blood. Now the largest stain on the dais was mine.

As I drew closer to the meeting room, the murmur of voices drifted through the dark wooden door left ajar. I was aware I should cough—should make some noise to announce my presence—but I didn't. Instead, I peered through the half-open door to find my father and brother deep in hushed conversation. I couldn't hear their words, but as I watched my father's mouth twist into a wicked smile, I knew whatever they were discussing was not good. Hands trembling, I pushed at the heavy door, announcing my presence.

"Father?" I called, forcing confidence into my voice. "Am I late?"

The king looked up, his burgundy eyes flitting over me

before turning away again, dismissing me. "No. It turns out I don't need you after all."

I stared at the back of his head, half-obscured by his immense black wings, unsure whether to feel relief or annoyance.

Fin turned, leaning against the iron-rimmed meeting table and folded his arms as he looked me over. "You don't look well, Sister. You should go to the kitchens and eat something."

My jaw clenched, my teeth creaking with the pressure. "A good idea, Brother."

His cruel mouth curved into a smile, and I turned to leave. As I did, I noticed the papers on the table. Parchment with gold lettering and another that looked like a letter, written in black.

"Goodbye, Sirain," my father said, his wings still to me.

Dipping a small curtsey, I turned and walked away. Had he really decided he didn't need me? Or had the entire meeting been a ruse to ruffle my feathers? Either option was equally plausible.

Gathering my skirts, I headed out of the throne room, making my way towards the kitchen. My brother was right. I hadn't eaten since yesterday afternoon. I hadn't eaten a full meal since my Rites. My diet consisted of apples and berries I foraged from the castle grounds and scraps from others' discarded meals. If Fin wanted to poison me, he'd have to poison everyone in the castle.

The kitchens were quiet, and I swept through, swiping crusts and half-eaten cake from the plates piled on the side for washing. If any of the kitchen staff saw what I was doing, they said nothing, their eyes averted, and their heads bowed until I left. It was almost laughable what I'd been reduced to. The future queen, sustaining herself on other Chaos' scraps.

Keeping to the shadows, I made my way towards my mother's rooms, hungrily gnawing at the stale crusts. I couldn't let them win. If I died, if my brother got his wings on the throne, it would all have been for nothing. Killing Dariel, Kreig, destroying Pace . . . I winced as I swallowed my food, a painful lump in my throat.

Standing outside of my mother's rooms, twice the size of my own, I brushed the crumbs from my dress and readied the façade of the future queen of Helle. A handful of servants were busying themselves tidying and dusting, but as I opened the door, they hastily dipped into deep curtseys and left.

As soon as I was sure I was alone, I made my way through the sprawling space filled with chairs, vases, and sculptures, and opened the door that led to the queen's bedchamber. My mother looked peaceful. Her onyx hair brushed and shiny, braided over her shoulder, a hint of pink on her pale cheeks. She didn't look ill. She didn't look like she was dying. She looked asleep. I was sure I looked worse.

I settled onto the red velvet stool at her side and took her limp hand in mine, swallowing the words I'd whispered to her a thousand times. *Why did you do this? Why didn't you run?*

What would my life have been like if she'd stayed in Liridona with Emeric Bickerstaff? What if I'd been born in the human world? Would the Fates have allowed it? Would the king? I closed my eyes. If his betrothed had run away, he would have sought her out. Every Hand would have been sent to look for her. There would have been no peace. No escape. Even though she wasn't awake to tell me, I knew it was the truth. Just as I was trapped, she had been, too. That knowledge didn't make it any easier, but then, nothing did. Nothing could.

Somewhere beyond the bedroom, a door opened, and I stilled as I listened to the heavy stomp of footsteps moving towards us. It wasn't Fin. Fin crept. I turned, surprised to find my cousin standing in the doorway.

"I've been looking for you," he said, his dark eyes flitting over his aunt before landing on me.

I sighed and turned back to my mother. "If it's about my birthday, I'm not in the mood."

Odio made his way around the bed and settled onto a chair on the other side, his long dark wings falling through the dipped gap as he rested an ankle on his knee. "It's not about your birthday. I've given up on that."

I raised an eyebrow. "Oh?"

Odio stared at me, his jaw tense and his eyes filled with an emotion I couldn't quite place. Concern? Doubt?

"What is it, Cousin?" I pressed.

He let out a long sigh. "The war has begun."

It took me a second to realise what he was talking about, but then a layer of ice settled over my skin. The humans. My father. My real father. Odio shifted, and I noticed he wasn't wearing his usual black leathers. Subtly different, hard black panels lined his chest and torso. Armour.

I swallowed. "How bad is it?"

"Bad."

My cousin had never been one for words, but a thousand questions lined up on my tongue. I needed to know more. I shouldn't—I shouldn't even care—but I did. Perhaps sensing my desperation, Odio uncrossed his legs and leaned forward, his voice dropping to a low whisper.

"I've just returned from orders in the Wendell Islands. The seas are filled with ships and the sky thick with smoke. My orders weren't on the main islands, but for one of the commanders on a ship. Even though I didn't get close to land, I could see things were not good. There were fires everywhere."

My eyes burned as my mind whirled. Was Liridona okay? Was Emeric okay? I knew Pace had wanted to help the humans. Had he found a way? Was he there amidst the fighting? I closed my eyes, exhaustion threatening to consume me.

A rustle of feathers sounded, followed by a strong hand on my shoulder. "Sirain? Are you all right?"

No. I was not. And I wasn't sure whether I ever would be again.

2
Pace

S weat trickled down my back as I strained, holding myself less than a foot off the ground, the tips of my wings brushing the whitewashed walls of my prison with every measured beat. With a grunted exhale, I allowed myself to drop to the floor, breathing hard. It may not technically be a prison, but it may as well have been. Ever since Tiesa had visited me, a herbal drink had been added to my meals, with a note informing me it would help with feather loss. I'd thrown the first two cups at the door.

When it became clear my brother wasn't going to be letting me out anytime soon, I'd moved the furniture to provide adequate room to spread my wings and get a few inches off the ground. It wasn't much, but it kept my muscles strong enough that I knew I'd still be able to fly when—if—Dashuri ever let me out. Tiesa had been to visit me twice, and both times I'd played my role. I knew Dash would ask her for details of our conversations, but he was yet to grace me with his presence. That was the most frustrating thing. I needed him to come and see me. I needed to convince him.

Standing in the middle of the room, my wings folded and my sweat cooling against my skin, I closed my eyes and calmed my breathing. It would be so easy to lose it. Being confined in a windowless room for several weeks was as close to torture as I could imagine. Every fibre of my being longed for a breeze, blue sky, the sun on my face . . . The isolation wasn't even the worst part. Being alone with my thoughts was so much worse, even more so than the lack of flying.

Over the last few weeks, I'd replayed every conversation, every action I'd taken since first entering the human world. Being locked away, it was almost possible to believe it had been a dream—that when I was finally let out, Dariel would still be alive. Sometimes I allowed myself the fantasy. We'd never visited the human world. The sequence of events that led to the death of my cousin and best friend had never been set in motion. I'd never met Sirain.

I blew out a slow breath. She was something I tried not to think about, but failed miserably each and every time. Haunting my dreams and slipping into my thoughts like rays of morning sunlight, I'd find myself longing for her, craving her, before remembering . . . Sometimes the memories were flashes; arrows striking a direct hit against my heart, so clear and sharp, they caused me to catch my breath. The scent of her skin, the soft curve of her hip as she lay beside me, the way the sun caught the amethyst strands in her hair, her laughter, the taste of her lips . . . I winced and closed my eyes. I'd risked everything for Sirain—I'd burned my world down—and she'd abandoned me. She'd stood on that beach and let me fall, knowing she was always going to walk away.

A knock sounded, and I opened my eyes. Another meal wasn't due for a while, and I stared at the door. If they were waiting for an invitation to my prison, they'd be waiting a long time.

"May I come in, Pace?"

My heart leapt even as my fists clenched at my brother's

deep, rumbling tones. "It's your prison, Brother," I called. "You're the one with the key, so surely you don't need my permission."

I could almost hear the answering eye roll through the thick wood. Grabbing my shirt from the chair, I slipped it on, tying it around my wings, as my brother unbolted the door and stepped inside.

His golden eyes flitted over me, his mouth bracketed, and his brow furrowed. "You look well, Brother."

I wasn't sure if he was impressed or disappointed, and my muscles twitched as I resisted the urge to fold my arms. "I've had a lot of time to reflect."

Dashuri nodded and closed the door behind him. I watched as he crossed the room, his navy-blue robes brushing the floor, before taking a seat on my bed. My heart thudded steadily in my chest. I'd waited for what felt like an eternity for this.

"Have you?" he asked, folding his hands in his lap. "Reflected?"

I pulled the chair from the desk and sat down, trying to keep my expression as neutral as I could. "Yes. I've done little else."

Dash nodded. "Would you care to share your findings?"

My jaw tensed at the familiar condescending tone, but I forced myself to relax. There was too much riding on this discussion for my pride to get in the way. "I understand why you needed to do this, Dashuri. I understand that what I did was wrong, and I want the opportunity to atone for my choices."

Dash stared at me, his face unreadable, so I took a deep breath and continued. "I think I was struggling to find my place. With you being heir, I felt my actions were not important. When our parents arranged my betrothal, I felt trapped, so I pushed even harder. I realise now that I should have spoken to

Mother and Father before things got out of control. I was reckless to travel to the human world. After what happened to Dariel, I understand that more than ever."

My gut twisted at the casual mention of my cousin's death. What would my brother say if he knew it was my fault? If he knew he'd been murdered by the female I'd given my heart to? I swallowed hard, wiping my clammy palms on my trousers.

"And what of the Fates?" Dash asked, his gaze so intense, I wondered whether he was trying to peer into my very soul.

"What of them, Brother?" I asked. "I have followed and respected the Fates my entire life. By visiting the human world, I was merely satisfying my curiosity. My intention was never to meddle with Fate."

Dashuri's jaw tightened. "Do you not think bedding a Chaos is meddling with Fate?"

My neck heated and I wiped my palms again. "I can only apologise for my actions. I know I'm a huge disappointment to you, but all I ask is that I be given the chance to redeem myself."

Dash sighed, the action making him look older than his twenty-five years. Perhaps some of that was my fault.

"If I let you out, how do I know you won't just fly straight back through The Crossing?"

Gathering up every scrap of pride I had left, tucking it away into the darkest corner of my soul, I moved from the chair and knelt at my brother's feet. "Dariel is dead. The Chaos betrayed me. Every action I took was a mistake. I see that now. I want to do better. Please allow me to prove myself to you."

I might have been only telling half the truth, but the thought that Dashuri might walk away and leave me in my prison had my eyes burning. I was so close to freedom I could taste it. What had happened in the world since I'd been locked away? My heart sped up as I wondered for the thousandth time whether Marlowe was okay. If anything had happened to him, I would never forgive myself. Ensuring his safety was the one thing I could do in Dariel's memory.

Dashuri stood, the gold embroidery of his robes brushing my fingers where they rested on my knees. "It will be a long road to regain my trust," he said. "If you stray again, please understand that I will not hesitate in telling Mother everything."

I looked up at him, plastering a grateful smile on my face as my heart slammed against my ribs. "Thank you, Brother. I won't let you down."

Dashuri stared down at me for a long minute, and I dared not breathe. The idea that my older brother was deciding whether to keep me locked up or set me free had my blood boiling, but I pushed down my rage. I was so close. So very close.

"I've told Mother and Father that you've been training in Liebe," he said, moving towards the door. "Please don't give them any reason to think I lied to them."

I got to my feet, swallowing the retort burning on my tongue. What would my parents say if they knew my brother had locked me up for weeks on end? They wouldn't be pleased, but when they found out the reasons why, it wouldn't matter.

"I won't," I promised.

Dash nodded, his eyes looking over me once more, as though he might find a lie pinned to my clothes or slotted between my feathers. "I've assigned a guard to you. They will inform me of your movements. Tomorrow morning, meet me at the palace and we will discuss your role."

"My role?" I echoed, deciding to let the fact that he'd assigned me a babysitter slide.

"Yes. The queen still expects you to take over from me, and things have changed since your detainment."

"How so?"

My brother tensed, indecision clear in the set of his jaw and the tightness in his shoulders. Worry flickered in my gut. What had happened that he would be so reluctant to tell me?

"War has broken out in the human world," he said carefully. "The Hands are busier than they have been in decades."

I frowned, my heart racing as I buried the news I'd been dreading deep down, where I would deal with it later. "I'll just have to work extra hard to catch up, then."

Dash opened the door and stepped to the side. "Don't let me down, Brother. Don't let the family down."

Every nerve was on fire as I stared at the open doorway, every muscle straining to run, to fly. I forced the feeling down, looked my brother in the eye and lied through my teeth. "I won't."

I stepped through into the hallway, almost in disbelief. Forcing my shoulders back, and holding my chin high, I eyed the two Hands who'd been standing guard outside my room. Had they been on guard before today? Had they heard me scream and curse in the early days of my confinement? Had they stood silently listening to me falling apart?

"This is Jacayal." Dashuri gestured to one of the two Hands. "He is to be your guard."

Tall and slim, with thick white curls that hung over his forehead, he looked to be about my age, and seemed vaguely familiar. I gave him a tight smile and he bowed in response.

"He'll keep his distance," Dash continued. "But until you've proven you can be trusted, consider him your shadow."

My skin heated at the reprimand, and I thought I might combust from the burning emotion I forced down my throat. More than anything, I wanted to get out of the palace. I needed air. Couldn't my brother tell I was drowning? Perhaps he could. He just didn't care.

The other Hand led the way down the corridor to the winding staircase, Dashuri just behind, and Jacayal already taking up his role as my shadow at the rear. My body tingled as I caught glimpses of light blue sky through the windows. I hadn't been sure what time of day it was.

It felt like an eternity to reach the courtyard, and the second the outer doors opened, the cool breeze rushing through, separating my feathers, I almost dropped to my knees.

I turned to Dashuri, expecting a warning look, but he gave me a small smile, his golden eyes filled with something I couldn't place.

"Go, Pace. Fly. Jacayal will watch."

I didn't need to be told twice. Four bounding strides into the courtyard and I snapped my wings open, leaping up into the air. Soaring high above the palace, I glided, stretching my wings —testing them. I could feel the difference with the feathers I'd lost, but I didn't care. There was too much to appreciate. Too much to be thankful for.

Rolling, diving, and swooping, I finally felt whole again. A whooping holler tore unwittingly from my lungs, and I howled with laughter at the sound of joy. My eyes burned as I flipped onto my back and basked in the delicate warmth of the sun. I was surprised to see the trees had started to turn their many shades of red and gold, the season further along than I'd expected. The Autumn Festival must be soon. Maybe I'd missed it. I had no way of knowing.

There were many things I didn't know. Like the fact that war had broken out in the human world. Whether Marlowe, Cove and Shanti were still alive. Whether Lord Bickerstaff was still alive. How long had the war been raging? How bad was it?

My gaze fell on the shimmering blue-green lights of The Crossing, but I didn't allow myself to linger. I couldn't afford to give it a second glance. Not when Jacayal was watching me from the courtyard, wings spread, ready to chase me down or report back to my brother if I put one feather out of line. No. The Crossing was something I couldn't consider. What I needed was to get to the Isle of the Fates. I needed to find a way to speak to Amare and get hold of the books she'd told Dariel were kept there.

What I needed were answers. But I needed to be more careful than ever about how I got them.

3
Sirain

The daylight had faded past the muted greys of twilight and into the cold quietness of night by the time I rose, stiff and weary, from my mother's bedside. I wasn't sure how long had passed since Odio left. He'd tolerated the silence for as long as he could before muttering about going to get something to eat. It took all my strength, both mental and physical, to stand—to leave.

Malin must have found someone else to accompany her to the city. I swallowed down my guilt. Such a large part of me wanted to give up. To curl up beside my mother and waste away alongside her. Not because I missed her, which carried its own guilt-laden burden, but because it was easier. The coward's way out. To keep going was hard and I hated that I found it so.

Pulling her bedchamber door open, I cast a final glance over my shoulder at her slumbering figure, even paler than usual in the caress of moonlight streaming through the window. No one knew why she wouldn't wake. Not a single Chaos healer could find the reason or a cure. I wondered whether the Cupids would know.

The servants hadn't returned while I'd remained at my mother's bedside. Or, if they had, I hadn't heard or seen them. Either way, no lamps had been lit, leaving the queen's outer rooms a maze of shadows coloured black and white by the moon.

"She's still alive, then?"

I straightened with a violent jolt, whimpering in pain as my pulse galloped, and my brother melted out of the shadows.

"No thanks to you," I hissed, closing the door behind me. "What did you do to her?"

Fin's dark eyebrows rose. "Why would you think I have anything to do with our darling mother's condition?"

My heart climbed into my throat, rage simmering as I took a step forward. Perhaps it was the exhaustion, the temptation to give up, that pushed me away from the door. Maybe I thought it would be easier if Fin followed through on his promise. My eyes dipped to his hands, half expecting to find a blade there. He tracked the movement and his grin widened.

"Oh, I'm not here to kill you, Sirain."

My fingers twitched at my side, my feathers rustling. "Why are you here, then?"

"Am I not allowed to check on the Chaos who brought me into this world?"

The grinding of my teeth was almost audible as I stared him down. "We both know that's not why you're here."

Fin stepped forward, closing the gap between us in a matter of strides, until he was close enough I could feel his breath on my face. "You know nothing about me, Sister. But I"—he chuckled softly—"I know everything about you."

I was suddenly reminded of the time he'd let himself into my rooms and I'd held a knife to his throat. If I had a blade on me now, I was sure it would have been lodged somewhere in his smug face already.

"You know nothing!" I hissed, straightening to my full height.

Fin's answering laugh was too loud for the empty, moonlit rooms. The rage that had been lingering in the dark recesses of my chest, coiling like a snake waiting to strike, burst from me with a snarl, and I shoved my brother as hard as I could.

His eyes widened, and he stumbled backwards, his black and burgundy wings flaring as he caught his balance. All too soon, the shock melted from his face, twisting into something far more dangerous. It took everything I had not to outwardly flinch as he came at me, eyes blazing. Inside, I baulked in horror.

"You filthy half-breed!" he screeched, spittle flying from his thin lips. "How dare you touch me!"

Blood roared in my ears and my fingers clenched at my side, my wings tensed. In all his eighteen years of existence, I had never once witnessed so much as a crack in my brother's cool, hard demeanour. Disgust and anger twisted his features beyond recognition as he raised his hand to strike me.

My body moved of its own accord, years of training and muscle memory causing me to duck, sliding out from between him and the door and into the open living room. He turned with a snarl, rounding on me again, too fast. My body may have remembered being a warrior, but a diet of half-stale crumbs and paranoia had depleted my strength and stamina to the point of rendering me near helpless.

When he pulled a dagger from his belt, I staggered backwards, my wings sending a vase crashing to the floor. Fin's boots ground the porcelain shards into the stone as he stalked towards me.

"I thought you weren't going to kill me," I said, despising the trembling note vibrating through my words as I edged backwards.

The cruel curl of Fin's lip was almost identical to my father. No. Not my father. *His* father.

"Who said I was going to kill you?" he hissed. "Death would be too kind a punishment for a disgusting half-breed like you."

He lashed out with the dagger, and I tucked my wings in,

twisting out of the way and slamming into a shelf, half concealed in shadow. Ornaments and trinkets clattered to the ground in a deafening cacophony, bouncing and shattering on the stone floor. Eyes wide, I stared up at my younger brother. His sneer twisted into a grin, dark eyes wild, as he licked his lips, turning the dagger in his hand.

My heart dropped to my stomach. I couldn't win this. Even as I searched the wreckage at my feet for a shard of something large enough to defend myself, I knew. He knew it, too.

Just as he lifted his hand to strike again, a crunch sounded behind me. I froze, watching, as the maniacal grin melted from the sharp angles of Fin's face, his gaze drawn up to something —someone—over my shoulder.

"Sheath your weapon."

Kwellen's rumbling tones bit through the shadows and my knees almost gave way with relief. My wings flared as I stumbled, but a strong hand gripped my waist, steadying me.

"She attacked me," Fin snapped. "I was defending myself."

My eyes widened in disbelief as my brother faded from terrifying to pouting teenager. If I hadn't been fearing for my life, I would have laughed.

Kwellen snorted. "Put that pathetic blade away and get out of here."

My brother's grip tightened on the dagger, his pale knuckles turning luminous in the darkened room. He stared up at Kwellen, his jaw working, and his eyes narrowed, and I wondered whether he would actually try to attack him.

At my side, Kwellen was a mass of stone. Unmoving and silent, the only sound from him was his steady breathing. Just as the tension became too much to bear, Fin let out a frustrated growl and stormed from the room, knocking his shoulder into Kwellen on his way past. It didn't have the desired effect, as my enormous friend barely moved and Fin stumbled. I watched my brother disappear into the shadows, waiting until the slam of the door echoed, before releasing my breath.

Carefully picking my way over the shards of glass and porcelain, I eased onto a chaise longue and rested my head in my hands, my blood still screaming in my veins.

"Sirain."

I exhaled into my palms; my eyes tightly shut. Kwellen had been my best friend for almost my entire life. I didn't need to look at him to read the unspoken question in that single word. Every muscle tensed, the pounding of my heart so ferocious, I trembled.

"Sirain."

"What?" I asked, through my hands. "Are you waiting for a thank you?"

Kwellen huffed a long sigh, and after a second, I felt his large hand on my knees. I peered through the gaps in my fingers to find him crouched before me, his dark feathers draped across the debris.

"Sirain," he tried again, his voice gentler than I'd ever heard it. "Why was your sweat stain of a brother calling you a half-breed?"

I closed my eyes. "Sticks and stones. You know how he is."

"Look, I've ignored this for too long. Odio and I thought perhaps you were just heartbroken after what happened with that Cupid, so we gave you space. But it's more than that, isn't it?"

I pressed my face harder into my hands. "Nice to know you and my cousin have been discussing me behind my back. How does one get an invitation to one of these tea parties?"

"Sirain." This time, the word was little more than a growl.

I looked up, my face hot and clammy. "What?"

Even crouched at my feet, I still had to tilt my head a little to meet his eyes. I didn't like what I found there. Not just concern, but pity. It made me feel weak. I hated it.

24

"What do you want me to tell you?" I bit out.

"Everything."

The laugh that left my lips was cold and empty, echoing around the dark space. "You're safer if you don't know."

Kwellen's dark brows creased, his eyes narrowing. "Let me decide whether I want to be safe or not."

"I can't."

"Don't you trust me?"

I laughed again. "This has nothing to do with trust."

"Oh, really? Because the only way you telling me will get me hurt is if I tell someone else, and you know I would take a blade through the heart before doing that."

I winced at his words, but Kwellen reached up and took my chin between his thumb and forefinger, tipping my face towards him.

"I would die for you, Sirain. You're my best friend. My family." His dark eyes burned. "Let me help you. Please."

Turning my head, his hand fell away, and I drew in a shaky breath. "Like I said, this has nothing to do with trust. If I tell you, you'll never look at me the same way again."

Kwellen pushed himself up off the floor and perched beside me. "You're wrong," he said. "That's everything to do with trust. You have to trust that there's nothing you could say that would make me walk away from you. Surely, you know that?"

I shook my head slowly, not in answer, but as the weight of what he was asking of me rolled around my skull like a spiked metal ball. "You can't tell anyone."

Kwellen tensed beside me. "You know me better than that, Sirain."

"I don't even know where to begin."

His hand reached out, clasping mine. "The beginning."

"My mother fell in love with a human."

"What?"

I looked up, almost smiling at the look of confusion and

awe on his chiselled face. "Before I was born, she went through The Crossing and fell in love with a human."

Kwellen scrubbed his hand over his face. "The queen was never a Hand."

"I'm not a Hand, either. Neither are you," I pointed out wryly.

"Okay," he said slowly. "So, the queen falls in love with a human. What does that have to do with him calling you . . ."

I watched as the pieces slotted together. Watched as his eyes widened, flitting from my face to my wings and back again.

"No," he breathed.

Turning to look at my mother's closed bedroom door, I nodded. "Yes. My father is human. I'm not a Hadeon and I have no claim to the throne."

Kwellen muttered a slew of curses vile enough that I raised an eyebrow. "How in all that's Fated did Fin find out? Does the king know?"

I raised my eyebrows. "Do you think I would be sitting here if the king knew? And Fin knows because he overheard me accusing my mother after I found out."

Kwellen pinched the bridge of his nose. "How did you find out?"

"I met him."

"The human? What? When?" He dropped his hand, his frown returning. "It was during one of your solo visits with the Cupid, wasn't it?"

My heart twisted as I nodded in answer. I'd had an hour with Pace at that party, and it had been one of the happiest hours of my life. One of my biggest regrets was leaving him to look for Emeric's office.

"You should have told me," he said, his voice soft.

"My whole life is a lie. I'm a lie. I'm not a Chaos. I'm nothing."

Kwellen's growl cut me off. "Stop it. You are a Chaos. You're the toughest Chaos in Helle. Don't you dare talk like that."

My eyes burned. "I'm not a Hadeon. I'm not related to Odio. He—"

"Won't care," Kwellen snapped. "I'm not related to you. Blood means nothing. You think that because you don't share the same blood as his Fateforsaken father, he's going to care about you less?"

I winced at the harsh edge to my friend's tone, and he sighed, reaching out and brushing his knuckles against my cheek.

"This changes nothing, Sirain. You need to tell Odio."

I gave the smallest of nods, the idea of doing what he was asking altogether too much to process in that moment.

"What I don't understand is why Fin hasn't told the king." Kwellen mumbled, more to himself than to me.

"I don't know," I admitted. "He told me during my final Rite that he was going to kill me. I'm also fairly certain he's responsible for my mother's current condition. I think he poisoned her."

Kwellen swore again under his breath. "Is that why you're not eating?"

My head shot up in surprise. I thought I'd hidden my paranoia well, but clearly, I'd underestimated my friend.

"I thought it was heartbreak," he said softly. "I was planning on speaking to you about it this evening. To tell you that enough was enough. It's why I came looking for you."

We sat in silence, Kwellen's thoughts as loud as my heartbeat while I allowed him time to work through my revelation.

"I still don't understand why Fin hasn't told his father." He shook his head, running his hand through his hair. "If he wanted you dead, that would be the way to do it. Even after completing the Rites, the king wouldn't allow you to take the throne. He'd find a way to get rid of you quietly."

"Thanks, friend." I huffed a laugh. "I'm sorry I didn't confide in you sooner."

"There's something we're missing." Kwellen tucked his long, dark hair behind his ear and turned to face me once more. "Who is it?"

"Who's what?"

"You know exactly what I mean," he said. "Who is your father, Sirain?"

I shook my head. "It might be better if you don't know."

"Too late. Tell me."

Holding his intense stare, I ran through all the pros and cons of revealing my father's identity, but before I could reach a decision, Kwellen sucked in a deep breath.

"There's something you should know."

I frowned. "What?"

"The Fates gave some unusual orders today," he explained. "Odio told me this morning. I was going to tell you tonight to see what you thought of it."

My stomach squirmed, slowly tying itself in knots. "What do you mean 'unusual' orders?"

Kwellen's jaw clenched, and he straightened. "Orders like the ones you were given for the Royal Rites."

The blood drained from my face, and I shivered as though a chill had settled in the room. "The Fates have ordered someone's death?"

Kwellen nodded.

"Who?"

"The ruler of Liridona. Lord Bickerstaff."

I was on my feet before I could think, glass sinking into the soles of my thin leather shoes. I didn't care. Shock and despair swirled into rage as I stared down at Kwellen in disbelief.

"They can't do that," I hissed. "Since when did the Fates start ordering deaths? We alter emotions; we don't murder people."

Kwellen stood, gripping my shoulders, his eyes darting amongst the shadows. "For Fate's sake, Sirain. Keep your voice down."

"Why?" I snapped. "You think the Fates will order my death, too? This is wrong. You see that, right?"

Kwellen took a deep breath, looking over his shoulder at the doors to my mother's chambers as though expecting to find my father's guards marching in to drag us to the dungeons. "Yes," he whispered. "But you need to be quiet."

A pained moan built in my chest, but I pressed my lips together and turned away.

"It's him, isn't it?" Kwellen sighed. "Bickerstaff is your father."

I closed my eyes. "How did you know?"

"Besides your reaction to the orders?" Kwellen snorted softly. "A gut feeling. There was something weirdly familiar about him."

Pulling my hands over my face, I turned to face him. "Do you think that's why the orders have been given?"

He shook his head. "Maybe it's nothing to do with you. He's the ruler of a country. It might be logistical."

"I can't let this happen," I said, a quiet calm settling over me. "We have to warn him."

Kwellen's eyes bulged. "You can't be serious, Sirain. Not only is there not a chance in Helle you'd be able to sneak through The Crossing, you're talking about actively going against the Fates."

I snorted. "Maybe it's Fated that I go against the Fates."

"You're delirious. The lack of food is clouding your judgement."

My fingers clenched into fists at my sides. "If I can't warn him, I need you or Odio to do it. Even if you can't get to Liridona, perhaps you could tell Marlowe or his sister. They could warn him instead."

Kwellen turned away, shaking his head. "You're asking too much."

"Am I?" I said, stepping up behind him. "If his death is Fated, it will happen whether I interfere or not, right? I didn't kill Marlowe and nothing's happened, has it? Maybe me trying to kill him was Fated, but Dariel's death was the intended outcome."

Kwellen's shoulders sagged. "I'll speak to Odio. See if we can get a message to him somehow."

A pang of relief settled in my chest. "Thank you."

"Don't thank me yet," he said. "There's a chance we're already too late."

I may as well have been sliced by Fin's blade. As we left my mother's chambers and made our way through the castle, it took everything I had to hold the flayed pieces of myself together. I'd been so angry with Bickerstaff—with my mother —but I hadn't decided whether I wanted him out of my life. Now, the choice was being made for me, and I wasn't prepared to let that happen without a fight.

4
Pace

Freedom was harder than I'd thought. In my room—my prison—I'd been alone with my thoughts. So removed from reality, Dariel's death had begun to seem like a bad dream. Out in the world, there was no escaping it. Over the last few days, his laugh had sounded around corners, glimpses of his face lurking in crowds. I saw his death in my mother's eyes and in the set of my father's shoulders.

A day after my release, I discovered the reason for Dashuri's change of heart. The Autumn Festival of Fates. There was no way my parents would have allowed me to miss the Festival, and no excuse Dashuri could have made on my behalf. My eyes flitted to the cracked section of the doorframe around my front door. It had taken every ounce of self-control not to release my anger on Dashuri's face.

Just as my brother had said, my parents believed I'd been training in the far northwest of Hehven. If they'd noticed my patchy wings or slightly paler pallor, they didn't show it. Perhaps having me gone for a while had been a relief to them. I gripped the edge of the wooden dining table and sucked in a breath. I'd never forgive my brother.

Although it had been wonderful to fall asleep in my own bed, nightmares had plagued my sleep. Endless dreams of being back in the castle behind a locked door, screaming and banging against the wood until my hands were little more than bloodied stumps. I dragged a hand over my face with a shiver.

When I wasn't dreaming about being trapped, I lay awake thinking about Dariel. There had been several times, usually during the middle of the night, when I'd almost flown to his home in the mountains, just to look through his window, to check that it was real. Then I would remember that I wasn't as free as it seemed, and even that small trip wasn't a possibility.

Even though Jacayal took shifts with other Hands at night, he was everywhere I turned. To his credit, he kept his distance as much as he could, but his presence was a constant reminder that my freedom was little more than an illusion.

Pushing away from the table, I strode to the front door of my cottage and pulled it open, looking around until I found him leaning against a tree at the water's edge. "Do you want some breakfast?"

Jacayal turned, his hazel eyes wide in surprise. "Thank you, Your Majesty, but I shouldn't."

"You should," I said, stepping back and gesturing towards my kitchen. "You'll need your strength if you're going to be following me all day."

Still unsure, he gave a small nod and pushed off the tree. I left the door open and set about placing plates of bread and cheese on the table, along with the last of the fresh fruit Tiesa had left in my cupboards, along with a note welcoming me home.

A smile played on my lips as I recalled how she'd only just restrained herself from tackling me to the ground when she met me back at my cottage that first night. I hadn't seen her so excited since we were smallwings. Jacayal had given us privacy to talk, but I don't think Tiesa had been prepared for what I wanted to talk about.

She'd confirmed the human war, and begrudgingly

answered my questions, after I assured her I wouldn't be venturing near The Crossing ever again. Then, when she'd told me she was headed on a mission that following morning, I'd thrown caution to the wind and asked her to check in on Marlowe. To my complete shock, she'd agreed. Of course, she'd said she would only do it if she had a mission in that area. That was days ago. I'd been waiting for news ever since.

"You don't have to do this, Your Majesty," Jacayal said, shifting from foot to foot as he looked over the plates of food.

Grinning, I gestured to an empty stool. "Please, have a seat, Jacayal. If you are to be with me every passing hour for the fore-seeable future, it makes sense to get to know one another." And earn your trust.

"You can call me Jac, Your Majesty," he said, offering a tentative smile.

I took the seat opposite him and leaned my arms on the table. "Okay, Jac. Then you must call me, Pace."

His hazel eyes widened, his light brown skin reddening. "I couldn't, Your Majesty."

I shook my head and started placing food onto my plate. "Well, if you ever change your mind, I really do prefer it."

Jac nodded, his eyes still wide. "Okay, Pa—" He shook his head. "No. I can't do it, Your Majesty."

A laugh rumbled from my chest, and I popped a piece of cheese in my mouth, considering him as I chewed. When I'd been freed, I'd thought him a similar age to me, but now, after watching him and noting his mannerisms, I decided he must be younger. Not by much, but a little. My eyes went to the golden Hand markings on his brow.

"How long have you been a Hand, Jac?"

"This is my fourth season," he answered, his shoulders straightening.

I considered his answer as he tentatively bit into a piece of bread. Hands finished their training at seventeen, which meant he must be eighteen or thereabouts. It was strange that Dash wouldn't place someone older as my guard. Why trust someone so new to the role?

"Do you like being a Hand?" I asked.

He nodded. "Very much so. Although, the newer Hands aren't getting many orders due to the war."

I raised my eyebrows. "How so?"

"The captains are sending the more experienced Hands to carry out orders," he explained. "We're to undergo extra training, both in combat and emergency healing measures, before we're allowed."

"I imagine war is quite dangerous," I said, hoping the uneasiness swirling in my gut wasn't visible on my face. "It's a good idea to be better prepared."

"It's not just the war," Jac said, taking a sip of water. "After what happened to Dariel, things have . . ."

His words trailed off, his eyes moving to where my fist had closed around the piece of bread I was holding. I swallowed, releasing the mutilated chunk onto my plate as my pulse skittered erratically.

"I'm sorry," Jac stammered. "I didn't mean—"

"It's fine," I said, dusting the crumbs from my hands. "I'm glad measures are being taken to prevent it from happening again."

The lie was ice against my tongue. What happened to Dariel had nothing to do with the humans. At least, not in the way the captains thought.

"I trained with him a few times," Jac said quietly. "He was an excellent captain and Hand."

I swallowed; my gaze fixed on my plate. "The best."

We ate the rest of our breakfast in silence. Perhaps Jac found it uncomfortable, but I was too lost in my own thoughts to care. Each day, I would spend most of my time at the palace, getting back up to speed with Dash's role. I listened, I recited, and helped as much as I could, hoping against hope I could earn a sliver of my brother's trust. My wings itched at the thought of getting to the Isle of the Fates and closer to my answers.

"Have you heard what time my brother wishes to meet with us today?" I asked.

Jac nodded. "We need to leave within the hour, Your Majesty."

I tried not to roll my eyes at the formality. It seemed it wouldn't be going away anytime soon.

The front door to my cottage burst open and I leapt to my feet; Jac doing the same, his sword singing free from its scabbard.

"Pace!" Tiesa's green eyes widened, her mouth falling open as she stared at us. "Sorry."

"At ease, Jac." I sank back down onto my chair with a chuckle. "It seems knocking is no longer required between friends."

Tiesa's eyes narrowed as she moved to close the door behind her.

"Wait," Jac said, sheathing his sword. "I'll give you two some privacy. I'll let you know when it's time to go, Your Majesty."

I nodded my thanks, smirking as he sidestepped past Tiesa and out of the front door, closing it behind him.

"He's adorable," Tiesa whispered, slipping onto Jac's vacated stool.

I raised an eyebrow. "You're welcome to him."

"No, thank you." She snorted. "You are more than enough trouble on your own." Before I could retort, she leaned forward on the table, her voice dropping lower. "I visited the Wendell Islands."

My heart leapt into my throat, and I glanced out of the window before looking back at my friend. "How? It's barely midmorning."

She shrugged. "I went at dawn. My orders were near the main island, so it didn't take long."

"And? How is Marlowe?" I leaned towards her, simultaneously craving and dreading her answer. In all that was Fated, I needed the young ruler of the Wendell Islands to be alive.

"Marlowe is well," she said, a knowing smile on her lips as I sagged in relief. "As are Cove and Shanti. The war is mostly at sea and in Liridona so far, from what I can tell. Only the outer islands seem to have been affected."

I closed my eyes, a long sigh warming my clasped hands as I hung my head in relief. "Thank you, Tiesa. Thank you."

She reached out and placed a hand over mine, waiting until I looked up. "There's more."

"What is it?" I searched her face for answers, finding nothing comforting in the line between her brows and the slight narrowing of her eyes.

"Odio visited them."

My eyes widened as I waited for my friend to tell me she was joking, or perhaps for my brain to register that I'd misheard. "Odio?" I repeated.

Tiesa nodded. "Apparently, he just showed up, knocking on their balcony a few days ago."

My mind reeled. "Why? What purpose could he possibly have to speak to them?"

The last time I'd seen Sirain's cousin, he was dragging her off Marlowe's ship after she'd murdered Dariel. My fingers moved to the small scar on my neck from his blade as he'd prevented me from stopping her.

"He was delivering a message," Tiesa said, her voice so quiet I had to lean closer to hear. "The Fates have ordered another death."

Bile rose in my throat, and I choked it down, shaking my head. "No. That's impossible."

Tiesa sighed. "It seems they're questioning it as well. It's why he was warning Marlowe."

My heart stuttered. "No. It's not—"

"It's not for Marlowe," Tiesa said. "It's Lord Bickerstaff."

I stared at my friend as her words sank in. This was wrong. So very wrong. I'd never heard of the Fates ordering deaths before Sirain's orders, and now it was happening again. But then, I hadn't known that the Chaos had Royal Rites either. Were the Fates giving kill orders to Cupids? The thought sent a violent shiver down my spine. No. Cupids were not killers. That was all Chaos.

"Why?" I managed, my voice little more than a rasp.

Tiesa shook her head. "Only the Fates know. You know that."

I almost laughed, before remembering my newly reformed Fate-abiding self, and swallowed it down. I wondered whether Sirain had confided to her friends that Emeric was her father. Perhaps that's why the Fates had ordered his death. Why would she warn Marlowe, though? The thought had my jaw clenching. She'd been happy enough to turn up with an arrow for him, but when it was her own flesh and blood, it appeared she'd go against the Fates to intervene.

I was vaguely aware of Tiesa talking, but I couldn't drag myself out of the spiralling pull of my thoughts. What would it mean for the war if Emeric was killed? As much as I remained annoyed with him for what happened at Plumataria, I considered him a friend, and I didn't want him to come to any harm. Perhaps he was already dead. If the orders were days old, it didn't seem likely that he would still be alive.

Did Dash know the Fates were giving the Chaos orders to kill? There was no way I could ask him without finding myself locked back in that room, and there was no way in Hehven that was ever happening again.

"Pace?" Tiesa's face swam into view. "Are you okay? You're shaking."

Pushing back my stool, I stood and moved to the window, the sky outside reassuring as I sucked in deep breaths, my heart hammering in my chest.

Tiesa's hand gently gripped my shoulder. "I'm so sorry, Pace."

I glanced at her out of the corner of my eye. "For what?"

"Your brother. He should never have locked you up. I begged him every day almost the entire time you were in there to let you out. I told him you wouldn't be the same." She shook her head, her voice hardening. "He said that wouldn't be a bad thing."

"I'm fine," I said, aware of how weak the words sounded.

"You're not. And that's okay. No one would be after being isolated for so long. I know Dashuri is a pain, but I had no idea he was capable of being so cruel."

I sighed, pushing my hair out of my eyes. It needed cutting. "He thought he was doing the right thing."

"Are you honestly defending him?" Tiesa asked, leaning against the wall so she could see my face.

I shrugged. "I don't know. A little. I made some dangerous choices. He did what he thought was best. He could have told my parents."

"Maybe that would have been better. I considered telling the queen what Dash had done so many times." She looked away. "I'm so sorry I couldn't get you out of there sooner."

A knock on the door halted my response, and I glanced at the door before turning back to my friend.

"Will you keep an eye on them for me?" I whispered, holding her pale green gaze.

"The humans?"

I nodded.

Tiesa sighed. "I'm not going to talk to them."

"You don't have to talk to them," I said. "Just keep me updated. I need to know they're okay. If you have orders for nearby . . . ?"

She stared at me for a long moment before nodding. "If I'm nearby."

I gave her a grateful smile and she rolled her eyes.

"Your Majesty?" Jac called. "It's time to go."

5
Sirain

"**Y**ou look a little better."

I paused in my pacing and squinted at my best friend. "Excuse me?"

Kwellen rolled his eyes from where he was sitting on his bed, before returning his attention to flipping a short blade over and over in his hand. "I was trying to be nice."

"Yeah, well, don't. It's disconcerting."

He snorted, and a smile tugged at the corners of my mouth as I resumed the path I was circling in front of the window. I knew he was right. Since confiding in him a week ago, I felt infinitely better. Kwellen had taken it upon himself to personally fetch me food from the kitchen three times a day, which I relentlessly teased him for, despite my gratitude. Already, I could feel my strength returning—a bounce in my step I'd forgotten I could muster. He'd also insisted on sleeping in my room. I'd put up the feeblest of fights as he commanded the servants to put a bed together in the corner of my room. His snoring could wake the dead, but I had to admit, I slept so much more soundly knowing he was there.

Odio had taken the news as Kwellen had; the anger and disbelief at Fin's actions overshadowing any feelings of disappointment towards my lineage. My cousin had also been more than willing to visit the humans and warn Emeric.

I paused in my pacing once more and gripped the wide window ledge, the smooth stone cold against my palms. When Odio had tried to deliver his warning, he'd returned, saying he couldn't get to Liridona. There were too many Chaos carrying out their orders amongst the ships resting in the seas, paused in their battles for the night. Instead, he'd travelled to the Wendell Islands, where the battle was yet to reach the innermost islands, and delivered the warning to Marlowe. It wasn't ideal, but it would have to do. Last night, he'd had a mission in the Midnight Queen's land, Dalibor, so he'd promised to try again.

"He's fine," Kwellen said, causing my fingers to tense against the stone. "You know that, right?"

In answer, I glared at the sun rising over the horizon. Odio was an excellent Hand. Ruthless, quick, and little more than a shadow. He'd never delivered orders during a war before, though, and I'd added another layer of danger by asking him to check on my father. My shoulders stiffened at the term.

Bickerstaff should be dead. The orders were given a week ago. But then, Marlowe's orders had been given months ago and he was still very much alive. I screwed my eyes shut as my thoughts pounded against the inside of my skull. Why hadn't the Fates reissued orders for Marlowe's death? Had Dariel been the real target all along? Would the Fates order a Cupid's death? What would that mean? I winced as my head throbbed painfully. I wasn't sure what would happen if the king discovered Marlowe was still alive. If I managed to convince him he'd made a miraculous recovery, would he send me to finish the job?

Even though I couldn't see it from my window, I opened my eyes and looked in the direction of the far-off isle. Who were these beings that they should have so much power? Was every single decision Fated? Was my decision to tell Odio and Kwellen the truth Fated? Had Pace and I been Fated?

A shiver ran down my spine, my wings trembling. Part of me was certain of it. The chances of us running into each other so many times in the human lands and then finding each other on that cliff. . . Yet, if it had been Fated, why? Why put us through so much pain for nothing? The king and my brother knew nothing of the Cupid prince. The only effects it had wreaked upon my life were the devastated remnants of my barely beating heart.

At the sound of wings, I looked up, my throat tight as I searched the skies. The king and my brother hadn't attempted to enter my room since I passed the Rites, but the sound still set me on edge.

"Out of the way, Cousin," Odio called as he descended.

I stepped back into my room, exhaling in relief, as he glided through my window, a mass of black feathers and armour.

"Told you," Kwellen said, stabbing his blade into the small wooden table beside his bed.

I shot him a glare before turning my attention to my cousin, giving him a once over.

"I'm fine, Sirain," he said, squeezing my arm as he shook out his wings before tucking them in. "It'll take more than a few humans to get rid of me."

"It would seem so." I watched as he swiped a piece of fruit left over from my breakfast and perched on my bed. "How is the war?"

He grimaced. "Bloody. I thought Chaos were ruthless. It's not pretty down there."

I raised an eyebrow at his turn of phrase. I'd never considered the human world as 'up' or 'down' before. "Did you speak to anyone?"

Odio shook his head. "I'm sorry, Cousin. Liridona is still

unreachable and when I went to the Wendell Islands, Marlowe wasn't there."

My stomach tightened. Was it done? Was Emeric dead? Which Hand had delivered the arrow? Odio had said, after his first trip, that orders were being given out faster than Hands could deliver them. I pictured the night sky, filled with midnight-clad Chaos delivering arrows to the warriors fighting below.

I frowned. "If you can't get to Liridona because of all the Chaos, maybe we need to go when there aren't any."

Kwellen barked a laugh. "There are so many problems with that suggestion, I don't even know where to start."

"Yeah," Odio scoffed, tossing his apple core onto the plate. "If you're suggesting going through The Crossing during the day, you must still be addled from the blood loss."

"It's the 'we' part that I'm worried about," Kwellen said, leaning forward and resting his arm on his leg. "There's no way you can travel through The Crossing, Sirain. You realise that, right?"

Ignoring him, I turned and stared out at the shimmering lights—a mix of pale purple and pink at that moment. "I thought that after I passed the Rites, I would be tied up in meetings and escorted around the clock." I huffed a laugh. "I thought I'd be Queen."

"You are," Odio said slowly. "As soon as the king decides he can no longer rule, you—"

"Do you want to know how many meetings I've attended since I recovered from the final Rite?"

My two friends stared at me, their dark eyes wide and eyebrows raised.

"Two," I finished, not bothering to wait for a response. "Recently, the king has taken to inviting me to meetings and then sending me away again. I don't know what game he and my brother are playing, but it's as though they've decided I'm not worth worrying about."

My cousin's expression hardened. "I wish you'd just let me kill Fin."

"If anything, we should be thanking him," I said, earning an incredulous look from my friends. "He thinks he's broken me—made me weak. No one is concerned about me, no one is looking at me. Between Fin and Malin holding their courts, I honestly think no one will notice if we sneak through The Crossing."

"You're not going through The Crossing." Kwellen sighed. "And during the day, too? You could be killed."

I raised my eyebrows. "I could be killed here. Fin would have done so already if you hadn't stopped him."

Shame filled me at the thought, but I pushed it away. I'd not seen my loathsome brother since, so as far as he knew, I was holed up in my room, weak and powerless.

Odio shared a glance with Kwellen. "Is this about that Cupid—"

"No," I snapped. "This is about Emeric."

"Are you sure?"

"How can you even ask that?" I stalked across the room, stopping in front of my friend, and shoving his shoulders. "I murdered his cousin. Do either of you honestly think he'd ever want to see me again? The kindest thing I can do for Pace is stay out of his life."

Kwellen stood with a grimace, forcing me to step back. "Fine. But you need to be honest with us, Sirain. Things might have worked out differently if you'd just told us what was going on from the start."

I knew he was talking about more than what happened with Fin at the final Rite. Was he right? Would things have worked out differently if I'd told them I was visiting the human world to meet with Pace on an almost daily basis? I pressed my lips together, my blood heating. I'd been raised as the crown princess, which meant I'd been told since birth that I shouldered the responsibility of Helle. When I'd discovered the truth about my father, the burden my mother had placed upon my shoulders in an attempt to save us both, I'd shouldered that responsibility, too.

Being queen meant making difficult decisions. I'd been told that since before I could walk. When the king had handed me the details of my first Rite, I'd added it to the existing weight dragging me down, doing what needed to be done to survive. For Helle.

"Wait," Odio said, looking between us. "Did Kwellen just agree to this? Are we going to the human world during the day?"

I frowned. "Did you?"

He shrugged his broad shoulders, tucking a strand of his long, dark hair behind his ear. "I've known you forever, Sirain. You're going whether I agree or not. At least if we go together, the chances of you being killed are a little slimmer."

Odio clapped his hands together, his garnet-flecked eyes gleaming. "So, when are we going?"

"Time is of the essence." Kwellen peered out of my window. "We have to be prepared for the fact that he's already dead."

"Today, then?" Odio pressed.

I looked at Kwellen to find him nodding. "Now. While the humans are still preparing for another day of battle."

My heart lodged itself in my throat. "Now?"

"You wanted to go and check on your father," Kwellen answered with a shrug. "Let's go check on your father."

I winced at the term, still at odds with the idea of the unusual human's blood running through my veins. "Okay. Let's do it."

6
Pace

Soaring over the forests to the northernmost reaches of Hehven, I flexed my fingers, allowing the cool currents to flow between the digits. As I marvelled at the rush of feeling the air filtering through my feathers, filling my lungs, I knew I would never again take the open sky for granted. It was hard to keep the excitement off my face. For the past few days, my work with Dash had taken place at the palace, however, it transpired that the workload brought on by the human war was becoming an issue, so today, we would travel to the Isle of the Fates.

As the mist-soaked island rose from the pewter sea on the horizon, I rubbed my sternum as though I might dislodge the lump of anxiety building there.

"Are you looking forward to the Festival tomorrow, Your Majesty?" Jac asked from where he was flying alongside me.

I swallowed, the lump solidifying and moving up into my throat. "Sure."

"I can't believe it's Autumn already," my guard continued. "I swear the Summer Festival was just yesterday."

My eyes drifted closed briefly as I sucked in a tight breath. "Feels like a lifetime ago to me."

It wasn't a lie. My mind reeled as I thought of how things

had changed since meeting Sirain—or Thorn—at the cliff during the Spring Festival. I wouldn't allow myself to think of the Summer. Instead, I banked slightly to the left, climbing higher so I could see the sprawling hills and fields of Rakkaus in the distance. How was Caitland doing, I wondered. Perhaps she was to be married soon, now she was free of me.

"Did I say something wrong?"

I turned my head to look at Jac and forced a smile. "Not at all. I'm just not as enamoured by the Festivals as most are."

Jac nodded, a small frown on his face as he considered my words. Over the last couple of days, he'd relaxed around me a little more. We'd chatted and laughed, and I'd noticed that he would give me more space when he could. I was lucky; I realised. My brother's choice of babysitter was excellent. For me.

The chill in the air was noticeable as we moved out over the cliffs and across the open sea. Casting my gaze over the infamous island, I suppressed a shudder. With every wingbeat closer, the mists thinned, and as I laid eyes on the Temple of the Fates for the first time, my breath caught in my throat. It was so much bigger than I'd imagined. Jagged spires of silvered rock pierced the sky, but smoothed as they reached the ground, forming an archway framed by two vast stone wings. As we dropped to the ground, I stared up at the intricately carved feathers, each one longer than I was tall. I had to crane my head back to see the top of each wing; the size causing my mouth to hang open.

"It's impressive, isn't it?"

I started at the sound of my brother's voice, snapping my mouth shut as he landed beside me, shaking out his wings. "It's intimidating."

A deep chuckle rumbled in his throat, and he squinted up at the enormous entryway as his accompanying Hands shook out their wings. "It's supposed to be. It's where every decision that has shaped the human world has been made. If you don't feel small and insignificant standing before this, you need to rethink your place in this world."

I nodded; my teeth clenched. Somewhere within this temple were the beings who'd given the orders to kill Marlowe and Emeric. The beings who hid away in this foreboding cavern and played with our lives. I regretted so many of the decisions I'd made over the last few months, but standing at the entrance, my heart slamming against my ribs, it all felt right.

"Come on," Dash said, folding his wings and marching up the slick, grey stone steps, his two Hands on either side.

With a final shudder, I shook the residue from my own wings and followed. The silence was deafening. Footsteps and the occasional drip of moisture to the stone floor were the only sounds as we stepped beneath the stone wings. Windows were carved high in the walls; small, jagged slats that sent streams of pale silver light cascading down across the worn narrow path. My breathing quickened as we descended further into the temple, the beams of light becoming fewer and further between.

"Are you okay, Your Majesty?" Jac whispered.

The sound of his voice jolted me, and I cast him a quick, reassuring smile. "Yes. Just cold."

His answering frown told me he didn't believe me, but that wasn't my problem. I fixed my eyes on my brother's retreating wings, focusing on measuring my breaths. I'd never been bothered by enclosed spaces before. Never been affected by the dark. My jaw tightened as I watched Dashuri stride forward, his head high. Would he even care that he'd damaged something deep inside me by locking me up? I shook my head. It didn't matter. It was just another broken part of me I'd learn to live with.

Slowly, the narrow pathway widened until we stood in a large circular space, the sound of our breathing echoing against the cavernous walls. Large stone doors were set into the walls, each one carved with letters and symbols I couldn't quite make out. I arched an eyebrow at Jac, but he lifted a shoulder in response, his own eyes wide as he took in the space.

Just as I took a breath to clear my throat, one door heaved open, the groaning scream of stone on stone far too loud in the reverent silence. My hand moved to my hip in reflex, but found nothing there. Dash had confiscated my sword when he imprisoned me, and I hadn't thought to ask for it back. After all, what need did I have for a weapon when I was tamed and leashed?

Two figures stepped through into the dimly lit space, their white wings luminous, almost glittering, in the trickling rays of light cast down from above. Dark cloaks hid their faces in shadow, the thick, rough material brushing the ground as they approached. The Fated. The Cupids dedicated to serving as the link between the Fates and Captains.

"Your Majesty." The two figures spoke as one, sending a shiver down my spine, rippling to the ends of my feathers.

"Greetings," Dashuri said, inclining his head a fraction.

If I'd been waiting for a conversation, I would have been sorely disappointed. As one, the Fated turned and heaved open one of the other three doors. One stepped through, while the other stood to the side, waiting.

Dashuri turned to me, his golden eyes narrowed. "No one is allowed beyond the atrium besides the Fated and those with royal blood."

I raised an eyebrow, hearing Jac shift beside me.

"Jacayal and the others will wait here," Dash continued. "Refreshments will be brought for them, but we will not be staying very long."

I smiled an apology at Jac, disappointment clear in his hazel eyes, before following my brother through the gaping void beyond the stone door.

It heaved shut behind us, enclosing us in darkness, and I

closed my eyes, curling my fingers against my palms, trying to calm my pounding heart. The sounds of breathing, rustling feathers, and cloth on stone echoed around the space until the quiet roar of flame broke through. Opening my eyes, I blinked at the sudden brightness illuminating the corridor. One of the Fated had lit a torch, already continuing down the path in silence. The flame licked at the towering walls, sending shadows bending and dancing across the rock.

I frowned, watching the hooded Cupids. Could one of these silent, mysterious guides be Dariel's sister? A chill swept through me as I wondered, would she even be allowed to speak to me? It hadn't occurred to me that Dariel could ask her about the books because of his royal blood. His wings had borne the same royal golden tint as mine. He would have been allowed to visit his sister, but it had probably helped that he was a Captain of Fate, too. My heart twisted and I lifted my hand, rubbing my chest as though it might soothe the sharp ache.

Amare had been there at Dariel's final flight, but I hadn't spoken to her. We'd embraced briefly, but I hadn't been able to bring myself to stay longer than a few seconds in the presence of Dariel's family. The guilt had been too much and the pain too raw.

The Fated slowed, and I realised we'd reached yet another door. Unlike the previous ones, this was much smaller and crafted from wood. Questions filled my head, leaking onto my tongue, but I swallowed them down. Were there Chaos on the other side of the door? Did the Chaos enter the temple the same way? Did the Chaos Fated work with the Cupid Fated?

My many, many questions halted, however, as the Fated gripped the door and hauled it open with near-silent ease. Dash stepped forward, and it took me a second to follow, my breath halting in my throat.

"Hurry up, Brother," Dash said, a hint of amusement bleeding through his annoyance. "We haven't got all day."

Nodding, I stepped through into the enormous space. I wasn't sure what I'd expected, but it wasn't what lay before me. Unlike everywhere else I'd seen so far, the space was brightly lit by dozens of sconces. Enough golden light filled the dome-like room, that it felt warm and homely despite being roughly hewn from rock. Tables lined the walls, piled high with parchment, quills, and ink. Dozens of Fated moved about the space, some with hoods up and others with them around their shoulders. Each of them, male or female, had their heads closely shaved, a single golden circle marking their brow. All of them had white wings. Not a single black feather in sight.

I followed my brother as he strode through the room, watching with fascination as the Fated murmured to each other, voices low, as one would expect in a sacred space. I hadn't realised there were so many of them. As we moved across the echoing chamber, I frowned at a familiar sound. It only took me a second to find its source. A slow, rippling river ran along the far wall of the room, each end leading into a tunnel of gaping darkness. I suppressed yet another shudder and wondered whether the Fated were given a tour before they chose this life.

"Dash?"

My eyebrows rocketed at the sound of a female's voice uttering the nickname I relentlessly inflicted upon my brother, rising further still as a Fated gathered up his hands and squeezed them before letting go.

"Amare," my brother said, his voice tight as he addressed our cousin. "How are you?"

She bowed her head and dropped his hands. "I'm well, Your Majesty."

I didn't miss the teasing lilt to the way she said his title, and I pressed my lips together as I watched the exchange with silent glee.

"I hope it's not too much of an inconvenience, but I've

brought Pace with me." Dash gestured in my direction, and I straightened, trying not to frown at his burdened tone.

"Pace?" Amare turned to me, lifting her head just enough for me to see her blue eyes widen beneath the shadows of her hood. "It's so good to see you."

She gathered up my hands, squeezing them between hers in the same way she had my brother's, but all I could do was stare. I'd forgotten. She was so like Dariel. My throat burned, but I forced a smile.

"I thought I was the only one who called him Dash."

A flustered grumble came from my brother's direction, and Amare chuckled gently. My chest tightened at the sound. I was glad she could still laugh. Dariel's sister was often in my thoughts, the guilt suffocating.

"You forget, Pace," she explained. "I'm a year older than Dash. We grew up together, much as you and my brother did."

I tried to hide the flinch as her words sucked the air from my lungs.

"Of course," she continued. "When I took the oath to become Fated, our paths diverged."

Dash grumbled something under his breath, and I pressed my lips together. I had never seen him so flustered.

Amare leaned forward and whispered in my ear. "I think he's glad of that."

"We have business to attend to," my brother said, folding his arms across his chest. "I thought Pace could help with your problem."

Amare studied him for a moment before looking back at me. "Sure."

She gestured to a small door I hadn't noticed, set into the rock, and turned, leading the way over. Inside was a smaller version of the main room, with two large wooden desks filling the space, each piled high with scraps and rolls of parchment.

"It's not usually this overwhelming," Amare said. Closing

the door behind her, she took hold of her hood, lowering it to her shoulders, her hair a thin layer of silver against her brown skin. She gestured at the tables with a sigh. "The war has changed everything."

Tearing my attention away from my cousin, I stepped further into the room, picking up a piece of paper, knowing already what I'd find.

Noxon Smithe. Enstanton, Liridona.

Orders. From the Fates.

"These are the completed orders," Amare said, coming to stand at my side. "We record them, then burn them."

My mind scrambled around the new information. "How do you know they were carried out successfully?"

Amare raised her eyebrows. "The Hands only return them to their captains once they are completed. The captains bring them here when they come to collect new orders."

I opened my mouth to ask how anyone could be sure they'd been carried out, but my brother stepped up to my other side, speaking before I could utter a word.

"Trust, Pace," he said quietly. "Hands do not question the orders given to them by the Fates. They carry them out without hesitation."

I swallowed, my neck heating at the fact that Dashuri knew me so well. "Why am I here?"

"There's a record keeper, but she's extremely old," Amare answered, examining an order before placing it back down. "She's only able to work a couple of hours a day, and we're not sure she'll be able to do that much longer."

"There's usually enough work for just one person," Dashuri explained, running his fingers over one of the piles. "Perhaps sometimes two. We were unprepared for how quickly the human war would affect us."

My eyes widened as I took in the heaped tables, noting the stacks piling up underneath, too. "This will take hours."

Dashuri clapped a hand on my back. "And that's why you're here. I will come and check on you later, but I must go and meet with the Fated."

I watched, speechless, as my brother swept out of the room without another word.

"Don't worry," Amare said, opening a large book and dragging forward the small glass pot of ink. "You're not expected to finish everything. It's straightforward. You just copy the order into the book and then put the paper in the chute."

"Chute?" I echoed.

In answer, Amare gestured to a small hole beneath the desk. I peered down, feeling a gust of warmth against my skin.

"It leads to the fire pits below. They not only incinerate the completed orders but heat the rooms. Incredibly useful as the weather cools."

I nodded, the tips of my ears burning as I took a seat behind the desk and picked up the quill. Dash must have been beside himself when he thought up this task for me. Something menial—degrading for a prince—in a secure room, miles away from anyone and anything. I sucked in a deep breath and tried to loosen my grip on the long, golden feathered quill.

"What if I make a mistake?" I said, frowning at the rows and rows of neat, cursive letters on the page.

When Amare didn't answer, I looked up and found her staring at a spot somewhere on the wall. I knew that look.

Reaching out, I placed a hand on top of hers. "I miss him, too."

Amare's eyes refocused, and she smiled down at me. "I still can't believe he's gone. Whenever the captains come to receive their orders, I expect to see him. Every single time."

I winced as my heart contracted painfully. There were no words I could say to ease her pain. I certainly hadn't found any to ease my own, so I just nodded.

"Oh, that reminds me," Amare said, her brow creasing into

a frown that severed the golden circle on her skin. "The last time I saw Dariel, he told me you were brushing up on your history. He wanted me to try to get some books for you."

My pulse quickened. I'd wanted to ask, but hadn't known how to bring it up. "That's right," I confirmed. "Did you manage to find any?"

"It was rather strange, actually," she said. "I spoke to the record keeper because I thought she'd be the best person to ask. She's almost ninety, so she would know."

I raised an eyebrow. "Ninety?"

"I know. She's a tough old boot. We've been trying to talk her into retiring for years." Amare shook her head, a small smile on her lips. "Anyway, she said there was a library where all the old books were kept."

"And?"

"And it's not there." Amare pursed her lips. "The space is there, but it's empty. Just a room filled with bare shelves."

My heart sank. "Thank you for trying."

"Oh, that's not all," she said, her blue eyes sparkling. "I told the record keeper this and she was outraged. She said that no one should have touched the books without permission. Whose permission she thought they needed I don't know."

Leaning forward on the table, I bit down on the inside of my cheek, my pulse quickening in anticipation.

"She said she'd been meaning to go to the library for years," Amare continued. "It turns out she had a couple of books she'd borrowed and never got round to returning. She initially put it off because the library is down a lot of stairs and she has trouble with her hips, but then over time, she just forgot about them."

My heart paused. "History books?"

Amare nodded, her eyes glittering with amusement. "More than twenty years, Pace. She'd been meaning to return the books for over twenty years!"

A laugh burst from me, too loud for the small room. "Please tell me she gave them to you?"

"Of course. I have them in my room." Her smile slipped, the light in her eyes dimming. "I was going to give them to Dariel the next time I saw him."

I sighed. "I'm so sorry."

"It's not your fault he's gone, Pace," she said, patting my shoulder, unaware of my inward wince. "I'll fetch the books for you."

"Could you not tell Dash?" I blurted, causing her to raise her eyebrows. My neck heated. "I'd like to surprise him. Show him I'm going above and beyond and all that."

Amare rolled her eyes as she pulled the dark hood back up over her head. "Fine. I'll try and sneak them to you before you leave."

I thanked her, waiting until she'd closed the door behind her, before sagging onto the table, my head in my hands. Any anger I'd felt at Dash for deeming this task a suitable way to keep me occupied dissipated as I realised the opportunity it had presented. I was on the Isle of the Fates, and I was going to get my hands on books that might just have answers I so desperately needed. Sucking in a deep breath, I straightened my shoulders and grabbed the quill.

7
Sirain

S ome would probably call it a death wish. The sad truth of the matter was, I was dying either way. If I was going to die, I would rather be shot out of the sky by a human arrow than slowly wasting away in the shadows, becoming a ghost of the person I used to be. Besides, it was hard to consider my actions as reckless when I felt so free.

Closing my eyes, I inhaled the cool autumn air as we soared high over the sprawling forests towards The Crossing. With the Festival tomorrow, it was even less likely that anyone would notice I was missing. My lip curled in a sneer. Fin was likely already drunk, testing the wines and liquor.

"Are you sure about this?" Kwellen called.

I opened my eyes and dipped, riding a crosswind towards the shimmering lights. "Not at all."

Odio's laugh carried to me on the wind. "What's there to be sure about? We've done this a thousand times."

I shot him a look he almost certainly couldn't see from where he was swooping below me. We might have travelled through The Crossing many times before, but never in the middle of a war, and certainly never with the weight of finding out whether my father was still alive hanging over us. I swallowed hard, my pulse a thrumming warning in my throat.

Kwellen scoffed. "We have most certainly not done this a thousand times."

I threw him a smile that showed too many teeth. "Today's as good as any other day to die."

"Well, I can't say I'm thrilled about that attitude."

Before I could reply, the dense lights of The Crossing swallowed me whole and I closed my eyes, losing myself in the nothingness, allowing it to carry me towards the human world. Towards Liridona.

I wasn't sure what I had expected of war, but as we emerged from The Crossing, I recoiled at the sight before me. I thought I'd seen the human seas in every variant of their savage beauty. From rolling pewter waves and calm crystalline turquoise sheets, to roaring icy maws large enough to swallow a ship. Yet I had never seen them like this.

Smoke lingered in the air, twisting between dozens of ships scattered across the water. Smouldering sails flicked embers into the dawn light as half sunken hulls bobbed listlessly. The smell of death was heavy on the breeze, and my eyes widened as I flapped my wings, turning to take the scene in fully.

"They're preparing for another day of battle," Odio said, nodding towards the fleet of ships behind us. "They're from Newbold and Dalibor. Do you see the flags?"

I squinted, just able to make out dark grey flags on some of the ships, although most bore a black flag dotted with stars. When I turned back to the wreckages before us, I noted few dark flags. Most were green or blue. "This is not good."

"Come on," Kwellen muttered. "The sun is barely over the horizon, but that doesn't mean we're safe. Cupids will be here any second."

My heart skittered at the mention of the white-winged beings, and I found myself staring up at The Crossing, as though expecting them to emerge. As though Pace might materialise from the lights.

"Come on," Odio called.

Dragging my eyes from the shimmering green ripples, I bowed my head and sped after my friends.

A far less impressive armada clung to the Liridonan coast. We soared over the damaged ships, occasionally spotting humans fixing rigging or patching sails. Weariness and helplessness rippled from them in waves. I supposed it made sense. The Chaos Hands would have been firing at them all night. At least the Cupids would come with hope today. Although, I knew they would share that hope equally between the four lands. The Fates didn't choose sides.

As we flew inland, I expected the signs of war to diminish. But as the charred skeletons of houses and ransacked villages passed beneath us, my stomach churned. This wasn't war. It was decimation. Silence settled over us as we soared above the muddied fields and scattered clusters of tents. Pace had wanted to avoid this. He'd wanted to help. I clenched my teeth as I recalled Marlowe's words the first time I'd spied on them. You would leave us all to die. From the sight below, I could only assume Pace and his friends hadn't found a way to help.

A slew of curses drew me from my spiralling thoughts, and I shot Kwellen a questioning look. When he didn't respond, I followed his narrowed gaze to the horizon, and any hope I'd been cradling within the recesses of my mangled heart flickered out like a candle in the wind.

Black smoke billowed from Emeric's manor, lingering in the air like a tattered blanket. I beat my wings faster, riding the currents, my heart pounding as I looked between the small licks of flame eating at the outer recesses, and the crumbling walls. It had been such an impressive estate, but now it was barely more than rubble.

"Fated Fates," Odio breathed as he drew level with me. "The orders were to kill him, not to destroy every trace of him."

My head snapped to him. "You think Chaos did this?"

"I don't know." He frowned, dipping lower. "It might just be a coincidence. Let's go and find out."

I opened my mouth to protest that someone might see, but tearing my attention away from the devastation, I realised there was no one around. Not a soul could be seen on the grounds that had been thrumming with life the last time I'd visited. A lump settled in my throat as I recalled the last time I'd flown towards Emeric's mansion.

Sucking in a steadying breath, I followed my cousin, surveying the damage as I came into land. The fountain that had once gleamed in the pristine courtyard was splintered, the winged statues in pieces, scattered across the courtyard. The wide steps leading to the gilded front doors were shattered and folding in on themselves. I folded my wings, staring up at the charred walls of the mansion, the ransacked rooms and smoke-stained walls inside visible even from a distance.

Gravel crunched at my side, accompanied by a heavy sigh. "I'm sorry."

"The odds were never good," I said, shooting Kwellen a sideways glance. "It's been days since the orders were given. I just wasn't expecting..."

His jaw tightened as he watched Odio pick across the rubble. "I doubt this is the work of Chaos. It's likely just the result of human war. He might even have left before this happened."

Even as the flicker of hope kindled in my chest, I extinguished it. Hope was a cruel and dangerous thing. Hope wound itself around your heart, seeping into your bloodstream, leading to nothing but reckless decisions and heartbreak. "I've known you for over a decade, and never once have you been so optimistic."

Kwellen opened his mouth to retort, but Odio's shout stopped him before he could utter a word.

"Stay back! There's someone here!"

Eyes wide, I stepped forward to see. If it was a human, we definitely shouldn't reveal ourselves, but perhaps they knew something. Hope reared its traitorous head, fluttering dangerously beneath my ribs. Kwellen thrust out his hand, as though ready to hold me back, and I shoved it aside.

"It's a looter," Odio called.

I peered around the wreckage of the fountain, my eyes widening as I found my cousin holding a human male off the ground by his shirt.

"What is he doing?" I hissed.

Kwellen's frown deepened as he shook his head. "Being a demon. Likely no one will believe the human if he's stupid enough to tell anyone."

My fingers gripped the stone wing of one of the broken figures, straining to hear what was being said, but they were too far away and their voices too low. Just as I shifted my weight to move around the rubble, Odio lifted his fist and brought it down in a right hook that sent the human's head lolling on his shoulders.

Dropping him unceremoniously in the dirt, my cousin strode over to us, dusting off his hands. "Do you want the good news or the bad?"

My fingers tightened on the stone wing. "Just tell me what he said."

"Newbold's army did this." He waved a hand at the smouldering wreckage as if it was nothing more than a broken tile. "They're the ones who took Bickerstaff."

My heart stumbled. "Took him?"

"Yes. It seems no arrows were fired." Odio turned and frowned over his shoulder at the unconscious human. "At least, not any that belonged to us. That piece of garbage says he witnessed the entire thing. He claims he's staff."

A wave of relief merged with confusion as his words collided inside my head. The orders hadn't been carried out. What did that mean?

"So, Bickerstaff is alive?" Kwellen said, looking every bit as confused as I felt. "Why would they take him?"

"To bargain with probably," Odio said, plucking human arrows up off the ground and studying them. "Perhaps Newbold thinks they can force Liridona's surrender if they have its leader."

I snorted. "Do you honestly think Newbold are worried about losing? You saw their ships."

"Why, then?" Kwellen asked. "Why not just kill him?"

My stomach lurched. "I don't know. I don't know enough about this war to even guess. Odio?"

"Don't look at me. I just shoot my arrows and leave." He flexed his wings and squinted up at the brightening sky. "Speaking of which, we need to get back. The human world will be swarming with Cupids soon."

"No," I said quietly. "I need to know more."

Kwellen stiffened at my side. "What are you thinking?"

"I don't know whether I'll be able to get away so easily again. This might be my last chance to visit the human world." I clenched my fists at my side as my plan solidified. "I know someone who'll be able to tell us more and perhaps give us insight into why Newbold might have taken Emeric."

Odio's mouth fell open. "You're surely not suggesting—"

"Not a chance," Kwellen barked. "They'll kill us on sight."

I shook my head. "I don't think they will. They didn't when Odio went to tell them about the order for Emeric."

Odio huffed a laugh. "I went in armed to the teeth and didn't give them a chance to argue. You asked me to deliver a message, and I did."

"Yes, but you still spoke with them," I persisted. "We'll be careful. If they don't want to help us, we leave immediately."

Odio swore under his breath but spread his wings and launched into the air. I raised an eyebrow at Kwellen, but he just shook his head and followed. It was reckless. Stupid. But that's what hope did.

8
Pace

After two hours, my fingers started to cramp; the embellished metal grip of the quill imprinted into my thumb and forefinger. The hundreds of entries I'd added were nowhere near as neat as the looping scrawl of the record keeper, but they were legible. Focusing on my task had been the only way I'd managed to subdue the panic of being shut away inside the small room. Twice, as my breathing had quickened to the point I'd felt lightheaded, I'd rushed over to the door and opened it, checking it wasn't locked, before closing it and returning to my desk.

My head snapped up as the door eased open, and Dashuri stepped inside, closing it behind him with a sigh.

"How goes it, Brother?" I asked, eyeing him as he slumped a little against the door. It was rare to see the future king in any state other than rigidly vertical.

He pushed away and strode over to the desk beside mine, sliding onto the stool. "I'm fine, Brother. How are you finding your task?"

I placed my quill down and laced my fingers together, stretching them. "Calming."

Dashuri stared at me as though weighing the truth in my response, then turned to the pile of orders on the desk in front of him. Without a word, he picked up the quill and started writing.

I blinked. What was he doing? My lips parted, about to ask the question, but I forced them closed. If the future king of Hehven wanted to partake in such a menial task, so be it. When it became clear that our brief exchange was over, I picked up my own quill and resumed my work.

It wasn't boring. It should have been. But the truth was, the orders fascinated me. With each piece of parchment I took between my fingers, I'd stare in wonder at the gold ink, wondering who the person was and why the Fates had chosen them. I'd noticed more orders went to the Wendell Islands and Liridona than the other countries. In fact, I was yet to come across an order for Newbold. I resolved to ask Amare about it if we were ever alone again.

A few times, familiar names had appeared on the orders. My hand had trembled as I'd written out the names of the humans I'd come to call friends. With each one, I wondered how many Chaos orders there were. Whether they'd counter-acted the orders given to the Cupids. I couldn't even be sure that some of the orders I was recording were Chaos orders. The opportunity to ask where the Chaos Fated worked hadn't presented itself, and probing questions like that belonged to the old Pace. Now, I was reformed. A placid puppet of Fate.

Biting down my questions, we worked in silence, the only sound that of the scratching of quills on thick cream paper and the occasional rustling of feathers.

Just as I placed down my quill, shaking out my cramping hand once more, the door eased open and Amare poked her head in, looking between us.

"Everything okay in here?" she asked.

Dashuri stowed his quill and stood. "We've done as much as we can, but it's time to leave. There are matters to attend to at the palace."

Amare stepped fully into the room, closing the door behind her. Her lip quirked as she folded her arms over her chest. "I don't think I'll ever get used to how stuffy you've become, Dash."

I baulked at her informality, coughing to stifle the laugh that tried to escape my lips. My older brother had been born 'stuffy'.

"I'm not 'stuffy'," Dash said, raising a dark eyebrow. "I'm Crown Prince and I have many responsibilities, all of which I take extremely seriously."

Amare pursed her lips together and squinted at him. "If that's true, why are you hiding away in here? No one is expecting you to do this work."

I raised my eyebrows as my brother flexed his wings, the feathers ruffling. Was that what he'd been doing? Hiding? I stared at my brother. Dash didn't hide from responsibility. That was my speciality.

"I'm not hiding," he gritted out, staring her down. "I'm helping. I thought you'd be grateful."

"And I am." Amare raised an eyebrow. "When will you visit next?"

Dash sighed. "I'm planning to try and return at some point this week."

"What about him?" she asked, nodding at me.

"He's shadowing me," my brother explained. "Learning the role."

Our cousin raised her eyebrows. "Learning the role? If that's the case, why has he been shut away in here?"

"Amare," Dash warned.

"I mean," she continued, "Surely that's a waste of time?"

"Should I be insulted?" I said, getting to my feet.

Amare shook her head. "No. I mean, with the war going on, surely it's a waste of time for you to be shadowing Dash. He's clearly overworked and you're obviously able."

Dash frowned. "What are you talking about?"

"I'm saying, why don't you let Pace take on some of your responsibilities? He's not a little kid, Dash. He's a capable adult. Delegate."

I watched the exchange, focusing all my energy on keeping my face neutral as Dashuri looked between me and our cousin. What she was saying made sense, and I hoped he couldn't detect the anticipation fluttering in my chest. If he agreed, it would grant me the slither of freedom I so desperately needed.

"No," Dash said, shaking his head. "He needs—"

"You need to put Hehven first," Amare said, her tone a little harsher. "With the war going on, we all have to pull together, and we both know your tasks don't include this."

"Amare," my brother's voice took on the familiar tone that meant he was reaching breaking point, and I knew we'd be leaving any second.

"I want to help," I said, taking a tentative step forward. "I know you don't trust me to be alone, but you trusted me here today. You shouldn't be bookkeeping, but I don't mind helping."

Dash stared at me through narrowed eyes. "Excuse me?"

"This," I said, gesturing at the remaining piles of orders. "Why don't you let me help here?"

Amare stared at me for a long moment. "If that's what you really want, I could try and convince the record keeper to take some time to rest. I'm hoping she'll realise the wheels will continue to turn without her and she'll finally retire."

Dash shook his head. "Amare, you don't understand. I—"

"Pace can shadow you for most of the day, but why don't you let us have him for a few hours?" She gave him a look that dared him to find a reason to argue.

"You can trust me, Dashuri," I said, willing a calm I certainly wasn't feeling into my words. "I'll be safe here on the Isle. What trouble can I possibly get into? The Fates are surely even better babysitters than you."

Amare's eyes narrowed at my words, questions swimming in her gaze, but I kept my attention focused on my brother.

"Please, Dashuri," I said, stepping closer to him. "I want to help."

"I'll take responsibility for him."

My brother made a noise that sounded a lot like a snort, and I turned to look at Amare.

"What?" she said, looking between us.

Dashuri sighed heavily. "Will you give us a minute, Amare?"

"Sure." She looked between us one more time before shaking her head and pulling the door open.

Once we were alone, Dashuri stepped close enough I could feel the warmth of his breath on my skin. "Do you realise what you're asking?"

I lifted my chin, holding my ground. "I'm asking for a chance, Brother."

"A chance," he echoed. "You make it sound so simple."

"It is simple," I snapped. "You can't keep me on a leash for the rest of my life. At some point, you're going to have to learn to trust me. How can we possibly get to that point if you don't let me prove that you can?"

"It's been a handful of days," Dash said, shaking his head. "Hardly enough to—"

"You had me locked up for weeks," I said, my words barely more than a whisper as I fought to contain my anger. As much as I wanted to grab the front of my brother's robes and haul him up into the air, I would not—could not—lose it. Not when I was so close.

"This is hardly a task worthy of a prince," Dash blustered, gesturing around the room.

I baulked. "Yet, you deemed it worthy of me today. And what exactly have you been doing for the last hour?"

"Fates help me," he muttered, pulling a hand over his face.

"Fine. No more than four hours a day. Jacayal will escort you to and from the Isle."

I inclined my head. "Thank you, Brother."

"Just don't let me down."

He turned and heaved open the door, stepping back out into the main circular room. Even though the Fated moved in near silence, just the sound of footsteps, feathers and the shuffling of papers seemed uncomfortably loud after hours of isolation in the record room.

Following Dashuri back through the space, I wondered where the Fates were. The idea that the beings responsible for the events of human history were so close sent a thrill down my spine, rippling through my wings. I couldn't even begin to imagine what they looked like. Only the Fated knew, and the question joined the ever-growing list I planned on asking Amare the next time I visited the Isle. Another jolt of excitement snapped at my chest. Tomorrow.

"Before I forget, Pace," Amare said, placing a hand on my shoulder. "I found these things of Dariel's."

I turned as she placed the leather strap of a worn flight satchel in my hand. "Oh?"

"He would have wanted you to have them," she said. Her ice-blue eyes captured mine, willing me to understand what she couldn't say, and my own eyes widened.

"Thank you," I said, looping the strap of the satchel around my waist. Even without opening it, I could feel the shape and weight of the books inside.

Dashuri narrowed his eyes, but said nothing, and I breathed a small sigh of relief as we continued to the dark pathway that would lead us back to Jacayal and the other Hands.

"I'll see you tomorrow, Pace," Amare said, inclining her head. She leaned a little closer, her hood keeping her face in shadow as she whispered, "And you can explain exactly why your brother thinks you need a babysitter."

My neck heated as I straightened with a cough. "Thank you, Amare. I'll see you tomorrow."

Dashuri grunted his goodbye and two Fated lifted torches from the wall to light our way. I had no idea whether they were the same ones as before, their faces obscured by their heavy hoods.

With every step back down the dark, damp tunnel, the weight of the books against my hip seemed heavier, my fingers twitching at my sides. Where had all the books in the library gone?

"Tomorrow," Dashuri said, his deep voice bouncing off the stone walls. "You will attend the Festival before completing your duties at the Isle."

My jaw tensed. "I don't mind missing the Festival."

"You will not miss the Festival," he said, his voice resigned. "Our parents will expect you to be there, if only to show your face. This means, of course, you will abstain from any wine—"

"When have you ever seen me drink at a Festival, Brother?" I gritted out.

He lifted a shoulder in response, and I fought the urge to shove him into the rock. I could count the number of times I'd partaken in alcohol on one hand, the last time being Plumataria. My brother's constant low expectations were a tight, heavy chain around my neck weighing me down, even as I clawed at them, slicing skin and flesh in an attempt to free myself.

I was still breathing hard, my teeth painfully clenched as the Fated hauled open the stone door to the atrium. Jacayal and the other hands stood waiting, and I wondered what they'd been doing. Had they been standing there the entire time? The thought irked me. It was cold and damp beneath the dingy stone. My brother had said refreshments would be brought for them, but he'd also said we wouldn't be staying long. We'd been here for hours.

"Is everything okay, Your Majesty?" one of the Hands asked, bowing as my brother strode forward.

"Yes. Let us make haste. There's a lot to do in preparation for the Festival tomorrow."

Jacayal caught my eye, raising his eyebrow at my brother's terser than usual tone, and I shook my head. Whatever had happened during his meeting with the Fated had him acting an even bigger ass than usual, and I planned on putting as much distance as possible between us at the first opportunity.

"Will I be allowed to return home to freshen up and have some food, Brother?" I asked, barely concealing the contempt in my tone.

Dashuri huffed. "Fine. I expect you at the palace one hour after we arrive in Dragoste."

I inclined my head, my teeth gritted, and as the stone door scraped closed, we left the atrium behind. Our footsteps echoed against the walls, the smell of the sea carrying on cool bursts of air, and as we drew closer to the entrance, I found it difficult not to hurry my steps in sheer desperation to spread my feathers.

By the time we reached the carved stone wings, my heart was pounding, my hairline damp. I inhaled the chilly sea air and extended my wings, exhaling as the harsh breeze separated my feathers. My brother said nothing as he spread his own wings, launching into the air, and immediately disappearing amongst the mist, his Hands close on his heels.

"Are you okay?" Jac asked, his voice low.

The concern in his voice twisted in my chest, and I forced a smile. "Yes. I'm fine. I hope you don't get sick from waiting around in the cold for so long."

Jac frowned. "Yeah, I wasn't expecting it to be so long. Next time, I'll bring a book."

"Ah, yes." I grimaced. "We're coming back tomorrow. I got offered a job."

Jac's eyebrows rose beneath the white curls covering his forehead. "Congratulations?"

"Thank you." I smiled, shaking out my wings. "My first shift is tomorrow afternoon. I'm afraid you're to accompany me, which means you'll miss most of the Festival."

Jac shrugged, extending his own wings. "It's okay. There's always Winter. That's my favourite, anyway."

A shudder ran through me at the mention of the Winter Festival. Not only would it take place just two days after my birthday, but it would have been my wedding. Before I could let the thought settle, I bent my knees and flexed my wings, launching into the air. I had one hour, and I wasn't planning on wasting a single second of it.

9
Sirain

By the time the tropical waters surrounding the Wendell Islands came into view, I'd all but talked myself out of going. With the war raging, the chance of Marlowe being home was slim, but I had to chance it. If he could give me any information at all about Emeric, I had to know.

The smaller islands protected the inner cities, with what looked like the majority of the country's forces stationed amongst them like outposts. We flew as high as we dared, drifting between clouds, until the largest island spread out beneath us.

"What will you do if he's there?" Kwellen asked, dropping to my side.

My heart crumpled in on itself. I knew he wasn't talking about Marlowe. On the journey from Liridona, a million scenarios had played out in my head. Each one ended the same way. I'd broken us. Whether I'd meant to or not, I'd taken something from Pace that I could never replace. If he was there with Marlowe, I'd leave. I owed him that much, at the very least.

"He won't be," I said, sucking in a breath and diving towards the walled city shimmering just beyond the thin cover of cloud.

We were still twenty wingbeats from the top balcony when Odio and Kwellen drew their weapons.

"Put them away," I hissed.

Kwellen glared at me. "I don't think so."

"The last time he saw me, I tried to kill him," I snapped. "Do you honestly think showing up armed and ready to fight is going to inspire him to help us?"

Kwellen's jaw worked as he stared at me, back-beating his wings. I knew he wanted to keep me safe, but there was nothing he could do. We were visiting the human world during the day, in the middle of a war. If he'd wanted to keep me safe, he should have locked me in my room.

"We can't spend all day here," Odio called, diving towards the balcony. "If you two aren't going to knock, I am."

My heart leapt into my throat as my cousin landed silently on the narrow balcony, the stone covered in twisting green vines, reaching out a fist to knock on the thickly framed glass. Shouts sounded from within as I landed beside him, my hands raised and empty.

It took a second for my eyes to focus on the dimly lit room within, the stone and dark wood in stark contrast to the bright dawn outside. When they did, I stumbled back a step, causing Odio to hiss. Marlowe was indeed home, his twin blades in his hands and his dark brown eyes aflame. At his side, Cove had her weapons drawn too, her plump lip curved in a snarl.

It was exactly what I'd expected.

"Please," I said carefully, calling through the closed doors. "We just want to talk. I swear we bear you no ill will."

Cove snorted, spinning her twin blades in her hand. "And you think we would believe the word of a demon?"

Kwellen and Odio's towering presence was a steady drumbeat behind me, and I knew they were ready to pull me into the sky, just as they had done on Marlowe's ship months ago. I sought Marlowe's wary gaze and tried to arrange my thoughts.

"I know there are no words that could atone for what I did —what I took from you," I said. "But please know that I'm sorry. I never wanted anyone to get hurt."

"Well, they did." Cove all but snarled, taking a step towards me.

"I know." Standing my ground, Kwellen stepped close enough that I could feel his breath on my scalp. "I'm not here to ask for forgiveness. I'm here about Emeric."

Cove's dark eyebrows rose, and at her side, Marlowe exhaled, his swords lowering. He looked older than the last time I'd seen him. His rich brown skin bore a greyish tint, dark circles claiming his eyes, and a short dark beard covered his chin. Shaking his head, he stepped to the doors and pulled them open.

"You mean your father," he said, eyeing us carefully. "You're not here to carry out the orders yourself, then?"

I winced at his bitter tone. "As far as we know, the orders are yet to be completed. We went to Liridona to see if he was alive."

Marlowe's expression hardened. "And?"

"He's been captured."

Cove swore and sheathed her swords. I raised my eyebrows at the gesture, but kept my hands raised.

"Captured?" Marlowe asked. "By whom?"

"The Newbold army took him."

Marlowe slid his swords into their scabbards and retreated into the room. Sinking onto a dark blue cushioned chair, he rubbed a hand across his face. "Why?"

Something in his tone implied he wasn't seeking an answer, so I pressed my lips together instead.

"We wanted to know more about the war," Kwellen said, his deep rumbling tones echoing against the stone balcony. "Liridona is being decimated, so why would they bother to kidnap its leader?"

Marlowe sighed and waved his hand at the sofas and chairs opposite him. "Come in. Sit."

I couldn't move. Even as Odio and Kwellen strode around me, perching on the soft seats, I remained frozen to the spot. This was a mistake. I shouldn't have come here. My attention flitted around the room, my thoughts louder than thunder. A chest of drawers up against a far wall was so like the one that had been in the guest room where Pace and I had spent the night together. He and Dariel had spent a lot of time here. Had they lounged on the chairs Kwellen and Odio had claimed? The ghosts of them taunted me with such clarity, the loss hit me anew. Pace might not be dead, but he may as well be. Hadn't those been his words, after all? Just like death, there was no coming back from what I'd done.

"Sirain?"

Marlowe's weary tone broke through my thoughts, and I turned to him, my hands quivering where I still held them in front of me.

"I know you were going to miss," he said quietly. "I won't forgive you for turning up on my ship armed and ready to take a life, but I understand that Dariel's death was never your intention."

I nodded.

"So, sit down and we'll see if we can figure out who might have Emeric and why." Marlowe's brow creased into a deep frown. "He's become an exceptionally dear friend, and if I can prevent his death, I will."

Lowering my hands, it took all my strength to put one foot in front of the other and sink onto a seat. The plush cushions were uncomfortable against my wings, but I perched on the edge, happy to take the pain as punishment for being there in the first place.

"What do you know of the war?" Cove asked, resting an ankle on her knee as she regarded us with narrowed eyes. "I'm sure the Fates have our deaths mapped out by the tens of thousands."

"You know we have no control over the Fates," Odio replied, boredom lacing his tone. "We are pawns to them, just as you humans are."

"Oh, really?" Cove sneered. "Do you go around shooting yourselves with arrows?"

Odio opened his mouth to retort, but Marlowe held up a hand. "Bickering will get us nowhere. You're right. It makes no sense for them to kidnap him. If they have, we need to think about where they might have taken him."

"There are only two logical options," Kwellen offered. "Either he's still in Liridona somewhere, or he's on a ship. Whether that ship is headed for Newbold or not is another question entirely."

Marlowe fixed me with an assessing gaze. "You said you wanted to see whether he'd been killed. He hasn't. So, what is your plan now? Do you intend to rescue him?"

My mouth fell open, but words failed me. Did I? When I spoke, my voice didn't sound like my own. "I hadn't thought past finding out whether he was alive. The likelihood of him being dead . . ."

Silence settled across the room. Did I want to rescue him? I certainly didn't wish him dead. After all, it wasn't his fault he'd been kept a secret. My mother had made the choice to raise me as another man's child. I knew that Emeric would have done anything to keep my mother with him.

"Newbold is concentrating the majority of its forces on Liridona," Marlowe said. "Emeric and I were going to provide a united front, but they attacked too soon. We weren't ready, and you saw firsthand the armada that Dalibor has put together."

Kwellen sat forward, resting his arm on his knee. "I think it's safe to say that after today, Newbold will have Liridona. Their ships are few and with Emeric gone . . ."

"What do you think their next move will be?" I asked, although I already knew the answer from the tense set of the Wendell leader's shoulders.

"They'll concentrate on us," Marlowe said, glancing at Cove. "We're further away, and with our outer islands and reefs making the waters hard to navigate, it was the better choice to leave us until last."

"I thought you were working on a plan with the Cupids to push the war off course." The words tumbled from my traitorous lips, chilling my skin, and freezing my lungs before I could suck them back in.

"We were." Cove reached out and placed a hand on her brother's knee, where he had gone deathly still. "Then someone showed up with a bow and arrow and they stopped coming."

My heart somersaulted in my chest. Ignoring Cove's pointed stare, I decided to push for the information I so desperately wanted. They already hated me. I had nothing to lose. "They stopped coming?"

Cove's eyes narrowed. "Yes. We met with Pace once after . . . After what happened. He promised to return, but we never saw him again."

My heart thumped a steady beat, so loud it vibrated in my throat. Months. He hadn't been back for months.

"That's probably because of me."

My head snapped to where Odio was sitting, picking at his nails with the edge of a narrow blade. "What do you mean?"

He looked up at me, his eyebrows raised. "I was worried he'd try to kill you after you murdered his cousin, so I took care of it."

I flinched at his bluntness, a sharp intake of breath coming from Marlowe.

My words were little more than a whisper. "What do you mean, you took care of it?"

"The next orders I had, I waited around until dawn and found a Cupid Hand. I told them that their second prince had been sneaking into the human world and scheming with them. I also told them he'd been getting down and dirty with a Chaos."

My hand was on my blade before the final word left his lips, but Kwellen was faster. He leapt from his seat, his dark wings unfurling with a snap as he turned on Odio.

"Watch your mouth," Kwellen snarled, standing in front of me.

I stood and reached up, placing a hand on his shoulder until his wings relaxed, folding. Odio smirked up at him, his eyes glinting with amusement.

"A little sensitivity, Cousin," I snapped.

"It obviously worked." Odio shrugged. "It's not like you have to worry. They're Cupids. They won't hurt him."

My teeth ground together as I held my cousin's gaze. The Cupids might not be as ruthless as my father, but I knew about Pace's family. I knew how disappointed his parents were with him and how his brother never missed an opportunity to make him feel every shred of it. His actions would not have gone unpunished.

"He's fine," Marlowe said, so quietly I wondered if I'd imagined it.

I turned slowly. "Pardon?"

"Not long after Odio came to warn us of the orders against Emeric, Tiesa came to see if we were okay."

Relief stole the breath from my lungs. "And she said he was well?"

Cove snorted. "She didn't say much at all. She turned up, checked we were all alive, and left. We had to call after her to tell her about the orders for Emeric."

I sank down onto my chair. Pace knew about the orders.

Pressing fingers to my temples, I closed my eyes and tried to sort through the emotions rocketing through my veins.

"We need to go," Kwellen said softly. "We've already stayed too long."

I pushed to my feet, Cove and Marlowe following suit, their justifiably wary gazes tracking our every movement.

"We'll do what we can to find out what Newbold wants with Emeric," Marlowe said. "But with the war pressing in, you understand, I have to put my people first."

I nodded. "Of course."

Cove pushed open the balcony doors and as Odio climbed up onto the railing and jumped, his wings snapping, I turned.

"I truly am sorry," I said quietly. "I thought I had no choice —that I had to do things alone. I realise now that wasn't true. My choice cost me everything."

"No," Marlowe said, a hard glint flickering amidst the sadness in his deep brown eyes. "Your choice cost me everything."

I pressed my lips together, and with the slightest nod of admission, stepped out onto the balcony. The cool autumn air filtered through my feathers, and as I climbed up onto the railing and jumped, I didn't look back.

10
Pace

Although the Autumn Festival of Fates was arguably the most beautiful of the four celebrations, it did little more than stir the unease already roiling in my gut. Sitting at my parents' side, listening to speeches, and watching Cupids enjoying the vast amounts of food spread across tables adorned with red and gold, felt wrong. On the other side of The Crossing, humans were being slaughtered in their hundreds—possibly thousands—while we celebrated.

"Are you all right, my love?"

I blinked, turning at my mother's voice. "Yes, Mother. Just a little distracted."

She raised her eyebrows, concern flitting across her features. "What's wrong?"

"Nothing." I reached out and placed my hand on top of hers. "I'm just anxious to get back to the Isle of the Fates. There's so much work to be done."

My mother's frown melted into an easy smile, but my chest failed to warm at the pride glistening in her golden eyes. Not when it was a lie. I was anxious to get to the Isle—that much was true—but not to put quill to parchment.

Stifling a yawn, I squeezed my mother's hand and returned

my attention to the celebrations. My head was heavy from lack of sleep and the overwhelming amount of information I'd subjected myself to the night before. Pale blues had licked at the horizon by the time I'd finished poring over the books Amare had given me. They were ancient. So much so, I'd handled each page as though it might disintegrate beneath my fingertips.

"You may go if you wish, Brother," Dashuri said from where he was seated on our mother's other side. "If you're not too tired afterwards, there should still be time for you to attend the end of the Festival."

The queen bestowed a loving smile upon my brother, and it took everything I had to keep the sneer from my lips. She thought him so caring and thoughtful. What would she think if she knew he'd locked me in a windowless room for almost two months?

"Thank you, Dashuri." I stood, dipping a small bow to my parents. "Enjoy the rest of the Festival."

Even my father gave me a smile that might have bordered on pleased as I descended into the crowd, knowing Jac would follow close behind me. Their low opinion of me used to physically hurt. So many times, I'd walked away from them, my wings heavy with shame, filled with a hollowness I didn't know how to fill. It was that hollowness that had driven me to the cliff —that had pushed me to the human world. Now, as I walked away from them, I was filled with grim determination.

"I'm going home to change first," I called over my shoulder as I spread my wings.

The echoing wingbeats confirmed the presence of my constant shadow as I soared into the sky above the celebration and across the water surrounding the palace.

"I'll wait here," Jac offered, as we landed a mere minute later.

Nodding in response, I stalked into my cottage, my thick brown and gold tunic already half unbuttoned. There was no need to get changed. My Festival attire wasn't uncomfortable. The real reason I wanted a few minutes at home was sitting in the top drawer of my bedside table.

Taking the stairs two at a time, I burst into my bedroom, shedding my clothes on the way to my bed. Jac was patient, but I knew he wouldn't wait too long before he checked on me. I sank down onto my bed, breathing hard. The fatigue that had pulled at my limbs all day had vanished, adrenaline racing through my veins as I pulled open the drawer and stared at the two books that could change everything.

The first book had been interesting. A history of the ruling families of both Hehven and Helle, it detailed both the Dragoste and Hadeon rulers, right back until the very first. Who they were and how they came into being wasn't stated, but it was fascinating to see thousands of years of my history. When I'd reached the most recent ruling families, my attention had lingered on King Nemir Hadeon, Sirain's father. Of course, none of his children had been written into the book, as it had been stashed away in the record keeper's room for the last two decades, but it was strange nonetheless to see her family on the page before me in black and white.

At the end of the book, almost as an afterthought, had been a brief history of the human world's ruling families. Leafing through the few pages dedicated to the cause, I'd found it infinitely more interesting than my own family's history. It was harder to follow, as the rule in Liridona, Dalibor and Newbold changed between families several times due to war—the victor taking the country amongst their spoils.

The only remaining ruler was Emeric and the only land which seemed to have retained familial rule consistently was the Wendell Islands. Marlowe and Cove had not been added, although I was sure they'd been born before the record keeper had removed the book. Perhaps it had only been updated every few years.

The Midnight Queen had been listed as a child, along with a twin brother. Luna and Sol Berch. I'd been a little disappointed to find she had a real name, the mystery somewhat tarnished. The strangest thing of all was there was no mention of Lord Diarke, the enigmatic leader of equally mysterious Newbold. I couldn't find him amongst the names of the family who ruled during the war. Perhaps he'd taken hold of the country by force from within.

The second book had been interesting for an entirely different set of reasons. A shiver ran down my spine, tingling down to the ends of my wings as I reached for the ancient tome, placing it carefully down beside me. The leather cover was so worn, it was hard to tell what colour it had been originally. Perhaps black or dark brown. Deep swirls marked the front in a pattern that must once have been inlaid with gold, but now only tiny flecks remained.

Carefully lifting the cover, I turned the pages until I found what I was looking for. The book detailed what was known about the Fates, which was surprisingly little, but still infinitely more than I'd known before. There were four Fates. According to the book, two were linked to Chaos and the other two to Cupids. My eyes skimmed over the words I'd read so many times, they were ingrained in my eyelids. Only royalty could see all four Fates. Others could see only the Cupids or Chaos Fates. Only one illustration had been included amidst the text. I hadn't been expecting it after pages and pages of waffling, but the sight of it had stopped my heart in my chest.

Gripping the thin parchment between thumb and forefinger, I steeled myself for the image that both thrilled and terrified me. Two Fated stood on each side of the illustration, their dark hoods concealing their faces, so that only the colour of their wings identified them as a Cupid on the right and a Chaos on the left. Between them were the Fates. Four identical figures, also shrouded in cloaks, although white in contrast. They came up to the Fated's shoulders, but what sent yet another thrill scattering goosebumps across my skin was that they had no wings. Their robes concealed any feet, yet they floated above the ground, leaving only a shadow beneath them. If they had been standing, they would have been the size of children. My fingers lingered, not quite touching, over the worn illustration. Three of the Fates' faces were completely obscured by the large hoods they wore. One, however, had their head tilted as though they knew someone was looking. It was the strangest sensation. Just the smallest sliver of a chin could be seen, perhaps even the hint of a smile. I leaned closer, barely breathing, as I stared at the tiny detail.

Closing the book with a forceful exhale, I tried to make sense of the image in my head. They were nothing like I'd imagined, but also everything I'd suspected, all at the same time.

A knock sounded at my front door, and I started, leaping to my feet, and quickly replacing the book in its drawer.

"Coming!" I shouted.

Knowing how cold it was on the Isle, I made sure to wear an undershirt and grabbed a thick jacket before half-flying down the stairs to where Jac was waiting.

"Did you remember to bring a book?" I teased, shrugging my wings through the slits in the jacket and fastening it around my waist.

His eyes widened. "No. I completely forgot, with the Festival and everything . . ."

"Hold on." I retreated to the shelves beside my fireplace and grabbed a book, thrusting it at my babysitter as I swept past him into the brisk autumn air. "Don't lose it."

"Oh, no, Your Majesty," he said, tucking it inside his jacket. "I promise I'll take care of it. Thank you."

A smile pulled on my lips as I launched up into the air, heading north, with the sound of music from the Festival drifting across the water on the breeze. I only had half a plan, but it was something.

Without my brother breathing down my neck, I hoped to find out where the Fates were. I would ask Amare as much as I could without raising suspicion, but I had to be careful. Judging by her surprise when my brother had been reluctant to let me return without him, she was unaware of my current status as wayward prince. She would want answers today, of course, but I would be the one giving them.

When the Isle of the Fates finally emerged from the fog-laden sea before us, I sucked in a breath, steeling myself. For most of my life, I'd stretched the truth—lied by omission. I'd bent the rules to my whim, but it had been a delicate line. My outright lies had been few and far between and had never placed anyone other than myself in danger. Now, everything had changed. My lies were a means to the truth, and I no longer cared about the consequences. My sights were set on answers, and I was prepared to snap the rules in two to get them.

Alighting before the towering stone wings, I marched forward into the darkened hall without hesitation, Jac at my heels. Although I'd been given the freedom to return, I knew my brother would be watching the hours and if I didn't show my face before sundown, he'd send Hands to check on me. Time was of the essence, and I didn't plan on wasting a single second.

When we reached the atrium, I paused. How had the Fated known to greet us last time? Had my brother told them he was coming? I frowned up at the stone door they'd appeared through, my mouth opening to ask Jac what he thought, when stone on stone cried out, echoing across the cavernous space.

Adrenaline coursed through my veins, my fingers trembling a little as I unfastened my jacket, shrugging it off over my wings. "Here," I said, holding it out to my shadow. "It's much warmer where I'm going. Take this."

Jac's eyes widened almost comically as he looked between my face and the jacket in my outstretched hand. "Your Majesty, I can't."

"Fates and feathers, Jac." I chuckled. "It's not a marriage proposal, it's a jacket. What will I do if you catch a cold and are unable to mind me?"

Uncertainty still painting his features, Jac took the jacket with a breathy thank you, and I returned my attention to the door. Two Fated emerged, bowing before me, but before I could utter a greeting, they turned to the same door as last time and heaved it open.

My eyes flitted briefly to the third door. What was behind it? Was that for Chaos? Did it lead to the Fates? Curiosity bubbled in my blood as I forced my focus to the task at hand and followed the hooded Cupids into the long, dark tunnel.

This time, prepared, only the briefest flicker of panic settled under my skin as darkness consumed us, and I swallowed my sigh of relief when the torch roared to life. The silence was hard to bear. I had so many questions, but I had no idea who the Fated were before me. It was impossible to tell, even if they were female or male. I watched their wings and the back of their heads as we trudged down the damp stone corridor, wondering how many times they'd seen the floating child-sized Fates. Of course, if the book was correct, they would only ever see two of them.

Lost in my tumultuous thoughts, I was surprised how quickly we reached the wooden door that led to the Fated's room. It was exactly as before, a hive of quiet activity, and I silently took it in, my eyes lingering on the river that stretched along the far side. This time, a small, dark, wooden boat bobbed on its surface, tied to a gleaming metal post.

"Pace!"

I tore my eyes from the strange little vessel, a genuine smile gracing my face as Amare stepped towards me, her hood up, but back enough for me to see her eyes.

"Cousin," I replied. "It's good to see you again."

"Indeed. I wondered whether Dash would go back on our agreement. He didn't seem entirely sure."

I hefted a heavy sigh. "He's having trouble letting go. He's been the overprotective older brother for so long, he can't see me as an adult."

"I got that impression." Amare pressed her lips together, her eyes narrowing. "Why did he seem to think that you were so untrustworthy?"

My skin heated, despite myself. "I may have been a little lax on my timekeeping in the past."

It wasn't entirely a lie. It also wasn't the entire truth.

Amare eyed me, but if she had her doubts, she kept them to herself. "Come on then, let's get you settled."

We made our way to the room I now knew belonged to the record keeper, but my gaze kept returning to the small boat. Just as we reached the door, a Fated stepped into it, releasing the rope that kept it moored. My footsteps slowed to a halt as I watched them gently push away from the side, the ever-moving current sweeping them towards the dark tunnel cleaved into the rock.

"Where does that go?" I asked, sensing Amare waiting patiently at my side.

"What would your brother say if he knew you were asking questions like that?"

My head snapped round to look at her, but my tensed muscles relaxed as I found a teasing smile on her lips. "Is it a secret?"

Amare opened the door to the record room and nodded for me to enter. Once she'd pulled it closed behind us, she lowered her hood and folded her arms across her chest. "Tell me the real reason Dash doesn't trust you, and I'll answer your question about the boat."

Pressing my lips together, I sorted through my many offences. I couldn't risk losing Amare's trust, but I needed to give her something big enough to accept as the whole truth. It was a dangerous game. Fated were only allowed to leave the Isle with special permission from the Queen. Amare had only left the Isle once since being sworn in as a Fated. Dariel's final flight. If she wanted to find out the whole truth, she could ask the captains when they came to retrieve their orders, but I was sure they wouldn't gossip readily about the royal family. Captains were strict in their morals, not easily swayed, and trusting in that was a risk I was going to have to take. Reaching up, I scratched the back of my head, shooting Amare a sheepish look.

"There are these tournaments that happen in secret," I started, watching my cousin carefully. "He found out I'd been fighting in them and wasn't pleased. He threatened to tell our parents and, I agreed to a temporary personal guard to prove that I'm back on the right moral path."

Amare's eyebrows rose slightly, but then she exhaled and shook her head. "That sounds like Dash. So dramatic."

"He was right, though," I said quietly. "I took my role within the family too lightly. I risked bringing shame upon the Dragoste name."

"Wow." Amare squinted at me. "He really got under your skin."

My own eyebrows shot up. "You're a Fated. Aren't you supposed to be the purest of the pure? I thought my actions would shock you."

"I chose this life," she said softly. "You didn't choose to be a prince. You're young. It's normal that you want to explore what life has to give. Your actions weren't severe enough to warrant the consequences he's inflicted upon you."

Guilt tightened my chest. My brother only knew half of what I'd done. I looked away. If Amare knew my actions had brought about the death of her brother, she'd likely drown me in the river I was so curious about.

"It takes the Fated to the Fates," she said. "The river runs in a loop around the centre of the Isle. The Fated are in the heart of the temple. We go, receive the orders, and return to give them to the captains."

I swallowed, willing nothing more than sated curiosity to show on my face as I turned to her. "What are they like?"

"The Fates?" Amare shook her head. "I answered your question. Time to get to work."

Insistence was heavy on my tongue, but I bit it back and slid onto a seat behind the same desk I'd used the day before. The stacks of orders had been replenished, towering both on and below the desk.

"I'd best get started, then," I said with a sigh.

"Pace," she said, pausing in the doorway. "I hope I don't need to say this, but you can't tell anyone what you see here. You know that, right?"

Despite the chilly room, my skin burned so hot, I wondered whether she could see the heat rippling from my skin in waves. "Yes." I swallowed. "I know."

My cousin stared at me for a moment, but just as she turned to leave, I shivered, rubbing my hands up and down my arms. The action caused her to pause, but I kept my eyes on the desk, picking up the quill and drawing the pot of ink nearer.

"You should have brought a jacket," she said. "Did you forget how cold it was the last time?"

I looked up with a grimace. "I came straight from the Festival. It must have slipped my mind."

Amare tutted and shook her head. "I'll fetch you a spare cloak. Hold on."

As she walked away, I closed my eyes, guilt and adrenaline a painfully nauseating cocktail in my stomach. I was a terrible, awful Cupid, but my plan was unfolding, and there was nothing anyone could say or do to stop me now.

II
Sirain

S omething wasn't right. My fingers dug into the black leather armrests of my throne as I surveyed the crowd before me, a heaving mass of black, red, and orange. Of the four Festivals, the Spring and Autumn events carried a heightened sense of celebration. Chaos started earlier, finished later, and drank considerably more. The air was thick with a carnal heat as people embraced their desires beside the many fires burning throughout the courtyard. Despite the reckless abandonment of my future subjects, however, I was on edge.

Casting my gaze across the crowd once more, I exhaled, my eyes burning from more than the thick smoke filling the air. I hadn't seen Odio or Kwellen all day.

When we'd returned from the human world, we rested in the forest to discuss possible plans of action. Whether it was conceivable to even entertain the idea of searching for Emeric, let alone rescuing him, amidst the human war.

After a few fruitless hours, we'd returned to Hadeon for lunch. Odio had excused himself shortly afterwards to train, and Kwellen had joined him. That was the last time I'd seen them. I waited up for hours for Kwellen. I wandered the castle, checking the kitchens, the training grounds, the cellar . . . All to no avail. It was as if they'd vanished.

Equally troubling was the fact I hadn't seen my father all day, either. One of his advisors had rapped on my door early this morning to tell me I would preside over the Festival as heir. Such was how I found myself seated on a leather-clad throne on the outdoor dais, watching the Chaos of Helle dance, drink, laugh and rut as though they might all die tomorrow.

A ripple of laughter carried on the breeze, and I turned to where my sister was perched, resplendent in a burgundy gown that highlighted the Hadeon red in her wings and hair. She was surrounded by a small crowd as she regaled them with what appeared to be an extremely entertaining anecdote. I had no doubt that any of the males and females surrounding her would not hesitate to walk over fire if she commanded it. She was every bit the future queen I knew my parents had hoped I'd be.

Despite my better judgement, I allowed my attention to wander to one of the fires, already knowing what I'd find. As though expecting it, my brother's eyes were already on me when I found him reclining in a pile of cushions. A lazy smile curved his lips, his long neck extended as a male licked and nipped at his flesh. At his chest, a female was unfastening his shirt. He lifted his glass of wine in a mocking salute, and I looked away.

The hardest part of the Festival was over. I'd given my version of the speech I'd heard the king give for as long as I could remember, thanking the Fates and welcoming the harvest. No one seemed to care that the king wasn't there. I'd briefly considered asking Fin where he was, as he almost certainly knew, but I'd refrained. He wouldn't tell me and would take great pleasure in withholding the information just to spite me if he knew I wanted it. There was a better chance of him telling me if I ignored the fact.

A servant paused, bowing low before me, a jug of wine in her hands. I nodded, extending my glass. I'd carefully watched her serve at least four Chaos before reaching me, including Fin, so if the wine was poisoned, we'd all go down together.

"Tell me, have you seen Lord Devland or Lord Hadeon this evening?" I asked.

The servant glanced up at me, fear in her dark eyes at having been spoken to. "No, Your Majesty. I have not."

I swallowed my thanks, gesturing with my hand for her to leave. Had she expected a punishment for not knowing the whereabouts of my guard and cousin? I'd never personally inflicted a punishment, but standing at my father's—the king's — side had seemingly caused an overflow of fear. Although almost every Chaos present had seen me kill Krieg in the arena during my Rites. I tried not to think about the fact that his family would be present somewhere. Kwellen had assured me that his family would consider his death honourable, but how could that be? Krieg had been someone's son. Someone's brother. Perhaps there was even a partner who grieved him, too.

Lifting my glass, I took a deep swig as Marlowe's parting words clawed at my heart. I should never have gone to that boat. It was a futile thought, and one that kept me awake most nights, but it didn't stop me from entertaining it. I'd felt so sure I had no choice. How different might things be now if I'd refused? Perhaps I'd be dead. My gaze flitted over to where Fin was now almost indiscernible beneath a heaving mass of pale flesh and dark wings. Would it be so bad if he was king? Perhaps he wouldn't have passed the Royal Rites. I honestly couldn't imagine him winning in the arena or surviving a night atop Mount Hadeon. Although his Rites would have been different, according to my father. I cringed. Not my father.

Closing my eyes briefly, I took a breath, letting my attention settle on the fluttering autumnal banners adorning the castle courtyard. Smoke and embers mixed in the late afternoon air, and I watched the burning sparks wink out of existence one by one. I had no idea how to find Emeric, even if he was still alive. Short of searching each ship one by one, there was nothing we could do. I would just have to hope that his capture had disrupted the Fates' plans.

My gaze slid to the towering wall of shimmering colour that sliced across Helle, a vivid green in that moment. Was Pace all right? What punishment had his parents inflicted for his actions? Perhaps they'd enforced the marriage he'd managed to extract himself from. I dragged my gaze away. It would do no good to think of him.

"Your Majesty?"

I looked down, surprised to find a familiar male bowed before me, more grey streaking his long, dark tresses than the last time I'd seen him. "Lord Devland. How are you?"

Kwellen's father stood, inclining his head. "I am well. I'd hoped to see my eldest son, but I have been unable to find him."

Unease gripped once more at my heart. "I'm afraid I haven't seen him recently. I'm sure he's here somewhere, caught up in the festivities. When I see him, I shall be sure to tell him you were asking after him."

Lord Devland inclined his head again. "There was another matter I wished to speak to you about, Your Majesty."

"Oh?" My brow furrowed as I tried not to squirm in my seat. "And what was that?"

The older man's gaze flitted to the empty throne beside me. "I was hoping to speak to the king."

I pressed my lips together. With no clue what the official reason for his absence was, I was reluctant to give excuses. If I said he was visiting his wife or had been taken ill, and then he arrived spouting different reasons, I'd likely be punished. "The king is unavailable."

Lord Devland didn't look much like his son. They had the same long, dark, thick hair and the same midnight-blue eyes, but that's where the resemblance ceased. Where Kwellen was tall and broad, his father was a lean accumulation of angles. When his first son had been born with the lower half of his right arm missing, he'd disappeared into the taverns for a week. Or so I'd been told. He then made up for the embarrassment by producing three more sons, all with completed limbs, much to his pride.

Kwellen never seemed bothered that his father avoided him. After all, he'd grown up at the castle with me. As soon as he'd been old enough to wield a weapon, Lord Devland had sent his young son to train. He'd hoped living with the guards would toughen him up as he'd need it being only half a male. My fingers tensed against leather. I'd heard drunken tales of what had happened during those years living as a child amongst the guards.

"I'm sure I can manage to help with whatever issue you have," I bit out, the smallest sliver of civility lacing my words.

Lord Devland bowed deep. "I'm sure you can, Your Majesty."

I watched through narrowed eyes as he straightened and turned, beckoning to a Chaos who appeared to be a younger, shorter haired version of my best friend. He approached with confidence, a wine-red sash around his black tunic, bowing low before me.

"Have you met my second son, Jeqred?" Lord Devland asked as he straightened.

I blinked, wondering what in the Fates was happening. "A long time ago. When we were children, perhaps."

"I can assure you, Your Majesty, I am a child no longer." Jeqred smiled, a teasing glint in his eye that caused my shoulders to stiffen.

"The king is yet to announce your betrothal," Lord Devland began. "I was hoping to put my son forward for consideration."

If I had been able to open my eyes any wider, I'm sure they would have popped out of my skull and landed at his feet. "The king has not announced my betrothal because there is not one. I have no interest in marrying any time soon."

Lord Devland shared a look with his son that had my teeth grinding.

"My son is an excellent choice," Devland continued, oblivious to my chagrin. "Perhaps we could arrange a meeting for when the king is available."

"Perhaps you should turn around and leave of your own accord before I ask the guards to assist you. I'd hate for you to singe your feathers on your way out." The words spilled from my lips, slathered with all the venom I could muster.

Lord Devland blinked, but dropped into another bow, Jeqred stumbling a little as he followed suit. "Apologies, Your Majesty."

I schooled my face into a sneer and looked away as they turned and disappeared into the crowd. Although I might have seemed bored and aloof to onlookers, a profound wave of complete exhaustion consumed me from the inside. This would be my Fate. Sitting on a throne, my eyes dead and my lip curled, as I spewed poisonous threats at the Chaos deemed to be beneath me. It was a life I'd known was mine since I was old enough to fly, but I'd never wanted it. Not for one second.

Now, another weight tugged at my heart. Jeqred would be but the first of many over coming months, or even years. It would be expected that I took a partner. Even if I preferred females, I would be expected to also choose a mate so that I might produce an heir. Bile rose in my throat, and I washed it down with wine. The thought of being with anyone . . . I downed my drink, emptying my glass.

My wings twitched behind me, longing for escape. Far away,

the cool, calm quiet of the cliff called to me on the wind, but I blocked it out. This was my place now. The shackles around my ankles had always been there, but now I felt their full weight, and was powerless against them. I straightened my spine, lifted my chin, and raised my empty glass.

12
Pace

As I pushed open the door, the pounding of my heart was loud enough I was sure the Fated would hear it, and the trickle of sweat at the base of my spine had nothing to do with the coarse, heavy cloak Amare had given me. Every muscle tensed as I stepped out into the room, the hood obscuring my face. Closing the door behind me, I waited for Amare to appear—for her to demand to know what I was doing—but the only greeting was the low whispers of the Fated.

Swallowing hard, I stepped forward, trying to mimic the slow assuredness of the Fated. Of all the hooded Cupids muttering at tables and leafing through books, Amare was the only one identifiable by the royal gold flecks on her feathers. The same gold flecks I hoped would allow me to pass as her. I couldn't stand too tall, or it would be clear I wasn't her, yet, if I stooped too low, I'd draw equal suspicion. My best bet was to act without hesitation and hope for the best.

I barely dared to breathe as I moved purposefully towards the curious river flowing alongside the back wall. What would happen once I got on the boat; I didn't know. I'd pored over the book for any mention of the river or the boat, but there had been none. Now, mere strides away, my limbs trembled at the thought that this might be the last thing I did. If the Fates revealed who I was, or if another Fated realised, I would be left with no choice. I would not be locked up again. My stomach rolled, but I'd already resigned myself to the decision. If I was discovered, I would do whatever it took to escape—to make it to The Crossing—or die trying. Marlowe would hide me; I was certain of that. The rest, I'd figure out in due time.

Reaching the coursing black waters of the river, I paused, longing to wipe the sweat from my brow. The current was stronger than I'd expected, knocking the boat against the rock as though it was eager to get going. Perhaps it knew. Smiling to myself, I took a deep breath and stepped down into the vessel with as much confidence as I could muster. I released the rope, as I had seen the Fated do earlier that day, and the current grabbed hold of the boat, instantly pulling me towards the dark tunnel that loomed ahead.

Gripping tightly to the sides, I tucked my wings in tight. There was no getting off. No turning back. Whatever lay on the other side of the tunnel, I would have to face it no matter what.

For a fleeting second, I imagined finding myself face to face with Dashuri, and my stomach somersaulted. What if this job had been an elaborate test? One I'd failed miserably. An icy chill wrapped itself around my bones, and I shivered. If that was true, I would go down fighting. They would have to lash my wings down or shoot me to get me back in that prison again. I would not be taken willingly.

Sucking in a breath, I held it as the inky abyss enveloped me. The darkness within the tunnel was so intense—so all consuming—I blinked to check my eyes were indeed open. My grip tightened on the worn, damp wood as I tried to quell the slowly rising panic in my gut. How long did it take the Fated to grow accustomed to the sensation?

Before I could ponder further, pale blue light shimmered in the distance. My pulse throbbed in my fingertips where I gripped the boat and I forced myself to loosen my hold. I was under no illusion that I would be able to fool the Fates. They would know I was coming. They would have foreseen my actions, perhaps even before I was born.

Fear slashed down my spine as I sucked in a breath, the end of the tunnel almost within reach. The Fates knew I was coming, knew what I'd done, and that I was questioning their benevolence. Questioning what they stood for when they had witnessed the very creation of our world—perhaps even birthed it themselves. Doubt paralyzed me beneath the heavy wool of my cloak, pinning me to the narrow wooden seat, my heart slamming erratically against my ribs as the boat slipped through into the light.

Jagged rocks surrounded the boat on both sides, blue light painting their surface with an ethereal glow, although I couldn't tell where the light was coming from. I tilted my head back, trying to find the top of the sprawling cavern, but the cobalt haze mixed with shadows reaching as far as the eye could see. The boat continued its circular path, although seemingly slower than before. I leaned forward, attempting to see around the wall of rock, but there was no need. Before I could draw another breath, it whittled down to a few more inches above the river, revealing the centre of the cavern.

I stopped breathing. Unable to move a muscle, I stared at the four small wingless beings, their long white cloaks obscuring every feature, waiting for them to raise the alarm. To smite me. To do . . . something. There were four elaborately carved stone thrones behind them, but they stood in front of them, robes pooling on the ground around their feet, waiting, as though they'd been expecting me.

The boat slowed and my mind scrambled for words. Did they speak? They probably already knew what I was going to say. I pressed my lips together, forcing myself to wait. Next to the water's edge was a low stone plinth, a wide golden bowl atop it. As the boat drew near, one of the Fates lifted an arm, gesturing towards it. My mind whirled as I looked between the infamous Fates, responsible for influencing the choices of countless humans, and the simple bowl.

When the boat reached the plinth, it slowed enough that I was able to see into the shallow dish. Three pieces of parchment were laid in the bottom. My gaze flicked up to the Fates once more, who stood, watching silently, the bluish light casting an ethereal glow over their white robes. Reaching out, I plucked out the thick squares, expecting the boat to stop. It did not.

I frowned, my lips parting for words I couldn't find as the boat continued its path, taking me away from the motionless Fates, and back towards the mouth of the tunnel. Frantically, I opened the squares of parchment, looking for answers, but as I read the unfamiliar names in swooping golden script, my heart sank. They were orders. Nothing more.

As the darkness swallowed me, I pressed my fingers to my eyes, my head pounding. Had the Fates known who I was and not cared? There was no way I could have fooled them, surely? I squeezed my eyes shut, trying to steady my breathing as the water lapped at the sides of the boat. Soon I'd be back with the Fated, and I realised with a soft laugh that I hadn't expected to get this far.

Wiping my clammy palms on my cloak, I inhaled and straightened my shoulders, ready to disembark. What I was supposed to do with the three orders clutched in my fist, I had no idea.

When the flicker of firelight broke the darkness, I checked my hood, adjusting my posture, ready to blend back in. Clutching the orders in my left hand, I took hold of the rope in my right, preparing to loop it around the mooring post. My heart dropped into my stomach at the thought of missing and repeating the loop past the Fates. Fortunately, when I reached out to grab hold of the post, the boat slowed, knocking gently against the side. I wrapped the rope around and climbed out, my legs trembling.

No one seemed to notice, or care, as I moved between the tables, back towards the record room. Reaching out, I subtly dropped the orders onto an unoccupied table. Whether they would be found and carried out, I didn't know, and honestly, I didn't care. It took every ounce of self-control to move slowly across the room, measuring each footstep as though I had all the time in the world and hadn't just broken every law in Hehven and probably Helle, too.

When my hand finally grasped the handle to the record room, I pushed it open, relief flooding through me as I found no one inside. Pulling it shut behind me, my breathing quickened, my heavy cloak suddenly suffocating, and I shrugged it off, sinking to the floor beside it as I shoved my sweat-soaked hair back with shaking fingers and sucked in gulps of air.

I wasn't sure how to process what had just happened. Of all the thousands of scenarios I'd imagined, the Fates treating me as any other Fated had not been among them. Leaning my head back against the door, I loosened my shirt and closed my eyes, my chest heaving. Even though I'd seen the illustration in the book, I hadn't been prepared for the reality. They'd looked so small. So innocent. How could those four beings be as old as the word itself? How could they control the Fate of every human? A shudder ran the length of my wings as I imagined what might lie beneath the gleaming cloaks. The cloaks that had looked almost too big for them, pooling on the ground at their feet.

My eyes flew open, my breath halting in my throat. They'd been on the ground. Firmly, indisputably, on the ground. In the ancient book hidden in my drawer, they'd floated. Unease swirled in my gut as I pushed to my feet. I needed to see the picture. I needed to be sure.

Snatching my discarded cloak from the floor, I draped it over a chair and opened the door, scanning the room for Amare; but a quick look told me she still wasn't there. Marching to the door that led back to the atrium, I found a Fated waiting quietly.

"Will you take me back to the atrium, please?" I asked, willing calm into my voice.

The Fated dipped their cloaked head in answer.

"Will you please let Amare Dragoste know that I've gone?" I asked as they pulled open the door, plucking a torch from the wall just inside. "I haven't seen her since I arrived."

The Fated inclined their head again before stepping into the dark passageway. With a tightened jaw, I followed. The silence did nothing to help my spiralling thoughts, and each leisurely step was torture, with my hands clenching and unclenching at my sides. When we finally reached the large stone door, my shoulders ached from the effort of stopping my wings from flaring.

Jac scrambled to his feet, his hazel eyes wide and my book in his hand. "Your Majesty? I wasn't expecting you back so soon. Is everything okay?"

I turned to thank my Fated escort, but they'd already retreated, heaving the door closed, stone scraping on stone. The nicety died on my lips as I winced against the sound.

Once the noise finished echoing around the atrium, I gave Jac a reassuring smile. "I'm fine. I felt a little off, so I thought I'd perhaps put in an extra hour tomorrow."

Jac narrowed his eyes as he took in my dishevelled appearance. "You don't look great. Do you have a fever?"

"Truly, I'm fine. I think perhaps it was something I ate at the Festival."

Wariness still stretching across his face, Jac sighed. "Okay. Home, then?"

"No." I shook my head. "I need to check back in at the Festival first."

"Surely, if you're unwell, Prince Dashuri will understand?"

A dry laugh tumbled from my lips. "Have you met my brother? It's fine. I'll let him see that I'm feeling a little peaky and then I'll go home to bed."

Leaving no room for discussion, I turned and began walking back towards the entrance. It irked me that I had to check in with my brother, but I knew it would only take a matter of minutes, and that was preferable to him barging into my home with his Hands to check that I hadn't escaped.

Once we were in the air, the breeze cooled my heated skin, and I tried to focus on the sensation. It would be easy to let my thoughts wander, but I needed proof. I needed to know . . .

When we arrived back in Dragoste, the Festival was still underway, and I made my way directly to the dais, noting that only my brother was seated there. His golden gaze fell on me as I moved through the crowd, his eyebrows raising.

"Brother? I wasn't expecting you for at least another hour."

I grimaced. "I'm afraid I'm not feeling all that well. Amare sent me home."

His eyes narrowed, sweeping me from head to toe, searching for the lie in my windswept hair and flushed cheeks.

"Your Majesty," Jac offered, stepping to my side, and bowing deeply. "Prince Pace looked thoroughly unwell when he returned to me. Please disregard the effects of the flight home. I will stand guard at his home while he recuperates."

My brother stared at Jac before returning his dubious gaze to me. "I'll send an additional guard."

My jaw clenched, but I dipped my head so he wouldn't see. After all, he was right not to trust me. "As you wish."

"I hope you feel better soon, Brother."

"Thank you." I gave him a tight smile, my attention

returning to the empty thrones on either side of the crown prince. "Have our parents retired for the evening?"

Something passed across Dash's face, but he blinked, and his usual haughty expression returned. "They were called away."

My eyebrows shot up. "Called away? Where to?"

"They didn't say."

I stared, my lips pressed together, holding in a plethora of questions. The queen told Dash everything. Where would they have gone to in the middle of a Festival? My stomach slowly knotted. Was it to do with what I'd done? Had the Fates alerted them to my actions?

Forcing a smile to my face, I dipped a small bow. "Farewell, Brother. I'll see you tomorrow."

He nodded in response, and I turned, striding back through the crowd, painfully aware that everything might be crumbling around me.

As soon as we reached the edge of the courtyard, I spread my wings and launched into the air, flying low over the water to my home. A third set of wingbeats registered somewhere amongst my deafening thoughts, but I was too distracted to worry about the additional guard. As long as they stayed outside and away from my room, Dash could send as many guards as he wished.

"Is there anything I can get for you, Your Majesty?" Jac offered as I pulled open my front door, my wings barely folded from landing.

"No. Thank you," I called over my shoulder. "Please feel free to stay downstairs, though. It's far too cold outside."

Whether he would or not, I didn't care. I bounded up the stairs and into my room, closing the door behind me. My heart was a war drum in my ears as I fell to my knees in front of my bedside table, reaching with shaking hands for the book inside.

Lifting it out of the drawer, I rested it on my knees, turning the pages until I found what I was looking for.

All sound seemed to be sucked from the room as I stared at the carefully detailed illustration. Despite being in black and white, and faded with time, the differences were stark. The four beings I'd seen with my own eyes had been solid and grounded. Staring at the picture before me, it was clear the beings were not fully corporeal. They had a wraith-like quality, slightly elongated and angular despite the shapeless cloaks. Not only did they float, but the glow that seemed to emanate from them was from within, not from the light above.

Slowly, the feeling I'd felt in my gut began to solidify. It was a feeling I'd harboured for longer than I'd realised. But now, I had proof. I sucked in a shaky breath. If the beings on the Isle of the Fates weren't the Fates, what were they? I stared at the picture until my eyes watered and the book slid from my lap to the floor.

13
Sirain

Mild concern had long since shifted into simmering panic. There wasn't a day in the last decade where I'd gone more than twenty-four hours without seeing either Odio or Kwellen. Even the longest mission, or the most painful hangover, would never have kept them hidden for so long. Around me, the castle was quiet, despite the early afternoon. Such was the norm the day after a Festival, when the last fires had been doused at eight that morning. I'd lost sight of my brother not long after Lord Devland left. I had little doubt he was still in his rooms with his companions. Hopefully, he'd stay there all day.

Staring up at the milky white sky, my thoughts turned once more to one that churned my stomach. Kwellen and Odio weren't the only ones unaccounted for. My eyes searched the sky out of habit for the sight of large black-red wings. I didn't know where the king was and no way of finding out. As heir to the throne, I should know, and asking anyone would raise doubt I didn't have the strength to dispel.

Tearing my gaze from the open window, I turned back to my bedchamber, only to find myself staring at Kwellen's untouched bed. A snarl of frustration tore from my chest as I grabbed the nearest object and hurled it across the room. The apple hit the wall with a dull thud before dropping to the floor and rolling underneath the bed. My breathing grew ragged, my wings flaring as I wrestled with the building frustration, the walls of my room closing in on me.

My friends were missing, and both of my fathers. It was almost enough to jolt laughter from my throat. Although I hoped wherever the king of Helle was, he'd met with a nasty demise, it was far more likely that Fate had befallen the energetic and slightly quirky human who'd fathered me. Going to the human world had only brought forth more questions, and I couldn't fathom how to find answers to them.

A shout carried on the wind, causing me to turn back to the window. I squinted at the two black shapes whirling and diving further down the mountain, their wings parting the last of the morning mist. My heart leapt into my mouth, and I scrambled to my feet, but as they drew closer to the castle, gliding around to the training grounds, I recognised one of them by their short spiky black hair. A female Hand called Hargitsi, she was a Captain of Fate I'd trained with a few times in the past; mostly when Kwellen wasn't available.

Disappointment left me in a heavy sigh, and I leaned out of the window, tracking the pair until they disappeared behind the East Wing and out of sight. The training grounds would be quiet the day after a Festival, with only the most dedicated Chaos turning up to sweat out the excesses of the night before.

The seeds of an idea took root in my head and, before I could question it, I climbed up onto the window ledge and jumped. My wings snapped open, the chilled mountain air stinging my eyes as I dove, allowing the currents flowing around the castle to guide me to my destination.

As I'd expected, only a handful of Chaos were milling around the training grounds. Some wielded swords, the clashing of metal-on-metal echoing abrasively against the stone walls of the castle. I suppressed a grin as I took in the sweat-drenched winces of some of the participants. Others were lined up for target practice, their dark bows in hand and buckets of arrows at their feet.

My feet touched the ground, my wings folding, and I allowed my mask to fall into place. It had been a long time since I'd trained, and a blade hadn't sat between my wings since I'd killed Krieg. The grey woollen shirt and comfortable black leather pants I wore were certainly not training attire, but that wasn't why I was there.

Lifting my chin, the heir to the throne of Helle strode amongst the Hands, eyeing their training with the precise mix of satisfaction and disdain the Hadeon family had perfected over eons. I might not be Hadeon by blood, but it had been burned into the essence of who I was.

Dismissing their bows, I made my way to where Hargitsi was stretching, her bow resting, ready, beside her.

"Your Majesty," she said, dipping into a bow as she realised I was watching her. "I haven't seen you at the grounds for a while."

Raising my eyebrows, I allowed the silence to grow painful as I slowly looked her up and down. "I've been busy preparing to rule Helle, Hargitsi. Do you see my father at the training grounds often?"

"No, Your Majesty. Of course, Your Majesty," she blustered, bowing again for good measure.

"I have a question for you," I demanded, hoping I sounded calmer than I felt.

"Anything, Your Majesty."

"An unusual order was given by the Fates recently." I stepped closer. "I want to know which Hand it was assigned to."

Hargitsi's eyes, the colour of evergreen pines, grew wide with panic, her pale lips pressing together.

It was risky, asking outright. Hands were not supposed to discuss orders. They were carried out and never spoken of again. Officially. Having spent the last few years with Odio, and on the training grounds, I knew that wasn't the case. Even though conversations were reduced to hushed whispers when I was near, I still heard enough to know that unusual or high-profile orders were discussed at length. If the Fates had given orders to kill a human, I was certain there was no Chaos alive who'd have been able to keep it a secret.

Hargitsi shook her head. "I . . . I—"

"Will tell me immediately," I snapped. "You would refuse your future queen?"

She swallowed, taking a small step back. "No, Your Majesty. It's just the Fates—"

"Will not punish you as harshly as I will if you don't tell me," I pressed, my lip curling up in a snarl. "Tell me and do not make me ask again."

"Tumulto," she whispered, her dark-green gaze dropping to her black leather boots in defeat.

I smiled with more teeth than necessary as I backed away. "There. That wasn't so hard, was it?"

There was a small part of me that recoiled at how easy it was to play the part. How naturally I could channel the calm, cruel nonchalance of the Hadeon men. Perhaps it would be easier if I let that part become permanent. How much easier it would be to not care—to not feel.

"Hargitsi," I continued, wondering if the Chaos with her head bowed before me could be even more useful than I'd hoped. "Have you seen Lord Devland or Lord Hadeon recently?"

She glanced up before dropping her gaze back to her boots, shaking her head. "Sorry, Your Majesty. I haven't seen them since before the Festival."

Disappointment weighted my stomach as I strode across the training grounds. I quickened my pace into a run, spreading my wings and letting the air sweep under me, lifting me off the ground. I still might not know where my friends were, but at least I could do something to shake the feeling of utter uselessness.

Tumulto was a Captain of Fate. One of the older Hands, he lived in the city below the castle, near the training barracks, as he was one of the three Chaos who looked after the new recruits. When Hargitsi had said his name, I'd been surprised. I hadn't realised he was still carrying out orders. But then again, these weren't standard orders.

I hadn't flown into the city of Hadeon for quite some time. On my many trips to and from The Crossing, I'd always been careful to stick to the uninhabited parts of Mount Hadeon, gliding over the tops of the dense forest, instead of the peaked slate roofs. Of course, the city was dead—its inhabitants allowing themselves a day of recuperation after the Festival. The only Chaos in sight were the occasional smallwings playing in the gardens and streets, and a few Chaos who couldn't afford to take a day from their livelihoods.

My gaze snagged on a gathering of older Chaos grouped on a corner, likely gossiping about last night's events, and I dropped between the houses, blending into the shadows.

"Oh, I know," a hushed voice trailed on the breeze. "He's the fourth one she's bedded this week."

"Good for her," another voice croaked. "Make the most of your body while you're young."

One of the oldwings snorted. "Young Prince Fin is certainly doing that. My granddaughter's been invited to his bedchamber three times now. He rarely sleeps alone, you know. He's a strange one."

"Oh, hush. He's exactly like his father was at his age. Don't you remember?"

My eyebrows rose and I bit back a smirk. The four oldwings would likely keel over if they discovered the Crown Princess was eavesdropping on their conversation. I turned to leave, but a new voice halted me in my tracks.

"He needs a connection," a rasping voice commented. "Someone to make him feel like everything is worth it and tempt him to settle down."

"Settle down?" one of them scoffed. "Don't be soft. He's only young. Let him have his fun."

"Princess Sirain presided over the Festival, though," the croaking voice persisted. "Perhaps King Hadeon has taken ill like Queen Briga. There might be a change of ruler sooner than we think."

My stomach rolled. I might not have known what had happened to the king, but I was certain he wasn't ill.

"I'm trying to convince my son to vie for her affections," one of the voices whispered. "She's a beautifully fierce thing. With the throne ahead of her, she'll have to think about choosing a partner soon."

I wiped my clammy palms on my shirt, peering round the corner to better glimpse the Chaos discussing my Fate. Four females, all with long grey hair twisted into an assortment of braids, stood hunched with steaming mugs in their hands, half an eye on the smallwings they'd likely been tasked with watching.

Despite their topic of conversation, I smiled. This was how I imagined the Fates themselves. A meddling group of oldwings. Shaking my head, I turned and headed between the houses towards the training barracks.

As expected, the long, two-storey stone building was quiet. The younger Hands inside would either be asleep after delivering orders all night, or hungover. Either way, the captains were strict, and the sun was past midday. They'd be up soon.

I knew the training barracks well. While Odio had lived in the castle during his training, Kwellen had lived in the barracks from a frighteningly young age. There wasn't a way to sneak in or out of that building I wasn't aware of. Raising a fist, I thumped on the thick wooden door.

It heaved open after a matter of moments; the Chaos tasked with the job's jaw slackening as she realised who had knocked.

"Your Majesty?" she stammered, pushing messy strands of black hair from her face. She must have been barely seventeen. "Can I help you?"

"I'm looking for Captain Tumulto," I said, forcing the amusement from my voice. "Is he here?"

The young Chaos shook her head. "No, Your Majesty. He has yet to return."

"From The Crossing?" I asked, concern gripping my throat. Every order during the human war was a dangerous one, after all.

She shook her head once more. "No. From . . . from the Festival."

"Oh." I narrowed my eyes. "Where is he?"

"I . . . I don't know," the Hand stammered. "I can find out, though."

"Go," I commanded, shooing her away. "Find out."

As she turned and flitted away into the barracks, I stepped inside and helped myself to one of the many blades lying around. I'd forgotten the peace afforded by the comforting weight of a weapon in my hand.

After only a matter of minutes, the female returned, her cheeks flushed. "He's just down the street," she said. "Someone says he stayed the night at the tavern."

I raised my eyebrows, swallowing the words of gratitude on my tongue. The crown princess didn't thank Chaos for doing her bidding. "Where is it?"

After gathering stuttered directions from the Hand, whose skin had taken on a greenish tinge from our exchange, I strode down the street towards the tavern.

It wasn't far; a two-storey simple stone building, built for purpose. The windows were small, more for ventilation than viewing, and when I stepped inside, I found every inch of the main room filled with tables and chairs. Whether it was always so crammed, or whether it had been arranged as such for the Festival, I couldn't be sure. I was unsurprised to find several Chaos sprawled on and under the tables in various states of consciousness.

Moving amongst them, checking each one for Tumulto's telltale long, grey braid, and avoiding the puddles of drink yet to be mopped up, I made my way to the staircase at the back of the tavern. No one stopped me. Perhaps the owners were still asleep, or even one of the Chaos sleeping in the main room.

At the top of the creaking stairs were six rooms. I stopped and stared, dragging in a deep breath, and immediately regretting it as my lungs filled with the stench of stale ale, vomit, and something else I didn't want to think about. My hand gripping my borrowed blade, I stalked from door to door, listening for any sign that it might be the right room. If I didn't hear Tumulto, I'd have to force my way into each room one by one, and I certainly didn't want to have to deal with that level of drama.

When I reached the fourth room, I heaved a sigh of relief as the captain's deep, rumbling laugh drifted under the door. Raising my hand, I knocked hard, the noises inside instantly falling silent.

"Tumulto," I called. "I know you're in there."

A giggle sounded, immediately shushed, and I tightened my grip on my blade as my blood heated with annoyance. I wouldn't knock a second time.

Stepping back, I rolled my sword once in my hand, drew up my leg, and kicked hard, right beside the lock. The door swung open with a crunch, slamming against the stone wall to the sound of shrieks and squeals, and I strode into the room, my blade pointed right at the male I'd been looking for.

Sprawled on the bed, with two hastily covered companions on either side, Tumulto's face fell, his steel-grey eyes moving slowly from my sword to my face.

"Princess Sirain," he said, sitting up and causing the blankets to pool around his waist. "Is everything all right?"

"I need to speak with you." I looked pointedly at the two badly disguised lumps on either side of him, black feathers peeking out from under the blankets. "Alone."

The captain stared at me for a moment, then with a barely concealed sigh, shoved at the offending masses. I kept my gaze fixed on him as two naked females extracted themselves from under the covers, giggling and whispering as they gathered their clothes and stumbled past me out into the hallway. I reached out with my spare hand and closed the door behind them. No doubt, my visit would spur a flurry of fresh gossip, but it was too late to worry about that now.

"You received some unusual orders," I said, stepping closer to the bed.

Tumulto lifted his chin. "Hands of Fate are not permitted to discuss their orders, Your Majesty. As you well know."

Despite approaching fifty, he was an attractive male. His body was a mass of solid muscle, a smattering of black and grey hair across his bulging chest and trailing down his flat stomach. A single, thick, silvered braid hung over his shoulder, disappearing under the covers. I knew for a fact it reached his knees. I also knew, despite his revered status, he was not a nice male. Not that many Chaos would want to be considered as such, but he had been the captain in charge of Kwellen when he was first sent to live at the barracks to 'toughen up'. My grip tightened on my blade as memories of my friend, just ten years old, terrified, and bleeding, filled my head.

"If you don't discuss your orders," I said, stepping closer still. "How have I come to learn of them?"

He shrugged, his eyes narrowing. "How am I to know what you've learnt, Your Majesty?"

Before he could blink, I spread my wings and leapt up onto the bed, my feet straddling his waist as my sword pressed into the cleft of his chin. "You know exactly which orders I'm talking about," I said. "I want to know everything about your trip to Liridona."

Tumulto glared up at me through narrowed eyes. "Why?"

Barking a laugh of disbelief, I pressed my blade a little harder, crimson blood pooling at its tip. "You would dare question the next in line to the throne? Perhaps some time in the castle dungeons might loosen your tongue. Or perhaps my blade will do a good enough job of that."

A rumbling growl reverberated from the captain's chest. "You're asking me to incur the wrath of the Fates."

"If I were you, I'd be more concerned about my wrath." To punctuate my point, I removed my blade from his chin and swiped it lightly across his chest, drawing a stripe of blood that had him hissing in protest. I lifted it to his throat. "Tell me."

"Fine," he gritted out. "It took me two attempts to get to Liridona because of the war. When I finally got there, the target, Lord Bickerstaff, was gone."

"Gone?" I echoed.

"I waited around until dawn, listening for information, only to discover that he'd boarded a ship to meet with the ruler of Dalibor."

My sword pressed a little harder and Tumulto leaned back into the wooden headboard, his eyes wild. "What are you doing? I'm telling you what you want!"

"You're lying," I hissed.

His dark grey eyes stared up at me, pleading. "I swear, I'm telling the truth, Your Majesty. I returned a third time and tracked his ship all the way to Dalibor, but he stayed below deck the entire time. I couldn't get to him. When I returned the fourth time, I found his crew had been slaughtered and he was gone."

The captain's words swept around my head in a haze as I tried to reconcile them with what we'd been told in Liridona. He had no reason to lie to me. Had the human Odio questioned lied?

"And what of the orders now?" I asked.

Tumulto swallowed hard, and my blade shifted with the movement. "I went and spoke with King Hadeon. He told me it was of no matter and to forget about it for now."

I stared down at the captain, my knuckles white. Before he could draw the breath to speak, I leapt down from the bed and strode from the room, leaving him slumped against the wall, scarlet trailing the cleft in his stubbled chin and down his muscled chest.

As soon as there was enough distance between me and his room, I broke into a sprint, tossing my sword to the ground and racing towards the nearest window. Heaving it open, I dived out into the wind. I'd hoped taking action might grant me some comfort, or clarity, but it hadn't.

Only one place had ever been able to do that.

One person.

I didn't stop until I found myself at the cliff, unable to ignore the pull any longer. Our cliff. Staring out at the inky ocean, I closed my eyes and extended my wings, relishing every gust of freezing, salted air as it tossed my hair and snatched at my feathers.

Hours passed, my fingers numb with cold, but I didn't speak a word.

I'd already said my goodbyes.

14
Pace

For the most part, I'd been left alone. I wasn't sure how long I stayed on the floor, the proof that could undo everything lying at my feet, but my eyes still bore the ache. Jac had checked on me in the morning and I'd managed to convince him that I wasn't feeling well enough to leave. With my window slightly ajar, I'd heard him ask the second guard to send word and return with two more Hands. I was glad Jac was planning to rest, but the fact that despite our semblance of friendship, he still clearly didn't trust me, hurt more than it should. I frowned at my ceiling, wondering if Jac had been there when I'd been accosted by my brother. We'd never discussed the reasons I'd been locked up, and I had no desire to, but the thought that he might know the sordid details of my life twisted something in my gut.

Lying in bed, I turned my head and stared out of the window at the distant afternoon sun. It was an unseasonably cold autumn for the south of Hehven. I wasn't sure what to do. I'd considered going back to the Isle of the Fates and speaking to Amare, but I couldn't. Not yet. Dariel had told me often that I was impulsive and reckless. This time, I would not make that mistake. Although it pained me, I had lain in my bed, considering each and every option. Unfortunately, none of them seemed viable.

A knock sounded at my door, and I shifted, pulling the blankets over me, assuming my ruse of malady. It was most likely Jac bringing me food, as I'd heard someone moving around in my kitchen not long ago.

"Come in," I called.

Tiesa stepped into the room, her green eyes narrowed. "You're sick?"

I opened my mouth to reply, then closed it, looking pointedly at the door instead. She hesitated, concern flitting across her features, but then she pushed it to with a resigned sigh.

"You're not sick," she said, perching on the end of my bed.

Sitting up, I stared my best friend in the eye. "I won't lie to you, Tee. No. I'm not sick."

"Why are you hiding away in here, then?" she asked, her frown bunching the golden Hand markings on her forehead. "Did you overexert yourself at the Festival?"

I laughed. "How exactly does one 'overexert' themselves at a Festival?"

"I don't know." She shrugged. "You disappeared for most of it. I figured you were off drowning your sorrows somewhere."

I stared at her. "You seriously think my brother would have allowed that?"

"I don't know, Pace. I don't know anything anymore." She shook her head, her fingers picking at the cream woollen blanket on my bed. "I tried looking for you."

"I was at the Isle of the Fates."

Tiesa's head snapped up, her green eyes wide. "Why?"

"I work there now." I couldn't keep the grin from spreading across my face at her startled expression.

"You what?"

"Dash took me there as part of my training. There's a room where all the completed orders are recorded. The existing record keeper can't keep up with them all, so Amare convinced Dash to let me help while the war continues."

Tiesa stared at me, and I tried not to shrink under the scepticism in her eyes. Her mouth opened and closed several times as she sorted through the many questions I was sure were circling her mind. At last, she seemed to settle on one.

"If you're not sick, why are you in bed?"

I felt it as clear as day, then. A choice had been laid before me, so stark in its clarity, a shiver ran the length of my spine. Tiesa had been my closest friend for as long as I could remember. Although her family ruled Caracy, the land to the far northeast of Hehven, her mother had served on the queen's council years ago, bringing Tiesa with her. We'd only been five years old the first time we met, but by all accounts, we'd been inseparable. Advisors were only allowed to serve on the council for ten years, but when Lady Caracy's time came to an end, Tiesa had already decided she wanted to become a Hand and stayed while her mother returned. Almost fifteen years, we'd been by each other's sides. In all that time, I'd never hidden the truth from her. Although I had never gone into detail, Tiesa knew of the tournaments, and knew what I would get up to sometimes afterwards. She would often make her feelings on the matter very clear, but she never once betrayed my trust.

Guilt solidified in my throat as I thought of how I'd shut her out over the past months. Dariel and I had journeyed to the human world without her, time after time, saying it was for her own protection. That had been a lie. We hadn't wanted to weather her judgement because we'd known she was right. For weeks, I'd thought she'd been the one to betray me to my brother, when in fact it had been a Chaos. Not once in our life-long friendship had she given me reason to doubt her loyalty. Only shame and guilt had prevented me from sharing the truth with her.

My jaw set as I reached a decision. Leaning over to my

bedside table, I opened the drawer and pulled out the book that had stolen my sleep. "Have you ever seen the Fates?" I asked, resting the book between us.

Tiesa frowned at the worn leather cover before looking up at me. "Of course not. Only the Fated are allowed to see the Fates."

I pressed my lips together, my pulse a fierce, relentless beat beneath my skin as I opened the book to the illustration of the Fates and turned it towards her.

"Pace!" she hissed, turning away, and covering her eyes. "What is that?"

"For Fate's sake, Tee." I reached across and gently pulled her hands away from her face. "It's a history book Amare found for me. Look. Please?"

Reluctantly, she turned and peered at the picture, her features pinched as though she might be struck down for her actions at any moment. After a few seconds, however, her face relaxed into an expression of awe, and I smiled.

"That's really them?" she whispered.

I nodded. "Yes. I've seen them."

"You've what?" Tiesa's eyes widened. "How?"

Sucking in a deep breath, I prepared to throw myself off the proverbial cliff. "I pretended to be a Fated."

Tiesa leapt from the bed, her white wings flaring. "No. Pace. We're not doing this again."

"Tee—"

"No." She shook her head, her white hair brushing her shoulders. "Did you enjoy being locked in that room? Do you miss it? Because that's where you're going to find yourself."

Throwing back my blankets, I climbed out of bed to stand before her. "This is bigger than me," I hissed, taking hold of her arms. "Something's not right."

Tiesa stared up at me, fear and concern warring on her face. "Why would you do this, Pace? After what happened last time?"

"Because this isn't right, Tiesa." I squeezed her arms, my face pleading. "The Fates have given two sets of kill orders. They're sending Chaos with orders for humans Cupids have just delivered arrows to. It makes no sense."

"The Fates don't need to make sense," she said, shaking out of my grip. "The future is not ours to control."

I rubbed a hand over my face, wishing I'd managed enough sleep to make my words more coherent. "Tiesa, I went to see the Fates because I needed to know. Everything I've done should have angered them, right? There should have been repercussions far greater than Dash locking me away. Don't you agree?"

Tiesa sighed, her shoulders lifting in a half-hearted shrug. "I suppose."

"If that hasn't happened, surely it means the Fates wanted me to make the choices I've made."

"So, you went to visit them?" Tiesa inhaled, looking up at the ceiling before meeting my gaze once more. "What did they say?"

I huffed a laugh. "Nothing. They acted as though I was just a Fated. They handed me orders."

Tiesa frowned as she considered this. "Perhaps they knew it was you, but didn't want to talk to you. Maybe it was all part of the greater plan."

It took everything I had not to roll my eyes. "There's a bigger problem than that, Tee." I turned back to the bed and picked up the book, abandoned amidst my heaped blankets. "They didn't look like this."

Tiesa's gaze remained on the picture, her face pained. "What did they look like, then?"

"They didn't float, for a start," I said. "They didn't have the same ethereal glow they have here, either. They were solid. Real."

Pressing her lips together, she stared at the picture. She was quiet for so long I began shifting from foot to foot impatiently.

"Tee?" I pressed.

"This is an illustration from eons ago," she said slowly and carefully. "The person who drew this might not have even seen the Fates. It's probably just an interpretation."

Jaw clenched, I leafed through the weathered parchment until I reached the first page and thrust it towards her. "This book was written by Elsker Dragoste. A revered Fated, he was brother to my ancestor, King Cariad Dragoste, over three hundred years ago."

Her eyes flitted across the words I'd read a dozen times. Elsker had served as a Fated for sixty years and had seen the Fates over two thousand times during his life. I'd even returned to the other book, finding his name in the records of royal ancestry. He'd been the king's only sibling.

"This is not a work of fiction," I said quietly. "What I saw on the Isle is."

Sighing, Tiesa gently pushed the book back against my chest. "This might have been true three hundred years ago, but perhaps the Fates have changed."

"You're trying to find a reasonable explanation where there simply isn't one," I said. "The Fates are as old as time itself. Why would they change? It makes no sense."

Tiesa turned, pressing her fingers to her temples. "Pace. You're asking me to believe that the Fates are not the Fates. Do you have any idea how unbelievable that sounds? How could that even happen?"

"I don't know. That's the point."

Her eyes shimmered with unshed tears, and I took a step towards her, but she moved away, shaking her head. "I wish you hadn't told me. This is too much."

Guilt cleaved open my chest. "I know. I'm sorry. I don't know what to do, Tiesa. I need you to tell me what to do."

"I want you to get rid of that book and walk away."

I shook my head. "You know I can't do that."

A loud knock sounded against the door and we both star-tled, our wings flaring and our eyes wide. My heart in my mouth, I shoved the book back into my bedside drawer before scrambling into bed and pulling the blankets over me.

"Yes?" I called.

"Your Majesty," an unfamiliar voice sounded through the closed door. "A messenger has been sent from the palace. You are to attend dinner at sunset."

I frowned. "Did you tell the messenger I am unwell?"

"The messenger said it was not up for debate."

My frown deepened and Tiesa raised an eyebrow.

"You realise you're not actually sick?" she whispered.

Shooting her a withering look, I called out, "Fine. Thank you."

As the footsteps we'd not noticed approaching made their way back downstairs, I sat up and pushed my hands through my hair. "What do I do, Tee?"

She folded her arms. "Go to dinner."

"You know what I'm talking about."

Tiesa's gaze lingered on my bedside table, as though she could still see the book resting inside. "I don't know. Let me think about it. It's a lot."

"I know." I pulled my knees to my chest. "Thank you."

She opened her mouth to say something, but then closed it with a soft sigh. I watched her open the door and leave, wondering whether perhaps I'd been selfish sharing the burden of my discovery with her. Whether it was or not, I felt lighter, and I was glad of it. Leaning my head back with a sigh, I closed my eyes and wondered what Dashuri wanted that was so important it warranted dragging me from my fraudulent sickbed.

I hadn't meant to fall asleep. Roused by banging on my bedroom door, I'd opened my eyes with a groan to find the sky striped in red and gold. Ten minutes later, wishing I'd had time to wash away the dregs of sleep, we'd set off for the palace. Jac must have warned his replacement of my illness because the guard had watched me warily on the short flight across the water, as though afraid I might drop out of the sky at any moment, despite my reassurances to the contrary.

Now, walking down the white hallways, the lit flames painting the walls in streaks of buttery gold, my stomach set about tying itself in familiar knots. There was a chance Dashuri knew what I'd done. If he'd visited the Isle today while I feigned illness, someone might have told him. I longed for my sword, my fingers clenching at my side where it should hang. I didn't feel awake enough to fight my way out of capture, but I would find a way.

The door to the banquet room flew open and Dash stormed out into the hallway, his apparent fury easing as he found me approaching. "There you are."

"Apologies, Brother," I said. "I didn't realise I was late."

He narrowed his golden eyes. "The messenger told you to be here at sunset."

"It was not specified whether it was the beginning or end of sunset," the guard offered at my side. "This is my fault, Your Majesty."

I shot the guard a grateful look, but shook my head. "I'm here, Dashuri. The sun set less than three minutes ago. Surely you've not been waiting long."

My brother's jaw tightened, and he flicked his gaze to my guard. "You're dismissed. Wait at the end of the hall."

The guard bowed deeply before turning and striding back the way we'd come. As soon as he was a distance away, my brother leaned in close enough that I could feel his breath on my cheek.

"Mother has called for this dinner," he said, his voice barely above a whisper. "You will not embarrass this family. You will sit, you will eat, and you will keep your mouth shut. Do you understand?"

Each time I spoke with my older brother, I found that the self-restraint required to not punch him in the face increased.

"Yes, Your Majesty," I bit out.

Dashuri wrinkled his nose, stepping back to look me up and down, clearly finding me lacking. "If you so much as put one feather out of line, I'll tell them everything."

My fingers curled into fists at my side, the skin stretching painfully over my knuckles. "You have nothing to worry about, Brother. I assure you."

Dash stared at me a second more, then turned and stalked back to the banquet room, heaving the doors open. I couldn't remember the last time we'd eaten together as a family. Even at the Festivals, the meal was served over the course of the evening, between the speeches, and we were rarely seated together.

Although no fire was lit in the room, between the heavy golden drapes adorning the walls, and the many fat, white candles burning on towering candelabras, the room felt warm and welcoming. Our parents were already seated at the large circular golden table, a large, gilded platter of fruit at its centre. My mother lowered her wine glass, thanking the server who'd filled it, and stood to greet me. I strode across the room to her, placing my hands in her outstretched ones as she looked me over.

"Dashuri told us you were unwell?"

I inclined my head. "I caught a chill working at the Isle. Next time, I'll take a warmer jacket."

She squeezed my hands. "You look tired."

"I barely slept last night," I explained. "I'm sure I'll be all right by morning."

"Come, sit," my father said, reaching up and patting my arm. "You should eat."

My chest warmed at his concerned tone, and I turned to him, surprised to see something other than disappointment in his pale blue eyes. Dash had taken the seat to the queen's right, so I pulled out a chair at my father's left.

"Where is Amani?" I asked.

"She ate earlier," my father answered. "She's too young to be concerned with what we want to discuss with you."

A server placed a cup of steaming honey, lemon, and ginger in front of me, and I thanked them before returning my mother's smile. "Does this have something to do with why you were called away from the Festival?"

I watched my parents' faces curiously as they shared a worried look. Trepidation thrummed in my veins, but somehow, I knew it wasn't to do with my actions. If Dash was aware of what I'd done yesterday, he would have mentioned it in the hallway. If my parents knew, they wouldn't be looking at me with such sympathy.

Silence fell over the table as food was brought out, the richly spiced aromas of thick vegetable soup and freshly baked bread filling the room. My stomach growled its appreciation as I realised I hadn't eaten since the Festival.

"Go ahead," my mother said, nodding at the food. "Eat."

I picked up a soft, warm roll and tore off a chunk, soaking it into the steaming soup. As I placed the morsel on my tongue, my tastebuds singing in response, my attention fell on my brother, who was yet to touch his food. My gaze narrowed. He looked concerned. I thought back to the Festival—the worried look that had passed over him when he'd admitted he didn't know where the king and queen had gone.

"Should I be concerned?" I asked carefully. "Is this bad news?"

My parents shared another look and I watched as my father all but downed his wine in one gulp. I raised an eyebrow.

"We were called away to an unexpected meeting," the queen said, measuring each word as she kept her gaze on the narrow stem of her glass, her fingers gripping it tightly.

I cast another look at my brother, who was watching them, his expression tense. "Where?"

"Rakkaus."

My stomach clenched. "Oh? Is Lord Rakkaus well? Caitland?"

"They are quite well," my father said. "We were called there upon another's request."

I swallowed, my heart pounding anxiously in my chest. "Whose request?"

My mother looked up, her golden eyes looking first at me, before fixing on my brother. "Nemir Hadeon. King of Helle."

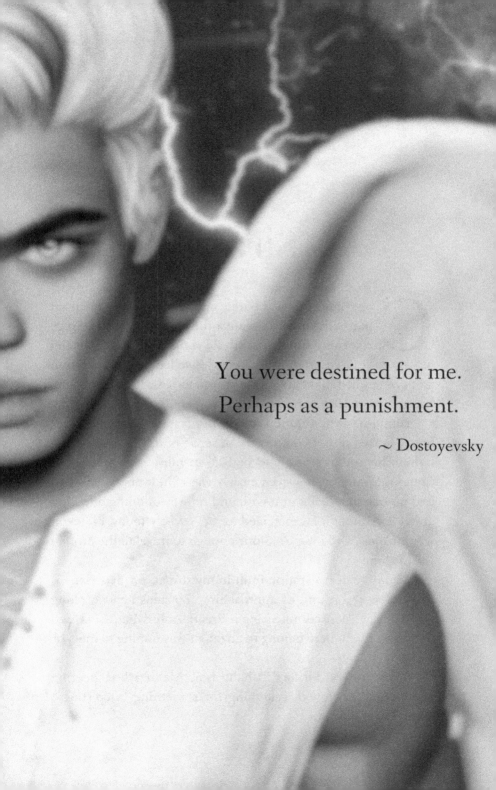

You were destined for me.
Perhaps as a punishment.

~ Dostoyevsky

15
Sirain

Common sense was barely enough to prevent me from pounding my fists against the cold stone walls. Since returning from the cliff, I'd stalked the castle, trying in vain to find any sign of Odio and Kwellen. My desperation had even pulled me to the throne room to see whether the king had returned. He had not.

Tumulto's words ran on a loop in my head, but no matter how I looked at it, I couldn't make sense of it. Why would the human lie and say Newbold had taken him? Why would the captain? Someone, however, clearly was. The worst part was, I had no one to talk about it with and no way of doing anything about it. Although I'd managed to move freely today, I knew it wouldn't last, and I wasn't idiotic enough to travel to the human world alone.

A rumble of frustration built in my throat, my fists clenching, but as the sound of approaching footsteps echoed along the hallway, I tensed, releasing a breath only when I realised they were too light to belong to anyone I was hoping to meet or avoid.

"Why are you lurking in hallways?" Malin asked, peering around me, as though searching for something interesting I might be looking at.

I opened my wings a little, leaning back against the wall. "I'm not lurking."

"It certainly looks like lurking." She raised a dark eyebrow in a way frighteningly like our mother.

"Did you enjoy the Festival, Malin?" I asked. "It certainly seemed it."

Her lips pouted. "Are you insinuating I shouldn't have?"

"Not at all." I held up my hands. "It was nice to see you having fun. As long as it's not the same kind of fun as Fin."

Malin's nose wrinkled in disgust. "Ugh. I have a lot more self-respect than that. He has no standards."

A smile tugged at my mouth. It was so hard to see her as anything other than my baby sister, even when it was clear she would be an adult sooner rather than later.

"Has Fin mentioned to you when Father will return?" I asked.

Malin glanced over her shoulder in the direction of the throne room, despite it being on the other side of the castle. "Is he not back yet?"

"No. I don't suppose he told you where he went?"

She squinted at me and tossed her dark hair over her shoulder. "Father doesn't discuss things like that with me. I would have thought he'd have told you, though."

I shrugged, my nonchalance disguising the disappointment swelling in my gut. "Where are you headed?"

"To bed," she said. "Do you not know what time it is?"

My smirk returned as I found myself being reprimanded by my teenage sister. "I'm afraid I don't."

"Well, I'm actually on my way back from visiting Mother, but the effects of the Festival seem to have caught up with me." She yawned for effect. "You should go to bed. You look awful."

My eyebrows shot up, but in all fairness, she was likely right. I couldn't remember the last time I'd eaten or bathed. As Malin sauntered off in the direction of her rooms, I gnawed on my lip, wrestling with indecision. I should go back to my own rooms, have a hot bath, and try to get some sleep. Perhaps I was more cowardly than I cared to admit, but all my room could offer me was stark reminders of how alone I was.

Turning on my heel, I headed in the opposite direction.

"I don't know what to do," I whispered, carefully re-arranging my mother's silken covers. "What would you want me to do? Try to rescue Emeric or stay here and keep safe?"

The words pulled a soft snort of laughter through my nose. Nowhere was safe.

"Lord Devland came to see me at the Festival," I continued, reaching out to wrap a strand of my mother's long blue-black hair around my forefinger. "He thinks Kwellen's little brother would be a good match for me." I smirked at the memory of their faces as I'd threatened them. "He asked me to think about it."

There was no need to think about Lord Devland's proposal. There was no way in Helle I was marrying my best friend's little brother. A wave of repulsion sent a shudder down my spine at the thought.

I stared down at my mother's peaceful expression, her eyes unmoving behind her lids, the thick dark lashes fanning across her pale cheeks. Unable to hold back, I reached out and stroked the backs of my fingers along her skin. It had been years since I'd spent so much time with my mother. What if she never woke up?

Taking her slender forearm in my hand, I pinched her skin, hard. Her eyelids didn't so much as flicker, and I dropped the limb back to the bed with a sigh of disappointment. I considered screaming in her face, but that would only draw unwanted attention.

My wings heavy at my back, I took her limp fingers between mine. I'd always been independent. Perhaps because I'd been left to my own devices for as long as I could remember. Acting time and time again without caution or fear of consequence, regret had never been something I acknowledged. Over the last year, however, my choices had left me filled with doubt. My world—my life—had always felt so certain. Inescapable. But there had been a comfort in that. I had been resigned to my Fate.

I brought my mother's fingers to my forehead and closed my eyes. That had all changed when I'd caught sight of white winged beings fleeing Cove's ship. I sucked in a sharp breath, squeezing my mother's hand.

"Does it still hurt when you think of Emeric?" I whispered, screwing my eyes shut tighter. "Does it ever stop hurting?"

I forced my eyes open and stared at the woman I thought I'd known. She'd spent years in love with Emeric. Years. Conceived a child with him. I pressed my hand to my chest, wincing at the heavy ache I couldn't shift. How had she just flown away? I'd had just four months with Pace and the pull to him was just as strong as it had been before I destroyed us.

And that was the vital difference.

If my mother woke and returned to Emeric, he'd welcome her with open arms. Whereas, despite the tug deep within pleading with me to find Pace, I knew I'd likely be met with a blade.

Letting my mother's hand drop, I rested my head on the bed, blinking back the tears before they could form. My days and nights consisted of a steady stream of 'what if's, and I was so very tired. Closing my eyes, I focused on the queen's soft, steady breathing and let exhaustion sweep me away into oblivion.

A sharp shove to the shoulder had me grumbling, my wings flaring to shield me from the intrusion.

"Sirain."

At the harsh, unfeeling tone, my eyes snapped open, and I sat up, cold dread spreading across my skin. "Father?"

It took me a second to get my bearings. Swiping a hand across my mouth, I blinked, taking in the dark window behind me and trying to make sense of the ache in my neck and back. Somewhere, a candle flickered, casting shadows across the room and I glanced at my mother, remembering where I was.

I pushed to my feet, trying, and failing to hide my wince as my muscles protested. On the other side of the bed, my father stood, a mass of foreboding darkness, the candlelight highlighting his sharp features.

"You missed the Festival," I said, immediately regretting saying anything at all as his frown deepened.

"I had important matters to attend to." His dark eyes lowered, sweeping over his wife. "Still no improvement."

It wasn't a question, so I said nothing.

"You should sleep in your rooms," he said. "I want you well rested for tomorrow."

My pulse quickened, though I kept my expression neutral. "What's happening tomorrow?"

The king of Helle ruffled his wings, drawing himself to his full height as he peered down at me, a cruel glint in his garnet eyes. "Tomorrow, you, my dearest daughter, are finally going to be useful."

Before I could gather breath to reply, he turned and swept from the room, the draft from his wings extinguishing the candle and plunging me back into darkness. Listening to his retreating footsteps, each syllable of his statement settled in my gut like lead. I rose, trembling, and walked to the window, peering out at the night sky, and wondering what time it was.

To the far left, I could see the shimmering purples of The Crossing, the familiar pull calling to me.

Just as every previous time I allowed my gaze to fall upon the monolithic wall of lights, I considered spreading my wings and letting The Crossing take me where it wished. It was a foolish notion. I could no more escape my father than I could my own Fate. Whatever use the king had found for me, escape was nothing more than the fading wisps of a dream upon waking. With a resigned sigh, I turned away from the window. Placing a kiss upon my mother's forehead—something I'd never once done when she'd been awake—I dragged myself back to my empty rooms to stare at the ceiling and wait for the king.

16
Pace

Soaring over the rolling hills and sprawling fields of northern Hehven, I replayed the events of last night's dinner in my head, trying to find answers when I knew there were none. After my mother's revelation, the soup had gone cold, and the waiting staff hadn't returned to serve the main course. It seemed my parents had just as many questions as me and my brother.

The queen had told us how a messenger from Rakkaus had arrived at the Festival with a letter from King Hadeon. I'd asked my parents how that was possible, but they'd refused to answer. I knew it couldn't have been delivered via The Crossing. After all, I'd tried to bring Sirain through to Hehven. I knew it didn't work.

It had been almost comical, listening to my parents explain that Helle was real and impart what little they knew about the Chaos, my face the picture of amazement. I hadn't dared look at my brother.

My mother had presented the letter to Dash, who'd read it with the same wary expression he'd worn the entire evening, before passing it to me. My fingers had trembled as I'd held the thick parchment; at the knowledge that the curling black lettering had been placed there by Sirain's father. Or at least, the man who believed himself to be her father. The letter stated the king wanted to meet in person the following evening. Tonight. My stomach dipped, and I beat my wings a little harder, anxious to reach my destination. Did Sirain know about the letter? Did the king know about us? I sucked in a sharp breath. There was no us.

"You should take it easy, Your Majesty," Jac called from my side.

I ignored him, wholly focused on reaching the Isle of the Fates. Sleep had evaded me again for most of the night, aided by the fact I'd stayed up, re-reading both books, scouring their pages for any mention of a link between Hehven and Helle. I'd found none and woken up, face down on the floor beside my bed.

Landing on the wide slab of rock before the arching wings at the entrance, I strode forward without hesitation. "I won't be long," I called over my shoulder.

"It's fine." Jac huffed as he jogged to keep up. "I snatched a book on the way out just in case."

When we reached the atrium, barely a second passed before the heavy stone door scraped open. This time, it was the door that led to the Fated workroom itself, but I didn't stop to question it; instead, continuing my purposeful journey further into the mountain. As we made our way down the now familiar dark passageway, I wondered whether there were lookouts somewhere to announce arrivals. Or perhaps the Fates themselves made it known. I frowned. It seemed when I answered one question, I unearthed two dozen more.

As soon as my guiding Fated opened the door to the main room, I thanked them and moved forward, searching for Amare. I found her leaning over a desk with another Fated, pointing at something on a large sheet of unrolled parchment. Quickly navigating across the room, my wings tucked in tight, I came to a stop beside her, clearing my throat.

"Pace!" She shifted her hood further back on her head so that I could see her face. "I wasn't expecting to see you today. I heard you were unwell."

"I need to talk to you." I looked pointedly at the record room.

Her eyes narrowing, she turned and excused herself before leading the way to the small room. Once inside, she pushed her hood down, her lips pressed tightly together. "What is it?" she asked. "What's happened?"

I realised, then, she was expecting bad news. I shook my head and stepped towards her. "It's nothing like that," I soothed. "Everyone's okay."

Amare's shoulders sagged and she pinched the bridge of her nose. "Thank the Fates. What's wrong, then? Why do you need to speak to me so urgently?"

"Do you deal with the Chaos?" I asked, deciding there was no point in wasting time on the preamble.

"Excuse me?"

"The Chaos." I took another step closer. "Do you see the Chaos Fated? Do they have a room like this? Or do they use this one? Where—"

Amare held up a hand, her blue eyes blazing. "Pace. Where is all this coming from? Why do you need to know about the Chaos?"

"Does it matter?" I tried. "Can't you just tell me?"

"No." She shook her head. "Explain yourself."

With a heavy sigh, I turned and slumped down on the nearest chair. "The king of Helle sent a message to my parents. He wants to meet with them. Today."

Amare's eyes widened to the point I could see the whites of her eyes clear around her sky-blue irises. "How?"

Disappointment settled on my chest. "I was hoping you could tell me. I know they can't come through The Crossing, so I wondered if there was some way here. The message was delivered to Rakkaus though, which makes absolutely no sense. Unless there's a point in The Crossing—"

"Pace." Amare crouched in front of me, her face crumpling with concern. "You're rambling."

I leaned my head back with a groan. "I'm sorry. I haven't properly slept for the last couple of days."

"Tell me what's going on." She placed a hand on my knee. "What's the real reason Dash is keeping you on a leash? Why did you want those books? Why is this Chaos business so important to you?"

I stared down at her, my heart in my throat. "Amare, I—"

"Tell me," she repeated. "Everything."

My world was already burning, and I was struggling to breathe through the thick smoke, so I resigned myself to letting the flames encompass what little remained.

I sighed. "You might want to sit down."

Amare stared at me for a moment, then rose and pulled a seat from behind one of the other desks. "How worried should I be?"

I studied her face and took a deep breath. "I convinced Dariel to take me through The Crossing. He did it out of guilt, because he was responsible for choosing the female my parents arranged my marriage with. I went back at night, by myself, to watch the humans, and Dariel came after me. We were spotted by Chaos, and they confronted us."

I paused, searching Amare's pained face as she processed what I was telling her.

"Go on," she murmured.

"Humans saw us. We became friends with Marlowe, the ruler of the Wendell Islands." I took a breath, deciding my cousin would want his sister to know how happy he'd been. "Dariel fell in love with him."

Amare's hands flew to her mouth, smothering the gasped

whimper that escaped her lips. My chest ached at the confession, but now that I'd started, I couldn't stop.

"The humans wanted us to help stop the war. We noticed that Chaos were carrying out orders that directly cancelled out orders Cupids had been given hours earlier. That's why Dariel asked you about the books. We were trying to find answers."

"You were questioning the Fates," Amare whispered, her eyes shimmering with unshed tears. "Oh, Pace."

I shook my head. "The Fates are part of the reason Dariel died."

Amare stood, her fingers pressing to her temples as she turned away from me, wings sagging under the weight of my truth. "What happened?"

"The Fates gave orders to the crown princess of Helle, to kill Marlowe."

Amare whirled; her eyes narrowed. "Impossible. The Fates do not order death."

I met her incredulous stare and nodded. "They do. They've done it twice that we know of."

"Is Marlowe dead?" she asked.

"No." I fixed my stare, unblinking on a spot on the floor as the pain of the memory threatened to consume me. "The crown princess couldn't carry out the orders. She was going to allow the arrow to miss, but Dariel didn't know. He died protecting the man he loved."

Amare crumpled back down onto the seat, her head in her hands.

"The Chaos were scared I would seek retribution for Dariel's death, so they told a Cupid Hand that I'd been sneaking through The Crossing. Dash was waiting for me the next time I arrived back in Hehven. He locked me away in a room for almost two months to teach me a lesson."

Amare swiped at her eyes, her hands trembling. "Who else knows all of this?"

"Just Tiesa," I said. "And the Chaos involved. Dash only knows that I was meeting with humans and Chaos. He doesn't know why."

Amare stared at me, reminding me in that moment of my mother—the way she seemed to see into my very soul. "What aren't you telling me, Pace?"

"The crown princess. I . . ." I exhaled, pulling a hand over my face. "I loved her."

The words felt jagged and painful on my tongue, and I grimaced.

Amare continued to stare at me. If she was surprised by my admission, she didn't show it. "Did you find anything in the books I gave you?"

Exhaustion pressed down on every inch of my body with the weight of a thousand boulders. "There was an illustration of the Fates," I said carefully. "In the book written by our ancestor."

"And?"

I stared back at my cousin, deciding in that moment to withhold one small piece of information. If it was discovered I'd sneaked onto the boat to see the Fates while under her care, she might face repercussions, and if I could prevent that from happening, I would.

"It showed the Fates as small, wingless beings. They float, at least a wing's width off the ground, and they glow with an almost translucent quality." I watched as Amare's face fell into a frown. "That's what they look like, right?"

Amare's eyes seemed to glaze, her body going perfectly still.

"The book also said that only Cupids and Chaos with royal blood can see all four," I continued, eyeing her carefully. "Which means you're the only Fated who can see all four. The others should see only two."

"The Chaos cannot cross into Hehven from here," she said, her eyes fixed, unblinking, on a point somewhere over my shoulder. "Although you can't see The Crossing over the sea, it remains. It only ceases at the front steps of the Isle of the Fates itself. The Chaos work through the night into the morning and we work from the morning into the early evening. Twelve hours each. Our paths do not cross. We are not allowed to communicate." She allowed her gaze to meet mine for a fleeting second. "I have never laid eyes on a Chaos."

I swallowed as her words settled over me. "Amare?"

Her gaze remained unfocused, but as I leaned forward to stand, the door swung open and my brother strode in, resplendent in glowing white robes trimmed in gold embroidery. His crown sat amongst his short, wavy, white hair, the jewels catching in the firelight.

"Dashuri," I said, getting to my feet as his narrowed gaze flitted between us.

"What's going on?" he demanded.

Amare stood, smoothing her hands over her robes. "We were just talking about Dariel."

Not quite the truth, but also not a lie. My brother's accusatory stare faded as he looked between us.

"Is everything okay, Dashuri?" I asked.

He gave a terse smile. "Our parents want to arrive early for the meeting. They've made arrangements with Lord Rakkaus and have arranged for suitable clothing to be brought for you to wear."

My eyebrows shot up. "I'm perfectly capable of going home and getting changed."

"You seriously expect to fly the length of the country twice in one day?" Dash stared at me, shaking his head. "Besides, there's no time. They're likely already there."

My stomach churned. I'd never once considered the possibility I might one day meet Sirain's father, and even though I knew the reason for the meeting could be a million different things, I couldn't help but wonder whether he knew. I didn't know what had happened to Sirain after she left Marlowe's ship, but I assumed she must have completed the Royal Rites if she was still alive to send a warning to Emeric. I pressed a hand to my stomach.

"Pace?" Amare stepped forward. "Are you all right? You don't look well."

I sucked in a breath, straightening my shoulders. "I'll be fine."

"Come on," Dash said, opening the door. "Let's get to Rakkaus and then we can find a healer to take a look at you."

I hesitated at the genuine concern in his voice. Sometimes it was easy to forget that somewhere beneath the disdain and arrogance, my brother cared about me.

"I'll see you soon, Pace," Amare said, touching her hand to my arm. "Tomorrow or the day after, perhaps?"

"Yes." I nodded, watching a thousand emotions swirling in the bright blue depths of her eyes and wishing we'd had just a few minutes more. "I'll see you soon."

As I followed my brother towards the atrium, I expected him to question me, but he remained silent. At first, I suspected he was annoyed with me, but as we reached the front steps, he gave me a tight smile over his shoulder before spreading his wings. It was then, I realised; he was just as nervous as I was.

17
Sirain

S
ix servants dressed me. My bedchamber had never been so full or felt so small. The silence was suffocating as twelve hands scrubbed and combed amidst the rustling of feathers and the jostling of wings. Even though the king had mentioned his plans pertained to the evening, the sun had barely breached the horizon when the servants had arrived. Dressed entirely in coarse, black dresses, they were indistinguishable from one another—wraith-like shadows, there to serve without being seen or heard. In my sleep deprived state, I hadn't questioned the hour, allowing them to do whatever they needed to do.

As one servant relieved me of my robe, another produced a dress I'd never seen before from a sleek, black box. It was beautiful. Two servants pulled the dress over my head, tightening the leather straps around the middle, and I stared blankly at my reflection. The criss-crossed top was a deep plum, with an intricate leather belt adorned with gold stitching. The floor-length skirts, which faded into a rich amethyst, would complement my hair and feathers perfectly. Perhaps they would also match the dark circles beneath my eyes.

I hadn't slept again. My insides were still knotted tightly with worry about the whereabouts of my friends and questioning the location of my human father following Tumulto's revelation. But then the king had added an additional weighty layer, which had caused me to toss and turn, my blankets abandoned on the cold stone floor, as I conjured a thousand different ways I might be 'useful' to him.

In the mirror, I could see a sliver of the window over my shoulder, the lights of The Crossing a jarringly bright green. I swallowed down the thoughts of my father—my real father. There was nothing that could be done now. I'd hoped Marlowe would try to rescue him, but we'd told him that Newbold had captured him. Had Emeric purposefully travelled to Dalibor? Had he made it?

Five of the servants stepped back, their heads bowed, and their wings tucked in tight, and I blinked, my reflection coming into focus. The sixth servant shuffled forward, her eyes downcast, a small black pillow in her outstretched hands and I turned from the mirror, staring at the tiara resting on the velvet. Made entirely from obsidian glass and black diamonds, it seemed to swallow the light, simultaneously breathtaking and devastating.

Reluctantly, I took the jewelled offering and placed it on my head. The servants had left my hair down in flowing waves, the heady scent of jasmine clouding my senses every time I turned.

"You look . . . presentable, Sister."

Every muscle in my body tensed at the sound of my brother's voice, but my heart dropped into my stomach when I caught sight of him. Dressed in fine black robes and a thick cloak lined with dark brown fur, a similar crown sat atop his short, dark hair.

"You're coming," I said quietly.

Fin stared at me, his eyes flickering with what looked like barely contained glee. "But of course, Sister. I'm here to escort you."

I gave him a tight smile. "And where exactly are you escorting me to?"

"Ah. It's not about the destination, it's about the journey."

My teeth clenched together, on the verge of cracking, but I gathered my skirts and swept from the room, my chin held high.

I expected Fin to taunt me the entire way to wherever we were headed, but his purposeful strides, just quick enough to cause me to struggle to keep up, were thankfully silent. We made our way through the castle, not stopping until we reached the entrance that led to the northern courtyard. I sucked in a gasp at the cold breeze, shooting Fin a questioning look.

"You should have brought a cloak," he said, his lips twitching. "It's going to be cold where we're going."

My eyes narrowed into a glare that only served to delight him further, but my biting retort was halted by the sound of approaching footsteps.

With barely so much as a glance, the king swept past us, his large wings snapping open as he took to the skies. He, too, was dressed in his finest black velvet robes, his ceremonial crown of polished onyx and black diamonds nestled amongst his thick, dark hair. I turned, looking for guards or servants, but found none. At my side, Fin spread his wings, purposefully knocking into me in the process, and took two running strides before swooping up after his father.

Panicked trepidation shook my body and my heart thumped loudly against my ribs. Something didn't feel right. It was as though a line had been drawn by the king, and I knew if I crossed it, there would be no going back. I couldn't begin to fathom what his plans for me might be, but I knew for certain they were nothing good. Why would we have no guards accompanying us? Perhaps this was all a ruse, and the king was merely leading me away from the castle so he could stage my accidental death.

Staggering backwards, I watched as the king and my brother's silhouettes shrank against the muted sky. Spreading my own wings, I took off into the darkness. I couldn't go through with this. I had to get away. Trapped within the confines of the castle—of my title—I could do nothing. If I could break free of those ties, perhaps I could find my friends. My father.

My heart raced as I decided; I was going to flee. I'd have to wait, though. Making a bid for freedom immediately would not be the wisest choice. Not this close to the castle, where I could be chased down by guards and Hands. I didn't know where we were going, but I resolved that as soon as there was enough distance between us and the castle, I would make my move.

It was a reckless and ill-thought-out plan, but the reality was simple. I could leave and live or stay and die. Angling my wings to catch an updrift, I rose higher into the air, catching up with the Hadeon men. Fin glared at me over his wing as I drew nearer, but I pretended I didn't see.

We flew north, over the snow-covered mountains, and I eyed the ivory peak of Mount Hadeon through narrowed eyes, my teeth chattering in my skull, as I recalled how close I'd come to losing my life at its summit. Squinting, I regarded the landscape below through my lashes as the cold air burned my eyes. The further north we flew, I rapidly ran out of ideas for our destination. Hadeon was the most northern city, with only towns and villages beyond the mountains along the coast. There were a few lords who presided there, but they were considered so inconsequential by the king, they were rarely invited to important meetings.

As the churning grey sea drew near, I shivered. Perhaps they were taking me to the Isle of the Fates for some sort of judgement. The idea of getting so dressed up, only to be punished, was ridiculous; but the king loved spectacle. If I was to die, I supposed it was of no consequence how I was dressed. My corpse surely wouldn't care.

We'd flown parallel to The Crossing, its shimmering light a burning constant in the corner of my eye, readying me for my escape. My heart hammered in my throat, every muscle tensing as I prepared to break away. With the sea ahead and nothing but sprawling forests below, I drew in a deep breath and, before I could change my mind, dipped my wing.

Banking hard to the left, I dropped lower, almost skimming the tops of the trees, before evening out in a glide. Only then did I pump my wings with every remaining ounce of strength, my heart in my throat, choking me.

I didn't dare look back. The precious seconds I had before they realised I'd dropped back and started towards The Crossing were already too few. Fin had been shooting me daggered glances every few minutes the entire way.

With each exhausted pull of my wings, I cursed the fact I'd let my brother wear me down to nothing. If I'd eaten, trained, and slept over the last few months, I would be twice as fast and easily able to outfly the both of them. In my weakened state, all I had was the element of surprise.

The Crossing shimmered, setting the tops of the trees alight with an ethereal glow. No matter how hard I beat my wings, it still seemed so far away. My lungs constricted at the thought of being thrust out into the human world in broad daylight, in the middle of a war. Where would I even go? Briefly, I considered the Wendell Islands, but pushed the thought away. No. I was on my own. I'd hide, scavenge, and spy. I'd do whatever it took to find Emeric. My heart ached. In doing this, I'd be leaving Odio and Kwellen behind, wherever they were. I'd have to sneak back through once enough time had passed.

A sharp pain shot along my wing, and I yelped as I dipped low enough that my feet touched the treetops. Righting myself, I turned in time to find Fin, his arm back mid-throw and his features twisted into a joyful snarl. This time, I was able to dodge whatever he threw at me, and I turned, bowing my head as I urged forward towards my salvation.

"You can't escape!" Fin's voice carried on the wind. "You'll only make things worse."

My lips pressed together as I pushed my wings harder. Worse. How could things possibly get any worse?

Another bout of searing pain slashed across my wings and I couldn't contain my shout as I faltered, the skirts of my dress tangling on the treetops. I'd thought perhaps they were knives he was throwing, but the dull, wide throbbing across the arch of my wing told me it wasn't. My best guess was rocks. Daring to cast a glance over my shoulder, I sucked in a breath as Fin slammed into me, his icy fingers gripping my throat and shoulder painfully as we plummeted to the ground.

"Let go of me!" I shrieked.

Fin said nothing as we tumbled, our wings bearing the onslaught of evergreen branches until the cold, hard ground of a small clearing reached up to greet us.

All air left my lungs in a grunt, and I gasped, eyes wide as I tried to breathe. Agony pulsed in my chest as I attempted to roll away, my fingers clawing at the layers of pine needles beneath me, but Fin shifted his weight on top of me, pinning me down, his long fingers still wrapped tightly around my throat.

"Get off me!" I snarled.

My brother glared down at me, his garnet-flecked eyes wild, as I continued my futile struggle beneath him. I grabbed and shoved, my fingers scrabbling, trying to pull his hands from my neck and attempting to grip his limbs through his thick robes. For so much of our lives, I'd been bigger, stronger. Now, Fin had the advantage, and I had nothing. My hands fell to the side in defeat, tears stinging the corners of my eyes.

"Just kill me," I croaked out.

Fin's grip loosened from my throat. "Trust me, Sister," he spat. "I would love to end this right now, but I can't."

"Why not? Tell me where we're going. Where's my guard? Where's Kwellen?" My hoarse yell rang out through the dense forest.

"You don't need guards where we're going."

My father's deep baritone saw Fin jump to his feet, brushing the forest debris from his robes as I scrambled backwards on my hands, my heart pounding.

I watched, chest heaving as the king stooped and plucked my tiara from the ground. He flicked bits of dirt from it, then stepped to my side, dropping into a crouch. It was all I could do not to flinch away as he reached out and secured the tiara back on my head. I could barely breathe as he remained, picking pine needles and leaf mulch from my hair. My gaze flitted to Fin, who watched through narrowed eyes, his features pinched.

"You marked her," the king muttered, his fingers touching the tender spots on my neck.

Fin shifted his weight, folding his arms across his chest. "They'll fade."

"Where is my guard?" I whispered.

The king stood, brushing off his own rich velvet robes. "Do you feel you need a guard?"

I pressed my lips together, pushing up to my feet. My wings ached, and I winced as I stretched them out, testing them.

"I asked you a question. Do you feel you need protection, Daughter?" The king all but spat the last word, as though it pained him to say it.

"You would know better than me, Father," I said, folding in my wings. "Do I?"

The king stared at me, the hint of a smile twisting at the corner of his mouth.

"Are you going to kill me?"

The smallest flicker of surprise passed over the king's

features. "If I was going to kill you, I'd have let your brother finish what he started."

"Tell me," I pushed. "Where are you taking me?"

The king peered down at me, stepping close enough that I had to tilt my head back to meet his gaze. "You are not to try and flee again. Do you understand?"

My jaw clenched, defiance simmering beneath the smothering swell of fear. "Tell me where we're going, and perhaps I won't feel the need to."

"Do you not see?" He gestured around us, his eyes lighting with quiet, cruel delight. "You don't have the power to make demands. You will do as you're told, without question, and if you so much as think about putting one feather out of line, know this: it will not be you that pays the consequences of your actions, but your friends."

My heart stuttered in my chest as I staggered back a step. "What have you done with them?"

"Nothing," he said. "Yet."

A soft snicker sounded behind him and it took all my willpower not to launch myself at my brother. Instead, I clenched my hands at my sides, a fresh wave of helplessness washing over me as my throat ached with blossoming bruises and my blood pulsed in my injured wing.

That was why I hadn't been able to find Odio and Kwellen. When had he taken them? Where were they? Were they okay? I pushed the questions back down my aching throat. He would never answer them and asking would only highlight the fact that he had the measure of me. They were my weakness.

"Can you fly?" the king asked, his gaze flickering to my wing.

I gave a single nod.

"Then let's go. We don't want to be late." He turned and opened his wings, then paused, glancing over his shoulder. "Don't do anything reckless."

The forest floor fluttered and shifted as his mighty wings beat the cool air, and I swallowed down the bitter taste of defeat as I watched him soar out of the clearing. This time, Fin waited, gesturing for me to follow.

Grimacing at the dull ache along the arch of my wing, I let the cool breeze caress my feathers as I pushed up into air, the sharp snap of wings signalling my brother's presence close behind. Any chance I'd had of escaping whatever lay ahead had been dashed. There wouldn't be a second opportunity.

18
Pace

Lord Rakkaus' home was a sprawling, red-roofed affair set into a large hill overlooking the rolling fields and orchards of the region famed for its farmlands. The last time I'd visited, had been to tell his daughter, Caitland, that I couldn't marry her, and the sweat beading at my brow had little to do with the short flight from the Isle of the Fates.

Several Hands were standing before the main entrance, dressed in their finest tunics, and they bowed low as we approached. One opened the large front door, and I nodded my thanks as I followed in Dashuri's hurried wake.

"Where are the second prince's clothes?" my brother demanded.

The Hand dipped into a shallow bow, pointing at another set of doors. "Just through there, Your Majesty."

Dash grunted his thanks before turning to me. "Get changed, and then we'll find our parents."

My mind whirling, I started in the direction the Hand had pointed. Two waiting staff, clad in white silk, whom I recognised from the palace, appeared at my side.

I paused, frowning. "I don't need any help, thank you."

They both stared up at me with wide eyes, but before they could insist, I slipped inside the room, pulling the door closed behind me. It was a small office, or perhaps reading room, judging by the walls of books and plush emerald velvet sofas. On one of said sofas, my clothes had been neatly laid out. I reached down and lifted the fine ivory tunic, running my fingers over the delicate golden embroidery. It reminded me of the one I'd worn for the Summer Festival, although this one was a lot thicker, with a soft, woollen inner layer.

My fingers gripped the material as memories from that night assaulted my senses. The scent of the bonfire. Sirain's laughter, her eyes closed, and head thrown back as we'd danced. The way her dress had pooled at her feet . . .

I shook my head, clearing it of the memory and forcing myself back into the present. As I shrugged out of my simple jacket and shirt, a wave of hysteria washed over me, and a booming laugh burst from my lips. I cast a quick glance over my shoulder at the door, but it remained closed. How had I found myself in this position? Preparing to meet the father of the woman I'd surrendered my purity to, in the house of my formerly betrothed.

What if Sirain was coming?

My chest tightened, my hand gripping my bare flesh as I froze at the thought. I'd been so concerned with the logistics—how a Chaos could even enter Hehven—that I hadn't considered the possibility that the crown princess might accompany her father. I swallowed, breathing hard, my wide eyes staring at the door. Was Sirain on her way to Hehven? Would I be forced to stand in a room with her? To sit at a table with her alongside my parents?

My stomach churned, the tunic slipping from my fingers to the floor. What if my parents were about to sit down with the female who'd killed their nephew? Sucking in a breath, I winced at the sharp pain in my chest. I couldn't do this. When Odio and Kwellen had dragged her from Marlowe's ship, I'd felt certain I'd never see her again. I knew she wouldn't try to find me to talk to me. After all, there was no point. The second she'd released that arrow, she'd set fire to everything we'd ever had.

I swiped at my sodden brow before striding over to a window and heaving it open. The frigid autumn air lashed at my heated skin, and I closed my eyes, trying to calm my racing pulse. She might not even be coming. It was likely just the king. My jaw clenched, wings flaring at the thought of seeing her and not being able to voice the things that plagued my mind during every second of quiet. The things that stole my sleep and hounded my waking hours. My chest rose and fell rapidly, my fingers gripping the wooden window frame. How could I stand in the same room as the person who'd ripped the beating heart from my chest and pretend like everything was okay?

"Pace?" Dashuri barked through the closed door. "Are you almost ready? Do I need to fetch a healer?"

A wry smile briefly twisted my lips. No healer alive could repair what was left of my heart. "One moment, Brother."

Steeling myself, I picked up the tunic from the floor, slipping my arms in and fastening it around my wings. I likely looked a mess, but at least I could blame it on being unwell. Glancing at the wool-lined trousers, I decided to keep on the ones I was wearing. They were both dark brown and I doubted anyone would notice. Taking a readying breath, I strode to the door and opened it.

Dash looked me up and down, his nose wrinkling. "Perhaps we should have arranged for a bath for you. Are you sure you don't need a healer?"

I shook my head. "I'm fine. Just a little feverish."

Dash's lips pressed together, then he turned to one of the waiting staff from the palace. "Fetch the prince some lemon balm tea to try and bring down his fever, please."

The server bowed and strode off into the house as if they'd lived here all their life. I frowned. "When did our parents arrive?"

"Early this morning." Dash fiddled with the neck of his robe and my eyebrows raised. I'd never seen my brother so nervous.

Looking around, I realised I was missing my shadow. "Where's Jac?"

"I dismissed him. I'll take responsibility for you while we're here." Dash narrowed his gaze on mine. "I've informed the Hands guarding the property that you are not allowed to leave without me or Jac under any circumstances."

Before I could muster a response, another servant stepped forward, a small white velvet cushion in her hands. It took everything I had to suppress the groan that built in my throat. Atop the cushion was a circlet, composed of two gleaming gilded feathers. I froze, my shoulders rigid, as Dashuri lifted it without any ceremony and placed it on my head.

"Let's go," he said, gesturing towards a hallway. "We're late enough as it is."

As I followed my brother, I noted it was a different part of the house than I had visited before. It was an impressive building from the outside, but as we moved through Lord Rakkaus' property, I realised I'd misjudged its size. Our footsteps sounded loudly against the polished, dark wood floors, each measured thud mirroring the pounding in my head.

It was too much. Between the Fates, my brother, the King of Helle and now possibly Sirain, I couldn't breathe. I longed for a minute of calm to clear my head. I longed for the cliff. Shaking my head, I clenched and unclenched my fists at my sides. Just another thing Sirain had ruined.

We reached a set of towering wooden doors and two Cupids I didn't recognise pulled them open. I smiled at them in thanks, but they stared back with glowering expressions that almost made me halt my stride.

"Who are they?" I hissed at Dash as the doors closed behind

us, enclosing us in a small, windowless area with several seats set against the walls.

He glanced over his shoulder, then back at me. "Two of Lord Rakkaus' sons. Why?"

I swallowed. "No reason. I didn't recognise them, that's all."

No wonder they had looked at me with barely concealed malice. I shifted uncomfortably. I'd known Caitland had at least one brother, because he was a Hand. I hadn't known there were others.

Dash stepped forward to another set of doors, fortunately unguarded, and knocked twice before opening them to reveal a large windowless room, surprisingly neutral in colour compared with the rest of the property. Ivory drapes adorned the walls, turning almost golden in the candlelight, with paintings of scenery placed in the gaps between. It was formal, yet comfortable. Impressive, yet humble. A large oak table took up most of the space, the white cloth on its surface filled with silver cups and a large glass bowl of fruit, but no one was seated at it. My parents stood talking with Lord Rakkaus at one end, looking up as we entered.

"Dashuri. Pace." The queen moved towards us, and I took in her appearance with raised eyebrows.

Both the king and queen were wearing their official crowns. I couldn't remember the last time I'd seen them wear them. They were large, heavy looking things, set with gleaming diamonds and made with twisting vines of gold and silver. My mother wore her finest robes, the shimmering white and gold silk trailing behind her as she walked. At her side, my father's hair was carefully braided, with threads of gold woven between the strands. When the queen took hold of my arms, smiling up at me, I noticed her dark brown cheeks had been dusted with a shimmering golden powder, her eyes also lined with gold. I blinked, unable to remember her ever wearing makeup.

Perhaps I should have taken Dashuri up on his offer to find a bath.

"You look beautiful, Mother," I said. "As do you, Father."

He rolled his eyes and my mother smiled, although it quickly faded to a look of concern.

"I hear you're still unwell. How are you feeling?"

"I'm fine," I reassured her. Not at all slowly dying inside.

Caitland's father stepped forward, dipping a bow, his long white hair falling forward. "Welcome to Rakkaus, Your Majesties."

I pasted a smile on my face as he looked me over, and I wondered what he saw. Most likely, a lucky escape for his daughter.

"Thank you so much for your hospitality, Lord Rakkaus." Dashuri inclined his head. "You have a beautiful home."

"Come," my mother said. "Let's sit. We have a lot to discuss before King Hadeon arrives."

"I'll send for some tea," Lord Rakkaus said, moving to the door.

Dash turned to him. "I requested some lemon balm tea for Prince Pace. If you could arrange for it to be brought here, we would be most grateful."

Lord Rakkaus bowed again, but when his eyes met mine, I found the same disdain I'd witnessed from his sons, and my pasted smile faltered.

As soon as the door closed behind him, I turned to my parents. "Why are we here? Why Rakkaus?"

The king and queen shared a look, and my wings flared.

"This is where King Hadeon wanted to meet," Dash said, speaking softly as though placating a child.

My jaw tightened. "I was asking our parents."

"Dashuri is right," the king said. "The reason for the location is unimportant."

"Unimportant?" I echoed. "I would say it's extremely important. As apparently, there's a way for Chaos to get into Hehven."

Dash reached out and gripped my arm, his fingers digging into my flesh. "It's unimportant for you, Pace."

I shrugged out of his hold, my fists clenching beneath the table. "Do you know why he wants to meet at least?"

The queen shook her head, the diamonds swinging from her ears catching the light. "No. We only know that he wishes to speak with us."

"How can you be so calm?" I demanded. "It's the King of Helle for Fate's sake! What if he's coming here with an army to slaughter us all?"

A strangled noise emitted from my father as my mother's eyes widened. Beside me, Dashuri leapt to his feet.

"Maybe you should step outside, Pace," he hissed. "Clearly your fever has worsened."

I shot him a withering look before returning my attention to my parents. "You should have Hands in here with you. You should have protection."

"Pace," the queen said, looking between me and my brother. "The stories that paint Chaos as ruthless killers are not true. They're just like us."

I tried, but I couldn't hold in the bark of laughter that burst from my chest. "How many Chaos have you met, Mother?"

Something that looked like hurt flashed in her golden eyes, but before I could begin to feel remorse, Dashuri dragged me from my chair. My wings flared as I protested, but I was on my feet before I could disentangle myself from his hold.

"Outside, Brother," Dashuri seethed. "Now."

My jaw clenched, my shoulders back as I stared him down, but I saw the threat in his eyes. If I didn't do as he said, he'd tell them the truth. There was more to that truth than they knew, though. They were oblivious to the fact they were about to meet with the most dangerous creature in existence. Whatever King Hadeon wanted, it was surely nothing good.

"Perhaps it's best if you wait outside," my father said, his brow furrowed. "We're going to meet with him alone first anyway. We'll call you in when we're ready for dinner to be served."

I opened my mouth to respond, trying to find words to warn them, but Dashuri hauled me out of the room. As soon as the door closed, I whirled on him, my wings snapping open. "What in Fates' sake was that?"

"Language!" Dashuri barked as he strode forward, backing me up against the wall.

I hissed, my teeth bared, as my wings bent against the satin wallpaper.

"I don't know what you think you're playing at," Dash said, his voice quiet enough that no one on the other side of the doors would be able to hear. "But this stops now. Unless you want our parents to know all about your exploits with the Chaos. Behave."

I pressed my lips together as his own curled in disgust. Didn't he know this wasn't anger, but fear? How could I stand by and allow my parents to put themselves in harm's way? Before I could formulate a response, the doors from the hallway opened and he stepped away from me, straightening his robes.

"Oh, sorry," Caitland looked between us, a tray laden with tea in her hands and her silver eyes wide. "Am I interrupting?"

I pushed off the wall, tugging at my tunic as I folded my wings.

"Not at all," Dashuri said, offering her a tight smile. "May I assist you?"

Caitland inclined her head in thanks as Dashuri pushed open the door to the meeting room, following in behind her. I exhaled, shoving my fingers through my hair. I hadn't meant to get so worked up. Everyone was acting like the situation was perfectly normal when it couldn't have been further from the truth.

The door opened again, but only Caitland emerged, a small porcelain cup in her hands. I gave her a sheepish smile and she winced, glancing over her shoulder at the door.

"The crown prince told me to tell you, you're to wait out here until you're called for." She held the cup out to me. "And this is for your fever?"

I sighed, taking the cup from her, and setting it down on a small side table. "Thank you."

"What did you do?" she asked, stepping closer.

"It doesn't matter." I sank down onto a chair. "How are you?"

I'd been a little nervous about seeing Caitland again, but now she was standing in front of me, I couldn't remember why. Just like the last time we'd met, her shyness was streaked with an undercurrent of confidence that reminded me not to under-estimate her.

"Fine," she said, a sadness flickering over her face. "You?"

I frowned. "What happened? Is your father giving you a hard time about the engagement?"

"No." She shook her head. "Not at all. Although my brothers were far from happy to learn you were coming here."

I chuckled. "Yeah, I got that impression from the two out there."

"I had to practically beg them to let me bring the tea in," she admitted, a small smile playing on her lips. "They're a little overprotective."

I leaned forward, resting my forearms on my thighs. "Why did you want to bring the tea in?"

"To see you." She gestured at one of the chairs. "May I?"

"Of course." I watched as she took the seat opposite,

smoothing her long pale blue skirts. "Why did you want to see me?"

Caitland stared at me for a long moment, and I marvelled at how the delicate female before me had once been unable to lift her head long enough to look at me. If things had gone differently, we'd have been married in just a few months.

"I wanted to see if you were okay," she said, keeping her voice deliberately quiet. "I was curious to know how things were with . . . you know."

My bemused smile evaporated and I looked away with a frown. "It's over."

"Oh." Caitland let out a slow breath. "I'm sorry."

I shook my head. "Don't be. It's for the best."

"If it makes you feel any better," she said softly. "Mine is over too."

My eyebrows shot up. "Oh? What happened?"

"It turns out, we were rather incompatible," she said, her cheeks flushing pink.

I stared at her for a moment, wondering whether to press for more information, but deciding against it.

"Don't worry," she said, raising her gaze to meet mine. "I'm not going to suggest we get married after all. If any two Cupids were the very definition of incompatible, it would be us."

Smiling, I reached up and rubbed the back of my neck. "I'd say you're probably right."

"Are you going to tell me what's going on before my brothers grow worried enough to come and drag me out, then?"

I opened and closed my mouth a couple of times, taken aback by her abruptness, before settling on a frown. "Everyone seems so calm about the fact the Chaos can get into Hehven," I explained. "I got a little worked up trying to convey just how serious this is."

Caitland surveyed me through slightly narrowed eyes,

weighing my words. "Why are you so worried? Do you think the Chaos have an ulterior motive for coming?"

I huffed a laugh. "Don't you? Why would they reach out to us now? There's no record of Cupids and Chaos ever meeting."

"There's always a first time for everything."

"Indeed. But there's only a first and last time to die."

Caitland's silver eyes widened. "You think they're coming to kill us?"

I shrugged, then pinched the bridge of my nose. "I honestly don't know. And no one will tell me anything."

"I'm sorry."

Caitland's quiet voice drew my attention, and I dropped my hand to my lap. "You know, don't you? You know why they're here in Rakkaus?"

In answer, she stood and took a step towards the door, avoiding my gaze. "I'm sorry things went badly for you and your love. I hope that next time, you find the right home for your heart."

Her words dragged blunt nails down the inside of my battered chest, but I dipped my head in thanks instead. "You too."

She smiled. "I'm sure I'll see you again before you leave."

"Caitland?" I stood, my eyes darting to the door as she lifted a hand to pull the handle. "Please, tell me. Why Rakkaus? I swear on the Fates I won't tell anyone you told me. You know I'll find out, eventually."

Her hand tightened its grip on the doorknob. "If you'll find out eventually, perhaps you should exercise a little patience."

"Patience has never been one of my strong suits," I admitted with a sheepish smile. "Please, Caitland."

Her hand slipped from the polished brass knob, and she sighed. "There is a tunnel that links Hehven and Helle. It runs under The Crossing. Thousands of years ago, the Fates placed the Rakkaus family in charge of guarding the Hehven side of the tunnel, ensuring no one left or entered."

I stared; my eyes wide. "I'm sorry. What?"

Caitland lifted her delicate shoulders in a small shrug. "Only the Rakkaus family knows about it. Even the King and Queen weren't aware until we sent my brother with the message King Hadeon brought."

"Why, though?" I managed. "If no one has been allowed in for centuries, why now?"

"I don't know." Caitland gave me a small smile. "King Hadeon is the first person to ever try and enter."

19
Sirain

Convinced we were heading to the Isle of the Fates, I stared in confusion as the king dropped, swooping down towards the thick forest and alighting at the edge of the trees. I followed, grateful to be out of the freezing currents, if nothing else. Fin landed softly behind me, his presence urging me to follow as our father wasted no time in striding between the thickly packed trees. I bit back the urge to turn around and see whether Fin was as puzzled as I was. It didn't matter. I had no choice but to obey. Chilled to the bone, I hoisted my skirts and followed.

We hiked through the forest for several minutes, until we came to a small clearing, a rocky expanse lining one side, although how high the rocks surged beyond the trees was concealed by their thick branches. A heavy sense of foreboding settled over me as I watched the king stride towards the dense, grey boulders, and promptly disappear. A small gasp tore from my lips, and I dashed across the clearing to see better. Fin snorted at my confusion, gesturing to a dark gash deep in the rock. A cave. Shaking his head, he shoved me forward, the darkness swallowing us both.

What was this hidden place? Why had the king brought us here? I started to wonder whether he'd lied to me; that he was going to kill me, after all. Perhaps he'd chosen the cave because then he could say I'd fled. Too weak to take the pressure of the crown—the throne. No one would ever find my body here. My hand moved to my thigh, grasping for the ghost of a dagger I hadn't worn in months. Breathing out a hollow sigh, I realised my folly; not even the sharpest blade could protect me from my Fate.

My fingers brushing against the rough, icy rock, I blinked, adjusting to the lack of light. A crackling roar startled me, and I staggered backwards as a torch burst into flame in the king's hand. Eyes wide, I stared at the small stack of torches near the entrance. This was not the first time he'd been here, and he clearly planned on returning. Fin's looming presence blocked the entrance, and as the king moved further into the cave, my muscles screamed at me not to follow. But I had no choice. I took a tentative step, wondering whether I'd ever actually had one at all.

We made our way along a dark, narrow tunnel, the only sound that of the crackling torch and our steady, echoing footsteps. The silence only served to taunt me with thoughts of my friends. I'd searched everywhere in the castle for Odio and Kwellen, but I hadn't thought to check the dungeons. After all, why would they have been there? My stomach twisted. Had they been below the castle the whole time? Odio may have been the king's nephew, but I knew that wouldn't make a difference. Wherever the king had put them, and whatever they were enduring, it was bound to be unpleasant.

Eventually, the tunnel widened, the space becoming broad enough that I didn't have to press my wings together. It was so dark beyond the flickering torchlight, I couldn't see how high up the cave went, but as my father spread his wings, I stared in awe as he pushed up into the air. I watched, fixed to the spot, until a rough shove knocked me forward.

"Hurry, Sister," Fin snapped. "We haven't got all day."

Scowling into the darkness, I jogged forward a few steps and leapt up into the air. With no breeze, it was hard work to keep aloft, and the effort of doing so with my injured wing meant my skin was soon coated with sweat.

We flew for what must have been over an hour along the endless pitch-black tunnel, with just the king's single dwindling torch for guidance. With every slight curve, I slowed, bracing myself, fearful that the rock face would emerge from the darkness and smite me. Shadows danced along the jagged walls, rising and falling with the flickering of the torch, conjuring images that grew more vivid with every passing minute.

More times than I could count, I considered asking how much further we had to go, and each time I swallowed the words down, internally cursing my stupidity. It didn't matter. I would have to face whatever lay ahead, regardless of my wishes.

When the king halted the beating of his wings, gliding downwards in a graceful arc, I followed, searching the surrounding cave for any sign of what might have prompted the action, but finding nothing.

We continued on foot, the cave gradually narrowing until we were forced to walk in single file once more, the king in front and Fin behind, trapping me between them. When King Hadeon came to a stop, I almost crashed into the back of him, catching myself just in time. He reached up and placed the torch into a sconce before turning to face me, the angles of his features sharply grotesque in the flickering flame light.

"When we go in, you are to behave," he hissed.

I frowned, noting a door behind him as I processed his command. The door was simple in style, made of solid wood with no handle to be seen. My pulse rocketed.

"What?" I asked, my voice a rasp from disuse.

He stepped closer, but I forced myself to stand my ground, aware of Fin behind me, close enough I could feel his breath on my wings. "You are the next queen of Helle, and I expect you to act as such. You'll speak if spoken to, but consider the weight of your words. I am still King, and I am in control."

I stared, my answer obstructed by the thousands of questions queued on my tongue.

He reached out and took hold of my upper arm, squeezing. "Do you understand?"

Defiance flickered under my skin, but I gritted my teeth and nodded. "Yes, Father."

His features twisting into a sneer, he gripped my arm tighter, forcing a whimper from my lips, before shoving me away, sending me stumbling backwards into my brother.

As I righted myself, flinching from Fin's unmoving mass, the king raised a hand and knocked firmly on the door, his shoulders back and his head high. The hammering in my chest filled the silence, echoing in my ears, and I wondered for a fleeting second whether my father had found a second way to the human world. But then, the door opened, and I blinked, squinting against the sudden onslaught of light.

"Welcome, Your Majesty. It is a pleasure to see you again."

My heart plummeted into my stomach as a middle-aged male with shoulder length white hair and slender ivory wings bowed deeply, before stepping back, gesturing at the room behind him. A Cupid.

The king strode forward, and I hesitated long enough that Fin poked a bony finger painfully between my wings, jolting me from my stupor. Blood roaring in my ears, I stepped through the doorway, trying to make sense of where I was and what was happening. The room was large, but not overbearing, with pale drapes adorning the walls. I could just make out a vast table, laden with fruit, over my father's wings. There were no windows that I could see, with paintings and candles on brass fittings, providing the ambiance instead.

"King Hadeon. It's both an honour and a pleasure."

My heart stuttered as my father stepped to the side, allowing me to see that there were others in the room. The female that approached, inclining her head politely as she looked at us, one by one, was stunning, with rich brown skin, delicate features and her white hair shaved close. When her eyes met mine, I faltered, forcing myself not to retreat. Her golden eyes were as familiar as my own. My eyes flicked to the stunning crown she wore as the pieces fell into place.

"Queen Maluhia Dragoste of Hehven, Your Majesty," the slender male who'd opened the door announced. "And King Armastus Dragoste of Hehven."

My attention flitted to the male at the queen's side, and what was left of my heart splintered further. Although his hair was long and braided, and his eyes a bright blue, his golden skin and sharp jaw were painfully familiar. I sank into a low curtsey, my head spinning. As I rose, my eyes scanned the room, relief sinking into my bones, my knees weakening, at the realisation that Pace wasn't here.

"As you know," my father said, inclining his own head. "I am King Nemir Hadeon of Helle. This is my daughter, Crown Princess, Sirain and my son, Second Prince, Fin. I'm afraid my wife, Queen Briga, is unwell and could not attend."

"I'm so sorry to hear that," the queen said, before offering me a warm smile that stole my breath, my own feeling stiff and awkward in return.

I tried not to imagine how those smiles would shift if they knew what I'd done to their son. To their nephew. A bead of icy sweat raced down my spine.

"This is our son, Crown Prince Dashuri," the queen said as another male stepped forward, bowing at the waist.

It was strange to put faces to the names I'd heard so much about. He didn't look much like Pace. Instead, a sturdy male version of his mother. I wondered if he knew just how much his judgement hurt his brother. Where was Pace? Was he okay?

Was he still being punished because of my cousin's reckless actions? Perhaps his family had forced the marriage on him once more and he was with her. My gut twisted as I realised it didn't matter. How Pace felt and what he was doing were no longer my concern and never would be again.

"Are you all right, my dear?" the queen asked, catching my eye. Her golden eyes were narrowed in concern. "You're trembling."

"I assure you, it's a lot to meet the infamous Cupids for the first time," my father said. "She's a little overwhelmed."

"As are we all," the queen said kindly, giving me a warm smile.

I dropped my gaze to the intricately woven rug.

"Come, let us sit," King Dragoste said, gesturing at the table. "We're all travel weary, and I'm sure there is a lot to discuss."

Fingers clutching my skirts, white-knuckled, I moved towards a carved wooden chair as my mind scrambled, trying to slot the pieces together. I was in Hehven. Somehow, the tunnel we'd flown and walked through must have gone underneath The Crossing. My throat throbbed with my heartbeat as I sat down. All this time, there'd been a way—a link between Hehven and Helle.

"You can wait outside."

My head snapped up, expecting my father's sharpened words to be directed at me. But they weren't. Instead, Fin stood, barely contained rage twisting his features, his hand clutching the back of the chair he was about to sit on.

"This is a matter for the current royalty and immediate heirs," he continued.

"Lord Rakkaus," the queen said gently. "Do you think you could escort Prince Fin to the waiting area and see that he is given refreshments?"

"Of course, Your Majesty." The willowy man bowed. "I have

arranged for a meal to be served after your meeting. Does that suit you, King Hadeon?"

My father leaned forward on the table, clasping his pale hands together. "That sounds wonderful, Lord Rakkaus. Let us talk business and then perhaps our meal can be one of celebration." He fixed Fin with a stare. "You may join us then."

The small bow my brother gave was reluctant and mocking, but my father didn't rise to it. He rarely did with Fin.

I watched as the man, Lord Rakkaus, led my brother out through a different door, closing it behind him, apprehension sending chills down my spine. My father had never sent Fin away before. Heavy silence enveloped us as I studied my hands, clasped in my lap.

"I suppose I should explain my reason for approaching Hehven," my father said. His voice was warmer and more polite than I'd ever heard it. One might even say he sounded 'charming'. My insides curdled.

Queen Maluhia smiled, darting a glance at her husband. "I will admit, we were unaware of the tunnel. The Rakkaus family claim to have been tasked with guarding it by the Fates for millennia."

"Indeed," my father said, a smile unlike one I'd ever seen curling his lips. "I discovered its existence in an old history book and scarcely believed it to be true."

I darted a look at the Crown Prince. His own hands were folded in front of him on the table, his brow furrowed in concentration as he listened to my father. Other than his eyes, and gold-tipped wings, he looked so different to Pace, it was difficult to believe they were brothers. Where Pace's demeanour was confident and warm, Dashuri's was intense and unapproachable.

"Why now, King Hadeon?" Pace's father asked. "What prompted you to call this meeting?"

My breathing slowed; my hands grasping tighter as I waited for his response. I couldn't begin to fathom his reasons.

"I have searched our libraries," my father began, "trying to find a reason for why Hehven and Helle have been separated all this time. Other than the obvious, The Crossing, it seems pointless. I thought perhaps it was the wishes of the Fates, but I have met with no opposition for my wishes, so I must assume they are happy for this to proceed."

"Would the Fates make their displeasure known?" Queen Maluhia asked. "We receive nothing more than orders for the Hands from them. Do they communicate with you?"

I watched my father, wondering how much information he'd give them. Would he tell them about the orders to kill Marlowe? To kill Emeric?

"No," he said. "However, all our actions are predetermined by them, so if I was not supposed to do this, I would not have found the book, or the entrance to the tunnel in Helle."

Queen Maluhia nodded slowly. "You're right. We can be assured in the knowledge that our actions have already been determined by the Fates."

My stomach lurched. If that was true, the Fates had planned for me to meet Pace. Planned for me to shred his world to pieces. I couldn't be sure if I was comforted or repulsed by that thought.

"I believe that finding the tunnel was a sign," my father said, sitting up a little straighter. "A sign of a new era for both Cupids and Chaos."

I dared a glance at the queen and king of Hehven, who watched the king of Helle, apprehension clear in their set of their shoulders and the tightness of their smiles.

"A new era?" the queen echoed.

My father nodded. "Indeed. We have been separated for too long when we share the same goal. Yes, the arrows we deliver have different purposes, but they are issued by the same Fates and carried out with the same dedication and belief. Why should our people be separated?"

I swayed slightly on my seat, although I wasn't sure whether it was from the words spewing with unheard enthusiasm from my father's mouth or from exhaustion. Perhaps both. I startled as the Crown Prince stood and reached for the ornate silver jug, pouring water into one of the delicate silver cups and sliding it towards me.

"Thank you," I said quietly, lifting the vessel with trembling hands.

It was all too much. My thoughts kept wandering to Helle, tormented by the uncertainty of Odio and Kwellen's lives. Knowing the king, I was sure whatever I was picturing, the reality would be far worse. Although, the version I knew of my father, the king, didn't seem to exist in Hehven—instead replaced by a friendly affable male who looked and sounded a lot like him.

"What exactly are you suggesting, King Hadeon?" the Queen asked.

"Please," my father insisted. "Call me Nemir. I'm suggesting that we form an alliance. That we unite Cupids and Chaos as one. We are all servants of Fate. Imagine how much stronger we could be together. How much we could learn from each other. Especially in times of human war, when we are all feeling the strain."

I gripped my water, staring at the liquid sloshing inside and forcing myself to take slow, steady breaths. Trepidation prickled along the inside of my wings, lifting the hairs on the back of my neck. The queen of Hehven seemed to be fooled by this version of my father and there was nothing I could do to warn her—to tell her that she should turn around and leave, bricking up the entrance to the tunnel at the first opportunity.

The king of Hehven leaned forward, his eyebrows raised as he looked between me and my father. "How exactly do you envision that working? We may have a tunnel linking Hehven and Helle, but there's still The Crossing."

"Uniting our people is not something that can happen quickly," my father said, shaking his head with a reassuring smile. "I would suggest a small step at first. A show of good faith if you will."

The queen tilted her head, the cascade of jewels hanging from her ears glittering. "A show of good faith?"

My father reached out and pried my fingers from the cup I was clinging to, taking my hand in his. I stared, trying to recall a time he'd touched me when it hadn't been with the intention of harming me.

His fingers squeezed. "I would like to propose a union between our first born."

My head snapped up, staring at him, wide eyed.

"What better way to show that the rulers of Hehven and Helle are invested in our joint future than to unite our families?" My father's grip tightened further, and I tried to erase the horror from my face, replacing it with a gracious smile. "I would like to offer my daughter, Princess Sirain as a wife for your son, Prince Dashuri."

My stomach rolled, the room tilting a little, but I forced myself to keep smiling for my friends' sake. Now I knew why he'd taken them. There was no way I'd have ever gone into this willingly.

"I'm not sure what to say, Nemir," the queen said, giving me a friendly smile. "This is a lot to process, as I'm sure you can understand."

My father nodded. "Of course. Please, take some time to discuss and think about it. We've waited hundreds, perhaps thousands of years for this. There's certainly no rush."

The queen stood, her husband and son following a second later. "Please, give us a few minutes. I'll have Lord Rakkaus send in some more refreshments."

As they turned to leave, I allowed myself to look at Dashuri. At first glance, he appeared nonplussed, but as I stared, I could see the tension in the set of his wings and the faint sheen of sweat coating his brow.

My stomach lurched as the door clicked shut behind them, and I clasped my free hand to my mouth, swallowing down the bitter taste of bile. I couldn't marry Pace's brother.

My father released me, wiping his fingers on his robes as his warm smile melted back into a familiar angry sneer. "You have until they return to pull yourself together. If they choose not to accept the proposal, you will have to convince them otherwise."

I stared at him, my mouth dry. "I can't force them to do something they don't want to do."

"If we leave here without an acceptance of this marriage proposal," he said, leaning in close enough that a faint tinge of sweat stung my nostrils. "You can decide which of your friends pays the price."

My heart stuttered. "You wouldn't."

He stared at me, knowing he didn't even need to dignify my statement with a response.

"Why me?" I managed, tentatively stretching my mangled fingers. "Why not Malin?"

"The people of Helle love Malin." My father barked a laugh before turning away and pouring water into his cup. "But you, Sirain? No one will even notice you're gone."

20
Pace

D espite the tea, and small plate of dried fruits, cheese and freshly baked bread provided, I couldn't even think about touching them. I couldn't sit still. My attention flitted between the two doors as I strode up and down the narrow room, my wings flaring. I'd already moved the chairs to give me room to work out my anxiety, but it didn't help that the windowless room seemed to be getting smaller with every lap I took, the walls pressing in on me, increasing the tightness in my chest.

I was aware I could probably leave, but how could I? If everything Sirain had told me was true, this meeting was a terrifying prospect. My parents were going to be in a closed room, unarmed, with the most dangerous man in Helle. My fingers twitched at my side, longing for the comforting weight of my sword.

Once again, I looked at the door Caitland had left through —the one guarded by her brothers—waiting for it to open, for the king of Helle to arrive. What would I do? What would I say if Sirain was with him? The urge to leave and find the nearest window built inside me, pulsing with every heartbeat, every intake of breath until I thought I might burst.

When the door to the meeting room opened, I whirled,

hoping for news that the meeting had been cancelled, or that my parents had changed their minds.

"Just in here, Your Majesty," Lord Rakkaus said as my breathing halted. "I'll send someone with refreshments."

I stared at the Chaos beside Caitland's father, every muscle in my body tensed tight enough to snap. There must be another door inside the meeting room. They wouldn't be coming past me. My world tilted a little and I reached out and grabbed hold of a chair to steady myself. They were already here.

My eyes raked over the unfamiliar Chaos, noting the burgundy highlighting his wings and hair. Everything about him was sharp. His short hair, his jaw, his nose—as though he'd been crafted to slice through the world with ease.

"This is Second Prince Pace Dragoste of Hehven," Lord Rakkaus said, gesturing to me. "Prince Pace, this is Second Prince Fin Hadeon of Helle. I'll leave you to get to know each other."

My grip tightened on the chair, my teeth pressed together so forcefully, my jaw ached. Still, I bowed at the waist as he did the same.

Lord Rakkaus excused himself, and Fin sank down into a chair, folding his arms across his chest as he fixed his narrowed gaze on me. I stood still, letting him assess as I forced myself to breathe. Fin. Sirain's brother. I had gone my entire life without feeling hatred until I'd learned of his existence. Yes, I'd been frustrated with people, annoyed, but never hated. Even after locking me in a room for weeks, I couldn't bring myself to truly hate my brother. Fin, on the other wing, was another matter entirely.

"Why aren't you in the meeting?" he asked, picking at a fingernail.

"Why aren't you?"

Fin huffed through his nose and turned his attention to the

room, his lip curling at what he found. "So, this is Hehven," he sneered. "Thrilling."

My lips pressed together, my wings tense. I didn't care that I likely appeared hostile. There was no conceivable way I could withhold how I felt about the male before me. My mind raced through the times I'd held Sirain in my arms as she'd recounted the ways he'd tormented her, hurt her. She was the strongest, fiercest female I'd ever met, but Fin had made her feel fear. I stared at him, sprawled confidently in his chair, and recalled the nights I'd lain awake, wishing I could meet him, preferably with a sword in my hand.

"What's wrong with you?" he asked, his dark eyes narrowing further. "Are you sulking because you didn't get an invite?"

"No," I bit out. "I'm wary because we've allowed demons into Hehven."

That got his attention. His eyes widened, his sneer slipping into a gleeful smile as he sat forward.

"Oh," he said. "Opposition. Perhaps we have more in common than our titles."

I didn't want to ask—didn't want to engage in conversation —but the words tumbled from my lips before I could suck them back in. "What are you talking about?"

"I don't want to be here either," he said, waving a pale hand at the room. "We have enough to occupy us in Helle without wasting time with Cupids."

"Wasting time?"

He huffed a laugh. "Indeed. What could Cupids possibly offer us? Spreading love and peace like it has any place in our world. Love clouds judgement. It addles the brain. It makes you weak."

"How would you know?" My eyes narrowed as I returned his sneer. "I doubt it's an emotion you've ever felt."

Fin's eyes flashed as his smile widened. "No. Because why

would I allow myself to be weakened? I know all about you Cupids. Saving yourselves."

My neck heated, and I forced myself to stand still as he dragged his gaze slowly up and down my body.

"Your abstinence is your weakness. I take what I want when I want it. That's strength. I long for nothing." He leaned back, folding his arms as he licked his lips. "Would you like me to tell you about the things I've taken, Cupid? I wonder if I could make you blush?"

It took all my energy to force myself to stay where I was, to not clench my fists, despite the ire causing my limbs to tremble. I could say nothing. Do nothing. He was the Second Prince of Helle, and his father was on the other side of the door. More than that, I certainly couldn't tell him that I knew more than enough of what he was talking about, and his sister was the one who'd shown me. My eyes flitted to the meeting room door once more. Was she in there? Surely not, if the king had brought Fin.

"You're weak," Fin continued, seemingly oblivious to my simmering rage. "All your longing and pining clouds your judgement."

"You know nothing about us," I scoffed. "This is the first time you've been to Hehven and likely the first time you've met Cupids. You think you have the measure of us after five minutes?"

"Oh, I have the measure of you, all right," Fin said, getting to his feet and taking a step towards me. "And I find it lacking."

I stood my ground, watching as he advanced another step. He was slightly taller than me and lean with muscle, but I knew he wasn't a fighter. That was my advantage. He was so sure he had me figured out, but I knew everything about him. I knew how he preferred wine and intimate encounters with multiple Chaos to training. I knew he preferred a dagger to a blade. I knew I could knock him to the ground with a single well-placed blow.

"My father wants to join our people," he spat as he stopped, leaving barely a feather's width between us. "But he's making a mistake. No good can come from sullying our lineage with Cupid blood. What could we gain from a race so scrawny and pathetic? Besides, you wouldn't know what to do with a female if we gave you one."

My hand reached out, grabbing hold of his robes, and dragging him towards me before I could think. "Shut your filthy mouth," I hissed.

Fin laughed, his breath warm and bitter on my face. "Make me, Cupid."

A knock sounded on the main doors a second before they started to open, and I gripped the fur-lined velvet of his robes tighter before shoving him away from me as hard as I could. His wings flared, correcting his balance but knocking my untouched tea onto the floor with a clatter.

One of Lord Rakkaus' sons stepped in with a tray of refreshments in his hands and he looked between us, his eyes widening as he took in Fin, his black wings still half spread and the spilled cup on the floor. I realised the waiting staff must not be aware of the tunnel's existence. So far, only Rakkaus and his children had set foot inside the rooms, and I wondered what they made of the Chaos' presence.

"Is everything all right, Your Majesties?" he asked, placing the tray on the table, and dropping into a deep bow, which I'm sure pained him.

"Yes, thank you," I said, breathing hard. "Just an accident."

He nodded, pulling a cloth from his belt, and stooping to clean up the spill. If he registered the tension in the room, he did a good job of ignoring it. The silence was deafening as he picked up the empty cup before backing out of the room with another small bow, closing the door behind him.

"You know what?" Fin said, his eyes lingering on the door. "Perhaps my father's proposal might have its perks after all. Most of the Chaos I find enjoyment with are already well versed in pleasure. I think it might be entertaining sharing my skills with those unfamiliar with desire."

Disgust wrinkled my nose and my fingers clenched at my sides, but as his earlier words settled properly, I stepped forward, my eyes narrowed. "Wait. What were you talking about before? Your father wants to join our people? How? Why?"

Fin shrugged, poking at the plate of food he'd been brought before placing a piece of dried fruit on his tongue. "I'm sure you'll find out soon enough."

"Peace between our families can only be a good thing, surely."

Fin dragged his gaze slowly from my clenched fists to my tensed shoulders, then up to where my eyes blazed with barely concealed wrath. "If you had a blade, it would be drawn, yet you talk of peace?" He snorted. "I hate the word. As I hate Hehven, and all Cupids. Especially you."

My jaw clenched, but I forced my shoulders to relax and let out a slow breath. There was no use in pressing the matter. The more I pushed him, the more loath he would be to give me information.

Folding my arms across my chest, I leaned against the wall, watching. The cruel arrogance that rippled off him in waves was suffocating in the small space. How had Sirain survived a lifetime with him?

My eyes flitted to the meeting room door and I wished I was alone so I could attempt to eavesdrop. Would my parents agree to a proposal as preposterous as merging the Cupids and the Chaos? How would that even work? Caitland had told me about the tunnel, but it didn't sound like it was an easy pathway, especially if it had been untouched for over a thousand years. An uneasy chill settled over my skin.

My parents were clever, but they were also Cupids. We were drawn to the emotions we were responsible for distributing to the humans. Could they genuinely say no to an offer of peace and unity, even if it was with the king of Helle?

The meeting room doors opened, and I pushed off the wall, straightening as my parents and Dashuri strode into the room. I immediately cast my gaze over them, finding no signs of distress or injury. "Mother? Father? Is everything all right?"

The queen placed a hand on my shoulder, offering me a reassuring smile. "Everything is fine. We just need a moment to discuss in private." She turned to Fin. "You may join your father now, if you wish."

Fin inclined his head, offering a shallow bow before retreating into the room and closing the door behind him as I tried and failed to peer past my family's wings.

"Pace," my father said. "Could you please give us a minute?"

I raised my eyebrows, gesturing at the room. "Where would you like me to go, Father?"

"This place is huge," Dashuri snapped. "Find somewhere that isn't here."

I baulked at his tone, my eyes widening. He had never spoken to me like that in front of our parents before.

"Dashuri," our mother chided, her eyes widening. "Take a breath."

Our father placed a hand on his shoulder as though offering comfort, and I stared between them in confusion.

"What happened in there?"

"We will tell you everything in due time," my mother said, running her thumb against my chin. "Why don't you go and find Lord or Lady Rakkaus and tell them we'll be ready to dine in fifteen minutes."

"Fifteen minutes?" I echoed.

She nodded and I exhaled, admitting defeat. With a last wary glance at my brother, I heaved open the main doors and strode down the corridor, purposefully avoiding looking at Caitland's brothers. Fifteen minutes. In fifteen minutes, I'd meet Sirain's father. My gaze fell on a large window, and I came to a stop, staring longingly up at the darkening sky. If I tried to leave, I'd be dragged back to the ground in seconds. Fifteen minutes. I rested my head against the cool glass and closed my eyes.

21
Sirain

Fin stormed into the room, looking decisively ruffled. Slumping into a chair on the opposite side of the table, he peered into the silver cups before making a derisive noise in the back of his throat.

"Please tell me there will be wine with dinner," he grumbled. "These Cupids are tedious."

The king stared at him long and hard. "This is one of the many reasons I didn't allow you in our meeting."

Fin's dark eyebrows shot up. "What do you mean?"

"You can't behave like this around the Cupids." Our father sighed, pinching the bridge of his straight nose. "If we don't act a certain way, they won't trust us. We talked about this, Fin. At length."

My brother held his gaze, his lip curling. "They reek of such righteousness, Father. I can barely tolerate the stench."

A low chuckle escaped the king, and I pressed my lips together, busying myself with tracing the patterns engraved on the outside of my cup.

"There's a washroom through there," the king said, dragging me from my thoughts. "Perhaps you should go and try to make yourself more presentable."

I blinked, glancing over my shoulder at the slim painted

door I hadn't noticed before. When I turned back, I realised it was not a request. They clearly wanted to talk and needed me out of the way. Reining in a sigh, I gathered my skirts and stood, crossing to the narrow wooden door.

Despite my annoyance at being sent away, once enclosed in the small, tastefully decorated washroom, I found myself grateful of a few moments alone. A large bronze-edged mirror adorned one of the walls and I cautiously stepped in front of it, bracing myself. Paler than usual, the shadows beneath my eyes looked more pronounced. I understood now why the servants had left my hair down. The king must have instructed them to do so, knowing any sort of style would have been destroyed by our long flight. Even so, my escape had caused more damage than I would be able to repair.

Frowning, I plucked out stray pine needles and tugged my fingers through the tangled strands, adjusting my tiara. I extended my wings, trying to assess the damage Fin had caused, but I couldn't see anything. The only evidence of my injury was the thumping ache that pulsed in time with my heart. Extending my arms, I noted the small scratches, pink against my pale skin. Not that I had any way of covering them, but it was doubtful anyone would notice unless they were looking for them. My fingers moved to my neck, the ghost of my brother's grip still lingering. He'd been right. The marks had faded, although I suspected purple bruises would be visible by the morning.

I held my breath, listening to see if I could hear the words being spoken on the other side of the door, but there was nothing. Staring at my reflection, wondering whether I'd achieved an acceptable level of presentable. The tips of my ears burned at the realisation that I'd met Pace's parents in such a state.

What must Dashuri have thought? I doubted he'd expected to leave the meeting with a wife. A violent shudder rippled through me, and I shook out my wings, goosebumps covering my arms. What if the king and queen said yes? Would I be expected to live in Hehven with Pace's brother? I swallowed hard. Perhaps Pace would kill me before he allowed it to happen. Perhaps he'd tell them everything. Prince Dashuri would not want to wed the female who stripped his younger brother of his purity.

My cheeks burned as the thought alone drew forth flashes of heated skin and taut muscle—the sound of my name breathed from between his plump, soft lips. I turned away from the mirror, closing my eyes. There was no way I could go through with this.

Aware I'd probably already taken too long, I straightened my shoulders and took a deep breath, stepping back to the door. As my hand closed around the handle, I heard voices, and my heart leapt into my mouth. The king and queen had returned. Closing my eyes, I leaned my head against the wood. I had no doubt my father would slaughter Odio or Kwellen if I didn't play his game.

Once again, I found myself trapped, and the over-whelming rush of loneliness stole my breath. It was akin to being in a maze. Every time I thought I'd found my way out, I was met by a dead end. Blinking back the tears, I pasted a warm smile on my face and pulled open the door.

The world dropped away at my feet, my vision blurring and the rapid beating of my heart thundering in my ears. I reached out, steadying myself against the door frame as Pace turned, his gilded eyes meeting mine.

"There you are, Sirain," my father said, the mask of pleasantness firmly back over his features.

The queen smiled at me, her eyes crinkling. "This is our other son, Second Prince, Pace Dragoste."

I dipped into a curtsey, although my eyes never left his. He stared at me, his jaw set and his gaze cold enough that the tears

I was so desperately trying to keep at bay threatened to fall once more.

My father coughed. "The king and queen have reached a decision."

"We have," the queen said. "Let's all take a seat."

I didn't move. I couldn't. How was it possible he was even more beautiful than I remembered? My fingers gripped the door frame as I stared at the reason I was no longer complete. The reason I had a gaping cavern in my chest. My eyes roamed over the way his snow-white hair, a little longer than when I'd seen him last, curled over his ears and forehead. The familiar, warm, golden brown of his skin called to me like home, a physical ache pulling me to nestle my face in his neck, inhaling his scent. Did he still smell like sunshine and beaches?

"Sirain," my father repeated, his voice a little sharper.

Dropping my gaze to the floor, I forced myself forward, returning to my seat at his right-hand side. "Sorry, Father," I said quietly.

"I think she's a little nervous," the queen said, giving me another warm smile. "It's understandable."

Nervous didn't begin to cover it. Fin took the seat to my left, with Dashuri taking the seat opposite me, his parents on either side. Pace took the seat beside his father, and I was grateful at least that he was out of my direct line of sight.

A knock sounded on the door and two white-haired males entered, carrying glasses and a large decanter of wine. At my left, Fin noticeably perked up. I kept my eyes on the table, not trusting myself to look anywhere else as the glasses were distributed and filled with rich, red liquid. Although it was likely only a minute or so, it felt like an eternity before the Cupids left, closing the door behind them.

"I thought we might need this," the queen said, reaching out and placing her hand over Dashuri's, as she raised her glass. "We've considered your offer carefully, Nemir. It is a momentous decision for both our peoples and not one to be entered into lightly."

I felt my father stiffen beside me, and I forced myself to keep breathing, the room unbearably warm.

"Dashuri also understands the implications and importance of such a proposal," the queen continued, "and we have taken his feelings into consideration, as I'm sure you have with your own daughter."

Out of the corner of my eye, I saw Pace shift to face his family. I didn't need to see his face to know he had no idea what was coming. My breathing shallow, I forced myself to look at the queen of Hehven as she sealed my Fate.

"We would like Dashuri and Sirain to spend some time together. Afterwards, if they both agree, we will accept the proposal of their union." She lifted her glass and everyone else followed suit.

"Wonderful," my father intoned. "An excellent decision, Your Majesty."

"Please," the queen said, her smile brightening even further. "If we are to be family, you must call me Maluhia."

I shifted my gaze to my potential husband, willing my pleased expression to stay where it was. Dashuri's answering smile was almost as warm and encouraging as his mother's, although I could see the trepidation in his eyes.

I tried. I really did. I tried not to look at Pace, but as I met his father's contented smile over the rim of his wine glass, my attention continued onwards. I don't know what I was expecting to see, but the expressionless calm Pace exuded as he fixed his attention on his family, wasn't it. Didn't he care? I was falling to pieces inside, barely holding myself together, and he looked like this was just another day. How was that even possible?

Another knock sounded at the door and the two Cupids from before returned, along with Lord Rakkaus and a few others who all looked to be related, flooded the room, carrying trays and dishes. Despite clinging desperately to the crumbling pieces of my own sanity, I wondered why the Rakkaus family didn't appear to have any servants. Perhaps no Cupids did.

As the food was served and the Rakkaus family left us to our meal, conversation flowed around me as easily as the aromas of the food winding their way through the room. I was grateful at least for a meal I could eat without having to worry whether it was poisoned, although I wasn't sure I'd be able to force a single mouthful down my constricted throat.

At my side, the king of Helle bellowed a laugh and I flinched at the foreign sound. What would the queen of Hehven think if I told her she was making a deal with someone who'd imprisoned his own nephew to coerce me into submission?

My gut churned at the thought of my friends. Where was he keeping them? Would he set them free now that the engagement seemed to be on track? No. A cold weight settled in my stomach. The king would not release them until it was a done deal. Of course, Dashuri could refuse after we spent time together. But that wasn't an option. It couldn't be.

As a fresh wave of despair threatened to crush me, I dared another glance at Pace, confident it would go unnoticed with everyone engaged in conversation amidst mouthfuls of food. Now, closer, I could see what I'd missed before. The small differences only someone who knew him well would notice. Someone who'd mapped and worshipped every single inch of skin.

Shadows lingered under his eyes, and his warm, golden skin was paler. Of course, the season could be held accountable, but something told me it was more than that. Especially with the amount of time Pace spent flying. He looked leaner, too. His body had always been a work of art, but I could tell the lines were harder beneath his tunic. He wasn't the same. But then, of course, he wasn't. He'd lost his best friend, his cousin. I'd taken that from him. I'd done this to him.

I swallowed the sob that built in my throat, drowning it with a gulp of wine. Sharp fingers gripped my knee, squeezing, and I startled, turning to my father, but his attention was focused on King Armastus, nodding at whatever he was saying. I squirmed, wanting to reach down and rip his hand away, but I knew I couldn't. His message was clear. I needed to pull myself together and play my part or risk losing the only thing I had left in my miserable life.

Taking another sip of wine, I fixed my attention on Dashuri, waiting until he turned to me with a smile. "So, Prince Dashuri, tell me a little about yourself."

My father's hand left my knee, leaving a throbbing pain I tried to ignore as I listened to the prince's response. Even as I smiled at his words, my mind stayed with Pace. Being so close to him was sheer agony, worse than any pain I'd ever endured. I thought I'd made peace with what had happened between us— that I'd accepted his hatred as a just punishment for my actions —but now, seeing him again, I couldn't bear it.

Bringing my glass to my lips, I nodded as Dashuri explained his role looking after the Captains of Fate. I needed Pace to know, even if it didn't change anything, that I hadn't been going to shoot Marlowe. That I would never have hurt Dariel on purpose. I needed him to hear those words. If that meant he took my life as payment, then so be it. I'd faced his unbridled rage before and fallen in love with him. I'd weather that same storm a thousand times more before I gave up. A calm settled over me as I decided; I'd find a way to talk to Pace, even if it killed me.

22
Pace

If even a shred of faith had remained in my heart for the Fates, the events of today would have destroyed it completely. Sipping my water, purposefully foregoing the wine in favour of keeping a clear head, I tried and failed to listen to the conversation happening around me. I hadn't been able to concentrate on a single word since my mother announced that Dashuri and Sirain were to be engaged. Bile rose in my throat, and I swallowed it down, wincing at the burn.

This couldn't be happening. I'd known there was a chance she'd be here—that I'd see her—but in the thousand ways I'd pictured it happening, it hadn't been like this. Cold sweat trickled down my back, the ends of my hair damp at the base of my neck, as I pictured my brother marrying the only female I'd ever loved. The thought of them together plagued my mind, leaving a stain I'd never be able to erase.

Darting a glance at my brother, he seemed to be just as nauseated as me. Part of me revelled in smug satisfaction that he was having a marriage he didn't want forced on him. If only it was with literally anyone else in existence.

Keeping my face straight when the news had been announced had been near impossible. I was painfully aware of Fin on the opposite side of the table, his taunting glances landing on me so frequently, I knew I couldn't give anything away. Sirain had made it clear how shrewd and calculating he was. If he even suspected I knew his sister . . .

I smiled in response to something that seemed like I should, allowing my gaze to sweep the table, lingering a few seconds on Sirain. Part of me had been sure my memories were exaggerated–that I'd built her up to impossible standards in my head.

I hadn't.

She was so beautiful my heart had faltered when she stepped through the door. Once the initial shock faded, however, I began to notice the subtle changes since the last time I'd seen her; the dark circles under her eyes, and the weariness in the way she held her wings. She'd lost weight too, no longer the fierce warrior I'd fought all those months ago. But it was the deep sadness in her eyes that stole my breath.

My mind was all over the place—another reason I was deliberately not touching the wine. For so many nights, I'd lay awake imagining what I'd do, what I'd say, if I ever saw her again. I'd harboured so much anger and so much pain, sure I'd want nothing more than to run her through with a blade if I ever laid eyes on her. Part of me still did. But I didn't want to kill her, I wanted her to know just how much she'd hurt me. My hand clenched into a fist below the table as I pictured wrapping it around her throat and hauling her against the wall, demanding answers.

I glanced again as she lifted her wine glass, taking a small sip, and my fingers tightened, cutting crescents into my palms. On her upper arm, faint enough that they were almost unnoticeable, were small red marks. I knew exactly what they were and how they would slowly turn deeper in colour.

My gaze moved, examining closer, finding small marks against her pale flesh and more against her throat. Who had gripped her that tightly? Was it her father? Fin? Or was I completely wrong? Perhaps it had happened in the throes of passion. Uncomfortably warm, I fought the urge to dab at my face with my napkin.

"What do you think, Pace?"

I flinched at my name, turning to my father. "I'm sorry, pardon?"

"Fin was just saying, he thinks his sister and your brother make a delightful couple." He smiled at Fin before looking back at me.

Glancing at Sirain's brother, mild panic flaring in my veins, I wondered if he'd noticed me looking at her. Had I not been careful enough? He smiled at me, but it didn't reach his eyes. I wondered if he'd ever given a genuine smile in his life.

"They certainly make a handsome couple," I offered, raising my glass in a salute to the Chaos prince.

Fin sneered at my cup before fixing me with his piercing stare. "Do you not partake in wine, Pace?"

He forced out my name as though it pained him to use it.

I gave him my most charming smile. "I've been unwell recently, so I thought it unwise to partake."

"Oh, yes." My father turned in his seat to look me over properly. "How are you feeling? Dashuri told me you had a fever earlier?"

"I'm fine," I reassured him. "Nothing a good night's sleep won't cure."

I could feel Sirain's eyes on me, the table drawn to our conversation. It took all my self-control not to meet her gaze, knowing that if I did, I might not be able to look away.

"I'm sorry to hear you're feeling unwell," King Hadeon said. "Your brother was just telling me how you're training to take over from him."

A chill gripped my spine as the king of Helle's garnet eyes fixed on me. He was being so warm and friendly, but I knew it was an act. Sirain might have lied about who she was, but I knew she hadn't lied about her family. Fin hadn't hesitated to show his true colours before, and I knew his father was so much worse. My parents were completely unaware they were sitting, eating, and laughing, across from a male who regularly beheaded and maimed his subjects just because he could.

"That's correct," I replied. "I've been assisting in the record room on the Isle of the Fates recently."

The king raised his eyebrows before nodding solemnly. "I expect things must be quite busy with the human war under-way. I know our Hands are feeling the strain."

"It's the same for our Hands, too," Dashuri said. "Hopefully, this war will not be drawn out."

I pressed my lips together, returning my attention to the untouched food before me. Tiesa had promised she'd let me know of any further developments in the human world, but so far there'd been nothing. After confiding in her about the Fates, I wasn't sure if she would. Perhaps I'd finally pushed the limits of our friendship too far.

The queen raised her glass. "Let us all trust that the Fates can ensure a swift settlement amongst the humans, so peace may resume."

"Indeed," my father said. "Times of war allow little time for courtship."

My brother flushed, hiding his discomfort behind a sip of wine, and I shifted in my seat, my stomach lurching. As much as I tried, I couldn't stop the onslaught of unwelcome images. Dash nuzzling the soft warm skin of Sirain's neck, inhaling her jasmine-laced scent. His fingers tracing the graceful curves of her hips. My gaze flitted longingly to my untouched wine glass.

"Will you stay?" my mother asked. "I'm sure it's a long journey back to Helle. Lord Rakkaus has assured me he has plenty of room if you wish to rest before your return."

King Hadeon smiled but shook his head. "It is a kind offer,

but we must return. As I'm sure you know, a country does not run itself."

"You will return soon, though, Sirain?" the queen asked. "I'm sure Dashuri can delegate some of his work to Pace, so you can spend some time getting to know each other."

I barely swallowed the groan that rose in my throat.

"I think perhaps you should take to your bed, Pace" Fin said, a smirk fighting the corners of his thin lips. "You look quite unwell."

"When I return, I'll bring you some tea," Sirain said softly.

My head snapped to her, my breath halting in my lungs. She wasn't looking at me, though, her gaze instead focused on the cup in her hand.

"There's a tea made from rosehips, which only grow on a particular cliff," she continued. "It's bittersweet, but it always clears my head and makes me feel better."

"That's so thoughtful," my mother said. "Thank you so much, my dear."

I couldn't breathe. There was no tea, I was sure of it. Roses and cliffs . . . it was no coincidence. She was asking me to meet her at the cliff. At our cliff. My mind whirled, trying to figure out how I could get there. Would she be able to get there? Did I even want to meet her? I sucked in a breath.

"Thank you," I said. "I would like that very much."

I was sure I didn't imagine the way Sirain's shoulders seemed to relax just a fraction.

"Wonderful," she said, nodding at her drink. "I'll order it tomorrow night."

Any doubt I'd had over whether I wanted to speak to her evaporated like morning mist on the sea. I couldn't leave so much hanging between us. I needed answers. Tomorrow night. A place and a time. Now, I just had to figure out how to make it happen.

23
Sirain

I f it weren't for the adrenaline coursing through my veins, the prospect of flying back through the long, dark tunnel and across the icy night sky to Hadeon Castle would have brought me to my knees.

"Thank you, Maluhia. Armastus," King Hadeon said, his charming smile sending a shudder down my spine. He inclined his head in Dashuri's direction. "I will arrange for my daughter to return to Hehven soon."

Dashuri dipped his head in response. "I look forward to it, Your Majesty."

"It was a pleasure meeting you all," Pace's mother said, her voice rich and warm like melted caramel. "Today has been historic for both our peoples and I'm hopeful for what lies ahead. This truly is the beginning of a new era."

I dipped into a low curtsey in response, hoping it wasn't obvious I was out of practice. In Helle, I preferred to bow if I was showing reverence to my parents. It was only when I was crouched, my hands gripping my thick skirts, that I allowed myself the briefest glance upwards, through my lashes.

Pace wasn't looking. His gaze was fixed instead on something to the side of the door, his jaw firmly set, as it had been all evening. I wasn't surprised. He'd only looked at me twice the entire evening and both glances had been borne of surprise.

As much as my heart ached at being so close, the possibility of speaking to him filled me with more hope than I'd felt in . . . Well, since before I'd flown to Marlowe's ship. There was every chance he'd use the opportunity to shout at me, but I didn't care. It was worth the risk. He hated me, that much was clear, but perhaps I could persuade him to help Emeric. After all, they'd developed a friendship before the war. My chest tightened at the thought of my real father. The chances of him still being alive were so incredibly slim.

The king of Helle lifted a fresh torch from the wall as cold damp wind whistled through into the meeting room.

"We wish you a safe journey back," King Armastus said. "Fly safe, fly true."

My father nodded, giving a final smile before striding into the darkness. Every fibre of my being pleaded with me not to, but I turned and followed, Fin close behind. The cavernous tunnel was colder and damper than I remembered, and I wrapped my arms around myself as we made our way back along the narrow crevice.

"I can't decide if you got the better end of the deal or not," Fin said quietly over my shoulder, the king several strides ahead, his torch held high enough to illuminate our path.

I tucked in my wings, not trusting my brother's closeness. "What do you mean?"

"Well, Dashuri is so uptight, he'll probably explode if you so much as kiss him on the cheek." He chuckled. "But I don't think he'll expect much from you. You'll just have to sit on the throne, smile, and have his babies. That is once he builds up the nerve to do the deed."

I sucked in a breath, itching for the tunnel to widen so I could spread my wings and put distance between us.

"The younger brother is more handsome, but a complete

idiot. The pretty ones usually are. And so easily riled. With all that pouting, you can tell he'd be needy. In fact—"

"Enough," I snapped. "It doesn't matter. I'm to marry Dashuri, so drop it."

"Maybe you could have an affair with the brother."

"It sounds like you want Pace," I bit out through clenched teeth.

Fin laughed softly. "I would take great pleasure in breaking him in, but I'd consider disobeying a direct order from the Fates before sullying myself with a Cupid."

I closed my eyes, inhaling deeply through my nose. Although the conversation was turning my stomach, it was ironically the friendliest exchange we'd ever had.

"You'll be lucky if I don't clip your wings after your performance tonight," the king snapped over his shoulder.

I stumbled, sure he was talking to me, but as the torchlight illuminated his face, I realised he was looking past me, at Fin.

"Father?" my brother faltered.

"You were an embarrassment," the king continued, coming to a halt as the tunnel widened out enough to stretch our wings. "If I deem it necessary for you to join me again, you will keep your mouth firmly shut. Or else."

Anger radiated off Fin in waves behind me, and I was glad we weren't alone, or he'd surely take it out on me. I couldn't remember a time my father had admonished my brother, especially in front of me, but there was no time to gloat as his narrowed eyes turned to me.

"And you," he said. "You will make sure this engagement happens."

Behind me, Fin snorted. "It shouldn't be hard. You're almost certainly the most exciting thing that's ever happened to the prince."

"I will do my best," I said quietly as my father spread his wings.

My father whirled, forcing me to stumble backwards against my brother. "You will do better than your best. Failure is not an option here. Do you understand?"

I swallowed hard. "Yes, Father."

He stared at me for a long moment, the angles of his face demonic in the flickers of amber firelight. "I have been planning this for a very long time. You should know, Sirain, people who get in the way of my plans pay the price. You are no exception."

"I still don't understand why we don't just kill her and use Malin instead," Fin huffed.

I spun, my eyes wide and mouth agape at the open discussion of ending my life, but my brother just stared right back at me, unabashed. Before I could think better of it, I turned to my father, perhaps hoping he would at least pretend to scold him for his words.

Instead, my father peered down his nose at me, his eyes as hard as stone. "Why would I auction off my own flesh and blood?"

My intake of breath turned to ice in my lungs as the king spread his wings and took off, disappearing into the darkness. Fin elbowed me out of the way, sending me stumbling as he followed. For a moment, all I could do was stare as the light of the torch grew smaller, the blackness of their wings merging with the shadows.

He knew. He knew I wasn't his. Had he known this whole time? My whole life? My breathing quickened as my head spun. Was this engagement the only reason I was still alive? Had I been part of his plan all along? Stomach churning, I looked back over my shoulder. What would happen if I turned around and walked back to Hehven? What if I told the king and queen everything and claimed sanctuary? Would my father come for me? Surely, dragging me back would go against his new friendly demeanour.

I took a step backwards.

But then I remembered. If I didn't return to Helle, it wouldn't be me that paid the price of my freedom. It would be my friends. I could barely live with the guilt of taking Dariel's life. How could I possibly live, knowing my choices had cost Odio and Kwellen theirs?

My wings a heavy weight at my back, I sprinted towards Helle, spreading my wings and letting the darkness surround me.

24
Pace

"I need to ask you a small favour."

Jac looked up from where he was seated at my kitchen table, a book opened in front of him. His brow furrowed. "A favour?"

We'd fallen into an easy rhythm, being around each other without it becoming an annoyance. We ate our meals together in amicable silence and he had finally forgone staying outside, taking up residence instead at the kitchen table until I went to bed. It was comfortable despite the awkward reality of why he was there. Although, he still wouldn't call me Pace.

"The meeting yesterday," I started, carefully, leaning against the windowsill. "It was—"

"No!" Jac held up his hands, his curls brushing his forehead as he shook his head vehemently. "I don't want to know. Prince Dashuri told us that even the fact we were in Rakkaus was on a strictly need to know basis. Please don't tell me anything."

My mouth twitched as I bit back a smile. "I wasn't going to spill any royal secrets. I was just going to say it was . . . a lot. My head is a mess and I need to try and sort through things."

Jac frowned. "Okay."

"This is where the favour comes in." I turned back to the window, letting my wings sag a little. The sun had disappeared beyond the horizon, each inch of creeping darkness speeding my heart. "There's this cliff, right at the edge of Dragoste, that I used to go to, to clear my head. Sometimes I'd even talk to the ocean. I know it sounds ridiculous, but it helped."

I waited, my skin tingling in anticipation. Had I laid it on too thick? My teeth gripped the inside of my cheek as I tried not to allow my tension to show in my shoulders.

A scraping noise sounded as Jac pushed back from the table. "So, what? You want to go to this cliff?"

I turned, nodding.

"That's not a favour. I have no problem escorting you to a cliff."

"It's a little more than that, though," I admitted, offering him a pained look. "If I'm going to be talking things through, out loud, you'll need to stay back enough that you don't overhear."

Jac's eyes narrowed. "So, you want to go to this cliff, but you want me to guard you from a distance?"

I almost laughed at his choice of words. Is that what he told himself he was doing? Guarding me? From myself, perhaps.

"Yes," I confirmed. "That's exactly what I'm asking."

Jac stared at me, almost visibly running my request through his head, trying to find loopholes or reasons to deny me. After a long minute, he shrugged. "Fine."

It took all my concentration to halt the curving of my lips. "Thank you."

"When do you want to go?"

I glanced at the window at the encroaching twilight. "Now."

Part of me hadn't believed I'd be able to convince Jac, so every time my mind had wandered to the enormity of what I was about to do, I'd pushed it away. Now, soaring over the night-cloaked pine forests towards the sea, I could avoid it no longer.

I had so much I wanted to say to Sirain, but also nothing at all. No matter the questions I asked, her answers couldn't erase the loss or pain of her actions. There was nothing she could say to justify what she'd done. I closed my eyes and inhaled the cold air, the dank salt-slick breeze stinging my eyes and dampening my feathers.

"I'll wait here," Jac called out, his voice distorted by the whipping wind.

Glancing over my shoulder, I nodded, watching as he descended to the treeline where he'd be sheltered, but able to see me. Ahead, the cliff drew closer, the lights of The Crossing a deep blue and pulsing lime green, too bright against the dark autumn night.

I landed on the sodden grass, pulling the neck of my wool-lined coat higher. There was a chance she wouldn't be here. I couldn't imagine she had the same freedoms she'd had before if she'd passed her Royal Rites. My gut twisted and I screwed my eyes shut, my fists clenching to match.

"Thorn?" I gritted out.

For a moment, there was nothing but the harsh rush of wind.

Then I heard her.

"Rose."

My breath left my lungs in a rush, my head spinning, and I opened my mouth to speak, but clamped it shut again. I didn't know where to start when we'd only ever been ending.

"I know it's worthless," her familiar voice rippled, distorted, through the lights, "but I'm sorry."

"For what?" I snapped.

"Everything."

I huffed, crossing my arms across my chest, and turning my back to The Crossing, even though I knew full well she couldn't see me. I'd forgotten how her voice sounded through the lights. The Spring Festival, when we'd first talked, seemed so long ago. A shiver of doubt flickered through me, frost coating my heart, and I turned, eyeing the lights suspiciously. "How do I know it's you?"

The silence was agony, and I stared into the waves of colour until my eyes watered; long enough that I wondered if she'd gone.

"The last words you said to me were that you would never forgive me. That's how I know my apology is worthless."

A plethora of emotions flooded through me at the memory of our last encounter. The relief I'd felt at seeing her after she'd fled Emeric's manor. The deep sadness at how lost she'd looked. The icy fear and molten anger as she'd pulled the arrow from her quiver . . .

"You should have come to me," I said, my own words surprising me.

"I know."

Frustration chased away the chill of the sea, my blood heating. "Why didn't you tell me you were Crown Princess?"

"You know why."

"Do I?" I laughed. "Because I'm thinking you didn't tell me, so you could have some fun before your duties kicked in. You used me."

"That's not true."

Pressing my fingers to my temples, I stalked back and forth in front of the lights. "You told me to risk everything for you. Why would you do that when you knew you wouldn't be there in the end?"

"I didn't tell you to risk everything for me."

My pacing halted, and I frowned at the bright green lights. "You did."

"No. I didn't. You were unhappy, trying to please everyone, and I told you, you had to make a choice. Either live the life people wanted you to live or choose yourself. It was never about me. It was about you."

A growl of frustration built in my chest, my breath clouding as the air cooled. "You knew you were part of that reason. I tried to let you go. I tried to walk away."

"Well, maybe you should have tried harder!"

My eyes widened, but then I stepped forward, forcing myself to ignore the way her voice had cracked. "I wish I had."

It was a lie. A cold, hard lie. Even if I'd walked away, the Fates would still have ordered Marlowe's death. Things could still have played out the same way. I knew that. I'd imagined every scenario possible as I'd lay awake in my prison, staring at the ceiling.

"Dash ambushed me," I said, glaring at the lights. "He was waiting for me when I came through The Crossing after visiting Marlowe. A Chaos had told him everything."

A heavy sigh filtered through the curtain of lights. "Odio. He thought he was protecting me. I'm sorry."

I stopped and picked up a rock, hurling it out into the churning charcoal waters. It was so dark I didn't see it land.

"What did your brother do?" she asked. "I'm guessing he didn't tell your parents?"

I snorted. "He locked me in a windowless room until just before the Autumn Festival. To give me time to reflect."

Even though I hated myself for it, the appalled gasp that echoed through The Crossing smoothed my feathers, vindicating my feelings in a way I hadn't realised I needed.

"Oh, Pace," she said. "I'm so sorry. That must have been . . ."

"Awful," I finished, my chest tightening at the sound of my name. "Yeah. I have a guard with me at all times now."

"Wait. Are they there now? Do they know?"

"No. He's waiting inland where he can see me, but not hear. I told him I needed to talk to the sea to clear my head."

I expected Sirain's teasing laugh to filter through, but there was nothing. As much as I wanted to nurse the coals of my anger, keeping the burn alive, I was finding it harder and harder to maintain. The sadness in her voice weighed on my shoulders and my memory wandered to the bruises I'd spied on her arm.

"What happened to you?" I asked. "Are you okay?"

A silence followed, long enough for me to launch four more stones into the sea.

"I'm fairly certain Fin poisoned my mother. She hasn't woken since the day before my birthday. The king has Odio and Kwellen; holding them hostage unless I go through with the engagement."

I swore, pulling my hand over my face. Part of me insisted I should find consolation in her pain—that it was deserved for taking Dariel from me, from Marlowe—but I found myself stepping closer, my chest tightening.

"Would he actually hurt Odio and Kwellen?" I asked. "Would he hurt you?"

A humourless laugh echoed through the lights. "He won't hurt me, no. Not when he needs me to marry your brother for this alliance."

My intake of breath stuck in my throat. "You can't marry Dashuri."

"You don't think I know that?" She barked a frustrated laugh, cold and harsh. "You think if I had any other choice, I wouldn't have taken it?"

I groaned, leaning my head back to stare at the moonless sky. There was nothing I could say. Although I wanted to tell her to run away, I knew it wasn't an option. Not when the king had the only people she cared about in his clutches.

"I went to see Marlowe," she said, the words so quiet, I squinted at the lights, not sure I'd heard correctly.

"What?"

"We went to the human world the day before the Autumn

Festival. No one seemed to care where I was or what I was doing, so we risked it to see if Emeric was okay."

My shoulders tensed. With everything that had been going on with the Fates and the meeting with Helle, the Liridonan leader had completely slipped my mind.

"Is he?" I asked. "Did you find him in time?"

"No," she said, the disappointment and concern clear despite the warping of the lights. "We made it to Liridona, but his manor had been razed to the ground. Odio interrogated a survivor, who told us he'd been taken by Newbold soldiers."

"Fated Fates," I muttered. "So, he might still be alive?"

"I honestly don't know. Yesterday, I went and found the Hand who'd been tasked with the orders, and he gave a completely different story."

"What do you mean?"

Sirain sighed, and I wondered where she was. Was she standing an arm's length from me? Was she sitting on the edge of the cliff?

"The Hand said he'd tried to carry out the order four times. Emeric had taken a ship to meet with the Midnight Queen and didn't come out from below deck."

"Well, someone's lying," I said.

"It doesn't matter," she said quietly. "I have no way of helping him now."

"Wait." I frowned, recalling her earlier words. "You said you went to see Marlowe. Why?"

A heavy sigh rippled through the undulating lights. "The war is awful. Getting around in the human world isn't like it used to be. We realised we were clueless as to what was happening with Newbold or Dalibor, so we went to the Wendell Islands to see if he'd tell us. To ask if he could help us rescue him."

A knot tightened in my chest, and I rubbed at it with my knuckles, sucking in a deep breath. I couldn't imagine what

Sirain must have felt, facing Marlowe after what she'd done, but the pain he must have endured at seeing Dariel's killer would have been worse by tenfold. "What happened?"

"Not much. Newbold and Dalibor had all but taken Liridona. Marlowe was certain they would concentrate their efforts on the Wendell Islands next. He said they'd do what they could for Emeric, but he had to put his people first."

I nodded, even though she couldn't see me. "And this was the day before the Autumn Festival?"

"Yes."

My slow exhale sent trails of half-frozen breath spiralling in front of me. It was the coldest autumn I could remember. Was Marlowe okay? The thought of him fighting, defending his island, outnumbered, knocked me sick.

"I just don't know what to do," she mumbled. "My hands are tied. I feel so damn trapped."

Before I could think, my hand reached up, trailing fingers through the lights. I closed my eyes. "We're both trapped. That's why I sent Tiesa to find out if Marlowe was all right. I haven't got a chance of getting anywhere near the human lands while I have my babysitter."

"I hate this," she said.

I didn't disagree, but I clamped my lips together as a heavy silence settled between us. After several minutes of shifting from foot to foot uncomfortably, trying to think of something to say, I glanced over my shoulder, checking that Jac was still keeping his distance. He was still by the treeline, but I opened my mouth to say that I should probably leave.

"This is why I didn't tell you," she muttered.

"Tell me what?"

"That I was Crown Princess."

A groan trickled through the lights, and I held my breath, waiting for the answer to the question I'd been asking myself since Marlowe's ship.

"I accepted that my life wouldn't be enjoyable from an early age. I knew what was expected of me, and you've experienced first-hand just how delightful Fin is." Her laugh was dry. "But when I was with you, I felt more. I was happy. Truly happy. I'd never felt like that before, and I knew I'd never get the chance to experience it again. It was selfish. I know that. But I just couldn't stop. I couldn't leave. You revealed a whole other world to me, Pace. One that I never thought was possible for someone like me. And it wasn't. It isn't. I'm so sorry."

I allowed her words to settle, one by one, in my consciousness, but not one syllable brought me peace or comfort. Shaking my head, I shook out my wings, clearing the drops of moisture.

"I can't forgive you, Sirain," I said, the gruffness of my voice taking me by surprise. "But I'm willing to help you. Both our hands are tied, but I've asked Tiesa to keep an eye on the human world. I haven't heard anything from her in a while, but I'll see if she can find anything out about Emeric, okay?"

"Thank you," she said.

"I know, by the way. About Emeric being your father."

"I figured he would have told you. I should never have left that day. I was just so overwhelmed. So angry."

Enough regrets existed between us to fill an ocean.

"There are a lot of things you shouldn't have done," I scoffed. My words were cruel and unhelpful, but I couldn't help but wield them like a blade in front of my bleeding heart.

"The king knows," she said, choosing to ignore my jibe. "I think he's always known."

I closed my eyes as the cold wind buffeted my skin. We were both prisoners, but at least the cage my family kept me in was safe. Sirain had lived her entire life in mortal danger, and I couldn't imagine what that must be like. Even though I wanted her to feel pain for her actions, I realised I didn't want her to endure physical pain. I didn't want her to die. Did that make me weak? Did I owe more to my cousin?

"At least he won't kill you while he needs you," I offered, the very words sounding ridiculous. There was no comfort in that statement. Not really.

She said nothing in reply, and I couldn't blame her.

"I have to go." I glanced over my shoulder at Jac, whose wings were spread, the white stark against the dark treeline. "When are you next in Hehven? Do you know?"

"No. But it'll probably be soon."

"Good," I said, surprised that I meant it. "We'll talk then."

I spread my wings, already leaning into the breeze that would carry me back towards the palace, when I heard Sirain's voice ripple through The Crossing.

"Goodbye, Rose."

Bowing against the wind, I allowed the current to fill my wings, carrying me up into the air, as I tried to ignore the agony those two simple words wrought against my existence. Jac's face was curious when I drew near, and I realised, it was at the pained expression on my face. After all, I'd told him I came to the cliff to clear my head, but now, my thoughts were more confused than ever.

25
Sirain

Lying in bed, I stared at my ceiling, replaying every word of my conversation with Pace, as a kaleidoscope of emotions took hold of my body. I'd known Odio was right—that Cupids wouldn't have physically harmed Pace for his actions—but by locking him in a windowless room for weeks on end, they may as well have. No wonder he looked as though he had a little less light in his eyes. Although, I knew I was responsible for that lack of light, too.

I closed my eyes and inhaled deeply. I can't forgive you, Sirain. Had I ever expected him to? From the way those words had slashed through the scar tissue of my heart, part of me must have. As my breath left my body in a shudder, I made a silent vow: I would do whatever it took to put the light back in Pace's eyes. Perhaps I could even use my courtship with Dashuri to persuade him to loosen his leash.

Rolling onto my side, my gaze settled on Kwellen's empty bed, and my gut clenched painfully. I'd wandered the lower levels of the castle for hours yesterday, trying to get close to the dungeons, but there had been too many guards. Of course, they might have let me pass, but they would have certainly reported it to my father.

A loud pummelling on my door caused me to sit up with a gasp, my eyes wide.

"Are you awake?"

I frowned at my brother's voice. It was unlike him to knock. "I am."

He pushed open the door, his dark eyes scanning the room before settling on me. "You slept in your clothes."

I had. When I'd returned from the cliff, I'd been too exhausted to change, falling asleep in my leathers on top of my covers. "What do you want, Brother?"

"Father has asked for you."

A wave of trepidation swept through me with a shudder. "Oh? And are you his messenger boy now?"

Fin took a small step towards me, his fists clenched, and I tensed, ready. But then he shook his feathers and lifted his chin. "You have five minutes to get to the throne room."

I watched, eyes narrowed, as he swept from my room. Perhaps the king had given him strict orders not to harm me. Resignation settled on my shoulders, as heavy as a leaden blanket, and I made my way to the washroom. With only five minutes to spare, knowing it would take at least four to make my way across the castle, I splashed some cold water on my face and gave my teeth the most perfunctory of brushes.

Every hurried step towards the throne room sent my mind flurrying through a thousand scenarios. The king hadn't spoken a word to me on our journey back through the tunnel, or the flight back to the castle, and I hadn't seen him since. My stomach rolled as his last words replayed on a loop in my head. How long had he known I wasn't his? My entire life? Perhaps the second I'd been born, and my wings hadn't displayed the royal red. Why hadn't he killed me at birth? I found it hard to believe it was out of love for my mother. Did he know who my father was? Perhaps he thought it was a random Chaos my mother had bedded before their marriage.

Lost in thought, I blinked in surprise as I found myself in front of the throne room, the heavy doors being heaved open by Hands. They bowed low, and I forced myself to ignore them, holding my chin high as I strode towards where the king was seated on his throne, my brother lurking at his side.

"Father," I said, bowing as the doors closed loudly behind me, leaving us alone. "You asked to see me."

He sneered. "I think it's time you stop calling me that."

My heart plummeted, and I stared, my lips parted as I scrambled for words.

"Fin told me of the conversation you had with your mother," he said, waving a hand dismissively. "Of course, it was nothing I didn't already know."

Part of me felt a twinge of satisfaction at the thought of my brother running to his father with his findings, only to discover it was of no interest or use to him.

"You are to return to Hehven," the king continued. "We don't need you here. Go and woo Prince Dashuri. Ensure that this engagement happens. You have one week."

Beside the king, Fin's smile was ear splitting and it took all my self-control not to react, instead linking my tensed fingers behind my back, beneath my wings.

"A week?" I echoed.

The king lifted a dark eyebrow, his gaze burning into me like searing coals. "You require longer to work your wiles? I'm sure it won't take much to tempt him."

I swallowed as my stomach rolled at the thought. "Of course."

"Cupids are strange creatures," the king said, his eyes narrowing as he tapped long, pale fingers against the arms of his throne. "They don't so much as kiss before marriage."

Fin snorted beside him, and I tried my best to look surprised, even as my heart ached at the memory of my first encounter with Pace; the fear in his golden eyes, wide, as I'd stepped close enough to kiss him before plucking a feather from his wing. I pressed my lips together. From the very beginning, I'd been nothing but bad news for Pace. I hated myself for not letting him walk away.

"If you can lure Dashuri in enough to kiss you," the king continued, "it would more than seal the engagement. He would have to marry you out of obligation."

My throat was dry as the Nefret wastelands as I croaked out, "You want me to seduce him?"

"I want you to do whatever is necessary, Sirain."

My thoughts frantically scrambled around my head like a creature in a cage, searching for a way out of the situation, but finding nothing. I opened my mouth to ask if there was anything else, but the malevolent glint in the king's eye halted my breath.

"You will need to be accompanied, of course," he said, leaning forward and threading his fingers together. "Fin and I have matters to take care of here."

"Of course." My eyes flitted to my brother, who was watching me with barely concealed glee.

"Bring them in!" the king barked, and I flinched as his voice echoed around the cavernous room.

The throne room doors heaved open, and I spun, my heart in my throat as four Hands dragged my cousin and best friend into the room.

I wasn't sure whether it was what I'd expected or worse as I stared at Odio's hands bound beneath his wings, and Kwellen's solitary arm strapped to his side by thick rope. My own wings tensed at the sight of the heavy chains weighting their wings, binding them closed at their backs. Both were shirtless, and my eyes burned at the sight of their pale skin, heavily marred with streaks of dirt and what looked like dried blood.

Odio's face was twisted in fury, his hair loose, hanging in limp, tangled strands around his face. As he barked out a curse,

Kwellen's features bore a similar expression, but they both halted in their struggles, falling silent, eyes widening, as they saw me standing in front of the throne.

"What did you do to them?" I choked out.

The king ignored my question, and as the Hands marched them closer, heated fury simmered in my veins. A bloodied gash slashed crimson across Odio's cheek and purple bruising striped Kwellen's ribs, causing him to grimace with each step.

When they reached the dais, the Hands shoved them to their knees, their breath leaving their lungs in a grunt as they met with the cold stone. My own breathing was slow and measured as I forced my expression to stay neutral, determined not to let the king see how much their pain was affecting me.

"Is that how you behave in front of your king?" Fin snarled, his dark wings unfurling. "Bow your heads."

Pure hatred radiated from them both, their jaws clenched as they bowed their heads.

"Your Majesty," they muttered in unison.

Now, up close, I noticed they were both trembling. It might have been with rage, but the dungeons were bitingly cold, and if they'd been held in their current state of undress, they must be chilled to the bone.

"Sirain," the king said, pulling my attention back to him. "You may choose one of them to accompany you."

My eyes widened. "What?"

"Don't make me repeat myself. Choose one."

Odio and Kwellen kept their attention fixed on the stone floor as my gaze flitted between them and the king in disbelief. "What will happen to the other?"

"They will remain here," he answered, a slow smile curving his lips. "As leverage. In case you get any ideas."

My stomach dipped. How could I possibly choose between them, knowing I'd be returning the other to captivity?

Kwellen tipped his head, enough so I could see his face

beneath his long dark hair. It was an almost unnoticeable movement, but his navy-blue eyes fixed on me, before glancing at Odio and back again. My chest tightened as I realised what he was asking of me.

"Choose, or I will choose for you," the king snapped, his patience waning fast.

Kwellen's eyes narrowed, leaving no room for argument. I didn't know why he was telling me to choose Odio, but there was no way I could make the choice alone and I trusted my friend.

"I choose Odio," I said, forcing calm into my words.

My cousin's head snapped up, his eyes wide and filled with outrage. "No!" he shouted. "Choo—"

His words were cut off as one of the Hands kicked him in the ribs. My hand flew to my thigh, reaching for a dagger that wasn't there, and my fingers curled into fists instead, my throat thick with anger.

"Take him back," the king said, waving a hand at Kwellen.

I watched, my lips pressed together and my eyes burning, as the Hands hauled my friend to his feet, dragging him back towards the door.

He caught my eye, his anger softening momentarily as he mouthed, "I'm okay."

I gave the slightest nod, choosing to take him at his word, because the alternative was too painful to consider. Before me, Odio remained on his knees, doubled over to the point his hair touched the ground as he slowly shook his head, muttering under his breath.

The king stood, dusting off his robes as he stared at his nephew through narrowed eyes. "See that he cleans himself up and then make your way to the passage immediately. I trust you remember how to get there?"

I nodded. We might have to spend hours searching the forest for a clearing I hadn't envisaged being alive to revisit, but I would do that before admitting I needed anything from him.

"Good. I expect confirmation of the engagement by the end of the week." He turned and descended the stairs, heading to one of the side rooms with my brother on his heels. "Don't disappoint me."

The door closed behind them, the room falling painfully silent against Odio's ragged breathing.

"I'm so sorry," I whispered, my vision blurring as I stared down at him.

My cousin kept his head down. "Why did you choose me? You should have chosen Kwellen."

I dropped to my knees beside him, moving to put a hand on his shoulder, then changing my mind at the last second, letting it rest on my thigh instead. "I didn't want to choose. If I had any choice, neither of you would be there."

Odio straightened, rage melting from his features as his eyes softened in a way that made my insides hurt even more. "Why, then?" he asked, shaking his head. "Why me?"

"Kwellen told me to."

His eyes widened momentarily before closing as he huffed a sigh. "I'm going to kill him."

"What happened?" I asked. "I tried to find you both before the Festival, but it was like you'd vanished."

"The king ambushed us while we were training," Odio explained. "We didn't know what was going on, so we didn't have time to react. I mean, why would we suspect the king would throw us in the dungeon without reason?"

"I mean, he has a lot of reasons." I snorted. "He just doesn't know them all."

A wry smile ghosted Odio's lips. "True."

Rising to my feet, I strode to the wall, where an ornamental blade was displayed, and lifted it free. Sensing my intention, Odio leaned forward again, raising his wrists. I took hold of his arm, wincing at his ice-cold skin, and sliced the blade through the rope, paying as much mind as I could to his bundled feathers.

He groaned, rotating his shoulders, and rubbing his wrists as I untangled the chains, letting them clatter to the ground. "Thanks, Cousin."

I offered my arm and he gripped hold of it, letting me haul him to his feet. "Come on, let's get you in a nice hot bath."

"That sounds incredible," he moaned.

As we walked slowly back to the main doors, I looked him over, assessing for any injuries I'd missed.

Odio turned to me, shaking his head. "I'm fine. Other than my face."

I frowned at the streaks of dried blood marking his pale cheek. "What happened?"

Odio grinned, although it turned into a wince as it pulled at the half-healed wound. "I may have provoked our guards."

"Shocking," I said dryly as he shrugged. "Is that why Kwellen told me to choose you?"

Odio tensed at my side, all humour draining from his face, but he didn't reply. He didn't speak again until we reached my rooms and a servant had been instructed to draw a bath and fetch a healer.

"Are you going to explain what the king was talking about?" he asked, slumping onto one of the plush chairs. "Or is it a surprise?"

I opened and closed my mouth a few times before shaking my head. "Cousin, I don't even know where to start."

26
Pace

The record keeper's room was chilly, despite the warmth trickling through from the furnaces below, and my progress through the towering stacks of orders was painfully slow. Staring at the open book, I winced at the error I'd just made, the scratched-out word glaring at me from the pristine page. How could I be expected to concentrate? I'd barely slept a wink last night, instead mulling over my conversation with Sirain, as I walked the length of my room until my thighs ached.

I hadn't told her about the Fates, and I wasn't sure why. Perhaps it was something to do with the gaping ravine she'd cleaved in my chest the last time she'd betrayed my trust. Placing the quill back in its pot, I raised my hands above my head in a stretch. It was hard to pretend that everything was continuing as normal when I knew a secret tunnel linked Hehven and Helle and my brother was going to unite our people by marrying the Chaos Crown Princess. A groan tore from my lips, loud in the empty room.

My gaze flicked periodically to the door, waiting for Amare to appear. I hadn't seen her since I'd arrived, and nerves crumpled my insides. We were yet to finish our conversation and I wanted desperately for her to confirm what I already knew in my gut: there was something wrong with the Fates.

When the door flew open, I jumped, almost knocking over the pot of ink, but it wasn't Amare.

"Dash?" I questioned, pressing a hand to my heart. "You almost scared the feathers off me."

He didn't respond, instead closing the door behind him, before beginning a determined path across the room. I folded my arms across my chest and watched, bemused, as the furrow between his brows grew deeper with each lap.

"Brother?" I asked. "Are you well?"

Dashuri grumbled something unintelligible, and I pushed back my chair with a sigh, before placing myself in his path, halting his stride.

I reached out and put my hand on his shoulder, lowering my head slightly so I could look him in the eyes. "Dash. What's wrong?"

He looked at me then, his eyes darting between mine, wilder than I'd ever seen them. "I understand."

"Understand what?"

He turned, my hand slipping from his shoulder. "How you felt."

"Words, Dash," I urged, trying to keep the frustration from my voice. "I need words."

His shoulders slumped, his ivory feathers brushing the floor. "I was so hard on you when you reacted badly to your betrothal."

I stiffened. "Yes. You were."

"I thought you ungrateful," he continued, turning to face me once more. "Caitland is a beautiful, intelligent Cupid, and I couldn't see past the fact that you should have thought yourself fortunate to have such an auspicious match made for you."

"I never said that Caitland wasn't a good match," I said carefully. "She just wasn't a good match for me."

Dash shook his head. "That's what I mean. I've always known I'd have to make a choice at some point in the future, but the crown came first. It was always the most important thing, with everything else following. I was going to wait. I thought I had time."

Pressing my lips together, I folded my arms across my chest, waiting for him to get to the point.

"I understand now. How trapped you felt." My brother lifted his golden eyes to meet mine. "I'm sorry."

My eyebrows shot up as I absorbed the first apology I'd ever heard my brother utter. I'd noted how unsettled Dashuri had looked at the dinner, but I had been so preoccupied with my own inner turmoil, I hadn't lingered on his feelings at being forced into a marriage with Sirain.

"Our parents wouldn't force you to marry her," I said quietly. "You know that. If they were going to do that, they would have accepted there and then."

Dash shook his head. "I know my role. This is momentous. A union between Hehven and Helle? How could I possibly turn that down?"

His words sent an uncomfortable chill down my spine, and I pressed my lips together to hold in questions that would likely awaken the version of my brother that had locked me up. Why was King Hadeon pursuing this union? What did he get out of it? I assumed he wanted control over the Cupids. But why? And more to the point, I couldn't figure out why my parents would agree to such a thing. Most Cupids didn't even know the Chaos existed. I certainly hadn't before I saw them on Cove's ship all those months ago. What did the Cupids have to gain from it?

I added my answerless questions to the insurmountable pile that already existed and focused on the crumbling Cupid in front of me.

"Surely, a union could be reached without a marriage?" I

eyed him carefully. "Especially if you weren't happy with the match."

"It's more complicated than that," Dash huffed. "I mean, it's not as though Princess Sirain isn't beautiful. She's truly breathtaking."

My fingers dug into my biceps, my jaw clenching. "Indeed, she is."

"But I'm not ready," he said, sighing deeply. "I don't have time for courting and wooing. Any spare time I have is spent preparing you to take over from me, so that I'm ready for the throne when Mother steps down."

I raised my eyebrows. "Mother plans to step down?"

Dash waved a hand dismissively at me before resuming his pacing. "She wouldn't be the first of our ancestors to do so. She's considering spending her twilight years enjoying life, rather than holding the throne until she passes."

"Twilight years?" I barked a laugh. "She's barely into her forties."

Dashuri ignored me, the furrow back between his brows.

"This is why you've been putting so much pressure on me to take on your role, isn't it?" I asked. "You're preparing to take the throne sooner rather than later, aren't you?"

Dash's strides slowed and he slumped down onto a chair with a sigh. "I've never minded the pressure," he said. "I've always known my destiny. Accepted it wholeheartedly. But part of me has always envied you. You've always been so free. So comfortable with who you are. You walk the world with an ease I could only dream of."

A laugh tumbled from my lips. "Excuse me?"

Dash stared at me. "Don't act surprised."

"Oh, trust me, Brother," I said. "I was under the impression you could barely stand to be in the same room as me. Why should I suspect you envied me?"

Dash leaned forward, his golden eyes wide. "You think I don't like you?"

I stared.

"I love you, Brother," Dash said, shaking his head. "I'm sorry if I ever gave you the impression otherwise. I know I'm hard on you, but it's only because I care."

"Hard on me?" I echoed. "Hard on me? You imprisoned me. You broke me."

I stood, staring down at him, anger roiling in my veins. At least, he had the decency to wince.

"I remember when you were born," he said, a small smile ghosting his lips. "I was almost six years old, and I was thrilled at the prospect of a brother. You were so tiny. All scrawny limbs and crumpled wings. I thought I was going to burst with excitement. Mother let me hold you and told me I had a job to do. A job even more important than ruling Hehven. She told me I was responsible for you—for showing you how to take the right path and being there for you no matter what."

I sank down onto my chair, swallowing the lump in my throat. "And yet, you robbed me of my choices and locked me up, torturing me for weeks on end."

Dash grimaced, dropping his head into his hands. "I didn't know what else to do. You'd strayed so far, and I couldn't see any other way to just . . . stop you. Things were spiralling out of control and I . . . I panicked."

"I have nightmares," I said, my voice hard as I stared at my brother. "I struggle in confined spaces. Something I never did before. Your 'panic' broke something in me."

Dash rubbed his hands over his face. "I'm sorry, Pace. I truly am. If I could go back, I'd find a different way."

I shook my head, looking away.

"Things don't feel right," Dashuri murmured, so quiet, I wondered whether he meant for me to hear. But when I looked up, his eyes were locked with mine. "Do you feel it?"

I pressed my lips together. "Again. Words, Brother. More of them, please."

"This alliance with Helle, out of the blue. The human war." He shook his head. "I don't know. Perhaps it's nothing, but I can't shake the feeling that something's not right."

I stared at him, wondering whether I could tell him. How would he react if he knew what I did? What I'd already done? As soon as the thought entered my head, I shoved it away. We might have just engaged in the most honest conversation we'd ever had, but that didn't mean I trusted him. I certainly hadn't forgiven him.

A loud knock at the door startled us both and Dash got to his feet, heaving open the door.

"Your Majesty," the Fated said, head bowed. "A messenger has arrived at the Isle. They want me to inform you that the princess has arrived in Rakkaus."

I stood, stepping closer as my brother stiffened. We both knew the princess was not our sister.

"Thank you," he said, and the Fated bowed again before turning away.

When Dash turned to me, the look of desperation on his face caught me by surprise.

"I'm not ready," he whispered.

My heart leapt into my throat, and I tried not to smile at the situation that had presented itself. Stepping forward, I placed a hand on his shoulder, squeezing. "Let me go and welcome her. I'll find out what's going on and send word to you here."

Dashuri sagged beneath my touch. "Thank you, Brother."

"No problem," I said, gathering my jacket from the chair and shrugging it on.

As I stepped back out into the main room, I cast a glance over my shoulder, finding my brother holding his head in his hands. A myriad of emotions flooded through me as I turned away. I didn't trust my brother as far as I could throw him, but I was beginning to think I wouldn't be able to hide things from him for much longer.

27
Sirain

"I can't believe there's a tunnel under the Fated Crossing," Odio cursed for the tenth time. "It's ridiculous."

I ignored him, concentrating instead on navigating the long dark passageway, the beating of my wings causing the flames of the torch in my outstretched hand to flicker chaotically. I'd quickly decided the damp, miserable tunnel was my least favourite place, but in a thick woven dress and a wool-lined cloak, I wasn't numb from the cold this time. If anything, I was bordering on too warm. My bag was heavy across my chest, despite containing only one change of clothes, and the weight caused me to work my wings a little harder than usual.

My stomach was in knots at the thought of a week in Hehven. Would I stay at the palace? Part of me leapt at the idea of seeing the place Pace called home, but equally, my insides shrivelled at the thought of being in forced proximity to someone I knew could barely stand the sight of me. I tightened my grip on the torch as it wavered. Pace had said he'd help me. Had there been any news from Tiesa? Not being able to find out what was going on in the human world was driving me to distraction, and I couldn't imagine it was much better for Pace.

Eventually, the tunnel narrowed, and I slowed the beating

of my wings, calling to my cousin over my shoulder. "We walk from here."

Odio dropped to the ground behind me with a grunt. "I still can't believe this is happening."

"Well, it is."

He left it at that, and whether he'd read the edge in my voice or heeded the rigidness of my shoulders, I exhaled in relief as we continued the rest of the way in silence. When the nondescript wooden door emerged in the torchlight, I reached out a hand to knock, and found it trembling. A hand closed over my shoulder, squeezing.

"You've got this, Cousin," Odio whispered at my ear. "You're the toughest Chaos I know. Wings up. Stand tall."

I rolled my eyes at the old turn of phrase, but his words rallied me more than I cared to admit. Raising my wings and my chin, I rapped my knuckles against the wood.

After several agonising minutes, Odio shifted, coughing awkwardly. "Are you sure this is the right creepy, never-ending tunnel?"

I shot him a withering look over my shoulder, a biting response on my tongue, but then the sound of bolts sliding echoed into the cave, and the door opened.

"Your Majesty," Lord Rakkaus said, bowing low. "Please accept my humblest apologies for making you wait. My son was guarding the door, but as we weren't expecting anyone, he went to fetch me instead of answering."

He moved to the side, gesturing for us to enter, and when I was sure we were alone, I let out a breath. The room looked different—felt emptier—with the large wooden table bare. My heart beat a little faster at the thought that the last time I'd stood within these walls, I'd been sharing a meal with Pace's family.

"I completely understand, Lord Rakkaus." I offered him a

small smile before gesturing to Odio. "This is my cousin, Lord Hadeon."

The slender, white-haired male baulked a little at the stitched slash across Odio's face, but bowed low, and by the time he straightened, a warm smile creased his face. "It is an honour to welcome you to Rakkaus, and to Hehven."

Odio stared at the Cupid with slightly narrowed eyes, his wings flaring just a little.

"Please," the lord said, holding out his hands to take my bag. "I've asked my sons to release our waiting staff for the day, so only my wife and children are in the house. Please make our home your own."

"Are we prisoners?" Odio said, the edge to his words clear, despite his casual tone.

Lord Rakkaus faltered. "Not at all, Lord Hadeon. It's just, Queen Dragoste expressed she wanted to keep the existence of the link between our worlds secret for now, as I'm sure you can understand."

I glanced at Odio in a silent order to stand down. "Of course. That is completely understandable."

Lord Rakkaus gestured for us to step through into a long, narrow room and I glanced around, realising it must have been the room where Fin and Pace had met. Part of me was surprised the furniture was still intact. The Cupid pushed open a set of larger, more ornate doors, and excitement fluttered in my chest at finally getting to see Hehven, if only from the windows.

"I hope you will stay with us longer than an evening, Your Majesty," Lord Rakkaus said. "We would be most humbled if you would honour us with your continued presence."

It was hard to gauge his sincerity. If we were in Helle, I would almost certainly be assured of his begrudging sarcasm, but Cupids were kind and gracious, right?

"A week," I said. "If that is amenable to you?"

Lord Rakkaus smiled, his brown, sun-weathered skin crinkling heavily at the corners of his eyes. "More than amenable, Your Majesty. I assure you, you are welcome to stay in my home for as long as you wish."

A young Cupid male, probably a year or two younger than me, rushed forward, trying not to gawk and failing miserably. I recognised him vaguely from the dinner. I wondered how many children Lord Rakkaus had that he could run the house without servants—or waiting staff, as he'd called them.

"Ah, Elsker. Go and tell the Hands that the crown princess is here," Lord Rakkaus instructed. "Then, find your sister and tell her to ensure the guest rooms are ready."

As the young Cupid turned and sprinted down the corridor, I wondered whether his speed was aided by his desire to distance himself from us.

"One of my sons," the lord explained. "The queen had two Hands stay on with us here in Rakkaus, ready for your return. They will send word to Prince Dashuri."

I smiled, although my stomach sank a little at the thought of the crown prince joining us. There was a chance he was busy with royal duties. Perhaps he wouldn't be able to come. A more persistent thought tried to worm its way to the front of my mind, but I knocked it away. There was no point wasting energy wondering whether Pace would come to see me. We'd said everything that needed to be said on the cliff.

"I'm a little disappointed," Odio whispered as we followed Lord Rakkaus down the hallway.

I frowned. "Why?"

"It looks just like Helle."

My heart stuttered a little as I realised, I'd been so caught up in my thoughts, I hadn't been taking in what was right in front of me. All along our right, long windows were cut into the hallway, lighting the dark wood and floral-patterned walls with muted afternoon light. Sweeping hills stretched as far as the eye could see, their slopes and valleys covered with fields and orchards in alternating oranges, reds, and yellows.

"It's been a good harvest this year," Lord Rakkaus said, slowing his stride as he noticed my attention. "Although this autumn is the coldest we've had in years, and I fear it means spring will arrive late."

I nodded absentmindedly; my gaze still fixed on the hills beyond the window. I may have been trapped within the four walls of the Cupid lord's home, but a sense of freedom still filled my bones, as though the sheer distance alone from the king and my brother was a loosening of the weight on my soul.

"Come, Your Majesty," Lord Rakkaus said gently. "You must be tired from your journey. Allow me to show you to your rooms and I'll have lunch brought to you."

I smiled graciously, and as we continued down the hallway, my wings sagging, I realised just how exhausted I was. It took several minutes to make our way through the house and up the stairs, revealing that Lord Rakkaus' house was much larger than I'd initially thought. But then, as guardians of a secret possibly as ancient as the Fates themselves, they must be a rather prominent family.

"Ah," Lord Rakkaus said as we turned a corner, revealing yet another endless hallway. "There you are."

Standing in front of a closed door, with a large tray in her hands, was a very beautiful Cupid with long white hair and large, pale silver eyes. She was so slim and delicate I wondered how she had the strength to hold the tray.

"Your Majesty," she said, curtseying as much as she could manage under the weight of the platters.

"Please, allow me," Odio said, striding forward and lifting the tray from her with a smile before she could open her mouth to protest.

She stared up at him, her lips parted and eyes wide. My

striking cousin had that effect on most people, but the look of awed terror on the Cupid's face was almost comical.

"This is my daughter, Caitland," Lord Rakkaus said.

My heart stuttered. Caitland. I'd thought the Cupid lord's name sounded familiar. I assumed it was because of the area named the same. But no. It was familiar because this dainty, pretty thing was the female Pace had been betrothed to when he met me.

"Come, make yourselves at home," Lord Rakkaus said, opening the door Caitland was frozen, wide-eyed in front of, and stepping inside. "This is our largest room. That door leads to a washroom, but the door over there connects with another bedroom. I thought perhaps Lord Hadeon would prefer to stay close."

"You thought correct," Odio said, placing the small mountain of food down on a table and flashing the older man a white smile. "Thank you."

"Yes," I said, forcing my attention away from Caitland. "Thank you."

Lord Rakkaus placed my bag down on a chaise longue and bowed. "I'll leave you to freshen up and eat. When the Prince arrives, you'll be the first to know, but please ask me or any of my children if you need anything at all before then."

As he disappeared into the hallway, Caitland dipped into a deep curtsey. "Is there anything else I can get for you, Your Majesty?"

I smiled, though I was sure it looked as fake as it felt. "No. Thank you."

She cast one last, terrified, look at Odio, dipping again before slipping out of the door and closing it softly behind her. My heart squeezed as I drew in an aching breath. Pace had been so loath to marry her, but he would have been so much better off if he hadn't fought it. She was beautiful, but more importantly, she was safe. Caitland certainly wouldn't have lied to him and ripped his world to shreds.

"Are you okay?" Odio asked, eyeing me with a frown.

I shook my head. "Not really, no."

He stared at me, long and hard, before shaking his head and pulling out a chair at the table. "Food will make things better. Come on, let's eat."

Taking a seat, I watched as my cousin uncovered the many plates, peering and squinting at each one.

"This doesn't look that different to the food we get in Helle," he simpered.

I laughed. "You've met Cupids before. You knew our worlds were more similar than not."

"I know." He shrugged. "But I still hoped."

"Caitland is pretty," I said, as casually as I could.

My attempt failed miserably as Odio stopped mid-chew to squint at me. "Excuse me?"

"I was just making an observation."

He continued to stare, chewing slowly. "She's pretty, yes. If you like bedding partners who might break."

I frowned, pointing at him with my fork. "I never said anything about bedding her."

Odio rolled his eyes. "What's this Prince Dashuri like? Is he anything like his brother?"

My heart kicked up at the mention of Pace, but I kept my eyes on my food, pushing some grains infused with garlic and spices around on my plate. "No. He's nothing like Pace."

Odio snorted. "That's got to be a good thing."

"It doesn't matter because I'm not marrying him," I snapped.

We continued eating in silence, although my appetite quickly waned to nothing and I stood, drifting to the window as though I might find answers on the horizon. Marrying Dashuri was just like everything else in my life: completely out of my control. Tilting my head back to stare at the white sky, I realised the only time I'd truly had a choice was when I'd flown to Marlowe's ship. Odio and Kwellen had been with me, safe from the king's clutches. I could have refused the Rites. I could have run. Pace would have hidden me. Protected me. But it was too late now.

A knock sounded at the door, and I turned, my fingers gripping the window ledge.

"Yes?" Odio called.

"The prince is here to see you, Your Majesty," Caitland called through the door.

Odio grinned at me over his shoulder and my heart plummeted into my stomach.

"Send him in," he called, tipping his head back and catching a berry in his mouth.

"I hope you choke," I hissed.

Odio rolled his eyes, not even deigning to stand as the door pushed open. But then, my already faltering heart stopped beating all together.

"Pace," I breathed, not quite believing my eyes.

He dipped his head in a bow, but then his gilded eyes settled on Odio, who was still reclined in his chair, wings draping on the carpet. Rage flickered across Pace's features, his wings flaring, but Odio just watched, chewing loudly.

"Can I get you anything?" Caitland asked, her gaze flicking curiously between us all as we stood in an awkward silent standoff.

"Actually, yes," I said, forcing myself to stand tall, despite the fact my legs were trembling beneath my thick winter skirts. "Lady Rakkaus? Would you be so kind as to show Lord Hadeon around your home? If we're to be staying here all week, I'd hate for us to find ourselves lost."

Caitland's silver eyes widened to moons as she stared at my cousin. "Of-of course, Your Majesty," she stuttered, curtseying.

I flicked my gaze to Pace, my mouth dry as I waited for him to say something—to contradict my request—lest he be left alone with me. Alone. I winced as my heart contracted.

Odio turned and glared at me, but I stared back, unfaltering. After an agonising minute, he stood, slowly brushing the crumbs from his black leather tunic, extending, and folding his vast wings. "Shall we?" he said, gesturing to Caitland.

I didn't miss the panicked look she gave Pace, but he didn't notice. His attention was wholly fixed on my cousin. I grimaced as Odio strode to the door, purposefully walking as close to Pace as he could without touching him. I half expected him to knock into him with his shoulder.

As Odio moved past, Pace's fierce gaze shifted to me, causing me to lean back against the window to steady myself. I looked away, locking eyes with Caitland, who stared between us, her eyes slightly narrowed.

"Thank you, Lady Rakkaus," I said, pulling her from her thoughts.

She blinked. "Please, Your Majesty, call me Caitland."

"Thank you, Caitland." I twisted my mouth into what I hoped resembled a smile. "And don't mind my cousin. His bark is much worse than his bite, I assure you."

My words did little to ease the look of panic on her face, but Odio grabbed hold of the door, pulling it shut and leaving me alone with the person who hated me possibly as much as my brother.

"I wasn't expecting you," I said, wilting under Pace's stare.

He arched an eyebrow. "Disappointed?"

I leaned back against the ledge, unable to respond as my gaze dropped to the carpet. The way he affected me, even after everything . . . I despised the power he had over my heart.

"Why are you here?" I asked.

Pace sighed, lowering himself onto one of the empty seats at the table we'd been eating at. "I heard the crown princess of

Helle had arrived in Rakkaus, so thought it only fitting that someone greet her."

I stared at him as he peered at our leftovers, memorising the sharp slope of his jaw, the broad expanse of his chest and the way his ivory hair contrasted with the rich golden colour of his skin. How could I ever have been expected to say no to him? Who could have walked away if he asked them to stay? Certainly someone a lot stronger than me.

He returned his gaze to me, and I turned away, my heart hammering in my chest. Clenching my trembling fingers, I leaned my forehead against the window, relishing the coolness of the glass against my burning skin.

"You can't look at me?"

I closed my eyes. It had been different on the cliff. Separated by the lights, unable to see him, I'd been able to speak freely, knowing I was safe. It was almost laughable. I'd never been safe.

"Sirain?" A ruffle of feathers sounded as he shifted. "What? You can't even speak to me now?"

I screwed my eyes tighter, each breath painful. "I'm glad you find it so easy."

He huffed a laugh. "Nothing about this is easy."

"Why did you come, Pace?"

"Dash is nervous. I offered to come and find out why you were here and for how long and then send word. Give him time to prepare."

I nodded against the window. "I'm here for a week. If I don't secure the engagement . . ."

"Kwellen?" Pace asked, his voice strained.

I nodded again. The king hadn't said as much, but his threat hadn't required specifics. "He made me choose."

Pace swore softly under his breath. "I'm sorry."

"Don't be. I deserve it. Perhaps this is all Fated. Punishment for not carrying out my first Rite. Comeuppance for lying to you."

Pace was silent long enough that I almost opened my eyes and turned, but I couldn't. It was so much easier when I couldn't see him.

"It's okay that you hate me," I whispered. "I understand."

Pace sighed and I could almost picture him pushing his hand through his thick, white locks, the way I'd seen him do a thousand times. "I wish I did hate you, Sirain. It would make everything so much easier."

A single burning tear escaped, searing a path down my cheek. I'd vowed to make Pace's life better, but what a foolish promise that was. I was as powerless to affect his life as I was my own.

More tears chased the first.

I let them fall.

"There's another reason I came," he said softly. "There's something I didn't tell you on the cliffs."

My mind raced, but I kept my back to him, my wings a shield between us. "What?"

"Sirain," he said, and I heard the brush of the chair against the carpet as he stood. "Please, look at me."

I shook my head. Didn't he understand I was barely keeping the pieces of myself together? How could I look at him when I'd only see everything I'd lost?

Maybe it was worse because I knew. I'd thought he was beautiful the second I laid eyes on him, but now I knew what those lips tasted like. I knew what those hands were capable of. I knew what it felt like to lie against his skin and feel whole. My chest ached as I searched for remnants of the cold, heartless Chaos I used to be—the mask I'd grown so accustomed to wearing in Helle—but it was broken, the pieces scattered to the wind the minute I'd surrendered my heart. The irony. Love had stripped me of my armour only to make me weak enough to need it.

Pace's steps were so quiet and my thoughts so loud, I didn't realise he'd moved until his fingers brushed the edge of my wing. I sucked in a breath, whirling, shrinking away from his touch as though it burned. It may as well have.

His eyes widened as he tracked the tear stains on my cheeks, the pain etched on my face. "Sirain . . ."

As he took half a step closer, I pulled further away, my wings crushed painfully against the wall. Pace frowned, his attention dropping to the rapid breathing causing my chest to heave.

"You're scared?" he asked, confusion clouding his honeyed eyes.

I swallowed. "Terrified."

After a moment, resignation dropped his shoulders and he returned to his chair. My throat constricted. All I wanted to do was make him happy, but I didn't know how. Everything I did made things worse. I sucked in a deep breath, trying to calm my erratic heart. He wanted to talk. I could talk.

I could try.

"Tell me," I said, forcing calm into my voice. "What didn't you tell me on the cliff?"

Pace kept his eyes on a fork, pushing at the tines with his finger, causing it to rock against the table. "Will you sit?"

I forced myself forward, pulling Odio's chair away from the table and lowering myself onto it.

Pace nodded, keeping his eyes down. "There's something wrong with the Fates."

My eyebrows shot up. I wasn't sure what I'd been expecting, but it wasn't that. "What do you mean?"

"I mean, I've seen a picture of them, and I've seen them in person, and they're not the same."

I stared, trying to grasp what he was saying. "Are you saying the Fates aren't actually the Fates?"

"I don't know," he admitted with a groan. "I'm saying that something's amiss and I need to know what it is."

A million moments raced through my mind—the conflicting orders delivered by Cupids and Chaos, the kill orders for Marlowe, for Emeric . . .

"There are just so many things that don't make sense," he continued. "I've been working in the record room, and I must have read two thousand orders from the Fates, but not a single one is for Newbold. That can't be right."

I nodded. "And Newbold took Emeric. Do you think they're linked?"

"I don't know," he admitted, rubbing a hand over the back of his neck. "But I want to find out."

"How?" I asked. "You have a guard, right?"

Pace nodded, almost lifting his head, then forcing it down. "He's waiting with the other Hands."

My heart swelled. He was trying not to look at me so I would feel comfortable. After everything I'd done to him, a part of him still cared. I pushed the thought away before it could linger. It wasn't that. He needed to talk to me. That's all it was. It wasn't personal.

"I think we need to tell Dash."

I gawped. "About us?"

Pace frowned, picking up the fork and stabbing it gently into the woven tablecloth. "About everything. It's the only way. We need freedom to find answers."

I blinked. "We?"

He nodded at the table, his knuckles white where he gripped the fork. "Yes. We. I was hoping you'd want to help me. Odio too. And Tiesa. Perhaps with the four of us, we can figure it out."

I shook my head, fear chilling my skin despite the warmth of the room. "What if he locks you up again?"

Pace's jaw clenched, and he stabbed the fork into the table hard enough that it embedded in the wood through the cloth. "I won't allow that to happen."

"No," I said softly. "We won't allow that to happen."

Pace's grip loosened on the utensil, his shoulders slumping. "I've tried to think of another way. I've even considered fighting our way out of Rakkaus and racing the Hands to The Crossing, but they'd follow and ruin our chances. Telling Dash is the only way."

I stared at him, my mind racing as I tried and failed to think of an alternative. After a moment, I sighed. "I think you're right."

Pace nodded, his mouth a thin line. "I'll send one of the Hands to tell Dash that you're here for a week."

Unable to find anything to say, I watched him stand and walk to the door without looking at me once. It closed softly behind him, and my gaze fell to the fork, still embedded in the table. Reaching out, I pulled it free and held it before me, staring at the finely crafted silver.

If Pace could convince Dashuri, could trust him, it would mean we had a week. A week to find my father. Seven days to find answers before I had to return to Helle. Because I would have to.

Trepidation pulsed in my veins. Was telling Dashuri the right thing? As much as the thought crushed my lungs and turned my stomach, I knew I had to return with an agreement to the engagement. The king wouldn't hesitate to execute Kwellen, and I would die before letting that happen.

Pace had seemed quietly confident. Maybe we could do it. Maybe there was a way through this. I had one hundred and sixty-eight hours of freedom. It might be enough. Tendrils of hope crept around my heart, but I pushed them back with a snarl, throwing the fork across the room. Hope was a luxury I didn't deserve.

28
Pace

I clutched the ancient book to my chest as I flew through the mist, my heart thudding against the worn leather binding. My wings were heavy as lead at my back as I allowed gravity to pull me, gasping, towards the intimidating entrance to the Isle of the Fates. Sirain was probably wondering where I'd gone, but I knew I needed to speak to Dash at the Isle. I still hadn't seen Amare since I'd told her of my suspicions, but I hoped against hope I could find her for this. I'd seen on her face that my words had struck doubt in her heart, and although part of me felt bad for it, it had to be done.

Flying all the way to my cottage and back up to the Isle had taken a lot longer than I'd anticipated and the afternoon had rather rudely slipped into evening before I could blink. It was easy to forget that my wings were still recovering from captivity, the journey much more gruelling than it should have been. Or perhaps it was because I'd barely slept in days. Landing on the icy rock, I stretched my wings out to their fullest, frowning at them over my shoulder. Perhaps it was time to ask the healers for some more of that awful tea they'd given me.

Pulling my jacket tighter around myself, I folded my wings and marched beneath the enormous stone carvings. Just as before, I barely had time to draw a breath before the doors were heaved open, a Fated stepping forward to lead me through the pitch-black tunnel to the main room.

I spotted my brother immediately, huddled over a table studying a large ledger, his midnight-blue robes and white hair in stark contrast to the heavy, dark, hooded robes of the Fated around him.

He looked up as I approached, his eyes widening a little. "Brother. I was starting to worry."

"Apologies," I said, coming to a stop in front of him. "May I talk with you?"

He nodded, his eyes flitting to the book cradled against my chest. "Of course."

I followed him across the chamber to the Record Keeper's room and he opened the door, gesturing for me to enter, before shutting it behind us.

"Is the princess well?" he asked.

"Quite," I assured him, even as the image of her tear-stained face assaulted my memory. She couldn't even look at me. My fingers tightened around the book, but I shoved my feelings down to deal with later. "She's staying for a week."

Dash nodded, wringing his fingers. I watched the absent-minded gesture in fascination. I couldn't remember a time I'd ever seen my brother so flustered. My stomach lurched. I had something that would certainly take his mind off the crown princess of Helle.

"Dashuri," I said carefully. "I need to talk to you."

Trepidation flickered across my brother's features, as clear as day. "What's wrong? Did something happen?"

A lot has happened. I pointed at one of the chairs. "Please, sit."

I stared at him as he warily sank down onto a chair, resting his hands on his lap. My list of confessions and admissions swarmed around my head in a deafening flurry as I tried to grasp at a thread of where to start. Perhaps this was a ridiculous idea. There were no Hands past the atrium, but would I be able to escape the Isle? I hadn't seen Dashuri's accompanying Hands on my way in, but that didn't mean they weren't around somewhere. He wouldn't have flown here by himself. Would the Fated themselves pin me down and take me prisoner if their future king demanded it?

"Pace?" Dashuri's voice broke through my spiralling thoughts, and I blinked, focusing on him once more.

"Sorry." I shook my head. "I need to talk to you about what happened."

"You're going to need to be more specific, Brother."

"The human world." Placing the book on the table beside me, I sat down, my fingers digging into my thighs in an attempt to stop them from bobbing. "My visits there may have started as mere curiosity, borne from the fact that I was feeling trapped by the engagement, but they became about something so much bigger."

I watched Dash's face, his lips pursing as though he was trying to keep his comments to himself. Ignoring him, I ploughed on. "I saw Dariel deliver an arrow, and then the same day, watched a Chaos deliver an arrow to the same human." I shook my head. "As you can imagine, I was confused. Why would the Fates send us to alter a human's emotions before an important meeting, only to contradict them later?"

"Ours is not to question Fate." Dashuri groaned. "You know this, Pace. I thought we'd moved past this."

My fingers gripped harder against my thighs, my skin burning hot beneath my clothes. "Do you know the Fates have issued orders to kill humans?"

"What?" he blustered, eyes widening. "That's impossible."

"It's not." I fixed him with an unwavering stare, even as my blood roared in my ears. "I was there when one of the orders was carried out by a Chaos."

Dash ran a hand over his brow. "You must be mistaken,

Pace. There's no way—"

"Have you ever seen the Fates?"

His mouth fell open, his frustration faltering at my inter-ruption. "Once. When I turned twenty and took over from Father as leader of the Captains of Fate, Mother sent me to present myself to them."

"Do you remember what they looked like?"

Dash stared at me for a long moment. "How could you possibly ask that? Do you think I could forget being in the pres-ence of such power?"

I reached for the book beside me and flipped it open to the illustration of the Fates. Turning it around, I handed it to him. "Is this accurate?"

His eyes flitted between me and the book, narrowing. "What is this?"

"A book written hundreds of years ago by one of our ances-tors. He was a Fated." I leaned forward, each breath painfully shallow. "Is that what they look like?"

A myriad of emotions played across his face as he stared at the page before him. "This doesn't mean—"

"It means something," I whispered. "That's what I was doing in the human world."

Dash's gaze lifted and he raised his eyebrows in a way that made my skin heat all the way down to my toes.

"One of the things," I muttered, leaning back. "The point is, there's something strange going on. I know that's not what the Fates look like. Close, but not quite."

"Why are you telling me all this?" Dash asked, placing the book on the nearest table and folding his arms. "You assured me you'd changed. You knew the consequences if you did anything to jeopardise this family. Are you trying to force me to lock you up again?"

My breath caught in my throat, but I forced the shudder of fear down into the pit of my stomach, glaring at my brother.

"You could try," I hissed, "but I'll never allow you to do that to me again."

Whether it was my tone or the look on my face, I couldn't be sure, but Dash paled, recoiling slightly.

"What do you want, then?" he asked. "Why even bother telling me these conspiracy theories?"

I swallowed. "Because the Fates have issued another kill order. This time for the leader of Liridona. The order hasn't been carried out, though, as far as we know. I have it on good authority that he's been kidnapped by Newbold."

Dash stood up from his chair with such force, it skittered backward, causing me to flinch. "I have the crown princess of Helle waiting for me right now with a historic alliance in the balance. I honestly don't have time to deal with this right now, Little Brother."

I stood slowly. "You need to have time for it. That's why I'm telling you. Helle coming to seek an alliance, the Fates, the human war. Everything's linked. I know it is."

A frustrated groan tore from Dash's throat as he turned away from me, pushing his fingers into his white curls. "Why must you test me like this? Why can't you just do as you're told for once in your Fated life?"

I stared at his wings, trying to steady my breathing. "You told me just a few hours ago that Mother told you to be there for me, no matter what."

Dash shook his head. "This is most certainly not what she was talking about."

"Dashuri," I pleaded. "You said yourself that things didn't feel right. Let me do this. Give me back my freedom."

He froze, silence settling between us as the echoes of my request sank into the walls of the room. "Your freedom?"

"I want you to release Jac." I took a step forward. "I need to be free to visit the human world and find out what's happening with the Fates."

Dashuri's shoulders shook, and I frowned, wondering whether the pressure of the crown—of me—had finally broken him, but then, deep rippling laughter filled the room, bouncing off the stone walls.

Anger exploded in my chest and I strode forward, grabbing his shoulder and turning him to face me. "This is not funny," I roared. "Do you have any idea how many lives are in the balance? How many lives might have been lost because of the Fates?"

Tears spilled from Dashuri's eyes. "And what? You think you're going to save the human world? You and your human friends?"

"No." My teeth clenched together hard. "Me, Tiesa, Sirain and her cousin, Odio."

Dash's laughter tapered off as confusion twisted his features. "Sirain? Why in all that's Fated would she be coming with you?"

I stared at him, waiting for him to figure it out. Waiting for him to put the final piece of the puzzle together so I wouldn't be forced to say the words.

The door flew open, causing both of us to jump back.

"What is going on in here?" Amare asked, her pale blue eyes widening as she looked between us. "I could hear shouting."

I grimaced. "Sorry, Cousin. We were just talking."

"You most certainly were not," she said, closing the door behind her. "No one has shouted on the Isle of the Fates in millennia, yet here you two are having a family spat. What's going on?"

Taking a breath, I turned to face my brother, but he was already looking at me with narrowed eyes, his lips parted.

"Sirain," he said softly.

I stared at him, waiting.

"She was the Chaos you lost your purity to?"

"Yes." The word was a rock in my throat, and I swallowed it down, knowing the next words would hurt so much more. "But it's over now."

My brother snorted a laugh, muttering under his breath as he turned away.

"You told him?" Amare asked, her slender fingers over her mouth.

"I've told him I'm worried about the Fates," I said, fixing her with a look that I hoped conveyed that I'd withheld some things. "And that I want him to let me go to the human world in search of answers."

Dash sank down onto a chair, shaking his head, before looking up at Amare. "You knew?"

She winced. "Pace wanted to know if the Fates looked different to the illustration in that book."

My brother groaned, pressing his fingers to his temples. "It's an illustration. Open to artistic interpretation. There's—"

"There's more," Amare said. "Pace said the book states that only those with royal blood can see all four Fates."

My heart slammed against my chest as I held my breath, waiting, although I knew what was coming.

"I asked six other Fated," she said quietly. "They thought I'd fallen down and banged my head or something when I asked them how many Fates they could see."

"What did they say?" I breathed.

Amare held my gaze for a moment before turning to Dashuri. "Four. All six of them said they could see four Fates."

A low moan tore from my brother's throat. "Pace. You're asking me to allow you to go to the human world in the middle of a war to try and prove that the very beings who brought about our existence are a lie."

I shook my head, my heart racing. "No. I'm not saying I don't think the Fates are real. I'm saying something's wrong.

Can't you see that? Didn't you hear what Amare said? If you'd just let me go—"

"You're the second prince," Dash barked. "I can send Hands to investigate. Tell me everything you know and your connections with the humans and—"

"There's no time," I snapped. "We have a week until Sirain and Odio have to be back in Helle, and we need answers before then."

"Why?" Dash pressed, his voice rising enough that Amare flinched, shushing him.

"I'll admit. There's a lot I haven't told you, Brother. But I need you to trust me." I stepped in front of him, pushing every ounce of confidence into my stare. "I've never asked anything of you. I'm asking now."

He stared up at me for a moment before turning to Amare. "What do you make of this, Cousin?"

She folded her arms across her chest and arched her brow. "I think you shouldn't have locked him up the first time, for starters."

"Amare—"

She held up a hand. "I think you need to let him go. The Fates give Cupids orders of love, compassion, and trust. What is the point if we can't manifest those things ourselves? If you truly believe, as I do, that all actions are Fated, then you have no choice in this."

He frowned. "What if my saying no is Fated?"

"I'm doing this," I said firmly. "I'm going back to the human world, Dashuri. Even if it's by force."

"Why ask me, then?" he huffed.

"Because I'm asking for your help!" I snapped. "I'm not asking for permission. I want your blessing. For you to help me do this. You wanted to be part of something historic? Perhaps it's not a marriage between Hehven and Helle. Maybe it's this."

Dash held his head in his hands, but I stood tall, barely

breathing, as I waited.

"I want to trust you," I said. "I want to go to the human world and know that I'm not going to return to an army. That I'm not going to come back to chains."

He looked up at me then, his eyes pink at the edges. "What if you don't come back?"

"I will." I crouched down, resting my hands on his knees. "I'll come back."

"If you get yourself killed." He sucked in a breath. "Mother—"

"Will know it was my choice," I said. "If it all goes wrong, you can deny you had any part in it. I earned your trust and then betrayed you. It won't be that big of a stretch for them to believe." The words, edged with truth, tasted bitter on my tongue.

"Why don't we just go to the Fates now?" he asked. "We could demand answers."

Amare snorted from where she was still standing in front of the door. "You want to question the benevolence of the immortal beings that created our world? Created us? To their faces?"

"Newbold," I said quietly. "That's where I'm going to get my answers. I'm sure of it."

Dash placed his hands over mine and it took everything I had not to sag to the floor as I witnessed the last shreds of his resistance crumble.

"I'm not happy about this," he said. "But I'll tell Jacayal to release you from his watch."

"Thank you," I breathed. "Thank you, Brother."

Dash squeezed my hands. "All I ask of you, Pace, is that you return safely."

I reciprocated his squeeze, staring up into eyes so similar to mine. "And all I ask of you, Brother, is that you leave me something to return to."

29
Sirain

Smoothing my hands down over the thick brown pants borrowed from one of Caitland's younger brothers, I glanced enviously at Odio next to me in his black leathers. He was standing, arms folded across his chest, his burgundy eyes narrowed to slits as he listened to Pace's plan, not even trying to disguise how unhappy he was at the thought of working with the Cupids.

Tiesa exhaled loudly from where she was leaning against the wall beside Pace, looking similarly disgusted. She was yet to acknowledge me. I understood why, but it added another layer to the smothering tension in the room that really wasn't needed.

Trying to keep my attention on the dark window behind him, I allowed myself fleeting glances at Pace, each one causing a stumbling heartbeat. He'd been gone for hours. I'd waited, staring at the door and out of the window, watching the sun slip beyond the hills, growing increasingly concerned with each passing hour. Despite his confidence, I'd convinced myself that Dashuri had managed to lock him up again.

When he'd finally arrived, I'd almost run to him. Holding myself back, my heart straining against my chest, had been like throwing myself against a cold, stone wall, and I shivered at the memory.

"It makes sense to go to the Wendell Islands," Pace insisted, mirroring my cousin's stance.

Odio stared him down. "Bickerstaff is either in Newbold or Dalibor, so that's where we should go. The only reason you want to go to the Wendell Islands is to check on Marlowe. Don't pretend it's because it's part of your plan, Cupid. It's only our lives we're risking here, after all."

"I'm well aware of what everyone is risking." Pace's jaw clenched. "But we can't just go storming into Newbold. Sirain and I have been before, and they tried to shoot us out of the sky. We need a plan, and Marlowe might be able to help us with that. The same goes for Dalibor. We don't know what we'd be flying into."

Odio curved a dark brow. "And what if the Wendell Islands are nothing more than smouldering heaps of ash?"

My chest tightened at the pain that flashed in Pace's eyes.

"If the Wendell Islands have fallen," Tiesa said, "then we go somewhere else and figure out our next move." Pace gave her a grateful smile, but she just shook her head in response. "Please let it be known that I think everything about this plan is ridiculous."

"Oh, your face has been doing a great job of making that perfectly clear," Odio said, a smirk playing on his lips. "Unless you're secretly sucking on lemon wedges over there."

Tiesa fixed him with a heated glare that only served to make Odio grin wider.

"Tee," Pace said, drawing her attention back to him. "I know you're not happy about this, but I need you on board. I mean, if Dashuri is, surely you can try?"

A loud laugh burst from his best friend's lips. "I can assure you, Dashuri is not 'on board' with this, and you know it. I wouldn't be surprised if there are lines of Hands waiting at The Crossing for us."

"And what would they do to you?" Odio sneered. "Tickle you to death?"

Tiesa pushed off the wall, her fists clenching at her sides. "You know nothing about what Cupids are capable of."

Odio opened his mouth, a retort on his sharp tongue, but I held up my hands, halting them before they could find their target.

"Can we please stay focused on the mission," I said, my skin heating as I felt Pace's eyes on me. "We're going to check on Marlowe and speak to him about our next move. That's final."

Odio shrugged, sinking down onto a chair, and I breathed a silent sigh of relief.

"When are we going, then?" Tiesa asked. "Morning? The human world will be crawling with Chaos right now." She punctuated the statement with a sneer in Odio's direction.

Pace shook his head. "I think it's best we go now. We can't afford to waste a second."

"Pace." Tiesa placed a hand on his arm, her brow creased in concern. "It can wait until morning. You've flown the length of Hehven twice today, and probably more. You'll be no good to anyone if you drown on the way there."

It was painful. A physical ache as I watched their exchange. I should be the one caring about him—looking out for him. My lips parted to agree with Tiesa, but I forced them shut again. Any suggestion I made would only serve to make things worse. I knew how stubborn Pace could be, and if I suggested he rest, he'd likely do the opposite.

"Dawn," Odio announced.

I turned, finding him staring up at me as though the pain of my innermost thoughts was etched on my skin.

"We'll leave at dawn," he repeated. "That gives us a few hours' rest, but we won't lose much time. Besides, dawn is the crossover between Cupid and Chaos missions, so the safest time for us to travel."

"Fine," Pace agreed. "Dawn."

I gave Odio a grateful smile, but he just stared at me in return, my insides shrinking a little at the intensity. "What?" I mouthed, but he shook his head.

"Right." Tiesa strode towards the doors of the sitting room we'd been using, her straight white hair swishing at her shoulders. "My room should be ready. See you all at first light."

She looked meaningfully over at Pace, who hadn't moved, but his attention was fixed on me. "I'd like a word with you, Sirain, if that's okay?"

Odio's wings flared as he stood, but I reached out and placed a hand on his arm. "Sure."

After pinning me with another indecipherable look, my cousin turned and followed Tiesa out into the hallway.

"What do you want to talk to me about?" I asked, my gaze fixed on the thick, red carpet.

Pace stepped closer until the tips of his brown boots invaded my vision. "You still can't even look at me."

"Self-preservation," I muttered. Looking at Pace was like looking at the sun. Beautiful, but painful. I could manage quick glances when I knew he wasn't looking at me, but the few times our eyes met, it stole my breath as though someone had kicked me in the chest.

"That's going to be a problem for the mission," he said. "I already told you, I don't hate you, Sirain. I honestly wish I did."

I frowned at the floor. "That's not comforting."

"It wasn't my intent to comfort you."

Drawing a deep, shaky breath, I lifted my head. He was a lot closer than I expected, and I leaned backwards a little, my eyes wide.

"I wanted to thank you," he said, his golden gaze roaming over my face before finally resting on my eyes.

I swallowed. He was right. There was no hatred in his stare. Pain. But no hate. "What for?" I asked.

"For siding with me against Odio." He shook his head with a heavy exhale. "It makes strategic sense to go to the Wendell Islands, because we should be safe there, but I can't deny the main reason is to check on Marlowe."

"I know," I whispered.

Pace's stare hardened a little. "I made a vow that I'd look after him. That I'd keep him safe. For Dariel."

My eyes burned as I looked away. My lungs were aflame with searing guilt, every fibre of my being aching with regret. More than anything, I wanted to hold him. I longed to reach up and place my hands on his broad chest, to smooth them round to his shoulders, pulling him in for an embrace. I wanted to press kisses to the soft skin of his neck while letting him know that I would do anything for him. Instead, all I could do was nod.

"I'll see you at dawn," he said, his voice thick with emotion.

I stayed still, listening to his footsteps as he walked away, pausing before closing the door behind him. After counting out a minute and a half, my breath held in my throat, I sank to the floor and cried.

The outer islands were burning. What was once lush green was now molten orange edged with charred black, while ships rested in various damaged states between the silvery waters. It was eerily quiet as we soared overhead, weaving through the plumes of smoke, eyes watering. My borrowed blade was a strange, yet familiar weight against my back, and every so often, the golden hilt of Pace's sword would catch the early morning sun, drawing my attention before I blinked and looked away.

We'd climbed through a window of the Rakkaus property, slipping into the muted dawn like shadows. Pace assured us that his brother would cover for our absence, along with Cait-land, but my unease was a weight on my chest, hindering my breathing. After everything he'd done, could we really trust him? Blind faith was ingrained in Cupids, but I couldn't be as quick to forget. Closing my eyes briefly, I tried not to peer too hard at the cracks in the plan. I knew it was our only chance.

The Wendell Islands might technically be the smallest of the human lands, but they knew the waters that surrounded them well, and the sea they worshipped paid them back in mutual respect. Dalibor and Newbold's ships were scattered, most of them moored on jagged rocks or half sunk near hidden sandbanks. The Wendell Islands was a siren, luring her enemy in to then destroy them one by one.

Most of the inner islands seemed to be intact, with the main island unchanged from the last time I'd visited. Relief shed weight from my wings, and I soared a little higher, knowing that Pace would be feeling the same. I was also relieved that the direction we were approaching the island from meant we wouldn't have to fly over the waterfall. Our waterfall.

A shadow dropped over me and I looked up to find Odio swooping to my side.

"We don't need them," he said, his eyes fixed on where Tiesa and Pace's white wings were outstretched ahead. "We can find your father ourselves. You know we're better skilled than them."

I stared at him. "How many humans have you rescued, Cousin?"

"That's not what I mean, and you know it."

"It's fine," I reassured him. "I want their help."

His mouth pressed into a thin line, turning his lips the palest pink. "Do you want to know what I think?"

I sighed. I'd known this was coming. Last night, I'd managed to avoid him, and I'd left my room before he woke. It wasn't as if I'd managed to sleep anyway.

"What do you think, oh wise one?"

Odio's eyes narrowed, glancing again at the Cupids. "I think the only reason you're doing this with them is because it hurts. You're in physical pain being around that Fated prince, and I think you think you deserve it. Like you're owed the pain because of what happened with his cousin."

I winced. "That's not true."

"Yes," Odio pressed. "It is. And you need to let it go. What happened to that Cupid was an accident. Kwellen and I both know you were never going to shoot that human. I saw you adjust your shot. I know he saw it, too. If the Cupid had been paying more attention, he'd have noticed. It was an accident. If you keep carrying this blame, it's going to kill you."

I stared straight ahead, my stomach churning as I processed his words. All this time, they'd known. Once again, I was hit by how much I'd kept to myself, not trusting anyone. Had my isolation been my own choice? My mother had always told me not to trust anyone. To never let anyone touch my heart. I suppose I understood now, it had been to protect me from the lies I'd been born into.

"He doesn't want you dead," Odio said.

I turned to him, pulling the dark wisps of hair that had escaped my braid from my face. "What?"

"Pace," Odio said, squinting at said Cupid. "He might not have forgiven you, but he doesn't want you dead. If he did, he'd have killed you already."

I laughed. "He can't kill me. Not with the alliance in the balance."

"If he wanted you dead, you'd be dead, and you know it. Or at the very least, he wouldn't have brought you with him. He can get his answers without involving you."

My heart shuddered in my chest. That much was true. He could easily have left me with Dashuri.

"What, then?" I asked, confusion coursing through my veins. "Why involve me if not as punishment for my actions?"

Odio sighed, tipping his wing, and allowing the current to pull him down towards Marlowe's butter-coloured mansion. "He still cares about you. If you actually looked at him for more than a second, you might see it, too."

Before I could refute the ridiculous statement, Odio dropped, soaring to the balcony where Pace and Tiesa had already landed. I swallowed, hope flailing for a moment in my battered chest, before I locked it away, landing beside Odio and tucking in my wings.

"These are stunning," Tiesa said, her green eyes wide as she reached out and traced the large, white roses sprawling along the railing and around the open balcony doors. "How is this even possible this late in the year?"

"They're actually early," a deep, booming voice called from inside. "Winter roses. Native to the Wendell Islands. They're the closest thing we get to snow."

"Marlowe!" Pace exclaimed, striding through the doors.

He met with the Wendell Islands leader in the middle of the room, their arms encircling in a fierce embrace that formed a lump in my throat.

"Pace," Marlowe mumbled into his shoulder. "I thought it was a mirage when I saw you flying in. I didn't know if we'd ever see you again."

"I'm so glad you're alive, friend," Pace said, holding the dark-haired man at arm's length as he looked him over. "I've been so worried."

Marlowe gave him a sad smile. "Alive, for now. My generals have said we need to start making plans to evacuate the larger islands."

"But where would you go?" I asked, before I could stop myself.

Marlowe's gaze lifted from Pace, as though finally seeing us all for the first time. His dark brown eyes assessed us one by one before settling on me. "That's the problem. We'd move them here, but it means Newbold and Dalibor are cornering us. Once they get through our last defences, we'll have to surrender."

A heavy silence filled the room, until Marlowe seemed to shake himself free of it, gesturing for us all to sit.

"I'll fetch Cove and Shanti and send word for some refreshments," he said. He paused, looking between us. "Do I need to worry about bloodshed?"

Pace laughed softly, shaking his head. "No. There's no need to remove our weapons this time."

Marlowe smiled, although tiredness lingered in his eyes. "I'm looking forward to finding out why you're here, friend."

As soon as the door closed behind him, the all too familiar awkwardness settled over us.

"Is this tension here to stay?" Odio muttered. "Because I'm going to start moulting soon and I am not okay with that."

"What do you expect?" Tiesa huffed. "With the number of times you've tried to kill us?"

My gaze flicked to the pale scar on her forehead, placed there by my cousin.

"The last time I saw you, Cupid," Odio said, resting his arms on the back of the chair he'd straddled, "my cousin was saving your life."

Tiesa's jaw tensed, and her gaze flicked to me. I held it for all of two seconds before looking away.

"Right," Pace said. He'd chosen a low cushioned chair, reclining with an ankle crossed over his knee. "We have until Marlowe comes back to air anything anyone wants to say, and then we all move on. Okay? Marlowe has enough to deal with, without adding our issues to it."

Silence followed his words, filling the room, punctuated

only by the distant sound of the ocean and screeches of the seabirds.

"Fine," Pace said, uncrossing his legs and leaning forward. "I'll start. Odio? I wish you no ill will. I understand that, when our blades crossed paths before, you were protecting Sirain. And whether you want my forgiveness or not, I hold no grudge for you telling my brother about what I'd been doing. Again, I know it was an action carried out to protect Sirain."

Odio mumbled something under his breath, before exhaling loudly. "My position hasn't changed. As long as your actions don't threaten my cousin, your lives are safe."

Pace raised his eyebrows. "Well, I suppose that's as close to a truce as I'm going to get from you."

A smile pulled at the corners of my mouth, but I pressed my lips together, halting it in its tracks.

"I won't lie," Tiesa said, her eyes burning into mine. "I'm grateful to you for saving my life that day on Marlowe's ship, but I don't think I can ever forgive you for what you did afterwards. However, I understand that we need to work together for Pace, so I'll try to put my feelings to the side for as long as this takes."

I nodded, aware that all eyes were on me, awaiting whatever I was supposed to say. Surely, Pace and Tiesa knew I bore them no ill will. A thousand thoughts fluttered to my lips, but before I could form a sentence, the door opened, and Marlowe strode back into the room, Cove and Shanti close behind.

30
Pace

Cove and Shanti wore wide, warm smiles, their arms open as they followed Marlowe into the room, and my heart swelled as I folded them into brief but firm embraces. For so long, I thought I'd never see any of them again. The relief of them being alive and well was almost painful.

As we returned to our seats, I caught Tiesa staring at me, her brow furrowed as though confused. Her eyes flicked back to the humans, and I understood. Where I had begun to crave contact as much as a fierce breeze beneath my wings, Cupids still purposefully avoided it.

Before I could stop myself, I glanced over at Sirain. She'd purposefully taken the seat furthest away from me. Self-preservation. I pursed my lips as I reclined on my seat. One of the things that had drawn me to her was her fearlessness. She'd faced down danger with her chin held high. I almost smiled as I remembered following her into the Dalibor jungle. It felt like a lifetime ago.

My chest tightened as I watched her warily eye her surroundings, speaking in a low voice with her cousin. Timid was a strange look on the Chaos princess, and I didn't like it. Of course, I understood why. But I didn't like it one bit.

I dragged my gaze back to the humans. "Where's Bertie?"

Marlowe paused in his pouring of steaming liquid into cups of polished grey stone, while Cove and Shanti shared a look.

"Is he okay?" I asked, worry tiptoeing along my spine. "Did something happen?"

Shanti chuckled. "Something happened, yes. But nothing bad. Bertie had . . . erm . . ."

"A growth spurt," Cove supplied. "He's a little bigger than the last time you saw him."

My eyes widened as I accepted a steaming cup of tea from Marlowe. "How big?"

"Wait. What is a 'Bertie'?" Odio asked, squinting at the human women. "And why do I feel like I should be worried?"

"Bertie is a dragon," Cove said, eyeing Sirain's cousin with matching trepidation. "And he's about the size of a small cow now."

"What?" I spluttered through a mouthful of tea. "How?"

Shanti shrugged, a bemused smile on her lips. "There are so few dragons. We still know very little about them. It's safe to say you don't want him curling around your shoulders anymore."

A laugh tremored along my wings. "Certainly not."

"Okay," Marlowe said as he finished handing out cups of the cinnamon spiced tea common in the Islands. "Please, tell us. To what do we owe this pleasure?"

"Well, I wanted to check on you," I admitted. "But we're also here because we want to find out what Newbold is up to and try to rescue Emeric."

The humans shared a look and I grimaced as I glanced at Sirain. No one needed to ask what they were thinking. The chances of him still being alive were almost non-existent.

"We still want to try," I said quietly. "And it turns out that the human Odio questioned might have been lying."

Marlowe's eyebrows shot up. "What do you mean?"

"Sirain tracked down the Hand who was given the orders,"

Odio explained. "He told her that Emeric had boarded a ship headed for Dalibor, to meet with the Midnight Queen."

"The Hand could have been lying," Marlowe said, looking between the Chaos and me.

I shook my head in frustration. "That's the thing. Neither of them had any reason to lie. But it does complicate things."

Cove snorted. "So Emeric, if he's still alive, could be in Dalibor or Newbold?"

"He could even be on his way back to Liridona," Tiesa offered.

Shanti shook her head. "I think you're overestimating how fast our ships can travel. They're a lot slower than your wings. But depending on how long he spent in Dalibor, it's a possibility he's back on a ship."

"Wherever Emeric may or may not be," I said. "I have suspicions that Newbold is somehow involved in more than instigating this war."

Marlowe sat forward, his cup cradled in his hands. "Oh?"

"There's still a lot we don't know, but I think somehow the Fates are involved." I frowned into my tea. "Ever since I first visited the human world, I felt something was amiss."

"And you think Newbold has the answers?" Cove asked.

I glanced over at Sirain, who stiffened at the acknowledgement, before nodding. "I've been working in the room where the orders given by the Fates are recorded. Even after checking the books I could, I couldn't find a single order for Newbold. The records didn't go back further than three years, as they're stored elsewhere, but the fact that there are none even in the last few years is strange enough, right?"

Shanti shuddered. "I've always said there was something strange about that country. It gives me the creeps."

"So, you're planning on going to Newbold?" Marlowe asked. "Is that wise? If I remember correctly, you pleaded with me and Emeric to stay away."

"Well, that's one thing we need to discuss," I said. "We need to decide whether we go to Dalibor or Newbold first."

"Surely it makes sense to check Dalibor first," Tiesa said, her frown scrunching her gold markings. "Out of the two, it's the least dangerous, right?"

I leaned forward a little so I could see Sirain. "What do you think?"

After a moment, she turned to look at me, her amethyst eyes wide, as though she hadn't expected me to address her directly. "What?"

"He's your father," I said gently. "The outcome of this mission affects you more than anyone. What do you think we should do?"

Beside her, Odio began a whispered chant of 'Dalibor' which she ignored as she nodded. "I agree, we should try Dalibor first. Like you said, Lord Diarke and the Midnight Queen are allies. If Emeric isn't there, perhaps we can discover more about Newbold. Find out what we should prepare for."

"Are you talking about interrogation?" Odio asked, his dark eyes flashing with what looked like glee.

Sirain shot him a warning look. "Possibly."

"Absolutely not," Tiesa blustered, turning to me. "You can't—"

"If it gets us answers, then yes," I said, before looking pointedly at Odio. "But no dismembering or killing anyone."

Odio held up his hands. "I can get answers without killing anyone."

"Perhaps we should come with you," Marlowe suggested, looking to his sister and her wife. "Make it a political mission. We could say we're seeking a truce."

"Absolutely not," I said, trying to ignore the hardening glint in his eye at my response. You need to stay here where you're relatively safe. Like you said, your people need you."

"I'm not letting it drop that easily," Marlowe huffed. "But

let's discuss strategy. I have procured maps of Newbold, although they're a little dated. I'd like to show you where their ships are in our waters, too, so you can familiarise yourselves with their weaponry."

Odio nodded. "That's a good plan. We can even sneak onboard a couple and eavesdrop."

Marlow's eyes widened. "What? No! They'd kill you."

"They wouldn't see us," Odio assured him with a smile. "The only reason you spotted us flying in is because you're used to us. Humans aren't supposed to see Cupids or Chaos. After all, you went most of your life before you saw us, right?"

"It's true," Tiesa said. "You didn't see us the first time Pace visited. Or when we eavesdropped on your conversation with Emeric."

Odio grinned at her. "Or me delivering an arrow to you later that evening."

"Or me watching Odio deliver that arrow," I offered with a sad smile.

Cove stared between us all. "You were all there that day?"

"Multiple times," I admitted.

"Well, that just makes me feel like an idiot," she huffed.

I reached out and placed my hand on top of hers, squeezing briefly. "It's just the way it works. And it's a good idea, Odio. We should spend today gathering information, so we know exactly what we're flying into."

"And then," Odio said, rubbing his hands together, "on to the Midnight Queen."

Sirain rolled her eyes, quiet laughter escaping her lips and the sound sent bursts of light to the darkened corners of my soul. When she sensed me staring, her eyes met mine, and the smile faded from her lips. The light that had ignited inside me extinguished as quickly as it had started.

As she broke our stare, returning her gaze to the steam rising from her cup, I tried to push aside my disappointment.

Not long ago, I was the reason she smiled—the reason she laughed. I was certain it shouldn't have irked me as much as it did. Swallowing a sigh, I returned my attention to the conversation flowing around me and the mission ahead.

War was loud and messy. I'd been expecting the violence, but in person it was so much more. By late afternoon, my ears were filled with ringing from the constant blast of cannon fire and my white feathers were coated with grey from the thick, ash-laded smog.

Marlowe had secured us dark scarves, which we wore under our hoods, around our mouths and noses to make it easier to breathe, and under an explicit agreement not to engage, we'd spent hours flitting between the boats, getting as close to the Dalibor and Newbold soldiers as possible in the hopes of overhearing something useful. So far, all I'd gained was an understanding that not all humans were as generous and kind as Marlowe and his family.

Even though humans never once glanced up at us, flitting amidst the layer of smoke, my pulse still hammered erratically in my chest as we swooped from mast to mast. The worst part was not being able to help the Wendell ships. Although they played their advantage of knowing the waters and having finely crafted vessels, their weapons were grossly outmatched.

A cry went up from a nearby ship and I squinted through the smoke from where I was perched amongst the rigging. The sails of a Newbold ship had come loose, falling in tatters to the deck below. It was the third time I'd seen it happen in the last hour.

"What's going on?" Tiesa hissed at my side. "That's not normal."

I gave her a look. "And you know what's normal on a ship during a human war?"

Tiesa shook her head and I grinned in response, although she couldn't see it beneath my scarf. It was most definitely not normal, and as I glimpsed two black winged figures between plumes of thick grey smoke, my suspicions grew.

"I'm going to get some answers," I announced, leaping from the rigging and into the air, soaring upwards until I broke through clouds of smoke and into the clear, silvered afternoon sky.

Yanking down my scarf, I gulped the fresh air into my lungs as I looked around for signs of the others. We were due for a check-in.

Tiesa burst through the clouds beside me, grimacing over her shoulder at her darkened wings. "I hope Marlowe has enough soap for us all. I don't think my wings have ever been this filthy in my entire life."

I smiled, but my attention was fixed, waiting for the sign of wings that couldn't be darkened by the smoke of war. After a few minutes, Odio and Sirain burst through the clouds a short distance away and I immediately took off in their direction. My heart swelled as I watched them play fighting, the smile on Sirain's face bright enough to light the dreary autumn afternoon.

"Did you find out anything?" Tiesa called as we drew near.

Immediately, the smile slid from Sirain's face, her entire demeanour shifting, and I bit back the urge to shove my friend in the shoulder.

"Nothing useful," Odio said. "You?"

I shook my head. "How about a swap?"

"A swap?" he echoed.

"Yeah," I said, trying to sound nonchalant and almost certainly failing. "Let's do one final round. You go with Tiesa, and I'll go with Sirain."

I didn't miss the way Sirain's eyes widened, and I could feel my friend's glare searing into the side of my face.

"Sure," Odio said, casting an uncertain look at his cousin.

After a pause that had me holding my breath, Sirain nodded. "Fine."

"Come on, then," I said. "We'll take a Newbold ship. Can you and Tiesa try and find one from Dalibor?"

Odio pulled his scarf up over his mouth and nose, and lifted his hand in a mock salute, before arching backwards into a graceful dive that saw him disappear beneath the clouds. I thought I heard Tiesa curse under her breath, but before I could check, she swooped after him.

Shaking my head, I turned to Sirain with a smile. "Shall we?"

"Sure."

I dove back down beneath the clouds, fixing my scarf and merging with the thick grey smoke as I tried to spy Newbold's black flag. It didn't take long. Glancing over my shoulder to check Sirain was still with me, I extended my wings, letting the sea air guide me down towards a towering mast. As soon as my boots touched the damp wood, I grasped hold of the sodden rope to steady myself.

It shouldn't have bothered me that Sirain was sad. I certainly shouldn't be trying to cheer her up. If you'd asked me while I was locked up, I'd have said with confidence that I hoped she was painfully miserable for the rest of her wretched life. However, wanting it and seeing it were evidently two very different things.

"You've genuinely heard nothing useful?" I asked, as Sirain wrapped a rope around her arm on the other side of the mast, tucking her wings in tight against her body.

"No," she said, peering down at the sailors shouting on the decks below. "I like humans a lot less, though."

I hummed in agreement. "I don't think war is known for bringing out people's good sides."

"You're probably right."

We stood until my muscles grew stiff, watching the Newbold soldiers load their enormous, heavy, crossbows, firing them at the Wendell ships with relentless pace.

"This is pointless," I said. "Do you want to cut down the sail?"

Sirain whirled, her eyes comically large. "What?"

I grinned. "That's what you and Odio have been doing, isn't it?"

The sheepish look on Sirain's face only served to widen my smile until I was almost laughing.

"You're not angry?" she asked.

I shook my head. "Why would I be angry? I hated that there was no way to help the Wendell Islands. I just wish you'd shared your plan with us."

"It wasn't really a plan," she admitted. "It just sort of happened."

"Oh?" I asked. "An accident, then?"

Sirain nodded, her eyes sparkling. "Exactly. We were watching the troops, and somehow a dagger found its way into my hand. I leaned against a rope, and the rest is history."

I'd known in my gut it had been her idea. As mischievous as Odio was, he wouldn't think to help the humans. Sirain wasn't like that, though. Perhaps it was because she was half human herself, or maybe she'd always been different.

"Shall we?" I asked, drawing my dagger from my boot.

Sirain gave me a small smile, her blade already in her hand. "Let's."

We hacked through the thick rope in silence, watching with bated breath as the heavy material raced towards the ground, sending humans scattering in a cloud of colourful curses. Then, before they could glance upwards in question, we were gone, soaring up through the clouds and out of sight.

Laughter burst from me as I looped backwards, my wings and arms outspread. "That was brilliant."

Sirain's laughter carried on the breeze, and I halted my swoop, desperate to catch the elation on her face before it inevitably faded.

I flew closer, taking in her flushed cheeks, as my own grin turned into a frown. "You're allowed to smile, Sirain," I said. "You're allowed to be happy."

She stared at me, liquid despair shimmering in her eyes. "How can I be?"

"I know you, Sirain. I know the guilt will never leave you completely." My fingers tensed at my sides, aching with the urge to take hold of her shoulders. I forced them to my sides. "I know that even if you're smiling and laughing, you haven't forgotten."

"I could never," she whispered.

I stared at her for a moment, too many words queued on my tongue. Exhaling, I pulled the scarf back up over my face.

"Come on," I said. "Let's find the others and get back to Marlowe."

31
Sirain

I t took two long, hot baths until the water ran clear; the dirt and debris finally washed from my feathers. Marlowe had given us rooms on the top floor, after giving his staff orders not to step foot there until further notice. Making my way back to the main room, I found the hallway eerily quiet, expecting Odio to be there already at least, but it was empty. Although the silence was unexpected, I was surprised to find a peacefulness settle over me, which was very much needed after a day of experiencing human war first hand.

Standing in the entrance between the large, dark wood doors, I let myself take in the space—the contrast of sturdy furniture, brightly coloured cushions, and intricately woven rugs. It was warm and comforting in a way no rooms in Helle had ever been. But then, it matched the personalities of its owners. How could Hadeon Castle be warm and comforting when its proprietor was vile, cold, and cruel?

Beyond the wide, thin windows, the sky was a muted orange, edged with rolling black clouds. I couldn't tell if they were the sign of an approaching storm or smoke, gathered from the battles on the outskirts of the Islands. With only an hour or so left until sunset, the ships would be ceasing their fighting soon, unable to see in the inky darkness that would settle amongst the islands once the sun descended.

A large copper teapot and a tray of stone mugs had been left out on the table, so, with a final glance at the empty, shadowed corners, I crossed the room and poured myself a cup. The rich scent of cloves and something I didn't recognise filled the air instantly and I smiled as I wrapped my still-wrinkled fingers around the warm mug and inhaled. After eyeing the scattered assortment of uncomfortable human chairs, I walked to the balcony doors, relieved to find them unlocked. Pushing them open and stepping outside, I wondered whether they ever were.

The scent of the winter roses immediately encircled me; a fresh, sweet smell that tickled my nose. I thought perhaps I smelled mint too, and leaned closer, taking one of the large white flowers between my fingers and drawing it to my nose. I smiled as the faintest hint of peppermint intermingled with the sweet floral perfume. They were truly beautiful.

Outside was just as quiet, feeling more like dawn than early evening, and I closed the doors, leaning against the cold stone rail as I stared out across the grounds to the city beyond. The gardens and trees between the wall that separated the mansion from the residents meant the city was far enough away that it was unlikely someone would spot my folded wings, so I attempted to relax as I sipped my tea.

Although the bath had soothed my aching muscles, and the quiet calm around me attempted to ease my thoughts, I couldn't keep out the creeping sense of worry. Even with such distance between me and the king, I could feel his presence. I shook my head as if to clear my thoughts of him, my still damp hair sliding over my shoulder.

I wasn't sure whether it was courtesy of Cove, Shanti or both, but when I'd left the bathing room, a selection of clothing had been left out for me with a note saying it was fine to cut the shirts to accommodate my wings. My eyes had stung with gratitude. The brown leather pants were so much more comfortable and familiar than the woollen pair I'd borrowed from Caitland's brother, and although I'd had to alter the flowing white shirt to accommodate my wings, the softness was more than enough to compensate. They'd also given me a leather waistcoat that tied around the neck and low at the back, which would work perfectly, but I'd left that on the bed for tomorrow.

Although, as a brisk wind whipped around me, rustling the dozens of roses twisted on vines between the balustrades, and sending chills across my skin, I considered going back for one of the colourful scarves they'd left out. It was much warmer in the Wendell Islands than Helle, but the evenings could become quite cool. I brought the mug to my lips, letting the hot tea warm me instead, not wanting to leave the calming solitude just yet.

Inevitably, my thoughts kept circling back to Pace. I frowned as I replayed our conversation after the ship over and over, just as I had in the bath—as I had every second since he'd said those words. You're allowed to be happy. Sure, I'd laughed today for the first time in forever, but happy? That was something I could only dream of.

I knew Odio had purposefully tried to coax smiles from me with his antics. Despite his default stance of disdainful nonchalance, he cared about me. I was fairly certain Kwellen and I were the only Chaos he cared about. My chest contracted at the thought of my best friend, cold, beaten and alone, in the dungeons of Hadeon castle.

That was one of the many reasons I could never be happy. My life was not—and had never been—my own. Perhaps the only other person who could understand that was Dashuri. I smirked at the thought, even as my stomach rolled. At the end of the week, we'd return, and I'd have to tell my father the engagement was on. Perhaps Dashuri would be okay pretending? Now that I knew Pace didn't want to kill me, maybe we could live peacefully. I'd be fine with Dashuri finding pleasure elsewhere. Cupids were the living embodiment of discretion, after all. And as for me? I snorted into my cup, endlessly amused at my own misfortune.

A faint sound carried on the breeze, and I paused, listening. At first, I thought it was coming from inside, and I turned, my eyes adjusting to the dark that had encompassed the main room, but it was still empty. Turning back to the balcony, I listened again. It was a faint muttering. Not a conversation, but as though someone was talking to themselves. Placing my mug down on the ground, I leaned over the railing, searching, and my heart immediately leapt into my throat.

On the balcony below, an all-too familiar Cupid was wearing a path into the stone as he strode back and forth. I smiled, relishing the opportunity to watch Pace, unseen. His loose white shirt was half untucked, as dishevelled as his thick ivory hair. It was uncommon to see him in such a state, and it unwittingly stirred a longing deep in my belly as I recalled the few times I'd seen him appear so undone. The times I'd been the cause of it. I swallowed, remembering the hard lines of his body and the sweet taste of his mouth; the deep rumbling groan I could coax from him by kissing the soft arch of his wing. My skin burned.

As if sensing my thoughts, Pace halted, and I watched, frozen in place, as he looked up, his eyes widening in surprise.

"Hey," I said.

He stared up at me, the breeze tossing curling waves of hair across his forehead and into his eyes. "What are you doing?"

"Drinking tea," I replied. "What are you doing?"

Pace's lips pressed together for a moment, then he shook his head and looked away. "Thinking."

"Ah," I said, nodding sagely. "A dangerous pastime if ever I heard one."

A faint chuckle reached me on the breeze, warming my

heart. I hadn't dared wish for this. That we could have a civilised conversation, or even be in the same room together. For the months following my Rites, I'd been convinced Pace would be the one to end my life. There had been times I'd welcomed the notion.

"Do you want some company?"

I blinked, looking down to find Pace staring up at me again. "Sure."

He bent his knees, his wings extending as he leapt upwards. My heart constricted a little at the sight. I knew each feather like my own and I'd noticed the thinner patches the first time I'd seen him at dinner. Now, I knew it was from being held captive, and the thought boiled my blood. Flying was like breathing to Pace, which was exactly why his brother had exacted such a cruel punishment.

I forced a smile as Pace landed gracefully on the railing, folding his wings, before jumping down beside me.

"No one else seems to be ready yet," I said, casting a glance at the still empty room behind us.

Pace frowned a little, but nodded.

"There's tea—"

"I'm fine," he said, turning and leaning his forearms against the railing as I had been. "Thank you."

My heart a pounding drum against my ribs, I stepped a little further away and mirrored his pose, staring out at the city but not really seeing it. As my fingers stroked the velvet petals of a nearby rose, my thoughts were consumed by the Cupid next to me. Even with a wing's width between us, I could feel the heat of him searing against my skin. It took every ounce of willpower not to shuffle closer—to soak it in.

"Do you think we should go to Dalibor tonight?" I asked. "Or do you think we should wait until morning? I don't want to waste—"

"I don't want to talk about Dalibor."

"Oh." I turned my head to look at him. "I thought perhaps that was what had you carving a path into the paving stones."

Pace huffed a laugh. "Not even close."

I waited for him to elaborate, but he just continued to stare out across the city, his jaw set. "Want to talk about it?"

He hung his head, resting his forehead on his folded arms. "I don't know if that's a good idea."

I turned, leaning my back against the cool stone. "We can stand back-to-back if it'll make it easier?"

Pace closed his eyes and my stomach clenched at the words that had tumbled thoughtlessly from my lips. Although seemingly harmless, those words carried memories of a choice we'd made—a choice we shouldn't have made.

"Sorry," I whispered.

Pace shook his head. "Don't."

Silence stretched between us, both our thoughts painfully loud as the autumn breeze whipped and pulled at the fabric of our shirts and the strands of our hair, ruffling our feathers.

I pushed away from the railing. "I'm going to—"

"Don't go," Pace said softly. "Please."

My eyes closed as I drew a shaky breath. This was too hard. Everything was too hard. I tensed at the rustling of wings, and then something warm brushed against my hand. My breath halted in my lungs as fingers intertwined with mine.

"Sirain."

I didn't want to open my eyes. This was surely a dream. Perhaps I'd fallen asleep in the bath. The fingers tightened around mine, squeezing.

"Sirain. Please."

My eyes fluttered open, widening at the sight of Pace standing in front of me. So close. His pale hair and wings were stark against the darkening sky, but his eyes were as warm as the summer sun.

"I miss you so much," he whispered, his eyes moving over my face as though memorising the shape of me.

My chest caved in as my eyes burned. "I miss you, too."

"I wish I could hate you."

"You should hate me."

Pace's features tightened, his fingers slipping from mine. The cold air stole the lingering warmth of his touch, and I cursed the wind.

"No." He shook his head. "I shouldn't. You were cornered, trapped, and you made the only choice you thought you could."

"I could have made so many others. I should have told you who I was. I should have confided in you."

Pace smiled sadly. "I didn't tell you who I was, either. You figured it out. Perhaps if I'd been paying more attention, I would have put the pieces together. As it was, I was a little . . . distracted."

I huffed a laugh. "Pace. You don't have to—"

"You were raised differently to me," he said, cutting me off. "Don't forget, I've met your father and your brother now, and quite frankly, they're terrifying. How you went twenty years without murdering Fin, I'll never know. I barely managed to refrain from squeezing the life from him and we were alone for less than an hour."

My lips curled into a rueful smile. "Yeah. He's pretty terrible."

Pace reached out to take my hand in his once more, but I pulled away, leaning back against the balcony. His face fell, and I looked down, focusing on the soft brown leather of my boots.

"I'm glad you don't hate me," I said. "And I hope that, in time, we can reclaim our friendship."

"Sirain . . ."

My heart ached at the gentle pleading in that single word,

but I shuttered my heart and pushed forward. "The memory of us, of how we were, Pace, is my most precious possession."

He stepped closer—too close—his boots edging into my vision as he stood before me. I raised my head to find his eyes fixed, searing into mine, his expression so serious it stole my breath.

Reaching up, he traced the backs of his fingers along my cheek. "I don't want to be a memory."

I pulled myself away, forcing distance between us, even as my body trembled from his touch. "I wasn't strong enough to walk away last time," I said, shaking my head. "I won't let you make the same mistake again."

"I'm a big boy," he said, a growl of frustration vibrating with the words. "I'm perfectly capable of making my own decisions."

I forced myself to meet the fierceness in his gilded eyes. "Things might be different, Pace, but nothing's changed. I'm still heir to the throne of Helle, and now I'm to marry your brother." I laughed hollowly. "If anything, things are even more impossible."

Pace stepped closer, taking hold of both my hands, and pulling me from the railing. "This time, we both know what we're getting ourselves into," he said. "The truth is laid bare before us. No secrets. Right?"

I shook my head. "That still doesn't change anything."

"Answer me," he said, squeezing my hands. "Is there anything you're not telling me?"

"No," I answered, the honesty behind the word lending a lightness to my heart I'd forgotten could exist. "You know everything."

He nodded, his brows drawn, as he stared down at me. "I've told you everything, too."

"Pace—"

"Do you want me, Sirain?"

I choked on my breath, my eyes wide, as I looked up at him.

"It doesn't matter what I want. I can't want. And more to the point, you shouldn't want me." I tried half-heartedly to pull out of his grasp, but he tightened his hold. "You should marry Caitland. She's beautiful. She's everything I could never be for you."

"Fates and feathers, Sirain." He groaned. "I don't want Caitland. I've never wanted her."

I pulled free of his grasp, turning towards the balcony doors, filled with the desperate need to extract myself from the conversation, but Pace grabbed hold of my wrist, drawing me back.

"Say the words," he demanded. "Tell me you don't want this. That you don't want me."

Frustration bubbled in my gut, and I rounded on him with such determination he stumbled back a step, his wings flaring. "I told you! It's not about wanting. I'll always want you, Pace. You know that. I want you more than I've ever wanted anything in my entire life. But I can't have you. I'm not allowed to have you. So, please, in the name of all that is Fated, let me go."

Pace stared at me, wide eyed, as my chest rose and fell, my hands clenched into tight fists at my sides and my shoulders squared. I thought then he'd leave, and although it was what I'd asked of him, my heart ached. But he didn't. Instead, he stepped forward and swept me into his arms, pressing me against the firm plains of his chest, heat seeping through the thin fabric.

After a moment, I exhaled, melting against him, and letting my arms snake around his waist, his feathers tickling the exposed skin of my wrists. The steady pounding of his heart was comforting against my cheek, and I breathed him in as he rested his chin on my hair.

"I'm sorry," he muttered. "I've never been very good at letting you go."

I closed my eyes.

"There's so much we don't know, Sirain," he continued, his

voice rumbling against my ear. "Don't ask me how I know, but I feel it in my bones that whatever we find in Newbold will change everything."

"It can't change everything." I sighed against the fabric of his shirt.

He pulled back, tipping my chin so I met his stare. "It can change enough."

I opened my mouth to respond, but Pace lowered his head, his nose brushing my neck as his breath warmed my skin, and all words were forgotten.

"Sirain," he whispered against my skin.

As his hands grasped my waist, the scent of him dizzying my senses, the carefully crafted walls of resistance I'd erected around my heart began to slowly crumble.

32
Pace

Breathing Sirain in, it was as though my lungs were full for the first time in months. It took all my self-restraint not to press my lips to the soft skin of her neck. My mind was consumed with the desperate desire to taste her lips, but I held back, waiting for her to push me away.

When her arms released me, her hands moving gently to my chest, I sighed, waiting for her to step back, but she didn't. Sweeping upwards, her thumbs brushed against my jaw before sliding into my hair, and I rested my forehead against hers.

"This is the worst decision we could possibly make," she mumbled.

I chuckled. "We're so good at making bad decisions. Why stop now?"

Pulling back a little, she stared up at me, frowning, even as her fingers stroked the hair at the nape of my neck. "I swear by the Fates, I'll never keep anything from you again."

I smiled, my heart leaping at what her words suggested. "Don't swear by the Fates, not when they can't be trusted."

"Tell me, then," she said, fingers sliding round to trace my jaw as she studied my face with an intensity that had my blood heating. "What should I swear by?"

I took hold of her hand, bringing her fingers to my lips

before placing them over my heart. "Don't swear by anything. I take you at your word."

She closed her eyes, a tremble running through her, and I gathered her against my chest once more.

"I stand by what I said," she mumbled into my shirt. "This is a terrible idea."

"Terrible." I smiled against her hair, my hands circling the space beneath her wings.

Lights flared in the room beyond the balcony, startling us from our embrace, and I sighed, biting back frustration at the interruption. "Come on. Let's go and figure out the next step of our plan."

Sirain's cheeks were flushed, and I raised a hand, gently stroking the warmth there, before taking a small step back. She was right. This was an awful idea, and I knew I should have let her walk away. But it was hard to believe my head when my heart was so full.

33
Sirain

Every tenth beat of my wing. That's what I'd rationed myself to. Every tenth beat, I allowed myself a glance at Pace, just to check he was still there—that this was real. After yet another night of fitful sleep, I wasn't sure if I could trust the memory of what had happened between us. It felt so fragile. Too good to be true. Even as the thought pressed on me, my doubt building, he turned, glancing over his shoulder from where he was flying ahead and gave me a small smile. The resulting blast of warmth around my heart pushed a smile onto my lips.

"What are you so happy about?" Odio smirked.

I looked away, squinting at the ocean as it spread out before us. "Nothing."

"Liar. I saw you and the prince out on the balcony. I'm not an idiot."

I glanced at him. "Oh? And what did you see?"

"I saw you looking awfully comfortable for two people who are supposed to hate each other."

"You were the one who told me he didn't hate me," I pointed out. "In fact, you're the one who told me to look at him for more than a second."

"Exactly. I told you to look at him, not kiss him."

283

My skin flamed. "I didn't kiss him."

"Oh?" Odio flipped onto his back, his black wings spread out beneath him as he soared below me. "That's not what it looked like from where I was standing."

I beat my wings harder, putting a bit of distance between us before the temptation to lower a foot and kick him in the crotch won over. "We were just talking."

"I talk a lot," Odio said, flipping back onto his front and letting the wind lift him to my side. "And that is definitely not how you talk."

"Just drop it, okay?" I snapped.

Odio held up his hands in surrender and I exhaled in relief. The truth was, I didn't know what had happened. We had talked. He'd told me he missed me. He'd held me. But then things had returned to normal. We'd moved back into the room as the others began to arrive and discussed plans for today. Pace hadn't sat next to me, taking a chair beside Marlowe instead, and I wasn't sure what to think. We'd talked about it being a bad idea, but what did that mean? Just talking on the balcony? Or was this the beginning of something more?

I cursed myself for even thinking it. I'd tried to tell him last night. This would never work. How many times were we going to throw ourselves onto the fire before we could no longer survive the burns? Shaking the thought from my head, I focused on what lay ahead. Dalibor.

We'd decided it best to travel by day, knowing that the Midnight Queen and her court would be asleep. After all, we didn't want to talk to her, we wanted to gather information and find out whether Emeric was there.

The all too familiar tendrils of hope began to coil themselves around my heart as the towering rainforest-covered mountains of Dalibor rose from the horizon. So many times, I'd replayed the moment I met the human lord at his manor during his festival, Plumataria—the festival he'd created so he could spend time in public with my mother. A lump built in my throat, and I swallowed it down. Although I'd thought him a little eccentric, he'd been so warm and welcoming.

With his greying hair and crinkled amethyst-flecked eyes, he was so different from the father I'd been cursed with. It was hard not to resent my mother for depriving me of his warmth, but I knew what it was to fear the king. He wouldn't have let his betrothed go without a fight, and King Hadeon didn't fight fair.

"Are you all right?"

I inhaled sharply, my heart leaping into my throat as I found Pace flying beside me, his eyes narrowed in concern. A quick glance around told me that my cousin had flown ahead, likely to torment Tiesa, which seemed to be his new favourite pastime.

"Sirain?"

"Sorry." I gave Pace a small smile. "I'm fine."

He gave me a look that said that he didn't believe that at all, but I kept the smile pasted on my face and stared ahead.

"I wanted to talk to you last night," he said.

Keeping my eyes forward, I did my best attempt at a shrug, which was hard mid-flight. "We did talk."

"You know what I mean. We weren't finished, but after the meeting, you left without so much as a glance."

"I was tired." The words came out harsher than I'd intended, and I caught Pace's flinch out of the corner of my eye.

"I knew this would happen," he said, the words so soft they were almost lost to the wind.

My attention snapped to him, finding his jaw set and his golden eyes narrowed, fixed ahead. "Excuse me?"

"It doesn't matter," he muttered. "I should have known better."

Before I could press the matter further, he angled his wing, catching an updrift and soaring away from me. I watched, my chest tight. This was what I'd wanted. For him to finally walk away when I wanted him to. But I didn't want him to. Not really. Despite everything I'd done, the impossibility that was us, he'd given me a second chance, and I was squandering it like a fool.

I pressed my lips together and worked my wings harder, a faint shudder of pain rippling through me with every beat as I raced to catch up with him.

"Is that it?" I asked, rising level with Pace.

He didn't look at me. "Is what it?"

Opening and closing my mouth a few times, I tried to find the right words and failed miserably. What did I want from him? I wasn't sure I even knew. Closing my eyes for a second, I inhaled deeply through my nose.

"You should know by now how utterly terrible I am at this," I said.

Pace snorted. "Terrible doesn't even begin to cover it."

"You're right," I tried. "Look, the truth is, I don't know what happened last night and I don't know where it leaves us. I have no idea what you want from me."

"I thought I made that pretty clear last night." Pace shook his head. "I want you, Sirain. But clearly, you're not as invested."

I frowned as he sped up, matching his wingbeats to keep pace. "What do you mean?"

"At the first glimmer of doubt, you shut down and run away," he said. "I've fought for us time and time again, chasing you and convincing you. You said you couldn't see how this would work, but maybe you just don't want it to."

We were close enough to Dalibor that the Midnight Queen's sprawling palace was clear on the side of the emerald-green mountain, the white-roofed city below gleaming a little in the pale morning sun. My gaze caught on a strip of golden sand that might well have been the same one we'd stood on all those months ago.

"I do," I said. "I do want it to work. I just don't see how."

Pace sighed. "I don't know if I can keep doing this."

Panic roared in my veins as I stared at him, his profile as fierce as when he'd come at me with fire in his eyes and a blade in his hand. "What are you saying?"

He closed his eyes and took a deep breath before turning to look at me. "I'm saying if you're scared, you need to talk to me. Stop running. Because the next time you run, Sirain, I'm going to let you go."

An icy chill that had nothing to do with the brisk sea air coated my skin. "Okay."

Pace held my gaze for a moment more, then looked away. We flew onward in a silence so tense my muscles began to ache.

"Where do you want to land?" Tiesa called back to us.

Pace squinted at the castle and its grounds before pointing at the same rocky outcrop we'd rested on when I first brought him to Dalibor.

Odio landed first, smirking at Tiesa as she touched down, folding her wings. She glared at him, which earned her a wink, and I bit back my smile.

"What's wrong with your wing?" Pace asked as we landed beside them.

"Nothing," I lied.

Reaching out, he gently took hold of the arch and extended it, running his fingers along the bone. "You're injured."

"What?" Odio barked, striding over and peering at whatever Pace had found.

"Perhaps if you spent less time tormenting Tiesa, you'd have noticed yourself," Pace replied, standing aside to let him see.

I snapped my wing closed, turning to face them. "I'm fine."

"What happened?" Odio demanded.

Narrowing my gaze at him, I folded my arms. "I flew here with no problem. You wouldn't even have noticed if Pace hadn't pointed it out."

Pace stepped forward, taking hold of one of my arms and

tugging gently until I unfolded them. He slid his fingers between mine, squeezing in a gesture that had both Odio and Tiesa baulking.

"Just tell us," he coaxed. "You know we're not going to drop it until you do."

I rolled my eyes with a groan. "Fine. The first time my father and Fin tried to take me to the passage under The Crossing, I didn't know where we were going. I thought they were taking me somewhere to kill me. So, I tried to escape. As you can imagine, I didn't get very far. Fin threw rocks to knock me out of the sky."

Pace's eyes blazed. "I'm going to kill him."

"You'll have to get through me first," Odio snarled. "He's been at the top of my list for longer than you can imagine."

"Fates and feathers," I grumbled, pulling my hand free from Pace's. "Can we drop it, please?"

Moving to the edge of the outcrop, I surveyed the palace below.

"I say we go to her balcony and just ask her where Emeric is," Odio said, his hands on his hips as he stood beside me.

Tiesa's laugh cut through the morning air. "Who? The Midnight Queen?"

"Why not?" Odio shrugged. "Take her by surprise. Why not go straight to the source?"

"Because we'd get ourselves killed," Tiesa replied, her eyes wide in disbelief.

Pace tilted his head, staring at my cousin. "What is it with you and this place, anyway? I noticed you were very keen to come here last night."

"My darling cousin has a little crush," I explained, grinning as Pace's eyebrows shot up.

"On the Midnight Queen?"

Odio shrugged, flicking his long black braid over his shoulder. "Go big or go home, right?"

"You know," Pace said, a mischievous glint in his eyes. "I have a book that lists all the human ruling families over the centuries. Did you know she has a twin brother? And I know her real name."

Odio turned to him, his white complexion turning even paler. "What?"

"Luna Berch," Pace replied, his golden eyes dancing.

My cousin wailed. "Why? Why would you do that?"

Laughter built in my chest, rising until I could contain it no longer. Even Tiesa chuckled as Odio kicked at rocks and cursed with impressive ferocity.

"It's not that bad," I said, reaching out to touch his arm.

Odio glared at me. "He just ruined the mystery. Gone. Forever."

"Just think," I said, fighting the smile pulling at my lips. "If she ever fell in love with you, you couldn't call her Midnight Queen. You'd need to know her name."

Odio grumbled under his breath, and I looked at Pace, who was beaming.

"Wait," Tiesa said. "Did you say she had a twin?"

Pace nodded. "Sol."

I stared down at the castle, trying to remember whether I'd ever heard anything about a brother. "Where is he, then?"

"Maybe he's dead," Tiesa suggested.

Odio's face lit up. "Maybe she killed him."

"There's something seriously wrong with you."

"And yet," Odio said, gesturing at his tall, muscular frame, "it all comes together so irresistibly."

"Okay, children," Pace said, cutting off Tiesa's reply before it could leave her tongue. "Back to our plan."

"There's no point asking the queen, anyway," Odio said, his gaze fixed on something down below. "She's not here."

"How could you possibly know that?"

"Her carriage isn't by the stables," Odio replied, nodding to the far side of the courtyard. "And the shutters to her bedchambers are open during the day."

"You just crossed the line into creepy," Tiesa muttered.

I glanced at the turret I knew belonged to the queen and found he was right, before looking up at the empty flagpole at the highest point of the castle. "The Dalibor flag isn't flying either. He's right. She's not here."

Pace sighed softly. "What now, then? We still need a plan."

"Easy," Odio said. "We ask one of them."

I followed his stare to where two guards were patrolling the outer wall, the hilts of their swords catching the light as they turned. "It's a much better idea than your previous one," I admitted.

Odio bent into a low bow, sweeping out his arms. "Thank you, Your Majesty."

"Okay," Pace said. "We have a plan. How do you suggest we—"

A bark of protest tore from my lips as Odio turned and launched himself off the outcrop and down towards the two guards. Tiesa muttered a curse that had my head snapping to her, but then she spread her wings, following my cousin.

I stared after them with wide eyes, before turning to Pace. "What do we do?"

Pace's eyes narrowed, his wings flaring as he prepared to follow. "Hope that he knows what he's doing."

I spread my wings, leaping with Pace, as Odio dropped silently down behind the two guards. Sliding his sword from the scabbard between his wings, one of the guards heard it and whirled, but Odio was too quick. With one swift move, he swung his blade, bringing the hilt down on the human's head. As he crumpled to the ground, Odio swung again, sending the second guard's weapon clattering to the ground. Tiesa swooped down and kicked it out of reach as Odio wrapped an arm around the human's throat, squeezing.

By the time we landed, both guards were in silent, crumpled heaps.

"How are we supposed to interrogate them now?" Tiesa asked, nudging one of the men with her boot.

Odio chuckled. "Pick one and let's take him somewhere more private. Then I'll wake him up."

Pace strode over to the smaller of the two human males and grabbed his arm. "Let's go, then."

Odio sheathed his blade and stooped, grabbing the guard's other arm. "Where to, Your Majesty?"

I raised an eyebrow. "Which one of us are you talking to?"

"Does it matter?" he asked. "Now that you're apparently on the same team again."

"The woods," Pace said. "On the other side of the wall. Let's go."

Lifting the guard between them, with Tiesa and I lingering beneath in case they lost their hold, they raised the human over the city wall and into the forest just beyond. As soon as we were ensconced by trees, the guard slumped against a trunk, Odio crouched down and slapped him hard across the face.

"Odio!" Tiesa protested as the guard groaned and rolled his head, his eyes fluttering.

My cousin stood, looking between her and the rousing guard. "What? He's awake."

The sound of a weapon being drawn had me spinning, and I drew in a breath as I found Pace's sword pressed to the human's throat.

"Where is the Midnight Queen?" he demanded.

The human stared up at him, light brown eyes wide through the strands of thick black hair that fell across his forehead. His mouth fell open as he took in the sight before him, his gaze moving to each of us one by one, until Pace pressed the tip of his blade a little harder.

"Answer me," he barked.

The guard pressed back against the tree, as though he might be able to escape. "I don't know."

Odio folded his arms, peering down at him. "He's lying."

"I don't know," the guard said, shaking his head. "Why would I know?"

"Maybe you should let me do this," Odio offered, drawing his own blade. "I have lots of ideas on how to make him talk."

Pace didn't respond. Instead, he unfurled his wings, lifting his chin. "You would dare lie to an angel?"

My eyebrows shot up. Angel? Whatever he was talking about seemed to have the desired effect, because the guard shuddered and shook his head.

"I'm sorry. I'm so sorry. I just—"

"Unless," Pace continued, "you'd rather the demon ask you our questions?"

On cue, Odio opened his own wings, a blood curdling smile gracing his face.

"No!" the human squealed. "The queen hasn't been here for days. She set sail for Newbold almost two weeks ago."

I frowned. "Two weeks ago?"

The guard tried to nod, but winced as his throat dragged against Pace's blade. "Yes. I swear it's the truth."

I turned and walked away; hopelessness heavy on my shoulders. Somewhere behind me, I could hear Odio demanding more answers, but I didn't care. I had the information I needed, but it had only served to make things worse.

The scent of summer beaches filled my senses a second before I realised Pace had followed me. I glanced at him, finding his sword back at his hip. A tremor of pity ran through me for the human guard, but at least Tiesa was there to keep Odio in check.

"Hey," he said, coming to stand in front of me. "You okay?"

I shook my head. "It doesn't make any sense. Why would Emeric come to Dalibor if the queen wasn't going to be here?"

Pace's eyes searched mine. "Maybe he didn't know. Her trip might have been unplanned."

I looked up at him, frustration pushing tears to the surface. "Where is he, then?"

Pace stepped forward and gathered me to his chest, wrapping his arms around me. "We'll find him. We still have time."

"Do we, though?" I murmured against his shirt.

"Yes."

I sighed. "You know, before I met you, I could count the times I'd cried on one hand."

Pace's chuckle rumbled against my ear. "I'm not sure I can apologise for helping you get in touch with your emotions."

I smiled and drew in a shaky breath. It wasn't even that I was scared for Emeric. Of course, I didn't want him to die, but I didn't even know the man. He was no more a father to me than the man who'd raised me. Kwellen and Odio had raised me. We'd raised each other, despite the odds stacked against us. Odds that seemed to grow more disproportionate every day. I huffed against Pace's chest.

"What's so funny?" he asked, his breath warm against my skin as he stroked my back, between my wings.

I pulled back enough to look at him. "I was just thinking. If we don't find Emeric and find out what's going on in Newbold, we'll have to return to Hehven, and nothing will have changed."

"That's not true," Pace said softly, reaching up and tucking a stray strand of hair behind my ear.

"Right," Odio announced, stomping over as he slammed his blade back between his wings. "I got everything I could out of him. Time to go."

"What did you do?" I asked, taking in Tiesa's slightly terrified expression.

Odio shrugged. "I followed the rules. No dismembering. No death."

"Fine," I said, glancing at Pace, who was peering through

the trees like he wanted to go and verify my cousin's claim. "Let's get out of here."

In silence, we made our way out of the woods, and almost as one, spread our wings and headed up into the sky. Pace gave me a reassuring smile as we coasted over the ocean, but it did little to calm the restlessness in my blood. Another day without answers. Another day wasted.

34
Pace

"You still have five days."

I glanced at Sirain before turning back to Marlowe, shaking my head. "No. On the fifth day, we have to return. So, in reality, we have just four days."

"Plenty of time," Cove dismissed as she twisted one of her long colourful braids around her fingers. "We can figure this out."

"Exactly," Shanti agreed at her side. "We can do this. Together."

I nodded, but any confidence I'd felt on the way to the human world had been severely diminished, and part of that was because of Sirain. The hopelessness emanating from her as we'd left Dalibor had lodged itself in my chest.

Pushing my hair out of my eyes, I frowned at where she was sitting, her arms wrapped around a bent knee as she stared out of one of Marlowe's narrow windows. The pale orange glow from the setting sun painted her skin in warmth, but the sadness etched on her face caused me to shiver.

"Tell us what you found out from the guard you questioned." Marlowe spread the only usable map of Newbold we had in our possession on the table in front of him, weighing down the ends with dark metal ornaments.

The question had been directed at Odio, but he remained silent, his narrowed eyes fixed on the corner of the room. My lips quirked in a smile.

Taking up so much space that chairs had been shifted out of the way, and radiating enough heat that we'd had to leave the balcony doors open, was a cow-sized Bertie. He was magnificent.

Asleep as usual, his large claret snout rested on his paws, black curling talons as long and sharp as daggers folded against the stone floor. His spiked tail was wrapped around him, twitching in time with his leathery eyelids as he dreamed, while tiny clouds of smoke rose in puffs from his flaring nostrils. It was incredible to believe the same beast had draped himself around my shoulders just a few months ago.

Despite Bertie's generally docile state, Odio had been eyeing him with a mix of distrust and awe from the second we'd stepped into the room.

"Odio," I pressed. "What did you find out from the guard?"

The Chaos turned, resting his chin on his hands, where they gripped the back of the chair he'd straddled. "He didn't know much. The Midnight Queen—"

"Luna," I offered, smirking.

"The Midnight Queen left on a ship eleven days ago, bound for Newbold," Odio said. "The Dalibor armada has been completely dispatched, with no ships or weapons remaining in their harbours or docks."

"So, they've given it everything they've got," Cove said. "Are they building any more ships or weapons?"

Odio shook his head. "No."

"That's not necessarily a good thing," Marlowe said, frowning down at the map. "It could mean they don't think there's any point because they've already won."

I groaned as I stood and stretched, making my way over to the open balcony. Closing my eyes, I relished the contrast of the warmth from within and the early evening breeze streaming between the doors. "We have to go to Newbold," I said. "We always knew it would come down to that."

Shanti hummed her agreement. "We just need to be clever about how we utilise these four days."

"Agreed," I said. "We'll use tomorrow to scout Newbold and decide where to go from there."

"Didn't you tell me that the last time you went there, they tried to shoot you out of the sky?" Tiesa asked, and I turned to respond, but Sirain spoke first.

"They have these tall stone watchtowers spread along the coast. We had to fly above the clouds to get past them, but that means you don't know what you're going to descend into."

"Which wasn't so bad before the war started," Marlowe said, his dark eyebrows pulling together in a frown. "But now, it's much more dangerous. You can't fly in blind."

"We might have no choice."

"You do have a choice," Tiesa said, her voice tight. "You can choose whether this is worth risking your life over."

"This? Do you mean the truth?" I asked. "If we don't do this, we return to Hehven, and everything stays the same. Cupids and Chaos continue to carry out conflicting orders. The Fates dish out demands of death as they see fit. With everything you know, could you actually sit back and allow that to happen?"

Tiesa pressed her lips together, holding my gaze for a moment before exhaling softly. "You're putting a lot of hope on Newbold. What if there are no answers there?"

"There has to be." I strode over to the table, forcefully placing my hand down on the map sprawled in front of Marlowe. "There's a reason no orders are given for Newbold. There's a reason they have watchtowers scouring the sky as well as the sea. There's a reason they keep to themselves except for when they're instigating wars. It has to be connected. It has to."

My ragged breathing filled the silence as my words settled, and Bertie stirred, mewling as he curled himself tighter.

"The prince is right," Odio said. "Newbold is the thread we need to pull to unravel this whole thing. And it needs to be unravelled." He turned to look at Tiesa. "You might be happy with your life, carrying out the Fates' orders blindly under the rule of a benevolent queen, but it won't stay like that. Hadeon is going to unite the Cupids and Chaos, whether it's via peaceful union or brute force. You know that, right?"

My heart stuttered in my chest. Although the thought had entered my mind, it had never properly manifested until Odio voiced the words. "You think Hadeon would attack Hehven?"

The Chaos shrugged. "He always gets what he wants. If Sirain doesn't secure this engagement, he'll kill Kwellen. Then he'll probably kill me."

"And me," Sirain added quietly. "If I don't secure the engagement, he has no use for me. It's the only reason to keep up the pretence that he's my father. There's no way he'll keep me around if he doesn't have to."

Odio stood and crossed to her, dropping to his knee at her side. "I'm not going to let that happen, Cousin."

She gave him a grateful smile, resting her hand on his forearm.

"We're not going to let that happen," I said. "Even if we have to hide you in Hehven, I'm not letting you go back to that monster."

Sirain's eyes widened as she stared at me, and I realised the weight in those words. It was something I hadn't considered, but I meant it with every fibre of my being. I wasn't going to let her go. Neither King Hadeon nor Fin would get their evil, malicious fingers on her ever again. The promise thrummed, red hot in my veins as I held her gaze, willing her to understand what I was saying.

Shanti pushed back her chair and stood. "Marlowe? Shall I fetch them?"

A shadow crossed my friend's face, pain flickering in his eyes, but then he nodded. Shanti squeezed his shoulder and left the room.

"Who is she fetching?" Odio said, voicing the words on the tip of my tongue as my wings flexed in trepidation.

Marlowe gave a half smile. "Not who, but what."

I turned an empty chair at the table and straddled it, searching his face for answers. "What are you talking about?"

"Do you remember when you and Dariel said you'd consider spying for us?"

My chest constricted, but I swallowed the sharp pain and nodded. "Yes . . ."

"We suggested at the time that perhaps the Chaos would be able to help in terms of armour to keep you safe."

I looked at Odio, who had straightened, following the conversation with interest. He was still wearing his Hand leathers, which had been enhanced with thick panelling for the war, the same as Tiesa's had been. Although, the Chaos' additions were black to the Cupid's dark brown.

"Our armour isn't much more than decorative," Odio said, rapping his knuckles against the thick leather panelling on his chest. "Because humans don't generally see us, the need isn't there. It's more an attempt to try and ease the minds of the younger Hands carrying out orders during a war than to protect us. To my knowledge, no Chaos has ever been killed by a human."

A wave of guilt broke against my chest as I recalled the concern Jac had shared regarding the dangers of being a Hand during a war. Tiesa had told my parents that a human had shot Dariel out of the sky while he carried out an order. There hadn't been time to think about the repercussions. She'd lied to save me. I glanced at where she'd gone still, and she met my gaze briefly before looking away.

"Well, before everything happened," Marlowe pressed on, "we had an idea. Just in case."

The door opened, and Shanti returned with a pile of material in her arms. She placed it down carefully on the table and I leaned forward to inspect it. It appeared to be some sort of fabric, a red so dark it was almost black, but as she took hold of an edge and lifted it, I realised it was a vest of sorts, with thick leather ties at the side. The material itself, however, had my attention flitting to the magnificent creature snoring softly in the corner.

Cove chuckled softly. "You recognise them, then?"

Wide-eyed, I looked back at the sheet of material, discerning the familiar pentagonal plates that covered it. "Bertie's scales?"

Shanti nodded, holding it towards me to touch. "When he grew, it was quick, and he shed twice within six weeks. Dragon scales are impenetrable, so Marlowe had the idea to make these."

Odio stood and walked over, touching his fingers to the hard scales. "They're a different colour to the beast."

"His name is Bertie. Cuthbert to you." Shanti scowled up at him. "But yes, when they shed, the scales darken."

As Odio carefully lifted a second sheet, holding it up to the light, I couldn't help but notice that the scales were almost the same dark colour as his hair and wings.

"What are those?" I asked, pointing to the strips of material remaining on the table, with small metal buckles attached to the sides.

Shanti lifted one, handing it to me. "Bracers."

I smiled, running my fingers over the smooth, hard scales before wrapping it around my forearm. "This is wonderful."

"The ties," Odio said, still inspecting the armour. "They're designed to accommodate wings."

Marlowe nodded. "Of course."

"Can you make any more?" I asked.

"We might have enough to make two more," Cove said. "We started making them when we thought you would be returning. When a month went by with no word, and war worsened, we stopped."

I glanced at Odio to find his jaw had tightened. It was the closest I'd ever seen to regret on his face.

"How long will it take?" I asked.

Cove sighed. "At least a full day. The metal mesh must be welded to the scales one by one. It's a delicate process."

"Okay," Odio said, holding it to his chest. "The prince and I will go tomorrow and scout. We'll formulate a plan, then when we have two more of these, we'll all go the following day."

"Absolutely not," Tiesa barked, rising to her feet. "We take tomorrow to rest and help to make some more, then we all go together."

Odio placed the sheet of scales down and turned to face her. "We can't afford to waste a day—"

"It's not wasting a day if it keeps us alive," she snapped, her fierce green eyes looking to me for agreement.

I looked between the two of them before turning to Sirain, who was watching the exchange, a small line between her brows. "What do you think?

"I think Odio and I should take the armour and go tomorrow," she said.

I sighed, tipping my head back to look at the ceiling. "Of course, you do."

"My opinion may not be of consequence," Marlowe said, "but I think Tiesa is right. You may feel the pressure of your time constraint, but if you're killed or captured by Newbold, you'll never find your answers." He reached across the table and wrapped a strong hand around my forearm, his dark eyes pleading. "Please don't risk your life unnecessarily."

I placed my hand on top of his and squeezed. "I won't."

"Can we test this?" Odio asked, still holding the armour.

Tiesa stepped to his side, taking a scale between her thumb and forefinger. "Are you asking someone to fire arrows at you?"

Odio peered down at her, a small smile lifting the corner of his mouth. "Potentially. Stabbing could be on the cards, too."

Tiesa nodded and snatched up a pair of bracers before turning towards the door. "Let's go."

Sirain unfolded from her seat and stood. "I'll go and make sure they don't actually kill each other."

"Probably a good idea," I said. "I'll come find you later."

She nodded, then turned to the humans and inclined her head. The simple act of deference twisted my heart.

"You still love her," Marlowe said softly after the balcony door had closed behind her.

I stared down at the table, the unspoken answer saturated in guilt that it should even be possible, but he lifted a hand, grasping my shoulder.

"I can see how much regret and guilt she carries," he said. "She's a shadow of who I met on my ship that night."

"You don't know the half of it. Her family . . . What she's been through." I shook my head, emotion welling in my throat as I lifted my eyes to meet his gaze. "Having met the people who raised her, it's a miracle she's even capable of compassion."

Marlowe stared at me, his eyes searching. "Do you love her?"

"Yes," I breathed. "Against all better judgement."

He chuckled softly. "Love doesn't care for our better judgement."

I looked to Shanti and Cove, expecting to see disappointment on their faces but finding nothing but understanding.

"Loving her isn't a betrayal of Dariel," Marlowe continued. "Or me. Does she still love you?"

Did she? The walls Sirain had built around her heart were so sturdy, I wasn't sure she could ever allow herself to fully acknowledge how she felt. "I think so."

Marlowe squeezed my shoulder. "Perhaps you should go and find out."

On the way to Dalibor, Sirain had assured me she'd stopped running, but we hadn't yet labelled what was happening between us. We hadn't even kissed. The thought set my blood humming beneath my skin, and I rose to my feet.

Marlowe stood, too, and I pulled him into a tight embrace. "Thank you," I said quietly.

As we pulled apart, he smiled. "Go. Don't waste a single second."

35
Sirain

Perching on the rooftop, my knees to my chest, I watched as Tiesa pulled back her bow, a fierce smile curving her lips, her green eyes blazing. Odio stood on the other end of the roof, facing her, the dragon armour over the top of his Hand tunic and his wings flared, ready.

"Not my face. Okay, Cupid?" he called out.

Tiesa raised an eyebrow. "Are you questioning my aim, Chaos?"

"Wouldn't dream of it." Odio winked.

I held my breath, my fingers gripping my legs tightly. I trusted the humans when they said they'd already tested it, but this all felt wrong. What if it didn't work? What if Tiesa killed Odio? Could it be some sort of twisted comeuppance for what I'd done? My heart pounded. If the Fates wanted it so, it would be. I lowered my chin to my knees, tensing as Tiesa let the arrow fly.

Odio grunted as the arrow smacked into his chest, stumbling back half a step. But then the arrow clattered to the roof.

"Fated Fates." Odio stooped and picked up the arrow, holding it aloft. "Look at this!"

He spread his wings and crossed the rooftop, landing in

front of me and thrusting the arrow in my face. I flinched back, adjusting my gaze to take in the bent tip.

"The armour is that strong?" I dragged my gaze from the ruined weapon to the scales covering my cousin's chest.

Odio's face was pure amazement. "This is incredible! Tiesa, do it from closer this time."

"Seriously?" I asked. "What are you going to do? Keep doing it until it pierces the armour, and you die?"

"Don't worry," Tiesa said, snatching the ruined arrow from his grasp. "I'm not aiming for his heart. If it gets through, it's unlikely he'll die."

I snorted. "Wonderful."

Odio ruffled my hair, then spread his wings and flew back across the roof, while Tiesa returned to where she'd rested her quiver.

The beating of wings sounded behind me, a second before a familiar scent flooded my senses.

"He knows what he's doing," Pace said, landing beside me.

I huffed a laugh. "Does he?"

Pace sat down, wrapping his arm around his bent knee. "If he doesn't, Tiesa does."

Exhaling, I focused instead on the horizon, the last remnants of the sun visible on the water before finishing its descent beyond the sea. Smoke rose from islands out of sight in the distance, tarnishing the white clouds with edges of coal black.

Odio cried out in triumph as another arrow bounced off the armour and Tiesa drew the sword from her hip, turning it in her hand.

The second the humans had revealed there were only two pieces of armour, I'd made up my mind. Tonight, while everyone was asleep, I would wake Odio, and we would go to Newbold. A grim determination coated my bones. If there was the smallest chance I could prevent harm coming to Pace and Tiesa, I would take it.

"I wanted to talk to you," Pace said, pulling me from my thoughts.

"Okay."

He nudged me with his wing, waiting until I turned to look at him. "Can we go somewhere private?"

I stared at him, emotions warring in my chest. Was this a good talk or a bad talk? I tried to find answers on his face, but found nothing.

"Sure," I said, getting to my feet. "My room?"

Pace stood and nodded. "Great."

"Please don't kill each other," I called out to where Tiesa was swiping at my cousin with a sword as he blocked the blow with the dragon scale bracers.

Odio grunted in response, and I paused long enough that Pace took hold of my elbow, tugging gently.

Spreading my wings, I followed as he jumped off the roof and down onto the balcony below. The humans had left the main room, but Bertie was still sleeping in the corner, his rumbling grunts punctuating the silence.

"He's incredible," I whispered, staring as we quietly crossed the room. "I can't believe that's the same beast that used to wrap around Cove's shoulders."

Pace smiled. "It makes me wonder what size he'll be when he's fully grown. Shanti told me there are only a handful of dragons in existence on the Islands, none of them adults. They were keeping track of them, but with the war, they haven't been able to.

"I hope they're okay," I said, taking a final glance over my shoulder at the slumbering beast.

Pace huffed a laugh. "I don't think we need to worry about them."

As we walked down the hallway to the rooms Marlowe had provided us, my body hummed with nerves. There were a thousand things Pace could want to talk about, and I wasn't sure I was ready for any of them. On the way to Dalibor, he'd told me in not so many words that I had one final chance. I wracked my brain, trying to think if I'd wasted it already. I hadn't run. I hadn't shut him out. Had I?

"Isn't this your room?" Pace asked.

I turned, blinking, to find him standing outside a closed door, a bemused smile on his face.

"Oh." My cheeks heated as I turned and headed back to him, pushing open the door. "Sorry."

I stepped aside to let Pace in, closing the door behind him. My chest was tight as I leaned back against the wood, watching as he shoved his hands in his pockets and peered out of the window on the other side of the room.

The fading fragments of sunset made it light enough to see, but as shadows stretched across the room, I knew I'd have to light the lamps soon.

"What did you want to talk about?" I asked.

Pace continued to stare out of the window, his feathers taking on a muted grey in the dimming light. "I wanted to talk about last night, and about what I said on the way to Dalibor. And, I suppose, about what I said during our meeting."

"Just a quick chat, then?"

Pace laughed softly and turned to face me, resting against the window ledge, and my heart stuttered. With his wings and broad frame eclipsing almost all remaining light, his eyes found mine, gleaming like golden twin flames.

"I know how hard it is for you," he said. "I understand you were raised without love. Without compassion. You find it difficult to trust those feelings, to believe that someone would feel those things for you."

I opened my mouth to protest, but his words had already buried deep into my chest. He was right. Hadn't I been surprised by Odio and Kwellen's loyalty when they discovered I wasn't a Hadeon by blood? My throat thickened as I realised Odio had never once stopped calling me 'cousin'.

"I meant what I said." Pace folded his arms across his chest. "By choosing you, I'm putting everything on the line—"

"I'm not asking you to do that."

He sighed. "Sirain. Listen to me, please."

Folding my own arms across my chest, I nodded. The door was uncomfortable against my wings, but I didn't want to move, to step closer. My survival instinct told me to stay away—to be near an escape—because pain was inevitably on its way.

"Sirain, I want to put everything on the line for you. You're worth it. I made that choice on the beach, and I'd make that same choice a thousand times again."

I drew in a shaky breath, my gaze falling to the floor, unable to bear the intensity in his eyes.

"It's going to be hard," he continued. "The path for us was never going to be easy. But I need you to trust me. I need you to be honest and come to me whenever you're feeling unsure or scared. Stop running from me, Sirain."

I nodded, my arms wrapping around my chest as I gripped my upper arms. A rustle of feathers sounded, and I looked up as Pace pushed off the window ledge and crossed the room, stopping a stride away from me, the evening shadows caressing his features.

"I'm choosing you, Sirain," he said softly. "But I need to know that you choose me. I can't leap again if you're going to just let me fall."

My heart twisted in my chest. "I don't understand why you'd still choose me after everything."

"Does it matter?" he asked, closing the space between us. "All you need to understand is that I do."

I stared up at him, the surety in his voice wrapping around me, settling me in a way that stole my breath.

"You don't have to worry." He reached out and gently pried my fingers away from where they were digging into my arms. "You're not going back to Helle. I don't care what I have to do, you're staying with me. We'll figure it out. I promise."

I exhaled, the idea so comforting but unbelievable. "What about Kwellen? What about—"

"We'll figure it out," he said, his warm fingers linking with mine. "But we'll figure it out together. You don't have to do it alone."

Exhaustion swept through me, and as I swayed a little, Pace lifted our joined hands, resting them against his chest. For so long, I'd existed on so little, and Pace's words offered something I wanted more than I could allow myself to.

"I need you to say it," Pace said, steadying me. "Tell me you're all in."

Darkness had almost completely consumed the room, shadows no longer discernible around us. I stared up at him, trying to imagine a world where we worked—where we could be together—but was impossible. We'd tried to stop this, but it seemed our worlds were destined to collide, no matter our choices. And I wanted him. I wanted him so desperately, it was a physical ache. Pace had said that I'd let him fall, but the truth was, I'd been falling since I'd held a sword to his chest on that Fateforsaken rock, and I didn't think I'd ever stop.

"I'm all in," I whispered. "I'm terrified of what lies ahead for us, but I trust you. I promise I won't run. I—"

Pace dropped my hands, taking hold of my face and halting my words as he pressed his lips to mine. My heart stopped, my knees weakening as I realised I thought I'd never feel his kiss again. Tears crept under my eyelashes as I slid my hands up his chest and around his neck, tangling my fingers in his soft, white hair. Pace sighed against my mouth, pushing me against the door as he parted his lips. My heart was as loud as thunder in my ears as I relished in the feel of his body, the soft slide of his tongue against mine.

As my hands roamed down his back, fingers dancing along the edges of his wings, he groaned, pushing harder against me, his teeth nipping my lip, drawing a soft gasp.

"I've missed you so much," he whispered against my mouth, his fingers sliding under the hem of my shirt. But then he pulled back, frowning down at me. "You're crying."

His hands raised, brushing away my tears with his thumbs, and I smiled, pushing his hair off his forehead, and trailing my fingers down the side of his face.

"Happy tears," I explained. "I thought I'd lost you forever."

Pace sighed, leaning his forehead against mine. "The Fates are welcome to try, but nothing is going to part us again. Okay?"

"Okay," I echoed, wrapping my arms around his waist and pressing my face against his chest.

After a minute, he stepped out of the embrace, taking my hand. "Come on."

I let Pace tug me towards my bed, watching as he climbed on and lay down, holding his arms out to me. Smiling, I knelt onto the bed and lay down beside him. He wrapped his arms under my wings, around my waist, tugging me against him as he rested his head beside mine. I waited, expecting him to say something, but as his fingers drew lazy lines along my side, his warm breath on my neck and the arch of my wing, I let myself relax, enjoying his embrace.

There was no way I could go through with my plan, I realised. I'd promised honesty—that we'd complete this journey together. There was relief in that realisation. The full weight of my burdens was no longer on my shoulders but shared with Pace—with my friends. Tomorrow we'd make the armour, and we'd still have time to get our answers. Together, we would make it work.

As Pace's breathing evened out, his movements slowing and his grip relaxing, I closed my eyes, a smile on my lips.

All things are subject to decay and when fate summons, monarchs must obey.

~ John Dryden

36
Pace

Something poked my shoulder painfully and I frowned, shrugging it away as it drew me from the warm embrace of sleep. It was too late, though. Even as I fought against it, I became aware of a cramping sensation in my left wing, and a numbness in the arm on the same side. I groaned as the same sharp prodding dug into my shoulder again and I opened my eyes, blinking as they adjusted to the heavy darkness.

My heart skipped as Sirain stirred in my arms and for a moment, the reason I'd woken was forgotten as I pulled her closer, burying my face in her soft dark hair, inhaling her warm, jasmine-laced scent.

"Pace!" a voice hissed. "For Fates' sake."

I turned my head to find a dark figure standing behind me and I flinched, before realising it was Odio.

"What are you doing in here?" I whispered.

By the faint light of the moon, I could make out the finger he lifted to his lips before pointing it at the door. For a second, I considered telling him to get out and slipping back into blissful slumber against Sirain, but I knew there had to be a reason he was waking me.

Slowly pulling my arm from beneath her and then

extracting my wing, I held my breath as she muttered, before curling into a tight ball. My heart full, I dragged a blanket over her sleeping figure before turning to where Odio was waiting in the doorway.

"What?" I asked as I pulled the door closed behind me.

Odio stared at me through narrowed eyes, the sparse lanterns along the hallway casting long shadows across his features. "You two are together."

"Yes," I said, daring him to push the matter, even though it clearly hadn't been a question.

His jaw worked for a second, and I waited for the words of warning—the threat on my life if I hurt her—but he just nodded once and thrust something towards me. I reached out and took it, frowning at the mesh of dragon scales.

Odio fixed me with a stare. "We're going to Newbold."

"Yes," I said, looking between him and the armour. "The day after tomorrow."

"Yeah, I have a problem with that." He crossed his arms across his chest. "First of all, we don't have time to waste. Second of all, I don't want to put Sirain in danger."

I frowned. "Neither do I."

"That's what I figured. So, let's go."

Before I could respond, he turned and stalked down the corridor, leaving me standing with the armour in my outstretched hands.

"Odio," I hissed, jogging after him.

As we reached the main room, the moonlight painting the dark furniture and stone floors in muted greys, he turned, his wings flaring at his back.

"You know this makes sense," he said. "If we leave now, we can be back before midday, hopefully with answers."

I glanced over my shoulder at the hallway, as though I might see Sirain standing there, disappointment gleaming in her amethyst eyes. Hadn't I just made her swear to be honest with me? Hadn't I told her we'd do this together?

"Look," Odio said with a sigh. "I'm going, whether you come or not. The choice is yours."

I narrowed my eyes, folding my arms across my chest as I stared at him. If I let him go by himself and something happened to him, it would destroy Sirain, and as much as I hated myself for it, the idea of keeping both Sirain and Tiesa out of harm's way was appealing. I knew they could both more than handle themselves, but if Odio and I went, I could concentrate on the task at hand without distraction. A voice in the back of my head screamed that those were terrible reasons, and that I should go and wake Sirain to tell her of her cousin's plan, but I found myself pulling on the armour and turning to let Odio tie the leather straps at my back.

A soft grunting caused us both to jolt, and I peered into the darkness to find a large pair of yellow eyes gleaming back at me. Relief sagged my shoulders. Bertie. Even though I could only make out his eyes, disapproval rolled off the enormous creature as he watched me pull on and fasten the bracers. Retrieving my sword from where I'd propped it up earlier that day, I avoided his gaze as I fastened it around my hips.

"Ready?" Odio asked, checking his own bracers.

Hesitation weighed heavy on my tongue as I inhaled the breath to reply. "I just need to fetch something from my room," I lied. "I'll meet you on the roof in five minutes."

Odio pressed his lips together, but didn't push the matter, instead striding to the balcony doors and opening them. I waited until the sound of his wingbeats faded before crossing to Marlowe's desk. Glancing over my shoulder to check Odio was out of sight, I grabbed a piece of parchment and a quill, hastily scrawling my message.

Gripping it in my fingers, shaking it dry, I strode down the hallway to Sirain's room, half hoping I'd find her awake and sitting up in bed. As I inched open the door, I realised I was out of luck. Still shrouded in darkness, Sirain remained curled up on her bed. I allowed myself one of my five allotted minutes to stare at her, drinking in the contrast of her dark lashes against her pale cheeks and the gentle slope of her nose. Reaching down, I swept her hair back from her face, brushing a feather-light kiss against her temple, before placing the note on the empty pillow. Uncertainty pulsing in my veins, I turned and walked away.

Less than a minute later, I landed on the roof beside Odio.

"We can't do this," I said. "Sirain will be furious."

Odio raised his eyebrows. "It doesn't matter if she's furious. We're doing this for her."

I opened my mouth to protest, but he bent his knees and spread his wings, shooting up into the air, leaving me no choice but to follow.

"How is this for her?" I pressed as I caught up, gliding at his side.

Odio peered at me. "Other than keeping her alive?"

"Sirain is perfectly capable of keeping herself alive," I said. "You know as well as anyone how tough she is."

"She used to be tough. You know she's different. She tried to shut me and Kwellen out, but we knew. Kwellen had to sleep in her room. Did you know that?"

My chest tightened as I shook my head. "Because of Fin?"

"And the king." Odio nodded. "After what Fin did to the queen, she was surviving on scraps stolen from leftovers in the kitchen."

I closed my eyes. She'd mentioned how scared she'd been, and I'd noted the hollowness in her features, but I hadn't realised the extent of it.

"Fin knocked her out of the sky," he continued, his words as sharp as knives. "That would never have happened before. He's a weak, lazy, drunkard who couldn't win a fair fight if his life depended on it."

Odio's words settled on my chest with startling clarity. Newbold was beyond dangerous, and we were flying into the mouth of the beast. If anything happened to her...

"Do you see?" he said. "We're doing this because we care about her. Yes, she'll be spitting feathers when she finds out we're gone, but she'll get over it."

Unease roiled in my gut, and I gulped at the cool salt air. She might eventually forgive her cousin, but I wasn't sure she'd forgive me so easily. Glancing over my shoulder, I exhaled as the island shrank under the night sky, Marlowe's mansion just a pinprick of light. It was too late now. I'd made my choice and I just had to hope we made it back with answers worthy of the betrayal.

37
Sirain

The moon woke me. Searing through my eyelids, I groaned at the brightness and curled away from it, pulling the blanket tighter around me. I could have got up and closed the shutters, but that would have meant facing the cold, and I was deliciously warm in the nest of blankets I'd built around myself. A sleepy smile curved my lips as I remembered why I'd fallen asleep with the shutters open in the first place. Pace. I listened for the sound of his breathing, and when I heard nothing, rolled over and found the bed empty.

I frowned, my attention snagging on a piece of paper glowing in the silver moonlight, lying where his head should have been. Pushing myself up to sitting, I plucked it up and squinted at the messy scrawl.

Sirain,

Odio and I have gone to Newbold. I'll explain when I return.

Please don't follow. Give us until midday.

Forgive me.

Pace

I read it four times, hoping that at some point it would make sense. They'd gone to Newbold. Without us. I kicked off the blankets and slid out of bed, glad I was still dressed from the night before as I wrenched open the door and stomped down the hallway to thump on Tiesa's door.

She opened after my second round of banging, her white hair sticking up on one side and a line etched into her cheek from her bedding. "What's going on?"

I shoved the note at her.

Unable to tame the restlessness coursing through my body, I pushed past her, stalking the length of her room as she stared at the square of parchment.

"This was absolutely Odio's idea," Tiesa said, scowling at the note.

I barked a laugh. "Oh, I know it was."

"When did they leave?" she asked.

I paused, throwing my hands out to the side. "While we were asleep. Could have been an hour ago or three, I don't know."

"No." She shook her head. "I saw Odio right before I went to bed, and I haven't been asleep long. Perhaps half an hour?"

A jolt of relief squeezed my heart and I leaned against her windowsill, gripping the edge.

"We need to go and wake Marlowe and the others."

Staring out of the window at the midnight sky, I barely registered her words. Betrayal didn't begin to cover it. I expected something like this from my cousin, but from Pace?

"Sirain?"

I turned to find Tiesa standing at the door. While I'd been lost in thought, she'd pulled on a shirt and leggings, the note still clutched in her hand.

"Come on," she said, something close to sympathy flickering over her features before they hardened once more.

Taking a deep breath, I followed her out of the room, but then stopped. "Will you wake them?" I asked. "I need a minute. I'll meet you in the main room."

Tiesa nodded and strode off in the direction of Marlowe's

quarters, leaving me staring after her. How could Pace do this? After his speech about honesty? I was well aware I'd planned to do the exact same thing, but I hadn't. I'd chosen to stay, and he'd left me. A maelstrom of emotions swirling inside me, I turned and walked back down the hallway towards the large room we would convene in. Just as fury rose to the surface, fear would leap and wash over it, leaving me confused.

Pushing open the doors, I walked over to my preferred bench seat near the window and sat down, leaning against the wall, and staring up at the stars. Where were they? Were they already in Newbold? The chance that they'd been shot down and killed already was far too high, and I sucked in a breath, my heart a tight and painful ball in my chest. It was taking all my self-control not to run out onto the balcony and launch myself into the air after them.

"Reckless!"

Cove stormed into the room, Shanti a second behind her. She reached out and shoved a chair, sending it skittering back on the stone floor, her colourful braids flying. A low growl came from the corner of the room and my breath caught as I realised the dragon was still curled in the corner, watching through narrowed eyes.

Shanti walked over to comfort the beast, while Cove leaned her hands on the table, her gaze finally falling on me.

"Did you know?" she demanded.

I shook my head. "No. Pace sneaked out while I was asleep. It was almost certainly my cousin's idea, though."

"It doesn't matter whose idea it was," Cove huffed. "We had a plan. If you go to the trouble of making a plan, you stick to the damn plan."

"Well, we are left with two choices, as I see it."

I tore my attention from Cove as her brother stepped into the room, Pace's note in his hand and Tiesa at his side. He looked at everyone in turn, as though getting the measure of the situation, before joining Cove at the table and peering down at the map of Newbold that was still unfurled on its surface.

"We either wait for them to return, as Pace has requested, and use the time to make more armour." He placed the note down on top of the map, frowning at it. "Or we go after them."

"'We' means two very different things," Tiesa pointed out. "Sirain and I could reach Newbold in a matter of hours, but for you humans on your ship, you wouldn't reach there until tomorrow."

"And that's only if the winds favour us," Cove muttered.

Shanti stood from where she'd been stroking the dragon. "And if we can navigate past the Newbold and Dalibor ships."

Marlowe leaned on the table, hanging his head.

"You need to stay here," I said. "For your people. You're far too important to go risking your lives over this."

The Wendell leader turned his head to look at me, a response on his lips, but I shook my head.

"Pace wouldn't want you to come after him. You know that."

Marlowe frowned. "So, it's okay for him to risk his life?"

"Yes," I answered firmly. "Pace isn't next in line to the throne. His death wouldn't unsettle Hehven permanently."

I was aware of all eyes on me, wide in disbelief at the callous fact I'd shared, but it was true. It didn't mean that Pace's death wouldn't rip the beating heart from my chest. I shuddered, drawing in a shaky breath at the thought.

"What about you?" Marlowe said. "You're next in line to your throne, aren't you?"

I shook my head. "I don't think that was ever the king's plan. If he succeeds in marrying me off to Dashuri, I think he'll try to put my brother on Helle's throne."

"Can he do that?" Shanti gasped.

I shrugged. "He can do whatever he wants. Rules mean nothing to a tyrant."

"Midday," Tiesa muttered, snatching the note from the table. "What's the earliest they could have left?"

"Does it matter?" I frowned.

Tiesa tucked her white hair behind her ears. "I'm trying to figure out if they're already there."

"We fell asleep around ten, so it's more than possible," I admitted. "But what difference does it make? The note says he thinks they'll be back by the afternoon."

Marlowe pinched the bridge of his nose, his eyes closed as he inhaled. "It's impossible to know how long they've been gone, but we do know we have eight hours until they return. How we spend those hours is what we need to focus on."

Shanti moved to Cove's side, placing a hand on her arm. "I think we have our revised plan."

"Indeed." Marlowe grunted and sank down into the chair at the head of the table. "We'll make what little armour we can in that time and if they're not back . . ."

His sentence trailed off into heavy silence, but a voice whispered in my head, repeating in a taunting continuous cycle. What if they're already dead?

Part of me was sure I'd know. I'd feel it in the very fibre of my being if Pace died. From the moment our paths collided, there'd been an indescribable link between us. Surely, if Pace no longer existed, I'd know. My breath caught at the idea. Had we had our last kiss? Had I fallen asleep in his arms for the last time? How could I carry on in a world where the white-haired prince didn't exist? The very idea caused my eyes to burn, and I turned away from the room, resting my head on my knees as I stared out of the window.

The sound of wings shifting filled the room and I lifted my head, expecting to see Tiesa on the balcony, but she remained by the table, poring over the map. Instead, the dragon had risen from his corner, scales shifting and rippling as he stretched his muscled forearms in front of him like a very, very, large cat.

No one else in the room seemed to pay the terrifying creature any mind as he rose to his feet and moved from his corner. Standing, he was much bigger than I'd thought, his tail half the length of the large room, slithering behind him like a vast snake. I watched, transfixed, for the beast to move to the balcony, expecting him to take flight. As far as I was aware, he hadn't moved from that corner since we'd arrived, so surely, he needed to eat or something. I didn't want to linger on what a dragon that size ate. But the beast didn't move to the balcony, instead, he lumbered across the room. Towards me.

My heart thrummed a warning in my throat as the dragon fixed me with his butter-yellow stare. I opened my mouth to alert the others—to perhaps ask one of the humans to call him off—but no sound left my lips. Sharp teeth, each one longer than my fingers, hung out the side of the beast's long snout, plumes of smoke drifting lazily from its nostrils.

When he reached my side, he stared at me, close enough that my skin warmed to an uncomfortable degree. I tore my eyes away, my body frozen, and glanced at the table. The humans and Tiesa were watching curiously but made no move to intervene. I pleaded with my eyes, but their attention was on the dragon, not me. The beast huffed, dragging my focus back to him, and I swallowed.

"Hey," I choked out. "Can I help you?"

The dragon blinked slowly, his gaze searing into mine. Then, he rubbed his warm snout against my thigh and sank to the ground with a huff, wrapping his large reptilian body around the bench seat.

I exhaled, eyes wide as he rested his head on the end of the seat, closing his eyes. With trembling hands, I reached out and touched my hand to his neck, flinching at the almost unbearable heat radiating from his scales. The dragon exhaled a plume of smoke before relaxing back into slumber, his vast, deep red body encircling my seat.

"Bertie isn't very trusting," Marlowe said, drawing my attention from the sleeping dragon. "He's unusually sensitive to emotions and generally an excellent judge of character."

I blinked, trying to understand what the human was saying. Was the dragon, Bertie, comforting me? Could he sense my despair?

"You should be flattered," Marlowe continued, a small smile on his lips. "His approval means a lot."

Glancing at the others, I realised they were all staring at me. Perhaps I was imagining it, but it seemed there was a little less hatred in their eyes. Resting my hand against Bertie's neck, I returned my attention to the window, searching desperately for any sign of wings.

38
Pace

Newbold was even more foreboding than I remembered. Soaring along the underbelly of the clouds, Odio and I circled, eyeing the tall, stone towers placed strategically along the coast. Flames flickered, warning beacons in the dense fog rolling in off the freezing sea. Thanks to Marlowe's map, we had an idea as to the where-abouts of Lord Diarke's fortress, but we first needed to ensure we got past the watch towers unseen. Even though we knew the arrows couldn't pierce our armour, the last thing we wanted was for the elusive human ruler to know we were on our way.

"If Marlowe's map is right," I called out to Odio as we looped back around. "Diarke's castle should be a ten-minute flight inland, northeast."

Odio nodded his agreement. "I hate this, but you're right. If we approach and then try to see where we are, we can adjust until we get it right."

Unease squirmed in my gut. Our approach was akin to opening doors and sticking our head into the room, hoping each time we didn't get an arrow in the eye.

"Remember," I warned him, wary of the glint in his eyes. "We're only getting an idea of what we're up against. How guarded he is—"

"What he looks like . . ."

I sighed. "Yes. What he looks like."

"If the opportunity presents itself," Odio said, soaring a little higher, "I'm going to interrogate a guard. See if we can find out whether Bickerstaff or the Midnight Queen are here."

My lips pressed into a firm line. Doing that would give us valuable information, but it would also alert Newbold to our presence.

"What's that look for, Prince?" Odio said, frowning at me over his shoulder.

"I'm just weighing up the pros and cons," I said. "If we reveal ourselves to a guard, we might as well just walk up to the castle gates."

"As if they'll believe the guard. They'll think he had too much wine."

I shook my head. "Newbold isn't like the other human lands. They tried to shoot me and Sirain out of the sky. It was like they were looking for us."

"You don't know that for sure, though," Odio pressed. "Perhaps they thought you were a large bird and shot at you for sport. Humans' enemies travel by land and sea. Not air."

I held his stare for a minute before exhaling heavily. He was right. We'd put a lot of weight on the fact that the archers had seen us, but it didn't mean they were looking for us. That was the thing about Newbold. It was so shrouded in mystery, appearing so foreboding, that you second guessed yourself out of fear. Perhaps that was the point.

"I'll go first," Odio said. "I'll camouflage better with dark wings."

I stared at him, wondering if I'd missed something, when he pointed below us through the thick cloud. I'd been so lost in thought, we'd already reached our first estimated location.

It was still dark, with probably a good couple of hours until sunrise, meaning the clouds remained a purpled grey against

the night sky. I opened my mouth to argue that we were probably similarly camouflaged when he dived, disappearing into
the clouds.

I swore, back beating my wings as I held myself in place,
waiting. No matter what we discovered beneath the cloud
cover, we'd have to find somewhere to land soon. My back was
aching from being airborne for so long, each wing beat a little
more demanding than the last.

Staring at the clouds, I watched impatiently for Odio's
return, trying to take solace in the fact that the dragon scale
armour reduced the chances of either of us being killed. I'd
seen the Chaos Hand fight, and I knew he was skilled enough
to avoid an arrow to the head, if nothing else.

Just as the urge to chase after him became unbearable, he
burst back up through the clouds a few metres away, and I
raced to his side.

"Well?" I asked.

He shook his head. "Nothing but fields and a small village.
It's too dark and hilly to see anything further away."

My heart sank. "Okay. We're definitely headed in the right
direction, but we must have incorrectly estimated the distance.
Let's fly another five minutes and check again."

As we continued onwards through the chilly sky, I tried to
keep my guilt at bay. It was likely our absence had been noticed
by now. I wondered how angry Sirain was. I knew Tiesa would
be furious. A shiver shook my shoulders, juddering all the way
to the tips of my wings, that wasn't entirely because of the
weather. It was colder in Newbold, but wearing heavier
clothing would have slowed us down and hindered our dragon
scale armour, so I just had to ignore the numbness in my
extremities and focus on the burning warmth between my
wings as I worked on keeping above the clouds.

The temperature wasn't the only thing we'd underestimated
about Newbold; the country was three times the size we'd

anticipated. Ten more dips below the clouds and over an hour and a half later, Odio returned with good news.

"It's down there. It's enormous. I can't speak for Hehven, but it's nearly twice as big as Hadeon Castle."

My jaw clenched as I glared at the clouds below us. The bigger his fortress was, the harder it would be to find any of the people we were looking for. "What about the layout? Is there anywhere to land?"

"Go look. There are a few guards on patrol, but it's still dark enough I could get quite low before I worried about being seen."

Shaking my head, knowing it wasn't worth reprimanding him for the recklessness that seemed to be bred into Chaos, I flipped and spread my wings, gliding down through the thick cloud cover. My clothes clung to me, sodden with droplets of precipitation, and I shoved dripping strands of hair from my face as Newbold spread out below me.

Odio hadn't been exaggerating. Lord Diarke's castle sprawled across the landscape, a mass of grey, weathered courtyards and towering stone walls. There were two walls encompassing the fortress. The high, outer wall was connected by four enormous turreted towers, taller than any building I'd ever seen. A lower wall, connected by walkways and marked with shorter towers, surrounded the main fore-boding building at its centre. The walkways were visible because of the guards marching their lengths, illuminated by flaming torches.

Large barren courtyards filled the space between both walls, and I wondered whether they were used for training. The word 'impenetrable' sprung to mind as I searched for some-where we could rest without being seen. Even alighting on one of the tall towers wasn't a viable option, as we'd likely be seen from one of the others. Grunting with frustration, I swooped back up into the clouds.

"What do we do?" I asked as Odio drifted over to me. "I can't see anywhere safe to land."

"We've got two choices, as I see it," he said. "We either retreat and set down somewhere further away, or we bite the arrow and land inside the outer wall."

"No." I shook my head. "We need at least a little height. What if we land on the inner wall and take out one of the patrolling guards?"

Odio's eyes widened as a wild grin spread across his face. "Look at the Cupid living dangerously. Let's do that one."

It was reckless and stupid, but after grossly underestimating how far we'd have to fly, we were both minutes from dropping out of the sky. I reached for the golden hilt of the sword at my hip as Odio slid his onyx blade from between his wings, his eyes ablaze. We could do this. We could surprise and incapacitate a human guard without drawing attention from anyone else. After all, we'd done it in Dalibor, and we could do it again. This would not be a problem.

As one, we descended below the clouds, aiming for a stretch of walkway to the east of the main building, where a guard was patrolling, almost at one of the towers. I shot Odio a look and he grinned, brandishing his sword.

Every sense was heightened as we plummeted towards the walkway, exposed to anyone who would care to see us. Speed was our only friend as we landed on either side of the human, our wings spread and our blades in our hands. The guard stared at me, wide eyed for a second, but before he could raise his weapon, Odio slammed the hilt of his sword down on the side of his head, sending him crumpling to the ground.

"Go!" Odio hissed.

I scooped up the guard and we half ran, half flew, to the shadows beside the nearest tower, pressing against the wall. The relief of folding my wings and feeling solid ground beneath my feet was such ecstasy I leaned my head back and closed my eyes, suppressing a groan.

"What now?" I whispered to Odio

He glared at the human, crumpled at our feet, his jaw set. "We rest here and then figure out a place we can properly hide. If we can get inside the castle itself, that would be extremely useful."

We stood in the shadows shivering in our damp clothes, our breath clouding the air, and I closed my eyes, trying to conjure the warmth of just a few hours ago when I'd woken with Sirain in my arms. Why had I left? With every passing minute, the weight of my decision grew heavier on my shoulders. This was a deadly game, and with every move we made, it grew more difficult to see how we could win.

A sinking sensation gripped my gut as I stared up at the looming towers on the outer walls. Even pressed into the shadows, we were still exposed, and I couldn't shake the feeling that we were being watched. Odio had insisted that the watchtowers had been a fluke, but my gut told me otherwise.

I was so lost in my own thoughts, my senses drowned out by my thunderous heartbeat, that I didn't see the crumpled guard's blade until it was too late.

Odio hissed as a short dagger slashed against his thigh, but before I could react, he drew back his gleaming black sword and buried it in the guard's chest.

My blood froze, my throat tightening as he withdrew his weapon, rivulets of red glistening on its length. "Fated Fates," I hissed. "What did you do?"

Odio wiped his blade clean on the guard's sleeve. "This is war. It's them or us."

My stomach churned as a pool of crimson blood spread out around our boots. I reached out and gripped his upper arm, rage bubbling beneath my skin. "You can't kill any more humans."

The Chaos gritted his teeth, yanking himself free of my grasp. "He attacked us, Cupid. If I'm forced to choose between my life and theirs, I will always make the same choice. If you ever thought this mission could be completed without a little blood being spilled, you need to readjust your expectations."

My chest heaved as I gripped my blade so tightly my knuckles ached. "I should never have come."

"It doesn't matter what you think you should have done. We're here, and we need to make our next move before it gets any lighter."

Pushing my rage aside, I glanced up at the sky, noting the paling clouds on the horizon. "What do we do with him?"

"We'll have to leave him here."

I stared down at the bloodied human, wondering whether he had a family—anyone that would miss him. "When he's discovered, they'll know someone's here."

"Then we'll have to move quickly."

Shoving the guilt into a dark recess of my chest, I peered out of the shadows at the enormous fortress. Grotesque stone statues guarded the windows and spires, masses of sharp teeth and cruel eyes watching, daring anyone to try to enter. They resembled dragons, but the way they perched, crouching, made their limbs look almost human.

"If we can time it with the guards, we could fly to the front of the castle and hide amongst the statues," I suggested. "We might be able to get inside through one of the windows."

Odio said nothing and I glanced at him in question. He was watching the walkway, a dangerously dark gleam in his eye, and I followed his glare to find another guard making their way towards us, a bow pulled and ready in his hands.

"Have they noticed someone's missing already?" I whispered.

Odio frowned. "They shouldn't have. If we'd had more time and a better place to hide, we could have watched and figured out the guard rotation and pattern. Something doesn't feel right, though."

My heart thumped in my throat. "We could capture this one. Get answers."

"Indeed."

We crouched in the shadows, watching as the human edged his way along the narrow walkway. If he suspected foul play, I was certain he wasn't expecting it to be an 'angel' and a 'demon'.

"You approach from the front and distract him as soon as he gets within a few metres," Odio whispered. "I'll fly up and land behind him."

I grunted my acceptance, tucking my wings in tight and adjusting the grip on my sword.

"Now," Odio breathed.

I stepped from the shadows, my sword braced, ready to disarm the human, while a gust of air ripped at my hair as Odio burst from the shadows behind me. The human's eyes widened, but instead of letting his arrow fly, he dropped to the ground and rolled to the edge of the walkway, covering his head with his arms.

Odio landed, our eyes meeting for a fleeting second of confusion, before the air filled with the sound of whistling. I whirled, dread weighting my wings as I found the courtyard between the castle and the inner wall filled with soldiers, their bows pointed at us and a wave of glistening arrows arching their way through the morning air.

Odio swore loudly and as one, we dove back towards the shadows beside the tower, curling our arms against our heads in hope that the armoured bracers would protect us.

"What in Fates' sake was that?" Odio snarled.

I couldn't think straight for the panic roaring in my ears, vibrating in my bones. The stone ground shuddered beneath our feet, the rhythmic thudding of heavy boots filling the air, as a wall of soldiers appeared at the end of the walkway, marching towards us.

"We're going to have to fly for it," I said, my chest heaving.

Odio leaned forward, peering over the wall, before slamming backwards as an onslaught of arrows followed. "Have you lost your mind?"

"I thought you'd be pleased," I snapped. "We're going to have to fight our way out."

A rumble sounded in the Chaos' throat, and he brandished his blade, knees bending. "Are you ready to die, Cupid?"

I gritted my teeth and raised my sword. "Not today."

39
Sirain

Nervous energy rippled from Tiesa, strong enough to rival my own, as the rolling fog gnawing at Newbold's coastline appeared in the distance. The sun was already sending pale tendrils of light along the horizon, turning the dark grey clouds a dank silver. We hadn't spoken in over an hour, instead focusing all our energy into flying as fast as we could.

Despite Marlowe's protests, we'd left well before dawn. I couldn't sit and hope. Hope was not a friend of mine, and I didn't trust it one bit. We'd spent just over an hour, together with the humans, welding enough dragon scales to make one bracer each and a small narrow strip wide enough to wrap around our chests. It wasn't nearly enough, but it would have to do.

Closing my eyes, I sent a silent plea to the Fates. Tiesa was certain they hadn't left long before us, and I hoped against hope she was right—that Pace's absence had stirred me to wake.

Rising further into the clouds, we soared over the watchtowers in the direction Marlowe's map had placed Diarke's stronghold. Once we were inland, we took turns swooping down, skimming the underside of the clouds to check our position. The movement reminded me of the dolphins that frequented the waters around the Wendell Islands. Although, with our wings, perhaps dragons would be the better comparison. A smile flickered across my face at the thought of Bertie. He'd lingered at my side for the rest of the night as we worked, his warmth causing me to shed my leather waistcoat and roll my sleeves. What I wouldn't give for that reassuring warmth now.

Glancing over my shoulder at Tiesa, I nodded once, then dipped below the clouds, the dampness coating my already sodden hair. My breath caught in my throat as what could only be Diarke's castle sprawled out against the barren countryside. My eyes widened as I scanned the gargantuan structure, the towers at each corner as tall as mountains. I had no doubt the humans could see all the way to the sea from the tops.

I angled my wings, gliding back up above the clouds and moving to Tiesa's side. "We're there. It's just a little further ahead."

She nodded. "Is there a place to land?"

"We'd need to get closer to tell for sure," I said. "It's more of a fortress than a castle. I've never seen something so huge."

Tiesa raised her eyebrows before dipping down below the clouds to see for herself. She returned moments later, a heavy frown etched on her face.

"This isn't good," she said. "I can't see anywhere safe to land."

"We can land on one of the tallest towers to start," I said. "And from there, find our next spot. If we don't linger for too long, we can hopefully avoid being seen."

Tiesa nodded in agreement and dove again. This time I followed her, and we silently glided down to the slated roof of the nearest tower. The sound of shouts, and metal on metal, carried on the biting breeze as we came into land, and I tucked in my wings before peering down over the edge.

"Fated Fates," Tiesa gasped at my side.

The blood drained from my face as I spied a familiar pair of black wings far below. I leaned forward, my own wings flaring, but Tiesa grabbed my shoulder, hauling me back.

"Wait," she hissed.

I opened and closed my mouth, my eyes wide as I looked back at where my cousin was fighting off four human soldiers. Arrows protruded from his wings and legs, his movements far more sluggish than they should be.

"They're going to kill him," I said, shrugging off her grip. "We have to help."

"And die in the process?" she snapped. "There are too many of them."

I wasn't listening. Instead, my fingers gripped the cold, wet tiles as I searched for another pair of wings. "Where are you?" I whispered.

Tiesa's whimper sounded a split second before my eyes fell on a figure sprawled on the ground below the wall where my cousin was losing his battle. Pace's wings were coated with blood, arrows along their arches, where he lay face down and unmoving on the stone courtyard. His ivory hair was marred with violent streaks of red, a pool of dark liquid inching out around his head, filling the gaps between the stones. I jolted backwards in horror, my feet scrambling for purchase on the damp tiles.

"No," I breathed. "No."

"We need to go."

I whirled to face her, noting the tears streaming down her brown cheeks. "You can't be serious."

"He's dead," she said, choking on the word as her body trembled.

My mind spinning, I forced my attention back to the battle below, to find that Odio had sunk to his knees, his blade kicked out of reach. The soldiers on either side of the wall appeared to have been called away, retreating into doorways along the wall, and my heart slammed against my chest as I watched two human guards haul my cousin to his feet.

"We need to get down there," I said, shaking out my arms and flexing my wings. "Take them by surprise now they think they have the advantage."

"What exactly do you think we can do?" she demanded, her green eyes wide and rimmed with red.

"We go down and take out those guards," I said, determination calm and sure in my bones. "I think Odio can fly enough to get over the walls if we can free him. Then we drop down, get Pace and get out of here."

"You're not thinking straight," Tiesa said, her damp white hair clinging to her cheeks as she shook her head. "We need to get back to Wendell. Maybe if we can come back with help—"

I stood, my jaw clenched. "I'm doing this with or without you, Tiesa. I'm not leaving my cousin to die and I'm not leaving Pace behind."

My throat closed at the unspoken weight of my words. Pace had already left, but I refused to leave his body. I wasn't sure if Cupids observed the final flight as Chaos did, but I couldn't deny him that option. I wouldn't deny his family the chance to say goodbye.

Without looking back, I fell forward, my wings catching the updraft as I swooped down, pulling my blade from between my wings. I would be the demon the humans believed me to be. I would tear the world apart to save those I loved; consequences be damned. I was done cowering in the shadows.

One of the guards looked up as my shadow fell over him, his blood splattered features widening in surprise. I drove my sword across his throat in one smooth motion before turning and slicing through another. Someone shouted, but I could barely hear over the blood roaring in my ears. Body after body fell, rage and despair fuelling every blow, until I was left gasping, dripping with sweat and blood.

"Sirain?"

Swiping at my face with the back of my hand, the dragon scales warm as they scraped against my skin, I turned. "Cousin."

Odio's eyes were wide with horror as he struggled to his feet, and I became aware of someone gasping for breath behind me. I whirled, ready to end another life, but found Tiesa, her white hair and wings splattered with blood, and a guard crumpled at her feet.

Remorse trickled through my veins for the briefest second, but I pushed it away. "Can you fly?" I demanded of my cousin.

He stared at me, pain flickering across his features in a way that sent a wave of foreboding skittering across my skin.

"Surrender," a voice called out. "You are surrounded."

I dragged my gaze from my cousin's face to find rows of human soldiers in the courtyard and more at either end of the wall, their arrows nocked and aimed at us.

"Drop your weapons," the voice demanded.

I looked at Odio. "Can you fly?"

He stared at me, sweat and blood dripping from his chin as his chest heaved with the effort of staying upright. "You shouldn't have come."

The deafening clatter of metal on stone sounded behind me and I whirled, my heart dropping to my stomach as Tiesa raised her hands in surrender.

"Sorry," she mouthed, her eyes brimming with fresh tears.

I looked back at my cousin, contemplating whether I could drag him with me, but as though reading my thoughts, he shook his head.

"It's over, Sirain," he said.

Tears stung my eyes as I let my blade fall to the ground. After everything, was this what the Fates had planned? Anger shook my shoulders and I clamped down on the inside of my cheek to keep my tears at bay.

"Sirain," Odio wheezed. "Did Pace . . ."

Shaking my head, I glanced at the edge of the walkway, trying not to think about what lay on the ground below. Odio's eyes closed briefly, and he hung his head.

"This is all my fault," he whispered.

As the sound of boots marching towards us filled the air, I met my cousin's gaze and willed him to see the devastation in my eyes. "Yes," I replied. "It is."

40
Pace

The throbbing in my head was beyond painful. The stench of blood filled my nose and I reached up to touch the source of the throbbing, finding a sticky gash on the back of my head. One of them must have taken me out with the hilt of their sword. Slowly, the agony of each arrow entrenched in my flesh broke over me in waves, as I remembered what had happened. I only just managed to lift myself a few inches off the ground before vomiting on the flagstones.

I turned my head, squinting up at the wall where I remembered seeing Odio last, but there was no one in sight. The courtyard I'd fallen into was empty, other than the bodies of the guards I'd felled in my failed attempt to escape, and I frowned, wondering where everyone had gone.

Guilt was an uncomfortable weight in my gut. Even though I knew they would have killed me if I hadn't defended myself, the stain on my heart was irreversible. I'd only made it a few metres into the air before the arrows had assaulted my legs and wings and I'd plummeted into the courtyard. The humans had approached me warily, eyeing me as though perhaps I might have some power over them they couldn't see. If only that were true. I'd taken so many lives. I closed my eyes.

They hadn't killed me, though. They must have assumed I was dead. I felt dead. I wasn't entirely sure why I wasn't. Three arrows protruded from the arch of my wings, and plenty more had torn through my spread feathers. Two were embedded in my leg, the pain a deep throbbing pulse. My chest felt as though it had been punched several times, and I could only assume it was where arrows had met with the impervious dragon scales.

Shifting away from my vomit, I rested my cheek against the cold stone, trying to filter common sense through the blinding pain. The soldiers might have gone, but they would certainly return to collect their dead. To collect me. I closed my eyes and hoped with every feather that Odio had managed to escape.

Voices sounded somewhere nearby, and I froze. There was no way I could get out of here in my current state. Opening an eye, I surveyed what little of the courtyard I could see. There was a door built into the inner wall, almost crawling distance away. If I could get to it . . .

The voices moved closer, the vibration of their footsteps shuddering against my body, and I closed my eyes, already silently repenting for what I knew I would have to do. My sword lay just within my grasp. Clearly, thinking I was dead, they hadn't bothered to move it.

"Can you believe it?" a human male said, coming to a stop nearby. "Angels and chuffing demons."

"I thought I was dreaming when it flew up off the wall," another voice said. "Can you imagine how much those wings will be worth?"

The first male scoffed. "Don't even think about it. Diarke will have your head, and you know it."

"Aw, come on."

"We're to move him. Nothing else."

"Just one feather. He'll never know."

"And how are you going to prove it's an angel feather?"

Hands roughly grabbed my wing, straightening it out, and I forced my face to stay relaxed despite the searing pain roaring through my body, beading sweat at my brow.

"Look," he said, tugging at one of my feathers. "Some have got gold on them. You name a bird that's got gold feathers."

"Fair point," the first voice said. "Get one for me, too."

Sweat trickled down my temple, and I held my breath as the men leaned over me. Just as I felt a tug on my feather, I reached out and snatched the sword, thrusting it upwards into the gut of the human holding my wing. The other man cried out, but before he could finish his warning shout, I rose onto my knees and sliced across his throat, silencing him.

I closed my eyes, wincing against the spray of blood as the humans crumpled to the ground beside me. With a laboured grunt, I carefully folded my wing back in, waiting and listening. No other shouts sounded, and after a moment, I allowed myself to turn my head, surveying the empty courtyard. It wouldn't be long before others came. I needed to move.

Pushing up onto my knees, I clenched my teeth against the pain drawing whimpers from my throat. Using the wall behind me, I dragged myself to standing and took a second, leaning against my shoulder, gasping for breath as I tried not to move my wings.

Each step was torture as I hauled myself forward towards the open door. I had no way of knowing what was beyond it, but the possible safety in the darkness it offered was the only hope I had. My hand pressed against the wood of the door, and I stumbled inside, closing it behind me as the sound of voices reached me across the courtyard.

The narrow space was faintly lit by a single flame halfway up narrow stone steps I presumed led to the walkway we'd fought on. I cast my eyes around the space, my heart beating so rapidly I had to grip hold of the wall to steady myself. Just beyond the base of the stairs was a stack of barrels. I moved to them, pushing them slightly further away from the wall, the effort drawing a low whine from my throat. As the voices drew nearer, I slid into the shadows behind them, the arrows invading my flesh digging deeper, and I bit down on my lip so hard I drew blood.

No one entered the stairwell. The humans chatted beyond the door, only the odd word discernible as they began removing the bodies from the courtyard. I leaned my head back against the wall, waiting, but they didn't seem to suspect anything. Perhaps they assumed the two guards I'd killed moments ago were casualties of the earlier battle. After all, I didn't know how long I'd been unconscious for.

When the voices finally retreated, I exhaled heavily, preparing myself for the task ahead. A fresh bout of sweat coated my skin as I grimaced, reaching around and unfastening my shirt. By pulling my arms out first, I was able to tug it off under the dragon armour, and I allowed myself a pained smile of triumph. There was no way I could re-tie the armour by myself, and I wasn't going to risk taking it off.

Taking my shirt between my teeth, I tore the material into strips, which I laid across my uninjured leg. I panted, eyeing the arrow protruding from my thigh, and swallowed. There had been many times I walked away from tournaments with injuries. My body was not free from scars. But this was the most pain I'd ever endured. Even as my brain screamed at me not to, I gripped the shaft with my clammy palm and pulled. The roar that built in my throat shifted to a low moan as I swallowed down the agony and I grabbed a strip of material and wrapped it around my thigh, tying it tightly over the wound.

There was no point pausing. This was not going to become easier. I gripped hold of the arrow embedded in my calf and pulled, the edges of my vision darkening as I leaned back against the cold stone to catch my breath. As warm blood pulsed from the wound, I shook myself back to my senses and tied another strip of material around my leg.

Against my chest and along my forearms, the dragon scales burned hot against my skin, and I swiped at the sweat soaking my forehead, wondering whether I was imagining it. Perhaps the scales had always emitted warmth, but I hadn't noticed because they were over my clothes. Or perhaps the blood loss was causing hallucinations.

It didn't matter. I allowed my fingers to move over my wings, gasping each time they brushed against an arrow. There were two along the arch of my left wing and one just above where my right wing joined my back. Steeling myself, I closed my eyes and reached over my shoulder, ripping the arrow free. There was nothing I could do to stem the bleeding from my wing, so I reached up and applied pressure as best I could, flinching at the pounding of my pulse beneath my fingertips.

The dragon scales seemed to throb in time with my heart-beat, the heat uncomfortable yet soothing. It reminded me of the dragon they'd come from, and I exhaled, smiling at the memory of a much smaller Bertie wrapped in comfort around my neck. My heart clenched as my thoughts turned to my cousin. If things had turned out differently, would Dariel be here with me now? Would it have been him instead of Odio fighting at my side? The 'what ifs' were deafening as I slumped against the wall, my eyes fixed on the door, waiting to be discovered.

"Have you seen them yet?"

I froze, my breath halting, as the words drifted down the stone stairs from the walkway.

"No. I was asleep. I can't believe I missed it."

"Do you think they planned it to happen during our guard change over?"

"Who knows? Angels and demons know everything, right? Being divine beings and all that."

The first voice laughed. "Not looking very divine in chains."

My heartbeat was thunder in my ears. Odio was alive. But as the wave of relief crested, the bitter realisation that he'd been captured doused the surge of hope.

"You've seen 'em, then?"

"Yep. I took some water before starting patrol."

"Where? Dungeons?"

"Nah. West Tower. Bloody hate those stairs. . ."

I leaned forward, trying to catch the rest of the conversation, but as they moved further down the wall, it was lost to the wind. West Tower. That's where I had to get to. My gut told me it was one of the four enormous towers at each corner of the fortress. I leaned my head back against the wall, awash with hopelessness. There was no way I'd be able to walk or fly any time soon. I may have escaped, but I was still trapped. It was only a matter of time before someone found me.

Shifting my cramped position behind the barrels, I peered down at the makeshift bandages around the deep wounds on my leg. It appeared that they'd stopped bleeding. A sigh of relief built in my chest, but as I exhaled, it was with a frown. I was glad the bleeding had halted, but it shouldn't have. Curiosity got the better of me, and I gently pressed two fingers to the wound on my thigh. When I was met with a dull ache rather than searing pain, I loosened the bandage, tearing the fabric of my trousers to better see the injury.

A soft gasp of disbelief escaped my lips as I found the skin already knitted together, as though days of healing had passed instead of mere minutes. My pulse racing, I extended a wing, bracing myself for the biting pain, but it didn't come. An uncomfortable aching spread along my wing, but more like a large bruise than a bleeding wound. What was happening?

As if in answer to my silent question, the armour against my skin pulsed with heat and I touched my fingers to the dragon scales across my chest. Marlowe had said they didn't know a lot about dragons, due to their near-extinct status, but as I marvelled at my rapidly healing wounds, I wondered just how much they'd underestimated their power.

41
Sirain

I held my chin high as the humans bound our hands at our backs and draped heavy chains around our wings. Not a single tear fell as they dragged us up what seemed like a thousand steps to the top of one of the foreboding towers. I stood, glaring at the humans who tore the arrows from Odio as he bit back his roars of agony, who dared even look at me as they placed water and bread in the barren cell before retreating out of the room and out of sight.

For as long as I could, I stood there, staring at the bars, my chin held high. I tried to keep the image of Pace face down on the flagstones from my mind, but it was no use. With every blink, his bloodied body filled my mind, squeezing my heart so painfully I couldn't draw breath.

Somewhere behind me, Odio sagged to the floor muttering a stream of curses, a plethora of soft sniffles emanating from Tiesa. And the dam burst. A gasping sob tore from my chest and I fell heavily to the ground, embracing the sharp pain of the ice-cold stone as it smashed against my knees. My shoulders shook with great rasping howls of agony—sounds I didn't know I was capable of making. If the humans heard me, I didn't care. The only light in my miserable life had been snuffed out.

The tiny sliver of hope I had for a better future shot right out of the sky.

Metal links dragging across stone sounded as Odio moved to my side, pressing his shoulder and arm against mine, the chains restricting him from providing any further comfort. On my other side, Tiesa shuffled across, resting her head on my shoulder, even as I trembled with loss.

"It wasn't supposed to happen like this," I choked out.

Odio heaved a sigh. "We knew this was dangerous. Death was always a possibility."

Tiesa whimpered.

I wanted to tell him he wasn't helping. I wanted to scream at him, blame him, but I knew it would do no good. A fresh wave of anguish rolled over me, and I closed my eyes, wishing I'd tried to fly away. I would have been shot out of the sky, but the pain would be less than this. Pace's death was a wound I knew I would never heal from.

"Sirain?"

I choked on my sob, sitting up with such force, Tiesa was flung backwards. Blinking through my tears, unable to push the damp strands of hair from my face, I listened, barely breathing.

"Did you hear that?" I whispered to Odio.

He nodded, staggering to his feet as he moved around the cell.

"Sirain? Is that you? Can you hear me?"

I stared at Odio with wide eyes, and he looked back at me in confusion. I had only heard that voice a handful of times, but I knew without a doubt who it belonged to.

"Emeric?" I croaked, my voice raw from my sobs.

A laugh sounded on the other side of the stone wall. "I'd say I'm glad to hear you, but I really wish you weren't here."

Thick iron bars lined the front of our cell, which was shaped like a wedge, narrowing to a shadowed corner behind us. Stone walls stood on either side, leaving our only view that of the tower wall. There must have been a window somewhere because it was light enough to see, but our captors had chosen to place us in a cell without the luxury of a view.

I stood and shuffled closer to the wall, looking over the stone bricks as though I might be able to find a way through. "What happened? We've been looking for you."

The human lord sighed, accompanied by the sound of chains. "I received a message from the Midnight Queen. She told me she wanted to meet at sea to discuss a surrender. Liridona was on the verge of collapse, so I went."

I pressed my forehead against the cold stone. "She betrayed you."

"Yes." He groaned. "I never saw her. We waited in the waters of Dalibor for a day and a half. I was on the verge of either sailing ashore or turning around when Newbold arrived. They killed everyone on board and took me prisoner."

Odio muttered something under his breath, and I closed my eyes.

"Why didn't your people know where you were?" I asked. "We came looking for you in Liridona."

"The Midnight Queen said explicitly that I wasn't to tell anyone of our meeting."

Odio barked a laugh. "You're an idiot."

"Not helpful," Tiesa hissed.

The scraping of chains sounded again, a little closer. "Who's there with you?"

"My cousin, Odio," I said, earning a glare from him. "And Pace's friend, Tiesa."

"I'm glad you're not alone," Emeric said softly. "Although I'd be happier if you were not here at all."

Odio snorted. "Wouldn't we all?"

Heavy silence fell over us, interrupted only by the roaring wind as it battered the outside of the tower. I swore it even swayed a little, and I let myself sink back down to the floor.

There was some hay scattered towards the narrow end of the cell, along with a bucket. I arched an eyebrow, wondering how they expected us to make use of it when we couldn't use our hands.

"Did you know there was a kill order out for you, Bicker-staff?" Odio said, his deep voice ringing around the tower.

I looked up at him, surprised at the offering of information.

"A kill order?" the human echoed. "From whom?"

"The Fates."

The silence that followed was laden with a thousand questions, and I hoped he didn't ask, because we couldn't provide a single answer.

"Is that why you were looking for me?"

I nodded, even though he couldn't see.

"There's something strange going on with the Fates," Tiesa said quietly. "Pace was determined to find out what it was."

Her voice broke over his name and I closed my eyes, swallowing the painful lump that immediately filled my throat.

"Was?" Emeric asked gently. "Is he—"

"Dead," Odio supplied gruffly, his chains shifting. "Newbold killed him."

Hearing the words spoken aloud seared fire across my heart, and I thought I might stop breathing from the pain. My eyes burned with fresh tears as I buried my face between my knees. Would Newbold execute us, too? They'd kept Emeric alive. A shudder ran through me as I conjured a thousand possibilities for what a cruel person like Lord Diarke might do to us. Perhaps he'd cut off our wings and pin them to his walls as trophies. I choked on my intake of breath as I thought of Pace once more. What had they done with his body? Bile rose in my throat, and I curled tighter, pulling against my bindings until it ached. I relished the pain.

"Sirain?" Odio asked, nudging me with his boot. "Are you okay?"

I groaned. "Stupid question."

I would never be okay again.

A realisation rose to the surface of the dark clouds surrounding my thoughts and I sat up, squinting at my cousin. He peered down at me, his face still blood splattered and the tears in his leather revealing patches of pale skin.

"What?" he asked, narrowing his eyes. "Why are you looking at me like that?"

"You should be in more pain," I said, sitting up and leaning closer to inspect his thigh as best I could with no access to my hands. "You could barely stand when they dragged us up here."

Odio held my gaze for a moment, the silent question hanging between us. "It still hurts," he said. "But I think the bleeding stopped."

"How, though?" I asked.

My cousin shrugged. "I'm just that indestructible."

Tiesa snorted softly from where she was curled against the wall, and I turned on my knees to face her. I barely knew the Cupid, knowing only that she hated me, and she was Pace's best friend. Other than his parents, she was possibly the only being who would feel his loss as deeply as me.

"Are you injured?" I asked. "Are you okay?"

She stared at me, her green eyes glowing in the dim light. "I'm not injured, and I think you know the answer to the second question."

There was no malice in her words, just pain. I nodded and turned away.

"Bickerstaff?" Odio called out. "Is there anyone else in here?"

My heart kicked up at the thought, watching as Odio pressed his ear to the other wall. I hadn't considered the option that we might not be alone.

"There's someone in the cell on the other side of me," Emeric said. "I hear them shuffling about and the soldiers bring food and water, but I've never heard a word. Trust me, I've tried."

I mulled over the information, but if whoever it was didn't want to talk, there was nothing we could do. If they'd been here longer than Emeric, they clearly couldn't offer any help.

Wherever the window was on the tower, the icy wind that blustered through whipped around the cells with intermittent intensity. I assumed they wouldn't be leaving us for too long bound as we were, but as the minutes ticked by, I began to doubt my logic and huddled in the corner of the cell to get warm. Odio wordlessly joined me, lending me his warmth as best he could.

"Come on," he called to Tiesa, who was still huddled near the bars. "We'll be warmer together."

The look of sheer defeat on her delicate features tightened my chest, but I shuffled slightly against my cousin, nodding for her to take the other side. She used the wall to push herself to standing and walked over, sinking down on my left. With a sigh, I rested my head against Odio's shoulder.

"Talk to me," I said to no one in particular. I couldn't take the silence. Silence allowed my mind to wander to places I didn't want it to go—to places I couldn't bear it to.

"Let me tell you about your mother," Emeric said after a moment.

I smiled gratefully, my lungs filling with relief, as I settled into the corner and allowed Emeric's rich, charismatic tenor to chase the shadows away.

A few hours later, what little sunlight permeated the tower had dissipated, leaving only a dusky grey. Heavy footfalls sounded outside the room, stomping up the stairs, and we all tensed, listening to the approaching humans. A door burst open, somewhere out of sight, and then six heavily armoured guards appeared in front of our cell. I eyed them, noting four males and two females, and counting their weapons. Our chance of escape was minimal, but I would be prepared to grasp any opportunity I had with both hands—even if they were tied behind my back.

A large, broad man, with more facial hair than I'd ever seen on a person, unlocked the cell, and the humans stormed in, hauling us up and out, one on each arm. I heard the movement of Emeric's chains as he moved, but I kept quiet. It was unlikely Newbold were aware we knew each other, and I wanted to keep it that way.

As they dragged us towards the door, I twisted, trying to see into the other cells, but I could see nothing but shadows.

42
Pace

It took forever for darkness to fall. Hours of crouching in the shadows, watching for the narrow slit of daylight at the top of the stairs to fade to black, had caused my limbs to cramp and my thoughts to spiral. Hiding, cowering, wasn't something I did well. Despite being well versed in the feeling of helplessness, I usually had options—even if it meant leaping into action headfirst. Being in the dark, dank corner of the stairwell did nothing but remind me of the confines of my prison, which in turn tightened my lungs, panic coursing in scuttering bursts over my skin.

Midday had come and gone, which meant Tiesa and Sirain would most likely be on their way. I doubted either of them had adhered to the time limit in the first place. The thought of them charging blindly into danger did little to soothe my restless nerves. I closed my eyes and pleaded with whomever might be listening to keep her safe—to stop her from coming here. What had happened was not a fluke. It had been an ambush. I didn't know how, but Diarke's forces had known we were there.

As the last of the day's light faded, replaced by the faint flicker of torchlight, I knew I would have to leave my hiding place. That much was certain. My chances of getting out of

Diarke's stronghold alive were beyond slim, but it was a risk I would have to take either way. I couldn't hide here forever.

In the hours I'd sat waiting, I'd allowed myself to consider the possibility of making a dash for the outer walls, leaving Odio behind. I could fetch reinforcements and we could try to rescue him together. But I couldn't do it. The chances of rescuing him were small, but I had to at least check to see if he was all right. Alive.

I shivered, despite the constant warmth of the dragon scales against my skin. My wounds had healed entirely, leaving only pale scars as evidence. I brushed my fingers over the dark red scales, hoping they'd worked the same way for Odio.

Up on the walkway, the sound of boots trudged past, and I waited, listening. Over the course of the day, I'd learnt the pattern of the guards. They patrolled the walkway in twos and ones, their paths crossing twice a rotation. Six guards patrolled each time and the change of shift had happened right after our attack. The next wasn't due for another hour, according to the grumbles of the last guard who'd marched past.

Pushing to my feet, my muscles screaming in protest at being used, I paused, listening; but there was no sound. It was time.

My plan was minimal. I would fly up over the outer wall and wait, making sure I was unseen, then make my way to the West Tower from the outside. If I remembered correctly, it was just marshland and sparse woods beyond the wall, so hiding should be simple. If I got that far.

Edging my way to the door, blood rushing painfully to my stiff limbs, I eased it open, holding my breath as I listened. The guards on the inner wall should be on the far side, leaving a gap for me to escape across the courtyard. I'd be exposed, but there was no other way. I realised now why the castle had been designed that way. If you escaped one wall, you were a sitting duck as you tried to make it to the second. I was grateful I'd fallen on the outside of the inner wall. At least I only had one wall to escape over.

Taking a deep breath, I started running, allowing my wings to coast over the low breeze, speeding my steps and sweeping me forward. I reached the outer wall faster than anticipated and as I pressed myself into the shadows, my heart trying to slam its way out of my chest, I waited for someone to raise the alarm.

After a few agonising minutes of near silence, my shoulders sagged with relief. Above me, one of the towers loomed impossibly large against the sky. Judging from the last lingering scraps of pale light in the distance, I was below the South Tower, which meant the West Tower was one over to my right. The moon was already bright in the sky, but the clouds that never seemed to leave Newbold were also racing across the sky at speed. I watched, waiting, and as soon as they muted the harsh light of the moon, I leapt into the air, my fingers touching to the top of the wall before dropping straight back down on the other side. I couldn't afford to be airborne for longer than a few seconds.

Landing amongst brambles, I winced as sharp thorns scraped and tore at my skin and feathers. My breath plumed small clouds of white as I carefully tucked in my wings, my face tilted to the tower, waiting for someone to raise the alarm.

After counting to one hundred, I breathed yet another sigh of relief and began slashing at the branches with my sword, extracting myself from the vicious thicket. It would be much faster to fly the length of the castle, but my wings were so large and white, I couldn't risk drawing attention from anyone looking out from the towers. Instead, I would have to walk, keeping close to the wall and the shadows that lingered there.

Each step mirrored the tumultuous pounding of my heart, damp grass licking at my legs, tickling the ends of my wings, and I shivered as the moon brought with it a frosty breeze.

When I finally reached the right tower, I tilted my head back, staring up at the foreboding monstrosity, a dense shadow against the night sky. There was only one window I could see, and I hoped that through it, I would be able to at least get a glimpse of Odio before launching to the clouds above.

My stomach churned as I flexed my wings, ready to leap into the air. Echoes of the searing pain I'd felt as arrows slammed into my flesh caused me to shudder in anticipation of enduring it again. Gripping my sword in my hand, I beat my wings, soaring up the side of the tower, keeping close enough I could touch the weathered stone. Even though it hindered my speed, I tried to keep the spread of my wings to the minimum, propelling rather than soaring, in the hope that it would make me less noticeable. It was a ridiculous notion. I was a 'mythical' being scaling their castle. I was, by very definition, noticeable.

When I reached the window, I gripped hold of the ledge with one hand, my sword still clutched in my other, folding my wings and letting myself hang. By some Fated design, the windows faced outward, looking at the vast wastelands of Newbold, so I was shielded from the other towers and the castle within. My fingers straining, I listened for any sign of guards.

Just as I started to lose grip of the stone, having heard no sign of humans inside the tower, I spread my wings and used a single wingbeat to thrust myself up onto the narrow ledge. Crouching in the small space, I peered inside, my sword poised and ready. I knew if any guards remained, they would have to meet their end.

"Pace?"

I almost fell backwards out of the window at the voice that hissed my name. Leaning forward, checking both ways before dropping inside, I stared wide-eyed at the leader of Liridona.

"Emeric?" I whispered, taking in the strange space. "We've been looking for you."

"So I hear," he said, rising to his feet and moving to the front of his cell amidst the clanking of chains. "I thought you were dead."

I faltered. "No. Almost, but not quite."

"Well, I'm glad of it."

He grinned, and I offered a strained smile in return. "Why did you think I was dead?"

"Odio told me."

A wave of relief washed over me, and I moved away from Emeric's cell to peer into the others. The layout of the tower was bizarre. A circle of cells took up most of the room, the individual spaces slotting together like segments, with a walkway around the outside.

There were four cells in total, but as I looped around, there was no sign of Odio. In the cell to Emeric's right, I could see a dirty, bare foot poking out from under a thick, grey, woollen blanket, and I stopped, staring.

"Hey," I hissed. "Are you okay?"

The figure didn't move, and after a moment, I continued my circuit, coming to rest outside Emeric's cell once more. The human lord was dirty and dishevelled, his neatly trimmed beard longer than I'd seen it and his silvered hair sticking up in tufts. Dark circles surrounded his eyes, his skin a worrying shade of grey.

Tearing my eyes from the heavy chains around his ankles, I shook my head. "What happened?"

Emeric rested his forehead against the narrow bars. "The Midnight Queen requested a meeting to discuss a peaceful surrender. Newbold ambushed me. I should have known it was a trap."

I frowned, tugging at the cell door to test it, but it held firm. "I was told Odio was being held here," I said. "We came together to find you and see what Diarke was up to."

Emeric nodded towards the cell to his left. "He was here,

but the guards took them about twenty minutes ago."

Something tugged at my memory. The way the guards had spoken about angels and demons. Ice-cold dread crept along my spine.

"Them?" I questioned. "Who else was here?"

Emeric's dark purple eyes widened, and I knew instantly what he was going to say before he could draw breath to say the words. "Sirain and Tiesa. They think you're dead."

My lungs constricted and I gripped hold of the bars of the cell, screwing my eyes shut as I tried to force the world to right itself. They shouldn't be here. This was my fault. If I'd just told Odio, 'no'.

"Are they okay?" I asked, my voice thick with fear.

He gave me a look that said there was no single answer to my question, and I nodded in understanding. Things were still so unsettled between me and Sirain, but I knew she felt the connection between us as strongly as I did. If she thought I was dead . . . I pushed away from the bars.

"Do you have any idea where they're taking them?" I asked, my mind painting a thousand gruesome options, each one more harrowing than the last.

Emeric shook his head. "I'm sorry. I haven't been out of this cell since they brought me here. Even Lord Diarke hasn't deemed me worthy of a visit."

I raised my eyebrows, then took a deep breath and tested the bars once more. "I need to go. But I promise you, we'll find a way to get you out."

"Thank you," Emeric said. "Be safe."

I looked away, knowing I could make no such assurance, and hauled myself back up onto the narrow window ledge. My plan had been to check on Odio, assess the situation and go for back up. Now, my backup was in danger, and I was on my own.

Bracing myself, I leapt from the window, my wings catching the air and halting my fall before buoying me upwards.

Keeping close to the tower, I flung myself onto the slanted roof and clung to the tiles as the freezing wind buffeted me.

Twenty minutes was a long time. I had no way of knowing how long it took to descend the length of the tower, and I couldn't begin to guess where they were being taken. There was no way I could sneak into Diarke's castle. We'd been fools to even consider it. It was already a miracle I hadn't been shot from the sky a second time. Panic gripped me with iron talons as I hauled myself forward to peer down into the vast courtyard below.

Sweeping my gaze over the guards patrolling the inner wall, it was a minute before a movement pulled my attention. My fingers gripped the slate tiles, almost prising them from the roof as I watched six soldiers drag Sirain, Tiesa and Odio across the inner courtyard. I watched for any sign that they were seriously injured, but other than resisting the rough way the guards were handling them, they seemed to be unharmed.

Crawling further along the roof, as though the few inches might allow me to see better, my gaze travelled across the sprawling space, trying to determine their destination. When I found a figure standing, waiting, on the wide steps of the castle entrance, my grip tensed against the tiles.

Dressed in long black robes, stood a dark-haired man, watching patiently as his prisoners were brought before him. There was no doubt in my mind he was Lord Diarke. Beside him stood a woman with long, black hair and a dark blue dress that trailed down several steps. The Midnight Queen. I scowled at the alliance that was tearing the human world apart.

As Sirain and the others reached the bottom step, the guards shoving them roughly to their knees, I looked about frantically, trying to find a way I could help them. They were completely at his mercy, and I didn't trust that the human lord would allow them to walk away with their lives. I had to find a way to help them; and I had to do it fast.

43
Sirain

I was sick to death of the frozen wind that whipped around Newbold like an over excited child. It was cold in Helle, especially so around Mount Hadeon, but the wind in this human land was damp and cruel in a way I imagined the Chaos king would love. I glared across the courtyard as the chains weighing down our wings dragged against the flagstones with every reluctant step forward.

Humans were predictable creatures, and during the hours we'd spent huddled in our cell, I'd noticed that Odio's hands were bound a lot tighter than mine. Judging from the number of male soldiers, humans clearly underestimated females. More fool them. Sitting back-to-back, Tiesa had helped me loosen my bindings a little, and as we were marched towards whatever awaited us, I continued to work my wrists, trying to break free.

Torches had been lit along the inner wall, and after being shoved through an iron gateway, we found ourselves being tugged across the central courtyard towards Diarke's fortress. It was a monstrosity of stone spires and foreboding archways, built with the same dull black stone as the walls. Guards were assembled on the steps to the castle, arranged in a cascading vee with two figures waiting at its centre.

With each halting step closer, my heart thudded in my

throat, the growling tension building in my cousin rippling from him in waves. These were the humans who had captured us. Even from across the gloomy courtyard, I recognised the long dark hair and gleaming crown of the Midnight Queen. Beside her stood a man who, despite being unable to see him clearly, reeked of familiarity.

As we trudged closer, the guards lit and raised torches, flooding the steps with flickering warmth. If I hadn't been captured and chained, squinting against the sudden burst of heat, I would have been impressed at the synchronised display. The soldiers gripping our arms shoved us further forward, stopping just before the brightly lit steps, and my world spun as Odio swore.

My father stood beside the Midnight Queen, his sharp features cast in shadow by the flickering torches and his dark eyes gleaming with menace as he peered down at us. How was that possible? I stumbled, not able to make sense of the sight before me, wanting to look at Odio to see what he made of it, but unable to tear my eyes away. Something was wrong, though. Something . . . not quite right. He half turned, offering an arm to the Midnight Queen, and as they descended the steps together, I realised what it was.

His wings were gone.

Horror and confusion tore through me, my exhausted brain trying and failing to understand what was going on. They stopped several steps above us, and I stared up at the man who'd raised me, noting a deep scar along one of his cheeks. His hair was a little longer and there was something different about his nose, too. I couldn't prevent the strangled gasp that escaped my throat as I realised. This male wasn't King Hadeon.

He raised his hands and clapped once. As one, the guards lining the steps turned their backs and took two steps away. In the same instant, the soldiers beside us dropped their iron grips, retreating into the shadows, but as the song of metal sliding from scabbards echoed across the stone, we were reminded that they were out of sight, but not out of mind.

"I must admit," the dark-haired male said, in a voice that sounded like the king, but slightly accented in a way I couldn't place. "I wasn't expecting to finally meet my niece today."

My mouth fell open as I looked up at him, noting more subtle differences to the man who looked so much like my father. Again, my eyes fell to where his wings should be.

"How?" I managed.

He arched a dark eyebrow. "How what? You need to be more precise, Sirain."

My heart stuttered at the sound of my name on his lips, and I was aware of Tiesa looking between us out of the corner of my eye, but honestly, I was likely just as confused as her.

"You're Lord Diarke," I tried again.

"Indeed." He spread his arms out to the side as he inclined his head. "Welcome to Newbold."

My gaze slid to the beautiful woman at his side, her pale face unreadable as her dark blue eyes flicked over us. I'd watched the Midnight Queen from afar many times, but standing before her, the coldness in her expression chilled me to the core. She was like a frozen lake: peacefully stunning, but prepared to drown you with one wrong step.

"Where are your wings?"

My head snapped to my cousin as he voiced the question lingering at the tip of my tongue. His eyes were narrowed as he glared at Diarke, and I leaned into him slightly, hoping to quell the violence I knew was flaming inside him.

Diarke was unflinching as he held Odio's menacing stare, a small smile playing on his lips, as though this was all a game to him. If it bothered him to be called out as a Chaos in front of the Midnight Queen, it didn't show. "To achieve greatness, sacrifices must be made."

"But why?" I asked.

Diarke descended another step, his eyes taking in my chained wings before moving on to Odio's. If I'd been expecting to find a wistful longing in his eyes, I'd have been sorely disappointed.

"These events are centuries in the making," he said, so quietly I had to lean forward to hear him. "The Hadeons were created for a purpose much greater than the confines of Helle allow."

My head throbbed as I tried to arrange the pieces of the puzzle into something that made even an iota of sense. "You cut off your wings to allow you to rule Newbold?" Even as I said the words, I winced, disgust strangling my stomach.

Diarke chuckled, the sound soft and dangerous. "Not just Newbold. Dalibor is mine. Liridona is mine. And before the week is out, the Wendell Islands will be mine." He turned to where Tiesa trembled beside me, slowly looking her up and down. "Meanwhile, my brother has been tasked with uniting Hehven and Helle."

"Brother?" I echoed. "My fath—the king—doesn't have a brother."

"It would appear you are wrong," he said. "Just as my brother was wrong to trust you with uniting our worlds."

I gave him a wry smile as I shifted beneath my chains. "It certainly might be a little more difficult now."

Diarke stared at me in a way that peeled the flesh from my bones. "Your disobedience is an inconvenience, yes. We'd hoped to take Hehven peacefully, as it would be the easier option. However, when the Fates command it, we'll take it by force."

"What?" I shook my head, blood roaring in my ears. "You can't. They wouldn't."

His smile widened and I realised with damning clarity that Pace had been unravelling something much bigger than either of us could ever have imagined. Something we were powerless to stop. My breath hitched as I recalled his lifeless body. Maybe it was kinder he would never find out just how badly we'd failed.

"Why would the Fates command such a thing?" Odio spat. "Even Hadeons can't control Fate itself."

"You remind me a lot of your mother." Diarke stared at him, tilting his head a little as his eyes moved over my cousin's features. "Our sister was an unfortunate sacrifice."

As his words found their home, Odio straightened, rage and disbelief rolling off him in waves. I recognised the intake of breath for what it was a second too late as he launched himself at his uncle. A scream tore from my lips as Diarke produced a long onyx dagger from his belt, holding it before him.

Odio's roar echoed around the courtyard as his chest slammed against the blade. In the shadows, the soldiers shifted but stayed where they were. Tears burned in my eyes, my throat raw, but as Odio staggered backwards, the blade remained unbloodied, and I gasped in relief.

"Dragon scales," Diarke mused, holding the dagger up to the light before dropping his gaze back to his nephew. "Interesting. Where did you find those?"

Odio glared at him, his chest heaving and his jaw clenched. "What did you do to her?"

"You harbour a lot of emotion for a female you never met," Diarke said, turning the dagger in his hand. "Perhaps you are not fully Hadeon either."

As his gaze fell on me once more, I glared back, focusing every ounce of hatred I could into the act.

"We'd at least hoped you would serve some purpose," Diarke continued. "My brother has communicated his disappointment several times."

I stood, seething, before the male who didn't know a thing about me—who I hadn't even known existed, yet had been involved in shaping the course of my miserable life from the start. I'd never stood a chance. Chaos are raised in the knowledge that our path has already been chosen by the Fates, but somehow, knowing I'd always been nothing more than a player in my family's twisted game of power, was so much worse.

"What are you going to do with us?" Odio asked, momentarily jarring me from the fury roiling in my blood.

Diarke tore his eyes away from me. "It will take time, but when a Chaos messenger next arrives, I'll send Sirain back with them. There's a chance she can still carry out our plan. Of course, she knows what will happen if she fails." He looked at Tiesa once more, who was eyeing him warily, before turning to my cousin. "You and the Cupid will have to die, of course. I'm sure you understand. Loose ends and all that."

Odio roared, lurching forward again, but Diarke lifted a knee and kicked, sending him tumbling backwards, where he landed on his chained wings with an aching thud. I winced, watching as he rolled onto his side, shoving back up onto his knees.

His eyes met mine and I shuddered at the reckless fury burning there. He didn't need to speak. The flames spoke louder than any words he could utter. We would take Diarke down or die trying.

A calm settled over me as I drew a breath. He was right. We were cornered, and that made us more dangerous than ever. The king's threat of harming Kwellen was null and void when Odio would die either way. I was loath to return to Helle and I certainly didn't want to help the king or his brother with their plans for domination.

For the first time, the choice lay in front of me with startling clarity. I would kill Diarke. Or he would kill me and take me out of the equation. I couldn't halt the war. I couldn't stop the king from attacking Hehven. But I could prevent the farce of my marriage to Dashuri. I could try to stop Diarke.

I rotated my wrists, biting my lip to hide the pain as I folded my thumb against my palm to pull my hand free from the slackened ropes. Pace had vowed I'd never return to Helle. Now that he was dead, I would have to fulfil that promise myself. The back of my throat burned as Diarke smirked, his dagger held loosely in his hand, while Odio struggled to his feet.

This is for you, Pace, I thought, as I pulled my hand free and lunged.

44
Pace

My heart launched into my throat as Sirain threw herself towards Diarke. She barely made it a stride before an arrow sliced through the shadows, sinking into her chest, the force of it sending her sprawling backwards down the steps.

My world stopped.

All common sense evaporated as I dove from the top of the tower, tucking in my wings. The wind roared against my ears, but it couldn't drown out the thundering of my heart as I plummeted towards the courtyard, not quite fast enough. I cried out, my anguish lost to the wind, as Odio charged at Diarke with his hands still behind his back. Somehow, he succeeded in knocking the dagger to the floor, where it skittered across the steps, but then soldiers were there, dragging Odio back.

Almost there.

The guards threw Odio to the ground beside Sirain. *Sirain.* Lying on her back, her head to the side, the arrow protruded from her chest in a nightmarish vision I would never be able to erase. All around the courtyard, the soldiers sped towards the commotion, but I barely noticed, keeping my attention on Sirain, watching, pleading, for any sign of movement.

So close.

Panic vibrated, a steady hum in my chest as Odio shoved at Sirain with his knees, his frantic cries reaching me on the wind. I whipped open my wings with a crack that echoed around the courtyard, the movement slowing my descent enough to allow me to draw my blade. Tiesa gasped, her green eyes widening as I landed beside them, my grief instantly smothered by rage as I bared my teeth at the soldiers forming a ring around my friends.

My breathing was slow and steady as I gripped my sword, the soldiers pausing for the briefest second in surprise. The price of that pause was death. I spun, taking down soldier after soldier, no longer caring about the consequences.

Out of the corner of my eye, I was aware of Diarke and the Midnight Queen still on the steps, a handful of soldiers at their side. Where Diarke's eyes gleamed with pleasure at the bloodshed before him, the human queen's face was impassive and cold. The fact that they hadn't bothered to leave—didn't even consider us a threat—irked me. He was so sure we wouldn't be able to fight our way out. I gripped my blade harder.

"Free me," Odio snarled, his wings to me as he held out his bound arms.

I brought down my blade, not stopping to check whether I'd caught any feathers, before turning back to the fray. Odio snatched a sword from a fallen human, and his bound wings brushed against mine as he joined me.

I waited for the arrows, but they didn't come. Somewhere someone was yelling, but the clarity of the command was lost amongst the clashing of steel and screams of pain. I could only guess the archers were unable to get a clean shot.

A yell sounded and I spun to find Tiesa breathing hard as she removed her blade from a soldier. At some point, Odio must have freed her, too, and she gave me the briefest nod before returning to the fight.

Every time I was granted a second to breathe, I glanced behind me at where Sirain lay, still and unmoving. She had to be okay. She had to be.

Rage narrowed my deadly focus until all I could hear, all I wanted, was the groan of a falling soldier or the warm spray of blood against my skin. The more that fell, the closer we were to escaping. They didn't have to fight me. They could turn and run. They should.

"You're not dead," Odio growled as we smashed together again, turning a small circle, wing to wing, as we surveyed the fresh ring of advancing human soldiers.

"Dragon scales," I bit out.

I pushed away from him and drove my sword into the nearest human, before pulling back and slicing across another.

"Sirain?" I grunted, rolling my neck as I eyed my next opponent.

Odio made a low, painful sound that wrapped itself around my heart, stealing my breath. When I finally managed to drag air into my lungs, I released it with a roar that I hoped rattled the Fates themselves. Carving my sword through the air in a deadly arc, I spun again, and this time, found myself face to face with Sirain's father.

I blinked, trying to make sense of what I was seeing. No. He couldn't be King Hadeon. He had no wings.

"Diarke," I hissed.

He stared at me, curiosity flickering in his burgundy eyes, but not a hint of fear. Two soldiers stood at his side, their short swords drawn and their eyes wide as they tried to keep track of Tiesa and Odio fighting behind me. Even as I watched, one of them looked at me, his mouth opening. He took a step forward, but I lunged, slamming the hilt of my sword down on his wrist, causing him to drop his blade. It had barely hit the ground before I drove my own up through his chin.

Turning to Lord Diarke once more, white hot flames of fury

flickering in my peripheral, I advanced, ready to end the life of the human who'd been the cause of so much death.

Before I could draw back my blade, a blinding pain slammed against my skull, and I stumbled. Arms wrapped around mine, fingers prising my sword from my hand, and I roared as I fought against the many pairs of hands gripping me, harsh breath and sweat stinging my nose.

"It's over, Dragoste."

Gasping for air, I glared at Diarke, who stood watching with that same curious expression. I wanted to rip it from his face. As I pulled against my captors, however, his words settled in my mind, and I stilled. He knew who I was. He looked almost exactly like King Hadeon. My stomach lurched at the realisation.

Sweat stung my eyes even as the freezing wind pebbled my skin, and I tried to think back to the book Amare had retrieved from the Isle of Fate. King Hadeon was the eldest of three. I knew Odio's mother had died when he was born, but I realised too late that Sirain had never spoken of an uncle.

A pained grunt sounded behind me and I tried to turn, but the soldiers holding me in place blocked my view.

"Odio?" I called out, replenished fear rising rapidly in my gut.

The clashing of sword against sword had stopped. and the absence of sound was deafening.

"Odio!" I yelled.

"Let him see," Diarke said, boredom permeating each syllable.

The soldiers shoved me roughly around and my chest tightened. Odio was on his knees, surrounded by three guards, a blade at his throat. Beside him, Tiesa was being held up by two soldiers, blood dripping down her face, her eyes closed.

"This battle was lost to you before you were even born." Diarke descended a step, stopping in front of me. "Even now, I only let this façade go on as long as it did out of curiosity. A Cupid, slaughtering humans? Whatever would Queen Maluhia say?"

"Don't you dare speak my mother's name," I snarled, gritting my teeth as I resisted the futile urge to strain against my captors. "Why are you doing this?"

Diarke sighed heavily. "I've already explained everything to your friends, and there's no point repeating myself to a corpse."

A movement to the Lord of Newbold's right caught my attention and I eyed the Midnight Queen warily as she drew closer. I'd teased Odio about his inappropriate crush, but I could understand now why he'd been drawn to her. Despite being a similar age to my parents, she was beautiful in a cold and dark way that both captivated and terrified me.

"Why are you helping him, *Luna*?" I snipped.

Her dark blue eyes widened at the use of her given name, her shoulders stiffening as she stared down at me. The soldiers gripping me tried desperately to force me to my knees before the human rulers, but I would not bend. I would not yield without a fight.

"Why are you helping him slaughter your own kind?" I demanded, a roar of frustration bursting from me as I threw one guard backwards down the steps with my wing. "Do you know he's not human? He doesn't care about you or your people."

The Midnight Queen continued to stare at me, her mask of cool indifference firmly back in place as she reached Diarke's side. I wasn't sure what I'd been expecting by reaching out to her. She was clearly as power hungry as him. After all, it was why he'd aligned himself with her instead of Emeric or Marlowe.

"Enough," Diarke barked. "I have much more pressing matters to attend to this evening than dealing with you."

"You won't get away with this," Odio's voice rang out from

behind me. "You can't just kill three members of the royal families without repercussions. The Fates—"

Diarke's deep laugh drowned the rest of Odio's words, rippling across the courtyard until it faded into the shadows. He raised a hand, sweeping it over us in a dismissive gesture that kindled the flames flickering in my blood. "Kill them."

A roar ripped from my throat as I pulled with all my might against the humans holding me, trying to get to Diarke. I would tear him apart limb by limb with my bare hands if I had to.

He stared at me, unblinking and unphased, but that only infuriated me more. Drawing a breath, I extended my wings with all my might, sending two guards hurtling to the floor. I tried to rip my arms from the others, but they held firm.

Terror built in my throat as the soldier holding his sword to Odio's throat withdrew his weapon, ready to strike.

Then, the human paused, looking past me with wide eyes. His arm dropped to his side, the tip of his blade clanking against the ground. Breathing hard, I tried to figure out what had happened—what I'd done—when a pained grunt echoed through the courtyard. I turned in time to watch as Diarke fell to his knees. His dark eyes wide, his mouth hung open as he clutched his chest, but it was only when he fell forward, slipping face-first down the remaining three steps, that I saw why. A long onyx dagger protruded from his back, sunk up to the hilt. I stared at it in confusion for a moment, before lifting my gaze to the only possible explanation.

The Midnight Queen stood, her eyes fixed on Diarke's body, as blood began pooling on the steps beneath him. Her chin was high, a defiance and hatred in her eyes that chilled me to the core.

"It's done," she said, her voice quiet but clear. "Release them."

The bruising grip around my arms loosened and then

disappeared as the soldiers stepped back. I stared at the queen, a million questions on my tongue, but I swallowed them down. They would have to wait. Turning, I raced to Sirain, dropping to my knees at her side.

45
Sirain

There was too much pain to catalogue, and I wasn't sure which was worse: the intense pressure on my chest making it hard to breathe, the freezing ground icing my bones, the pounding in my skull, or the unnatural way my wing was bent. The only comfort was the gentle caress against my cheek, the smell of sunshine and beaches washing over me like a warm summer's day. There was something about that smell that hurt more than any physical pain, though. A sense that I shouldn't be feeling that touch or smelling that scent. That I never would again. A hollowness echoed deep inside me, and I curled into the darkness.

"Sirain?"

Voices were growing closer, louder, and more insistent. I knew I'd have to answer them, but I was so far away. They'd arrive soon. I wasn't sure I wanted them to. If I did, I'd have to face something I was sure I didn't want to.

"Sirain. Wake up."

A drop of moisture fell on my cheek, and I frowned.

"Pull it out."

"No!"

"If you won't, I will!"

The voices were closer. Why were they angry? The sharp,

heavy, pressure on my chest worsened for a brief second and I winced, but then it released, and I sat up with a gasp, drawing in a breath as a wave of pain washed through my body.

"Sirain?"

I shook my head, trying to clear the haze as my eyes slowly adjusted to the flame-lit darkness. Turning towards the familiar voice, my heart stilled in my chest as I found a pair of gilded eyes searing into mine. Eyes that shouldn't be there. Was I dead? Was that why I was in so much pain?

Reaching out, I touched my fingers to his cheek, finding it warm but damp. I frowned as I took in his blood-soaked hair, more pink than white. His wings were filthy, stained black, grey and red, as was his golden-brown skin. I touched a finger to the warm, dark red scales across his bare chest and shook my head, hoping to clear the pounding, but it just ached more. Gingerly, I reached to the back of my skull and the wound that throbbed there, but when my fingers brushed the edges of the abrasion, I pulled back with a wince.

"Sirain," Pace said gently, pushing hair from my face and tucking it behind my ear. "Are you okay?"

I squinted up at him. "You're dead."

"Not the last time I checked." The corners of his mouth twitched before his brows dropped into a frown and he lifted my hands to his lips. "You, however, took an arrow to the chest. I thought you'd left me."

My gaze dropped to the band of dragon scales tied around my chest. One of them was heavily dented, as though it had caved in on itself. I touched a finger to it, pressing into the indentation and hissing as the bruise beneath throbbed in protest. My eyes burned as I looked back at Pace, my mind finally accepting that the Cupid in front of me was real, and I sat up, launching myself at him. Unshed tears seared the back of my throat as I wrapped my arms around his shoulders, burying my face in his neck. Pace's arms encircled me, gripping me to him as he pressed kisses to any skin he could reach. If anything was going to kill me today, it would be those Fated lips.

"I thought you were dead," I repeated. "I saw you in the courtyard. I—"

"I'm here," he soothed. "We're all here."

His words settled and I reluctantly pulled back, taking in the bloodied bodies strewn across the courtyard. My stomach twisted as I realised I'd lain on the ground, oblivious to the deadly devastation being wreaked around me. There were so many. My attention landed on a pair of black boots, and I looked up to find Odio standing beside me, relief stark on his sharp features. I raised a hand and he grabbed hold of it, hauling me to my feet. Even as my body protested, my wing straightening, I allowed him to pull me to his chest in a brief but fierce embrace.

As he released me, I turned, seeking out a different pair of wings. Tiesa gave me a small smile, her own hair and feathers streaked with blood and gore. I took a small step towards her, then paused as she raised an eyebrow. I inclined my head, a smile pulling at my lips as she did the same.

"As is law, Newbold is now mine."

I whirled to find that the Midnight Queen had moved to the top of the steps, her crown glinting like stars amongst her long, dark hair. Her voice rang out, a rich and melodic chime against the freezing night. I glanced up at Pace in confusion and in answer, he looked at a body lying face down on the steps, a dagger protruding from his back. My eyes widened as I arranged the pieces of what had happened while I'd been unconscious.

"No harm shall come to the angels and demons," she continued, her dark gaze landing on us. "I wish to speak to them, and while they are in Newbold, they are to be treated as guests. Anyone who disobeys my order will pay with their life."

After a beat, all the remaining soldiers stowed their weapons, and in a clatter of armour and grunts, they dropped to their knees, their heads bowed to their new queen.

"Come," the Midnight Queen commanded, turning towards the gaping entrance to Diarke's castle.

I looked at Pace, questioning, but he merely stared after the Midnight Queen, his eyes narrowed and his jaw set.

"We should leave now," Tiesa said, glancing up at the sky. "Escape while we have the chance."

Odio snorted a laugh at my other side. "How far do you think you'll be able to fly? You can barely hold your own head up."

"We can't abandon Emeric," I said, my gaze lifting to the tower we'd been imprisoned in, as I wondered whether he had any idea what had transpired below. Had the screams and clashes of weaponry reached that high?

Pace's fingers interlaced with mine, pulling me to his side. His eyes were still fixed on the queen's retreating figure. "Sirain's right. We can't leave without ensuring Emeric is okay. But Odio also has a point. If we try to leave now, we won't get far. Plus, the Midnight Queen has answers we need. She worked with Diarke for years."

Tiesa snorted. "And she just murdered him."

"Which means she's on our side," Odio countered.

"Or it means she can't be trusted." I sighed, glancing at the soldiers eyeing us warily through narrowed eyes. "Either way, we need to decide quickly, before revenge becomes a risk this lot decide is worth taking."

Pace stooped and picked up his sword, the golden hilt gleaming as he slid it into the scabbard at his hip. "Let's go."

Plucking an abandoned blade from a fallen soldier, I slipped it into place between my wings, sharing a look with my cousin as I did so. If we could be certain of one thing, it was that we would not be able to relax while we remained in Newbold.

Soldiers fell in around us, keeping their distance, as we marched up the steps and into the castle. The throbbing in my head had subsided, but my skin was tight with dried blood and my chest ached with every inhale.

"By the way," I said, admiring the large stone archway as we passed underneath. A curling dragon was carved into the side, its mouth open, mid roar, at the centre. "Not that it's not a good look on you, but where's your shirt?"

Pace smirked and shook his head, tugging me through the dark archway, and my eyes widened as I took in the sweeping atrium of intersecting arches. The gleaming black stone was lit by several flame-filled chandeliers, the light casting long shadows across the polished floor.

The Midnight Queen waited at the bottom of a wide set of stairs, soldiers at her side. "I will arrange rooms for you to freshen up in," she said. "Then, we can talk."

"No," Pace said firmly. "You may have killed Diarke, but that doesn't mean you've earned our trust. We talk now."

The human queen looked at him, her gaze unwavering, before turning to me. I met her dark stare with my chin high until she finally let out a small sigh.

"Fine. If you wish to talk while covered in blood and entrails, so be it." She turned, walking towards a gaping arch-way. "This way."

Our footsteps echoed as we crossed the atrium, entering the large open space, but it wasn't a throne room as I'd been expecting.

As the queen led us forward, leaving the soldiers at the entrance, I peered up at the ceiling, so high, I could barely make out the beams in the shadows above. Heat rolled around the room from an enormous fireplace, at least the height of two grown males, the flames as big as trees.

The Midnight Queen took a seat on a large, cushioned chair, the back and arms made of intricately carved wood. As we drew closer, I realised it was a dragon, its claws gripping the armrests as its wings sprawled across the back.

"Come. Sit," the queen said, gesturing to the array of seating spread out before her.

I selected a backless bench, lined with embroidered red and gold cushions, wide enough for Pace to sit beside me. Odio took a chair and spun it, straddling as he liked to do, while Tiesa perched on a chaise longue, her eyes flitting constantly to the entry arch. There was no door to close, though, and I wondered whether that was why the Dalibor queen had selected this room for us.

She smiled, her blood red lips pressing together as though pained. "I know you must have many questions."

I shared a look with Pace, and he squeezed my hand. "The leader of Dalibor, Lord Emeric Bickerstaff, is imprisoned in one of the towers," I said. "We'd like to request his immediate release."

The queen raised her eyebrows in surprise. "Of course. I've already given orders for his release. He will be given the same hospitality I've offered you."

Relief sagged my shoulders and I exhaled. "Thank you."

"Why did you kill Lord Diarke?" Pace asked, his grip tightening on mine. "I thought you were working together?"

The Midnight Queen's dark blue eyes drifted shut as she leaned against her chair and inhaled deeply. When she opened them, they were filled with such pain I sucked in a breath.

"You called me Luna," she said, tilting her head as she stared at Pace. "So few people remember the name given to me by my parents. How do you know it?"

"I found it in a book. I know you have a twin brother, Sol, too."

A sad smile curved the Midnight Queen's lips, and she turned her gaze to the roaring fire beside us, the wood cracking and spitting at the hearth. "My brother and I were inseparable from birth," she said softly. "Born as two sides of the same coin, Sol was bronzed and blond, full of smiles and warmth; while I was pale and dark, quiet and calm. I overheard servants talking about me once when I was small, saying it was unnatural for a child to never cry.

"Although Sol was born two minutes before me, we swore as soon as we were able to that we would rule together or not at all. Our parents told us it was preposterous, but we couldn't be swayed. War broke out when we were sixteen. Newbold attacked us while our country slept, breaching our castle's defences, and killing our parents. It was declared a miracle that we were spared.

"As the people of Dalibor looked to us for guidance, we made a pact. We would be the perfect solution for the unrest that had shaken our land to its core. Sol would rule the twelve hours of day and I would rule the twelve hours of night. We would never be unprotected again."

I swallowed, my throat dry, as I tried to imagine taking control of a war-ravaged country at sixteen—just a little younger than Malin.

The Midnight Queen stood and drifted to a cabinet against the wall, pouring a large measure of golden liquid into a glass and downing half before refilling it. She looked at us in question, but I shook my head, aware of the others doing the same.

"What happened to Sol?" I asked, as the queen continued to sip her drink, her distant gaze staring past the flames licking at the stone fireplace.

"To explain what happened to Sol, I must go back a step," she said, pinching the bridge of her nose. "Around my seventeenth birthday, I was in my bedchambers when I heard a strange sound outside. I grabbed a dagger from my dresser and opened the balcony doors. That was the first time I saw a Chaos."

Her eyes landed briefly on Odio, and my heart stuttered.

She'd referred to us as 'angels' and 'demons', but she clearly knew who we really were.

"Engano told me he was there to deliver an arrow, and that I mustn't tell anyone I'd seen him." She shook her head and knocked back most of her drink. "I was so young and naïve. We stayed up all night talking, and he promised he'd try to return."

"Diarke," Odio muttered. "Engano was Diarke, wasn't he?"

My eyes widened and I looked to the Midnight Queen for confirmation.

"It was all part of his plan," she said, her features twisting. "He lured me with friendship and the promise it might blossom into something more when I was older. I thought I was in love. It made ruling the nights so much easier to bear, knowing I would see him. It also made keeping it a secret from my brother easier, too.

"When I turned eighteen, Sol went missing." She shook her head, unshed tears causing her eyes to gleam in the firelight. "I was distraught. The country spent days searching for him, but it was as if he'd vanished. Then, Engano returned. He told me that if I ever wanted to see Sol again, I had to do exactly as he said."

The Midnight Queen threw her empty glass into the fireplace with such force, the flames erupted with a roar, and I startled, Pace jumping to his feet to shield me.

"Sorry," she muttered, turning away from us.

I watched the queen's shoulders rise and fall as she tried to regain her composure, the roaring of the flames slowly returning to their gentle crackle. Tugging at Pace's hand, he shared a look with Odio before cautiously reclaiming his seat.

"Where is Sol now?" I asked.

The human queen's shoulders sagged, and she braced herself against the cabinet. "He was being held in the West Tower."

"I'm sorry," Pace offered.

Something in the soft way he spoke caused me to wonder if he was thinking of his own imprisonment—of the damage that had been done after a couple of months. What would it be like to endure years of such torture? I squeezed his fingers and he offered me a tight smile, the clouds clearing from his expression.

"Are you satisfied that I mean you no harm?" the Midnight Queen asked, returning to her high-backed chair, and sinking onto it, a fresh glass in her hand.

"Diarke may have taken your brother," I said carefully, "but your actions since then have cost the lives of thousands."

She stared at me, her chin raised. "War ravaged our world long before Engano decided to use me and I'm sure it will again even now he's gone. People are greedy and power is all consuming. No one forced the soldiers to fight. There are hundreds of thousands of people in Newbold. If they'd wanted to make a stand against Diarke, they could have."

"You feel no remorse for the people who've been slaughtered because of your alliance?" Pace asked, incredulity lacing his words.

The queen exhaled, staring at the amber liquid in her glass. "Of course, I regret the lives lost. But I chose my brother, and I would choose him again. I'll do whatever it takes to save the ones I love."

My retort lodged in my throat. Would I do the same? If King Hadeon took Pace, would I allow thousands to die to keep him alive? If he hadn't taken Kwellen, the lives I'd taken today might have been spared. Swallowing, I gripped Pace's hand a little tighter. Perhaps we weren't so different after all.

46
Pace

"The rooms I've requested for you are yours for as long as you wish," the Midnight Queen said, settling back against her chair, her slender white fingers resting on top of the carved dragon claws. "However, I understand you are uncomfortable here, and if you wish to leave, I assure you may do so safely."

"Thank you," I said, inclining my head. "We appreciate your hospitality."

The dried blood had tightened against my skin, the smell of death worsened by the roaring fire heating the vast room. Glancing at the others, I knew the effects of battle were taking their toll, the adrenaline long since waned. I pushed to my feet, and Sirain rose with me. She hadn't let go of my hand since we'd entered the castle, and I was glad of it. I never wanted to let her go again.

An elderly human woman appeared in the entrance to the room, dwarfed by the tall archway. Her grey hair was pulled in a severe bun and her face deeply lined. She eyed us each in turn before dipping a shallow curtsey, her thick black skirts brushing the stone floor. "Your rooms are ready."

I looked at the Midnight Queen, and she nodded. "Go. Rest. Know you are safe within these walls."

My jaw worked as I considered our options. I believed what she'd told us. There was no reason to lie. Everything came down to the Hadeons and it seemed the human queen's life had been manipulated by their existence even longer than ours.

The elderly woman cleared her throat and with a sigh of resignation, I started towards her, the others following suit. Reaching up, I brushed the hair from my forehead and found the strands hardened with blood and sweat. Despite my trepidation at remaining in the castle, the thought of a hot bath had my heart quickening.

Sirain's fingers tightened around mine and I looked down to find her watching me with concern.

"I don't want them to separate us," she said softly.

"All the rooms are next to each other," the human woman assured us as we reached her. "Her Majesty has also ordered the soldiers to stay down here. If you'll follow me, I will escort you to your rooms."

Sirain nodded, the tension easing from her shoulders just a little, and a longing ravished my chest. I wanted to take away all her worry. More than anything, I wanted to give Sirain peace— a life where she didn't have to worry about her family trying to destroy her. An existence that involved her, me, and time to be together. It was a selfish and unrealistic dream, but I allowed myself to indulge in the fantasy a few seconds more, before pushing it from my mind.

"Come on." Bringing her hand to my lips, I brushed a kiss against her knuckles before following the woman.

She led us back to the wide staircase. It appeared she'd told us the truth, as no soldiers moved to follow us, and the only sound was that of our own weary footsteps as we trudged up the broad stone steps behind her.

Thick woven carpets of red and grey ran down the middle of the hallways, the walls lit by intricate sconces of weaving strips of metal, flames licking between the gaps. Sirain leaned into me as we followed the human, eyeing the closed doors we passed.

"Here," the grey-haired woman announced, turning and gesturing to doors on either side of the corridor. "These four rooms are yours for as long as you require them. Baths have been drawn, and an assortment of clean garments have been provided. Although, I'm not sure about the . . ." She gestured at our wings briefly, then pursed her lips. "The Midnight Queen has arranged for dinner in an hour. I will come and fetch you then."

Despite being so hungry my gut ached, I wasn't sure about sitting down to a meal in Lord Diarke's home; even if he was dead. I pressed my lips together, holding my hesitation at bay. We could discuss it together once we'd cleaned up.

"Are you even bothered Diarke's dead?" Odio asked as the human woman turned and made to continue down the hallway.

She paused, glancing at him over her shoulder as her chin lifted before continuing down the corridor. "I'm from Dalibor."

I met Odio's eye and raised an eyebrow in question. He shrugged, seemingly satisfied with the human's answer.

Tiesa pushed open one of the doors, peeking inside. "There's a window," she said, her serious tone implying it wasn't the décor she was complimenting.

"If anyone suspects foul play, yell," Odio said. "Keep the window unlatched and be ready to fly."

I nodded, watching Sirain reach out and squeeze his arm as he opened his own door. Once he and Tiesa had disappeared into their rooms, she turned to me.

"I don't want to leave you," I murmured, my hands finding her waist, pulling her to me.

"We're both covered in blood," she said, gently shoving me away.

I frowned, tugging her back to me. "You think I care about a little blood? I thought I'd lost you today, Sirain. I saw that arrow hit your chest and . . ."

I dropped my gaze, sucking in a shuddered breath as the pain of watching her fall down those steps hit me anew.

"You didn't lose me," she said, reaching up to stroke my face. "I'm here."

I closed my eyes, leaning my cheek into her palm. "I'm so sorry. I should have told Odio, no. I shouldn't have left you."

"No, you shouldn't have," she agreed, looking away as her shoulders sagged. "But we've both done things we shouldn't have done."

I leaned forward, resting my forehead against hers as the warmth of her breath caressed my skin. It was a sensation I would never take for granted again.

After a moment, she stepped back, reaching for the handle of one of the remaining rooms. I watched her, a thousand words on my lips, but before I could voice them, she gave me a reassuring smile and stepped inside, closing the door behind her.

47
Sirain

Exhaling, I leaned against the door for a moment. Even though I'd seen him, touched him, the sight of him face down in the courtyard, blood pooling around his lifeless body, haunted me every time I closed my eyes.

A moan fell from my lips as my gaze fell on a large, bronze, roll top bath, steam rising from the heated water within. I strode towards it, stripping off my blood-soaked clothes as I went, before climbing in and lowering myself down with a satisfied hiss.

The water was scented with cloves and cinnamon, and I leaned back, soaking my hair as I inhaled the warming scent, allowing it to soothe my aching muscles. A selection of soaps had been left on a raised wooden table beside the bath and I made use of every single one, scrubbing and lathering until I could no longer feel the blood and sweat that had permeated my skin and hair.

Even as I relished in the calm, shadows loomed in the silence, the sound of clashing blades and cries of agony echoing in my mind. I'd taken so many lives. I pressed my lips together as my throat thickened. How many had fallen at the end of my blade, my blind rage indifferent as I exacted revenge for Pace's death? A death that hadn't happened. Closing my eyes, I sank beneath the water, as though it might wash away some of the guilt weighting my heart. I stayed below until my lungs burned.

Bursting to the surface, I shoved my soaking hair from my face and sucked in a breath. We might have survived, but there were still lives at stake. The king would find out what had happened to his brother sooner rather than later, and he would seek vengeance. My heart quickened at the thought of Kwellen, alone in the freezing dungeons of Hadeon Castle. What if the king took his life as retribution?

A knock sounded at the door, and I froze, wondering if the hour had passed so quickly.

"Who is it?" I called.

"Pace. May I come in?"

I swallowed, staring at the door, as my heart beat a little faster. It wasn't like he hadn't already seen me undressed, but that had been before. Before I'd ruined everything.

"Sirain?" he called. "Are you all right?"

"I'm still in the bath," I answered, my cheeks heating. "Could you come back in a few minutes?"

The silence that followed was agony, and I held my breath, waiting for his response.

"Sirain," he tried again, his voice firmer than before. "May I come in?"

I could insist he come back later—perhaps I should—but I didn't want to. It seemed the Fates were determined to keep us apart, so why shouldn't I spend every second I could with him?

"Come in," I called, sinking lower in the water, so that it lapped at my bottom lip.

Pace opened the door, stepping inside and closing it behind him, before turning to look at where I watched him over the rim of the bath. My blood thrummed in my veins as I drank him in. He'd clearly bathed as quickly as possible, his hair still damp and hanging across his forehead. The white shirt he'd managed to wrangle around his wings—which were dripping onto the carpet—was untucked and wet in places, clinging to his torso.

"Didn't you like your bath?" I asked as he stalked towards me, fire gleaming in his eyes.

"I liked it just fine," he said, his voice low as he reached my side. "I just like you more."

His heated gaze trailed across the water, and I froze, unable to move, until his eyes found mine again.

"I'm almost done," I said, aware his breathing had quickened, his fingers gripping the edge of the tub. "I just need to wash my wings."

Pace's throat bobbed and he nodded, taking the sponge from my hand. His fingers grazed mine, leaving blazing trails of fire in their wake.

"Sit forward," he commanded.

I did as he said, the water sloshing a little over the sides, as I wrapped my arms around my knees and carefully extended one of my wings. My eyes closed, my breath hitching as Pace carefully and gently ran the sponge along the arch of my wing, his fingers stroking through my feathers.

"Are you injured anywhere?" he asked, his voice rough as he traced his fingers down the centre of my spine, causing me to shudder.

I shook my head. "No. It seems the dragon scales are more than just impenetrable."

Pace hummed in agreement. "They saved my life. It's a shame there aren't more dragons. They could save a lot of lives in the Wendell Islands."

I frowned, trailing my fingers through the water in front of me. "Isn't the war over now?"

"It depends on the Midnight Queen," Pace said, gently folding my wing and coaxing out the other. "She's taken control of Newbold. Who's to say she won't grow hungry for more power?"

Another shudder shook my body, but this time it was nothing to do with Pace's caress. "I still can't believe Lord Diarke was a Chaos. How ruthless does one have to be to cut off your own wings?"

"I saw in a history book that the king was one of three siblings. I knew Odio's mother had died, but it never occurred to me you didn't know about the third."

I frowned. "He said that Odio's mother had been an unfortunate sacrifice."

Pace paused in his cleaning, water dripping noisily from the sponge. "He killed her?"

"Just another question in a thousand we need answers for."

"You're done," Pace said, pressing his lips to the base of my neck. "Do you want me to go?"

I shook my head. "Pass me a towel?"

As he moved to the bed, picking up the towel that had been left out, I stood, twisting the water out of my hair over my shoulder. When Pace turned, his jaw slackened as his eyes slowly drank in every inch of me.

"Towel?" I repeated, a small smile on my lips.

Pace strode forward, the intensity on his face causing my heart to stutter. He held out the towel, and I stepped out of the bath onto the wooden step, smiling as I realised we were almost eye to eye as he wrapped it around me.

"You have a bruise," he murmured. Stepping back, he pulled the towel down a little to reveal a circular dark purple mark right over my heart. He shook his head. "If you hadn't had the dragon scales . . ."

"But I did," I said, tilting his chin to force him to look at me. "If we lived by 'what ifs', we'd drown."

He stared at me for a minute, his eyes searching mine, then dipped his head and brushed his lips over the bruise. My breath hitched, and when he looked up at me through thick lashes, he set my heart alight.

Reaching out, I took his face in my hands and pulled him to me, claiming his lips, his mouth, as though I might die if I didn't. Pace's arms moved around my waist, gripping me tightly against him as he returned the kiss with matching urgency. A low rumbling moan vibrated in his chest, and I slid my arms around his neck, winding my fingers in his damp locks.

Pace's hands swept down my sides, wrapping around my thighs, lifting me up, and I gasped as I hooked my legs around his waist.

"Sirain," he breathed between bruising kisses. "I won't ever leave you again."

I caught his plump bottom lip between my teeth before pulling his mouth back against mine. "You'd better not."

He walked us backwards towards the bed, but I pulled back, breathing hard.

"That woman will be knocking for us any minute," I said.

"She can wait," Pace grumbled, his lips caressing every available inch of skin along my jaw and neck.

I laughed, unwrapping my legs from around him and lowering to the floor. "I don't think Odio and Tiesa will appreciate waiting."

Pace groaned and reluctantly stepped back. "Fine."

Biting back a smirk, I watched as he sat down on the bed and picked up the shirt that had been laid out on the bed, carefully tearing slits into the back to accommodate my wings. My heart swelled and I bent down and kissed his temple before turning away to dress.

48
Pace

Finding things to occupy my hands and eyes while Sirain dressed was a test of self-control I barely passed, and when a loud knock sounded at the door, I leapt to my feet in relief. She'd been right, of course. I craved her more than air, but I didn't want a time limit when we could finally be together, and I certainly didn't want to be interrupted.

Odio and Tiesa were already in the hallway, and I noted that, just as I'd insisted with Sirain, she wore the larger dragon scale armour while Odio wore the thinner strip across his chest. Tiesa gave me a smile, and when it didn't quite reach her eyes, it took everything I had to hide my wince. The guilt I carried for dragging her into this with me—for the darkness that was now gouged into her heart by taking lives—I pushed down to deal with later. I only hoped that our friendship was strong enough for her to forgive me.

"I don't think I've ever seen you in anything other than black," Sirain said, frowning at Odio's thick brown shirt.

He wrinkled his nose at her, gently shoving her in the direction of the human woman who'd begun to head towards the staircase.

"And what's that?" Sirain asked, squinting over her shoulder at him.

Odio raised his eyebrows, evidently knowing what his cousin was talking about, as he pulled at his long black braid, twisted in a complicated style common in Hehven between his fingers.

"Tiesa did it," he said with a shrug.

My eyebrows shot up as Sirain choked on a breath.

"You're doing each other's hair now?" she hissed. "Does this mean you're . . . friends?"

"We didn't do each other's hair. I did his hair," Tiesa scoffed. "It means nothing."

Odio pressed his hands to his heart. "In Helle, braiding someone's hair is a declaration of love. I thought we were to be married."

Tiesa's green eyes widened as she looked between us. I fought back a smile, but Sirain immediately burst out laughing, and Tiesa's expression disintegrated into a glare as she punched Odio in the shoulder.

Sirain continued chuckling to herself, and my heart soared at the sound. Just a couple of hours ago, I thought I'd never hear her laughter again.

"Are we seriously going to eat?" Tiesa asked, drawing level with me, her eyes narrowed on the grey-haired woman in front of us.

I sighed. "If the queen wanted to kill us, why wait until we're bathed and clean? She could have ordered the soldiers to slaughter us in the courtyard after she killed Diarke. I don't trust her, but I don't think she's going to harm us."

"I agree," Odio said from behind me. "And I'm starving."

We descended the stairs and followed the woman down a wide hallway. All the rooms were large and the ceilings twice as high as any I'd ever seen. In a country as bitterly cold as Newbold, it would have made sense to make the rooms smaller and easier to heat. It would be possible to fly around the ground floor of the castle and I wondered what purpose it served, especially as its owner had hacked off his wings. I shuddered.

Before long, the smell of food curled its way towards us, and my questions were forgotten as I inhaled the rich, warm scent. The elderly human woman halted and gestured at a set of intricately carved wooden doors, opened to reveal a large dining room. A long table filled the space, two humans already seated at one end.

"Emeric!" My chest swelled with relief at the sight of the human lord, and he stood, clean and freshly shaven, beaming as we entered the room.

"There you are! I'm so glad to see you all."

Perhaps we should have taken time to bow before the human queen, but all niceties were forgotten as I strode across the room, the lord pulling me into an embrace. Exhaustion was evident in his eyes despite his warm smile, and I knew I probably looked the same. The relief of victory—of surviving—was just a thin coating, masking the grief and pain.

Sirain had remained on the other side of the table and when she gave her father a nod, he bowed low in response. Looking between the two of them, my chest tightened at the thought of how different her life might have been if she'd grown up with Emeric. If she'd been raised on love and praise instead of fear and disdain. Would I still have met her, though? Probably not.

"Please, sit," the Midnight Queen said, smiling as she gestured at the empty chairs. If she was irked at our lack of deference, she didn't show it.

I returned to the other side of the table, giving the queen a small bow on my way past to which she inclined her head, her red lips quirking.

"Are you okay?" I asked as I took a seat beside Sirain.

She nodded, leaning her shoulder against mine, and I placed my hand on her thigh, squeezing gently.

When a handful of waiting staff entered the room, lifting the lids from the plates and bowls of food, I realised we hadn't seen a single soldier on our way to the dining hall. The Midnight Queen truly was trying her best to make us feel at ease, and the gesture loosened the tension in my wings just a little.

Loading our plates, stomachs growling at the warm bread and hearty broth, a comfortable silence settled over the table as we ate. The whole experience was so surreal, I had to stop from pinching myself.

Emeric sat to the Midnight Queen's left, deep in conversation about what would happen to Newbold and how best to distribute resources to support cities in all countries affected by the war. It was a serious topic, but as they sipped red wine and smiled, anyone would have thought they were two friends discussing old times. That was Emeric, though. His jovial, confiding manner pulled you in.

I wondered how the queen's brother was. Her eyes still bore the hollowness of grief, and I knew wherever he was, he had a long road to recovery ahead of him. He'd been imprisoned for two decades. The thought sent an icy chill over my skin, my fingers tightening their grip on the spoon in my hand. I exhaled slowly, trying to quell the nausea rising in my gut, focusing on the people around the table instead.

Even more strange than the humans, was the sight of Tiesa and Odio sitting beside Emeric, immersed in their own conversation. I couldn't make out enough words to determine what they were talking about, but between Odio's smirks and Tiesa's eye rolls, it seemed light-hearted enough.

And that was the thing. The light-heartedness was so misplaced. Beyond the warm comfort of the dining hall, dozens of men and women had lost their lives. So many, I'd lost count. I didn't know which rituals the humans followed for their dead.

Had families been informed? How many tears were currently being shed as we filled our stomachs?

Sirain's fingers slid between mine where I was still gripping her thigh and squeezed hard enough for me to turn and look at her. She said nothing, but in the pained depths of her violet-flecked eyes I found understanding. The others weren't happy. Relieved, perhaps. But not happy. Talking and laughing was merely a distraction. I blew out a breath, and Sirain silently leaned her head against my arm.

"What I don't understand," Odio announced as soon as the plates had been cleared, "is why Diarke instigated war between the humans. Was it solely to gain control of all four lands?"

The Midnight Queen nodded.

"And meanwhile, King Hadeon intends to unite Hehven and Helle?"

She nodded again and my eyes narrowed at the Chaos, curious to see where he was going with his line of thought.

"What's their end goal?" he asked, looking at each of us. "To rule both the human lands, Hehven and Helle?"

"I think it's honestly that simple," Sirain said, frowning. "They want ultimate power. For everyone who exists to be under their control. Diarke said that the Hadeons were made for greatness."

I shook my head, my shoulders tensing. "It's over now, though. If we can stop the engagement, tell my parents the truth—"

"He'll take Hehven by force," Sirain said, her wings flexing at her back. "Diarke said the Fates would command it."

"How?" Tiesa demanded. "The Fates would never order Helle to do something like that."

My gut twisted. It was exactly what I'd feared. "The Fates wouldn't. No."

Sirain tensed at my side, her fingers gripping mine as the

awful truth settled around us. She looked up at me, her eyes wide. "Unless . . . the Fates answer to the king."

I will seize fate by the throat; it shall certainly never wholly overcome me.

~ Ludwig van Beethoven

49
Sirain

"I'll be fine," Emeric assured me for the tenth time. "Luna is confident that after a few days, word will have carried to all ships of Newbold and Dalibor's combined withdrawal. I'll be home in a week or so."

I winced. "I hope you're not expecting it to be in one piece."

"My manor was made of things," he said, lightly gripping my shoulders. "The bricks can be torn down, the mortar crumbled, but it will take a lot more than war to destroy the memories."

He pulled me into another embrace before stepping back and clasping arms with Pace.

"Look after each other," he said.

Pace nodded, glancing at me with a smile. "I don't intend to let her out of my sight."

"Time to go," Odio called, pointing at the stripe of grey sky on the horizon, signalling oncoming dawn.

The Midnight Queen stepped forward, inclining her head. "Thank you. If you hadn't come, I don't think I would have had the strength or the opportunity to end this."

I smiled, wanting to ask so much more, but pressing my lips together to hold in my questions. We'd talked all night and she wore her pain for all to see. She would need time to recover, just as her brother would.

"He looked a lot like you when he was younger," the queen said, turning to Odio and fixing him with her dark stare.

My cousin shifted uncomfortably, and I bit back a smile. He'd harboured a crush on the human queen for years, only to discover she'd spent two decades being blackmailed by an uncle we didn't know we'd had.

"Thank you, Your Majesty," Pace said to the queen, patting his pocket where he'd placed a copy of the official letter of surrender to give to Marlowe.

"We'll see you soon," I promised Emeric as we stepped further out into the courtyard, spreading our wings.

I took two running strides towards the wall and leapt, my wings beating as the breeze carrying me higher, soaring up and over. Exhilaration tremored through me at feeling the air moving between my feathers, whipping at my face and hair as we climbed up into the clouds. Even though the Midnight Queen had ordered her troops to stand down, we'd decided it wasn't worth the risk of getting shot down when we'd come so far.

I grimaced as the icy precipitation soaked my clothes, but I knew it wouldn't be for long. In just a couple of hours, we'd be soaring over the warm waters of the Wendell Islands. A longing built deep in my chest for the tropical islands—a place where I could feel safe.

"When we get to Marlowe's," I said, as Pace drew level with me. "I'm going to curl up around that Fated dragon until my hair singes."

Pace laughed, pushing damp hair off his forehead. "I might have to join you."

It was a strange feeling, leaving Newbold behind. We'd flown there to find answers, almost paying with our lives, but things were far from finished, and it seemed the tight knot of anxiety in my chest wasn't going anywhere anytime soon.

I glanced up at where Odio was flying above us, and the knot tightened further. We'd not had a chance to talk about what Diarke had said to him. How had Odio's mother been a sacrifice? Did it mean they'd killed their own sister? If so, why?

Tiesa was flying near him. Not beside him, but near enough that he wasn't alone. My lips pressed together as I imagined Odio allowing her to braid his hair, wondering how something like that could even happen. It appeared some sort of begrudging friendship, or at least understanding, was emerging between the two of them.

The knot in my chest twisted to the point of pain, and I sucked in a breath. Kwellen. Pace had promised I wouldn't return to Helle, but what about my friend? The image of him on his knees, dirty and bleeding, his long dark hair matted, and his wings bound with heavy chains, seared against my heart. We'd faced a monster in Newbold, but there was another still to face.

"Are you all right?" Pace asked, the tip of his wing brushing mine.

I shook my head. "I'm worried about Kwellen."

Pace's face darkened in the way it always did when the king or my brother were mentioned. It was strange to think that not only had they met, but had walked away from the meeting unscathed.

"You know," I said, a thought occurring to me. "Fin found you attractive. He said if he wasn't so disgusted by Cupids on principle, he'd have enjoyed 'breaking you in'."

Pace's eyes widened before scrunching with disgust. He shuddered and rolled, sweeping through a bank of cloud as though trying to cleanse himself. I laughed, the knot in my chest loosening just a little.

"Thanks for that image," Pace said, as he returned to my

side, still shuddering. "Definitely not going to have nightmares about that."

I smiled and tilted my wing, touching it to his. "Don't worry. I'll find a way to distract you if you wake up screaming."

Pace looked at me with a heated intensity that stole my breath, and I thought for a second, he might tackle me out of the sky.

"Come on," he said, beating his wings a little harder. "Let's get back."

We continued the rest of the way in silence, concentrating on riding the currents and soaking up the morning sun as we coasted above the tropical waters of Wendell. By the time we reached the main island, I was warm and dry, but thoroughly exhausted.

Pace landed on the balcony first, pulling open the doors and striding inside without so much as a pause. Tiesa landed just behind him, with me and Odio arriving last. I followed them inside, my heart warming as I found Pace already wrapped in a fierce embrace with the Wendell leader.

"I was so worried," Marlowe said, his eyes closed as he showed no sign of letting Pace go.

I dropped onto my favoured seat, my gaze flitting to the huge red dragon curled in the corner. Bertie opened a large yellow eye and looked at me, huffing a plume of smoke before returning to sleep, and I smiled.

"The dragon scales saved our lives," Pace said, as they pulled apart, still gripping each other's arms. "Did you know they speed up healing?"

Marlowe's wide-eyed expression said he didn't. We were still wearing our armour, just in case, and the human reached out and brushed his fingers over the large red scales across Pace's chest in wonder. "That's incredible."

Pace nodded. "If it wasn't for Bertie, we'd all be dead."

"Pace." Marlowe hung his head, still gripping his friend's

arms. "The war. Newbold's ships are almost here. I'm sure you saw them on the way in."

My smile widened, and I pulled my legs beneath me. "About the war . . ."

Pace grinned at me and reached into his pocket, fishing out the letter we'd brought from the Midnight Queen.

Marlowe took it with a frown, breaking the navy-blue wax seal and unfolding it. I watched his face as the queen's words sank in, his mouth falling open as he looked between us.

"It's over?" he asked. "Truly?"

"Truly," Pace assured him. "We're still trying to put all the pieces together, but it would seem the Hadeons have been orchestrating war between the humans for a long time."

Marlowe staggered backwards, sitting heavily on a chair. "What happened?"

Pace pulled up a chair, turning it round as Odio had with his. "Where are Shanti and Cove?"

"They're on one of our neighbouring islands assessing the damage of the latest attack. They're not due back until tonight."

Pace nodded, then drew a deep breath. "Diarke was actually Engano Hadeon, the king of Helle's brother."

"What?" Marlowe exclaimed. "Lord Diarke had wings?"

Pace winced and I tried to repress a shudder of my own. "No. He cut them off to appear human."

Across the room, Odio swore loudly.

"He manipulated the Midnight Queen," Pace continued. "He gained her trust when she was still a girl, then when she took the throne, he kidnapped her twin brother and used him as leverage."

Marlowe leaned forward, scrubbing a hand over his face. "This is a lot to take in."

"You're telling us," Tiesa muttered.

"What of Emeric?" Marlowe asked, his attention turning to me. "Is he alive?"

I smiled. "Yes. Diarke had him imprisoned but unharmed. He's staying in Newbold for a few days until word has spread of the withdrawal of troops, then he'll sail back to Dalibor."

Marlowe breathed a sigh of relief, slumping back in his chair. "So, what now?"

"Now," Odio said, "we need to figure out what Diarke meant when he said my mother had been an 'unfortunate sacrifice'."

Pace stared at him before darting a glance at me. "Do you honestly think they killed their own sister?"

"I wouldn't be surprised." Odio scowled.

"What else did he say?" Pace pressed. "How did it come up?"

"He brought it up after saying that the Fates would tell Helle to take Hehven by force."

Pace stood suddenly, moving to the balcony doors, and staring out through the glass. I wanted to go to him—to comfort him—but I knew it wasn't the time. Pace had questioned the Fates since his first trip to the human world, and now it seemed his doubts were justified. I wished he was wrong, but the more we uncovered, the deeper the problem seemed to go.

"How could that even happen?" Marlowe asked, tearing his eyes from Pace's brooding silhouette. "I thought the Fates' orders were only for humans?"

"It seems there's a lot we don't know," Odio muttered. "I knew the king and Fin were up to something, but I never imagined . . ."

"Do you think Fin knows all of this?" I asked, the idea twisting my insides a little more than perhaps it should. Had they been conspiring together, laughing at me, for years? My skin heated at the thought.

"This whole time, it's been about the Fates," Pace said, hanging his head. "The conflicting orders they give Cupids and Chaos, the kill orders . . ."

"At least we know why Newbold never got any orders," Tiesa huffed.

I nodded. "Because the king would have intercepted them."

"No." Pace turned, the mid-morning light behind him casting his face in golden shadows. "Because the Fates work for Helle."

My breath caught. "How would that even work?"

"We need to ask the Fates."

Tiesa muttered something under her breath. "How could we possibly do that?"

"It's not as hard as you'd think," Pace admitted.

He moved back to his chair, but then paused, his eyes drifting to me as he seemed to make a choice. I gave him a small smile and he crossed the room, perching beside me on the bench seat. I leaned into him, exhaustion sweeping through me, and a little of the chill that had coated my bones retreating as his soft feathers brushed mine.

"I've visited the Fates once," he said. "I can do it again."

Odio's eyebrows rose, and I would have said he looked impressed. "Seriously?"

Pace nodded. "My brother let me work in the record room. I borrowed a cloak belonging to a Fated and sneaked in. There's a river that circles the centre of the isle and a boat takes you through a tunnel to the Fates themselves."

"And you think you could just go and confront them? What would you even say?"

"It's ridiculous." Tiesa baulked. "These are the very beings that created the world—that brought us all into existence—and you think you can just march in there and start pointing feathers?"

"They have the power to snuff your life out of existence on the spot," Odio said, shaking his head. "They're immortal beings."

"I don't know much about the Fates," Marlowe offered, "but this does sound like an unnecessarily dangerous idea."

Pace braced his hands on his knees as he looked around the room. "And what else do we do? Warn Hehven that Helle might attack at any minute? I don't think they're going to believe that."

"What about the marriage?" I asked carefully, my voice calm despite the rapid beating of my heart. "If we convince Dashuri to agree to it, I can go back to Helle and—"

"No," Pace barked. "I vowed you'd never have to go back there, and I intend on holding that promise."

"It's okay. I'll be fine. There might not be another way—"

"We'll find another way." His eyes burned into mine with such ferocity, I swallowed and looked away.

"This other way needs to happen soon," Tiesa said. "King Hadeon is expecting Sirain and Odio back in Helle the day after tomorrow."

I glanced up at Pace, my gaze trailing the sharp line of his jaw, and the soft curve of his plump lips. Every time I looked at him, it felt like it might be the last.

"We have to go back to Rakkaus," Pace admitted. "I need to talk to Dashuri. Maybe he can offer some insight or suggest a way we can speak to the Fates."

"You're not going anywhere today," Marlowe said, his voice firmer than I'd heard in a while. It was the voice of a leader, not a friend.

Odio's black wings flared as he straightened his spine. "Excuse me?"

Marlowe fixed him with a look that said he wouldn't be tolerating anything other than acceptance of his orders. "None of you slept more than a couple of hours before sneaking off to Newbold and I highly doubt you slept last night either."

Pace opened his mouth to protest, but closed it again, his jaw clenching. Marlowe was right. We'd barely slept before I'd woken to find Pace and Odio gone, and there had certainly been no sleep last night as we fought for our lives. The realisation sent exhaustion barrelling through me, my wings sagging, and as Tiesa stifled a yawn, I knew I wasn't the only one.

"Go. Sleep," Marlowe commanded. "Leave tonight. Then you'll have a full twenty-four hours to figure out what to do next."

Odio looked at me, a dark eyebrow raised in question, and I nodded. It was a good idea and probably the reason we couldn't think of a reasonable solution. I was so tired I could barely remember my own name.

"I'll have food and drink left outside your rooms for when you're ready," Marlowe said, getting to his feet and gesturing to the door. "I'll wake you after sunset."

Wearily, we all stood, Bertie grunting as we trailed out of the room and down the corridor towards the rooms we'd abandoned two nights before.

"Sleep well," Tiesa called as she reached her room and slipped inside.

I gave her closing door a wry smile. Even though I was more tired than I'd been in my entire life, my mind was a whirring mess of half-constructed thoughts and theories, none of them making a feather's worth of sense.

"Sweet dreams, Cousin," Odio said, reaching out and gently punching my arm as we reached his door. "Make sure you do actually try and sleep."

I grabbed hold of his braid and tugged lightly. "What else would I do?"

Odio's eyebrows lifted, and he looked pointedly at Pace.

My cheeks burned and I wrapped his hair around my fist and yanked. "Sleep well, Cousin."

His laughter sounded even after he'd closed the door and I tensed, my skin uncomfortably hot as I found myself unable to look at the Cupid standing behind me.

Arms slid around my waist, and I parted my folding wings

to allow Pace to press himself to my back, his breath warm against my neck.

"I can leave you to sleep if you want," he said, pressing a soft kiss behind my ear.

I wrapped my arms over his, holding him tight and tilting my neck to allow him better access. "I don't want you to leave."

Pace exhaled, and I felt his relief washing over me. "Good. Because I don't want to, either."

Stepping out of his arms, I took the three strides necessary to reach the room that had been assigned to me and opened the door. As Pace followed me inside, my skin suddenly felt too tight for my body, my lungs too small. Hoping he couldn't see my trembling limbs, I moved across the room and pulled the shutters closed, blocking out the low late-autumn sun.

Behind me, the rustle of fabric sounded, followed by a clunk that told me he'd removed his sword and dragon scale armour. My fingers shook as I pulled off my own sheet of armour, reaching for the harness holding my sword between my wings. As my fingers lingered on the metal buckle, I wondered when things had shifted. There'd been a time when I'd been confident in Pace's presence. A time when I'd brought him to his knees with a smirk on my lips.

I closed my eyes, unfastening the leather strap and letting my sword fall to the rug with a thud. That had been before. Before the Rites. Before I'd discovered my entire existence had been nothing more than a part of the king's devious plans. I'd bled, I'd starved, and I'd been stripped of the confidence growing up as heir had instilled me with. Realising the world was more complex, and that I was capable of more than lust and exhilaration, had shaken me to my core, and I wasn't sure who I was anymore.

"Hey," Pace said at my shoulder, his fingers gently skimming the arches of my wings. "What's wrong?"

Turning around, I looked up at him, wondering if he felt the same. "I was just thinking."

"Dangerous."

"I'm not the same Chaos you fell for. You do realise that, right?"

The grin faded from Pace's face. "I know, and I'm glad."

"Oh?"

He took my hands and held them between us. "You were always strong. But now your strength is borne of experience and pain. You are who you are because of what we've been through together."

I stared up at him, processing his words, but then he bit his lip with a smirk.

"Plus, you're a lot nicer now."

I gasped and tried to thump his chest, but he held me firm, his eyes gleaming.

"Anyway," he continued. "I'm not the same either. The Cupid you met at The Crossing was lost and reckless. I was searching for something, and I hurt a lot of people in the process."

I dropped my gaze, my breath sharp in my lungs. He'd hurt people because of me. The choices he'd made because of me.

"No," he said softly, knocking our hands against my chin, forcing my head up. "I know what you're thinking, and that's not what I mean. I was searching for you, Sirain."

"Your life would be a lot simpler if you hadn't found me," I whispered.

"Not true. Like Diarke said; all of this was planned long before our births. The fact that we're caught in the middle of the storm doesn't mean we caused it."

I opened my mouth to argue, but Pace leaned down and stole my words with a kiss. Gently pushing me back against the window, my fingers gripped the front of his shirt as he parted my lips, and I moaned at the soft warmth of his tongue against mine. His answering rumble set fire to my blood.

Pace's fingers swept under my wings, unfastening my shirt, and my breath caught as he pulled it free. His eyes burned like molten gold as he tugged off his own shirt, casting it to the side, his heated gaze never once leaving mine. Cupping my face in his hands, he leaned in, pressing tender kisses to my forehead, my cheeks, my nose and finally my mouth.

I lost all sense of time and place as desire took hold. Shedding our remaining layers, my mouth and hands took everything they could, as though I might never touch or taste him again.

Pace lifted me, walking us to the bed, and I clung to him; my fingers knotted in his hair as I kissed my way along his jaw. Placing me down gently, his broad chest heaved as he moved over me, the chiselled dips and grooves of his torso gleaming with the heat of our embrace, and my body thrummed with anticipation.

Loving Pace was being swept up by a storm. The white of his hair and wings was silver as rain clouds in the darkened room, and the kisses he trailed along my bare flesh struck like lightning against my heart. I reached for him, my name a rumble of thunder on his lips, and allowed myself to be taken by the force of his passion until all thoughts of what lay ahead had been drowned or swept away.

As much as I tried not to think about it, a part of me wondered whether our shared bliss would always be pierced by a shard of fear. Even afterwards, lying warm and spent in Pace's arms, the truth was cold and painful beneath it all. He hadn't realised and I hadn't the heart to tell him. Our paths would be parting sooner than he thought, and there was nothing either of us could do about it.

50
Pace

A punch in the face from Odio would have been less painful. I stared at Sirain, the awful truth pinching her features. How had I been so foolish? How could I not have realised? A frustrated roar tore from my aching lungs before I could stop it and I clenched my fists in an effort not to pick up the nearest piece of furniture and smash it against the wall. The Crossing. The Fated Crossing, after everything, would be the thing to tear us apart.

When Marlowe had knocked on the door, waking us, a wave of blissful happiness had crested over me as I pulled Sirain's warm body against mine, inhaling her scent and relishing the feel of her. Being with her was everything, and the knowledge that she'd be there every time I woke, had filled me with such throat-choking happiness, I'd thought I'd burst.

Then my entire world had crashed in on itself.

"It'll be okay," Sirain soothed. She reached out and tentatively placed a hand on my arm.

Dread coursed through my veins with such ferocity I couldn't think straight. Just the idea of heading into The Crossing together only to be wrenched apart was enough to make my blood run cold.

"You have to stay here," I said, turning to her.

"Excuse me?"

"It's too dangerous." I shook my head. "You can't go back to Helle."

Sirain slid out of bed, pulling on her clothes, and I watched, measuring the annoyance in her movements.

"Why are you angry?" I asked, reaching for my own clothes.

Shaking her head, she grabbed her sword from where it had been abandoned and strode to the door.

Muttering a curse under my breath, I finished dressing and chased after her.

"What's wrong?" Tiesa asked, jumping to her feet as Sirain stormed into the main room, with me close behind.

As the humans and Odio also got to their feet, I realised we were the last ones to arrive.

"Sirain is annoyed that I'm asking her to stay safe, I think," I said, tucking in my shirt and running my fingers through my hair in an attempt to tame it.

"No." Sirain rounded on me. "I'm annoyed that you think hiding is even an option."

"It's not hiding."

"It is."

Odio stood and moved to stand beside his cousin. "Does someone want to explain what's going on?"

"The Crossing." I groaned. "I didn't even think."

"What about The Crossing?" Shanti asked.

I offered a weak smile and crossed the room to greet them. Both women knocked my hand away as I held it out, pulling me into a hug instead as Marlowe smirked over their shoulders.

"The Crossing separates Cupids and Chaos," Sirain supplied as Marlowe clasped my shoulder.

"Which means the four of us can enter it together, but once inside, it will force Sirain and Odio towards Helle and me and Tiesa towards Hehven."

My words hung in the air, and I sank down onto a chair as a

fresh wave of frustration rolled over me. Perhaps I'd known all along but hadn't wanted to face it. It had been a long time since Sirain and I had entered The Crossing together.

Holding my head in my hands, I didn't bother suppressing the groan that built in my throat. I was sick of feeling helpless. It seemed no matter what I did, the odds were always stacked against us. I'd blindly promised Sirain that she would never need to return to Helle, without considering it was never within my power.

"You're welcome to stay here," Marlowe said, and my chest tightened at the offer.

"Please?" I tried.

"I can't hide out here in the human world. What do you think will happen when I don't return to Helle? I know you care about me, Pace, but my life is not worth more than Kwellen's, and the king won't hesitate in executing him if I don't return with the promise of an engagement."

I stared at her, my heart in my throat, trying to decide which part of her statement to respond to first. Tiesa started to speak, but I stood and crossed the room, placing my hands on Sirain's shoulders.

"First of all, I more than care about you. Second of all, I don't think anyone's life is worth more than anyone else's and you know that. I just want to protect you from them."

"I'll keep her safe," Odio promised, pressing a hand to my shoulder. "When we arrive back in Helle, we'll head straight for the tunnel and meet you back in Rakkaus. Think of it as a small detour."

Sirain nodded, her eyes a glittering purple under the flames lighting the room. "We're just taking the scenic route, Pace. There's nothing to protect me from."

I closed my eyes, trying to make peace with the decision and failing miserably. Fear had gripped my heart and no matter how hard I tried, I couldn't pry it free.

She pressed a kiss to my lips. "I'll be okay."

Resting my head against hers, I wrapped her in my arms and hoped she was right.

Even though I thought I'd been prepared for it, having Sirain's hand ripped from mine as the swirling lights enveloped us had still taken me by surprise. As soon as Tiesa and I emerged in Hehven, I flew as fast as my wings could carry me. All my thoughts were consumed with Sirain, and every pounding beat of my heart was a stark reminder of each second she spent in Helle.

By the time I landed in Rakkaus, my lungs were on fire and my wings aching. I barely acknowledged the Hands who hurriedly pushed the door open, standing back to make way for me. Tiesa called my name, but I couldn't slow. Striding through the house, I made my way down the corridor to the room I knew housed the entrance to the tunnel connecting our worlds.

"She won't be here yet," Tiesa said, her breathing ragged as she jogged to keep up with me. "You know that, right?"

I did know that. The tunnel was long, on top of the flight they'd have to take to the northern reaches of Helle, but that knowledge did nothing to slow me. I pushed open the doors to the holding room, barely pausing before slamming my hand into the final door, causing it to open with so much force it banged against the wall. One of Caitland's brothers was guarding the ancient door to the tunnel, and he jumped up, his blade drawn and his eyes wide as I burst into the room.

Even before I looked around, I knew she wasn't there. I knew it was impossible for her to have arrived, but my heart still sank.

"What in all that's Fated is going on?"

I turned to find Lord Rakkaus staring between me and

Tiesa, his eyes wide. Dashuri stood beside him, his face unreadable as he looked us both over.

"Sorry," I muttered. "I was hoping . . ."

"Will you give us a minute please, Lord Rakkaus?" Dashuri asked, an apologetic smile on his face.

The elderly lord sniffed, but inclined his head in acceptance, gesturing for his son to follow him out. Once we were alone, my brother sank onto a chair and stared at us for a moment before scrubbing a hand over his face.

"You're alive." He exhaled, then seemed to shake the relief from his shoulders as he sat forward. "What happened?"

My gaze flitted to the door again, my fingers itching to heave it open and race towards her. Perhaps I could meet her halfway. What if something had happened to her?

"Pace?" Dash tried again. "What happened?"

Fingers gripped my arm and I blinked, finding Tiesa pulling me to a chair and shoving me down into it.

"Focus," she said firmly. "She's okay."

Swallowing hard, I pressed my fingers to my eyes before taking a deep breath and explaining what we'd discovered. I might have glossed over the fact that we'd all almost died, focusing instead on King Hadeon's brother and what he'd said about the Fates.

Dashuri stared at me as though I'd spouted another head. "That's preposterous."

"It's true," Tiesa assured him.

Dash stared at us a moment longer before getting to his feet and turning away, his fingers pressing to his temples.

"I know it's a lot," I said slowly.

A cold, harsh laugh burst from my brother. "It's more than a lot. Where is Sirain now?"

"We were separated at The Crossing." My chest contracted and I glanced over my shoulder at the door. "She should be here soon."

Dashuri turned, his face set in the dismissive scowl I was so used to. "How could Helle take us by force? The Fates would never allow such a thing."

Sirain's words were etched like a brand across my mind. What if the Fates answer to the king? The idea was as terrifying as it was impossible, but the niggling feeling that had lived in my chest since I first saw Odio contradict Dariel's arrow persisted.

"Hadeon's brother seemed fairly certain that the Fates would command it," I said.

"Ridiculous," Dashuri huffed. "The Fates only give orders for the humans, not us."

"But something's wrong with the Fates. You know that. I showed you the illustration. They don't look—"

"That means nothing," he snapped. "That can be explained."

I stood, frustration curling my fingers. "What about the fact that the Fated can see all four of them? You can't dispute that. What if Hadeon did something to the Fates? What if he's controlling them somehow?"

Dashuri stared at me for a moment, his expression blank. Then he started laughing.

Anger heaved in my chest, and I opened my mouth, ready to take a step towards him, but Tiesa stood, gripping hold of my arm.

"It's not easy." Her eyes searched mine, willing me to understand. "Trust me. To doubt the beings you've followed your entire life? It's a lot."

I stared down at her, my anger dissipating a little. She was talking from experience. I'd dragged her into this against her will, yet she'd stood by me, faced with questioning everything she stood for. Nodding, I forced myself to sit back down.

"Your Majesty?" Tiesa said. "Please sit. Let me tell you everything that transpired while we were away."

Shaking his head, Dashuri swiped at his eyes and sank onto a chair.

As Tiesa recounted the past few days, I struggled to take my attention from the door. How far away was the tunnel from where they'd arrived in Helle? How long was the tunnel? Sirain had told me it was high and wide enough to fly through most of it, but I didn't know more than that. We'd been back for almost two hours.

A knock sounded at the door to the holding room and Tiesa paused, looking at me in question.

"It will be refreshments, no doubt," Dash said. "Come in."

The door opened and Caitland stepped inside, balancing a tray laden with tea and food. My brother leapt to his feet with a speed I didn't know he was capable of and took it from her. I blinked, sharing a look with Tiesa, as he placed it on the table.

"Thank you, Your Majesty," Caitland said, averting her eyes.

"We've spoken about this," my brother said gently. "Call me Dashuri."

I turned to Tiesa, my eyes wide and she shrugged, fighting to keep the grin from her face.

"I'm glad to see you returned safely," Caitland said, pulling my attention.

I smiled. "Well, I did promise Dash."

My brother grumbled at the nickname but set about pouring tea instead of correcting me. I stared, wondering if I'd ever witnessed my brother pouring his own tea before.

Caitland curtseyed, making to excuse herself, but Dash stood, gesturing at the table.

"Why don't you stay?" he said. "You know everything that's going on, anyway. Tiesa was just filling me in on what occurred in the human world."

I shrugged, offering Caitland a reassuring smile, and as she took a seat beside him.

Tiesa picked up a cup of tea, glancing at me briefly, before continuing where she'd left off. "The Midnight Queen now has control of Newbold, which means the human war is over."

Dash reached for some sort of sponge cake and took a bite. "Good."

Glancing at the door once more, I circled back round to the issue at hand. "I want to visit the Fates."

Dash spluttered on his mouthful of cake, crumbs flying, and I tossed him a napkin. "You don't want to visit the Fates, Pace," he said, swiping at his mouth. "You want to accuse them."

"That's what I said," Tiesa muttered, sipping her tea.

I shot her a look before turning back to my brother. "Something is amiss with the Fates, and the only way we're going to get answers is by asking them directly."

Dash opened his mouth to speak, but his words were drowned out by frantic hammering against the door to the tunnel. I leapt from my seat and wrenched it open to find my worst fears realised.

Odio stumbled into the room, breathing hard, his dark hair slicked to his pale skin with sweat. "Ambush," he gasped.

My stomach rolled, my breathing quickening as I pushed my hands through my hair. "Where's Sirain?"

Tiesa handed Odio a glass of water and he gulped it down, swiping at his forehead with the back of his hand.

"There were Hands guarding The Crossing," he said, staring at the empty glass. "It was like they were expecting us."

Tiesa gasped. "Someone must have told Hadeon what happened in Newbold."

I rushed forward, fisting the front of Odio's shirt. The glass fell to the floor, shattering as I hauled him against the wall. "Where. Is. Sirain?"

Odio snarled, shoving against me, but I pushed harder, forcing his wings to splay behind him. "They took her."

My heart dropped into my stomach, and I let go. Odio

planted both hands against my chest and shoved me so hard, I stumbled backwards, knocking against the table, sending cups spilling over the surface. Rage roaring in my ears, I stepped forward again, but Dashuri and Tiesa grabbed hold of me, pulling me back.

"Don't you ever come at me like that again, Cupid," Odio barked. "You don't think I tried to protect her? You don't think I fought?"

I stopped straining against my brother's grip and looked at the Chaos. In my desperation to find out about Sirain, I hadn't noticed the blood crusting the arch of his wing or the slices along his arm.

"They're already healing," he muttered, following my gaze and tapping the dragon scales he still wore over his chest.

"What happened?" I croaked out, my gaze still flitting towards the door as though she might still appear. I should never have let her go. I should have made her stay.

Odio flexed his wings with a wince, shooting me a glare, then sat down beside Tiesa, leaning his elbows on the table. "Like I said, they were waiting when we arrived through The Crossing. We tried to out fly them, but they would have only followed us to the tunnel. I tried to distract them, fighting them off while Sirain escaped, but they were more focused on her than me. After a few minutes, it became clear they'd been told to capture her and kill me." He shook his head, rubbing his hands over his face. "Of course, as soon as Sirain realised this, she surrendered. She told me to go."

I turned away, resting my head against the wall as I tried to calm myself. There was nothing he could have done. I realised that. Even so, I wanted to scream at him that he shouldn't have left her, that he should have tried harder.

"I'm going after her," I said, pushing away from the wall.

Dash leapt up and stood in front of the door, blocking my way. "You most certainly are not."

I glared at him, anger pulsing in my blood. "Don't make me move you, Brother."

"Pace," Tiesa said, shoving against my chest until I looked at her. "You know you can't go."

I turned back to my brother, advancing in a way that made him flinch, but to his credit, he held his ground. "Why not?"

"Because you're the Fated second prince," Odio snapped, pushing to his feet. "Because you need to go and ask the Fates what they're playing at."

My jaw clenched as I stared at him. "I can't just leave her with him. You know what he's like. What he's capable of."

"I do," he said, crossing to me. "Which is why I'm going to go back and get her out. I only came here first because I knew it's what she would have wanted me to do. That you'd be losing your mind wondering where she was."

"You think you can get her out by yourself?"

"He won't be by himself," Tiesa said. "I'll go with him."

Dashuri swore under his breath and returned to the table, where Caitland was watching the proceedings with wide silver eyes.

"You can't go to Helle." I sighed. "Your wings and hair would make you a target from miles away."

"I'll wear a cloak," she said. "And I'll darken my wings. Ash or charcoal will do the job."

I didn't miss the wince as she suggested it, knowing the pride she felt about her pristine white feathers. "It's too dangerous, Tiesa."

"Everything about this is dangerous," she said. "We're way past dangerous."

"If it looks like we won't be able to do it, we'll come back," Odio assured me. "I won't risk Tiesa, I swear it."

I shook my head, but my friend fixed me with a look that told me she'd be leaving no matter what I said. My shoulders sagged and I looked away in defeat.

"I'll go and find you a cloak and something to blacken your feathers," Caitland said, getting to her feet.

I gripped Tiesa's shoulders, my chest so tight I could barely breathe. "I'm so sorry for dragging you into this."

She looked up at me, her eyebrows raised. "This isn't you anymore, Pace. You were right. Things are going on that are so much bigger than any of us and although your actions might have been the catalyst to discovering them, none of this is your fault."

I tried to take heart at her words, but I couldn't. Instead, I found myself wandering to the open doorway and peering into the dark tunnel beyond.

"Pace?" Dashuri warned.

"I'm just looking," I muttered. "Are you coming?"

"Where?"

I looked at my brother, who was eyeing the tunnel warily, as though I was suggesting we go picnicking in Helle. "To the Isle of the Fates."

Relief flickered across his features until the reality of my words sank in, and he sighed. "Yes. I suppose I am."

"Although," Tiesa said, frowning. "If the Fates are going to strike you dead on the spot, maybe it's better if the crown prince isn't there."

"Tee." I groaned. "Seriously?"

Dash stood and dusted off his pristine robes, lifting his chin. "If I demand an audience with the Fates, we have a better chance than you just sneaking in."

I raised my eyebrows, but nodded in agreement. "Then what are we waiting for?"

51
Sirain

Wearing my dragon scales beneath my shirt had been a last-minute decision before leaving the Wendell Islands. I hadn't wanted to worry Pace, having spent our final hour together convincing him I would be safe; so, to quieten the little voice in the back of my head, I'd hidden the scales. When we'd burst through the lights of The Crossing, I'd quickly discovered I'd made the right choice. I wrapped my arms around myself, wishing my last-minute decision had also included a jacket.

Leaning my head back against the icy stone wall, I wondered whether the sun had risen outside. It shouldn't have been a surprise that the king would deem it fit to throw me in the dungeon, but then, I'd been shocked we hadn't both been shot on sight. I sighed, wondering whether Odio had made it back to Rakkaus.

"What are you sighing about?" Kwellen asked. "Is it the quality of the breakfast or the lumpy bed?"

I glowered at him through the wall, even though he couldn't see me. Another kick in the wing, courtesy of the king. He'd put me in the cell next to my best friend, but not in front of him, so we couldn't see each other. Even though he'd assured me he was okay, I wouldn't believe it until I saw it with my own eyes.

I'd considered passing him the dragon scales, but if I dropped them, they'd be discovered, and I couldn't risk that.

At the sound of footsteps echoing against the damp stone, I curled tighter into the shadows. The Hands who'd accosted me had deposited me in here and then left without a word. It had been hours since and I wondered how long it would be before my family paid me a visit. I hoped against hope the approaching Chaos was a guard.

"Ah, Sister."

I groaned. No such luck.

"What?" Fin said, coming to a stop in front of my cell. "Not pleased to see me? After all, we've all been so worried."

"Oh, I'm sure," I muttered.

Fin kicked at some hay that had fallen between the bars, wrinkling his nose. "You've been a very naughty Chaos. Father destroyed two sitting rooms and burned all the tapestries in the throne room when he found out what you'd done."

My heart stilled in my chest, a fresh layer of ice coating my skin. "What are you talking about?"

"Don't play stupid," Fin snapped. "Father knows exactly what you've been up to. Instead of worming your way into that pompous Cupid's bed, you've been off meddling with the humans."

I swallowed, willing my face to stay neutral. "I still don't know what you're talking about."

"Why you have to make things so difficult, I have no idea," he continued, leaning against the bars, and inspecting his nails. "All you had to do was seduce the crown prince and you could have waltzed off into the sunset together."

I bit down on my tongue hard enough to draw blood, refusing to rise to his baiting.

"You're lucky Father hasn't been down to see you yet," he said, glancing into Kwellen's cell with a bored expression. "It's probably the only reason you're still alive."

Another set of footsteps sounded on the stairs and despite my best efforts not to react, I pressed myself against the wall, my heart pounding. When a Hand stepped into view, I exhaled in relief.

"Your Majesty," the Hand said, her eyes wide at seeing the second prince in the dungeons. "Apologies for interrupting. I was just bringing Princess Si—the prisoner—some food."

Fin peered down his nose at the guard, his lip curling up at whatever was in the bowls she carried. "Leave them with me. I'll make sure she gets them."

To her credit, the Hand hesitated for the briefest second before placing the metal bowls on the floor and walking away. Fin leaned silently against the bars until the footsteps completely faded away. When he turned to me again, the hatred in his eyes pierced my chest, halting my breath.

"Your days are numbered, Sister," he hissed. "Best enjoy what's left."

He turned to leave, his dark robes swishing against the floor, and just as I thought he might forget about the food and water, he kicked both bowls over, stomping his foot down on the bread and grinding it into the stone.

As soon as his footsteps faded away, I exhaled. I wouldn't have risked touching the food anyway, but I might have been tempted by the water.

"You okay?" Kwellen asked.

"I've survived worse."

A soft chuckle reached me through the wall. "Yeah, you have."

Smiling, I closed my eyes and thought over the world shattering events of the last few days. It seemed like a lifetime ago that I'd arrived in Rakkaus, unable to look Pace in the eye for fear of shattering the final fragile fragments of my heart. I hoped for the thousandth time that Odio had made it. The thought of Pace waiting for my return caused an ache in my chest more painful than the arrow that had almost ended my life. I could feel his rage. His hopelessness. It was mirrored by my own.

Pushing the image away, I focused on the memory of my hair wrapped around his fingers. The feel of his body against mine and the sound of my name on his lips.

"You know, if he wanted you dead, they'd have done it already."

I opened my eyes and frowned, annoyed at being pulled from the thoughts keeping me warm. "Thanks, friend."

Any further seething remarks were cut short by the sound of approaching footsteps. I needed no warning this time. The slow, measured pace, each step ringing with powerful purpose, was one I'd learnt to recognise, and fear.

Scrambling to my feet, I lifted my chin and wings. If I had any chance of making it out of here alive, I couldn't afford to show weakness. King Hadeon swept in front of the cell, the dim light casting his features in sharp angles.

"Your Majesty," I said, bowing before him to hide the grimace the bitter words brought to my mouth.

The king said nothing and when I straightened, I found him staring at me, his expression unreadable. I stood, waiting, knowing not to press him. He'd speak when he wanted to. I tried to stand still, without fidgeting—a statue under his unseeing stare. Just when my willpower started to falter, he spoke.

"You murdered my brother."

"The Midnight Queen killed your brother."

His eyes snapped to mine, and I sucked in a breath. "Was it worth it?"

"Was what worth it?" I asked, my voice little more than a whisper.

"Saving your father."

My skin was ice cold, but a bead of sweat trailed the length of my spine and I fought off a shudder. There was no right answer, so I said nothing.

"The reason you're not dead," he said when he realised I wasn't going to reply, "is because I haven't yet decided if you can be of use to me."

I stared at him, wondering what he knew. Diarke, or Engano, whatever his name was, must have been communicating with Helle somehow, but I hadn't considered the king would discover what had transpired in Newbold so quickly. How much he knew, however, could mean a world of difference.

"I'll do whatever I can," I said, lowering my gaze.

"I thought I'd instilled enough fear in you that you wouldn't disobey me, yet you still thought you could run away from Hehven, and I wouldn't notice." The king stepped closer to the bars, barely concealed rage apparent in his white knuckles and the tension in his jaw. "Perhaps you think my threats are empty?"

My pulse rocketed as he leaned away from the bars, peering into the cell next door. No.

"Is that why you chose to leave this one behind?" he sneered. "He's the obvious choice, of course. But did you truly think I wouldn't kill him if you failed me?"

Fear gripped my heart, squeezing until I couldn't breathe. "I haven't failed you," I rasped. "I can still get you the engagement."

"How?"

"He likes me," I said, stepping closer. "We spent time together. He even let me hold his hand, but then he got called away. That's when I left. If I went back, I know he'd agree."

I almost said 'please' but swallowed it down at the last second, knowing it would be the word that unleashed the king's fury. Please was ultimate weakness. Hadeons didn't say please. They took what they wanted when they wanted it.

"My brother's death has altered things," he said. "But humans are weak. They still need to be controlled."

The king fixed me with his dark eyes, and I stood tall before him.

"I will consider your role in things," he said, his lip curling as he looked me up and down. "I will also be clipping your wings before sending you back. I'm sure the Cupid prince won't care if you can fly or not."

"No!" All bravado evaporated as his words hit home and I rushed forward, falling to my knees before him. My mouth opened and closed with a thousand pleas. All of them were sure to have dealt me a worse hand, so I stayed on the ground before him, wilting under the disgust in his gaze.

He turned, heading back to the stairs, and my stomach rolled. I had to fly. If he took my ability to fly . . . I clutched at my stomach, bile rising in my throat.

"Oh, and I almost forgot," the king's voice carried down the stairs, even as he continued to climb. "Kwellen dies tonight."

52
Pace

When the towering stone wings adorning the entrance to the Isle of the Fates peered through the mist, I had the urge to smash them to pieces. I didn't care whether the beings inside were responsible for all life; I only cared that they had destroyed the lives of those I cared about.

Dawn had only just broken, and peering over my shoulder, as though I might see Helle on the other side of the invisible barrier separating the sea, I itched to turn around. Caitland had done an incredible job of making Tiesa's wings look black. She could do the same to me. I could go and help.

"Pace," Dashuri said, pulling my attention. "They'll be fine."

"You can't know that," I said, as we came in to land.

Dash flexed his wings before folding them. "You all just survived the human war. Surely this is no more dangerous?"

"You don't understand." I stared at him, trying to find the words to explain. "King Hadeon is nothing like the Chaos you met with our parents. He's cruel and ruthless. Murdering his own flesh and blood is something he'd do without a second thought."

Dash stared back at me, his gold eyes narrowing. "That may be true, but he raised Sirain. He's Odio's uncle. It may be dangerous territory, but it's familiar territory. You went to Newbold blindly. Odio knows Helle. He knows the castle. Have faith."

"That actually does make sense." A little of my tension eased at my brother's words, and I sighed. "Thank you."

Dash took a stride towards the archway, then stopped. "Before you left, you said that things were over between you and Sirain."

I opened my mouth, but he turned to face me, holding up a hand to halt my explanation.

"It's clear you've resolved whatever happened between you. Is it serious?"

I nodded.

"And you love her?"

"More than anything in this Fated world."

"Okay." He exhaled and continued towards the archway. "Then let's go and accuse the most powerful beings in existence of being corrupt."

Smirking at his tone, I didn't think it wise to mention that the Fates probably already knew we were here and what was going to happen.

We walked down the dark passageway in silence, led as always by equally silent Fated. Staring at the back of their cloaked heads, I wondered what they'd think if they knew the reason we were there. Would the Fates be angered enough to smite us? Could they feel emotion? My stomach lurched at the idea that we might not leave this place, but was quickly followed by a wave of sadness as I realised it meant Amani would have to take the throne. I wouldn't have wished that burden on anyone, but there was no other way.

The Fated pushed open the doors and I immediately spotted Amare's telltale gold-tipped feathers. Evidently, so did Dash, as he headed straight for her.

She looked up as we approached, her dark blue eyes wide beneath her hood. "You're here."

I took a breath, my eyes already looking towards the record room, to suggest we go somewhere private to talk, but Dashuri's voice rang out loud enough for all to hear.

"I demand an audience with the Fates."

The room had already been quiet, but the silence that followed my brother's words was deafening.

"Your Majesty?" Amare said, her gaze flitting between us. "What do you mean?"

"I mean, I want to speak to the Fates."

The Fated had halted in whatever they were doing, beginning to gather around us curiously. My fingers flexed at my side, but of course, there was no weapon to grab hold of. Not that I would have slain my own people.

Flashes of bodies impaled on my blade flickered through my mind, their grunts and death rattles sounding over and over. I blinked, pushing it away. I couldn't linger on the lives I'd taken. I'd done it to protect Sirain. To protect my friends. I'd do it again if I had to.

One of the Fated stepped forward, tall and broad, his hood shadowing his face. "No one speaks to the Fates."

My gaze drifted to the boat tethered to the side.

"As Crown Prince," Dashuri continued, drawing himself up to his full height. "I demand an audience with them. Whether they deign to speak to me is up to them."

A low murmuring rippled amongst the hooded Cupids, and I caught Amare's eye, pleading. She knew what this was about, had been implicit in most of it, but asking her to speak out for us publicly was another thing entirely.

"Let them go," Amare said, holding my gaze. "As Prince Dashuri said, it's up to the Fates whether they answer."

The murmuring started up again, louder this time, and I

wondered whether such a commotion had ever been had in all the Isle's history.

"I'll go with them," she said. "To make sure they hold to the rules."

This seemed to appease the Fated, although bursts of whispers continued even as Amare led the way to the boat. Dashuri eyed it warily, but I gestured for him to climb in.

"It's not as bad as it looks."

"I know," he muttered, his hands gripping the sides as he took his seat. "I've done this before, you know."

Amare looked at me with narrowed eyes from where she was already seated. "How do you know what it's like, Pace?"

I turned away, reaching for the rope, and tugging it free. Dashuri had barely taken his seat when the current swept us away into the tunnel. Sitting in the pitch black, I was grateful for the moment's reprise it gave me from my brother's and cousin's scorching looks. I wondered whether Dashuri had already planned what he was going to say to the Fates. I knew I certainly hadn't. It still felt like a dream. How does one start a conversation with an ethereal immortal being?

The light began to glow at the end of the tunnel, and I gripped the edge of the boat as it slowed, easing us out into the cave. All three of us tensed as we neared the edge of the rocks, and I could barely hear my own thoughts over the pounding of my heart.

"The boat won't stop," Amare said.

I turned to Dashuri, who was staring ahead, his expression frozen. "How did you do your captain thing?"

"What?" He blinked, turning to me.

"When you were initiated as leader of the captains," I pressed. "How did you do it?"

Dash frowned as he tried to remember. "There's a mooring post on the opposite side of the river. The Fated secured it there and we climbed out."

I peered ahead, trying to spot the mooring post he was referring to. It would mean we'd be on the opposite side to the Fates, though, and I planned on being a lot more up close and personal.

"I have an idea." Taking hold of the rope, I crouched, ready, as the boat approached the golden dish containing the orders.

Amare nodded, latching onto my plan, and as we drew close, she reached out and grabbed the plinth. I lurched forward, wrapping the rope around it, and tugging it tight. The boat jolted, like it was trying to free itself, so I climbed out onto the rocky ledge before it could. I held out a hand to help Amare up onto the platform as Dash clambered out beside her.

My heart slammed against my ribs with enough force it vibrated down my wings as I turned to face the beings who held all the answers. I'd forgotten how small they were, and as we stood before them, they stiffened, taking a tentative step backwards.

An icy chill ran over my skin. "The Fates shouldn't be scared of us," I murmured, reaching out to grab hold of my brother's sleeve. "Right?"

Neither my brother nor Amare answered as we stared at the Fates, their white robes shimmering in the otherworldly blue light filtering down from above. I took another step forward and almost as one, the Fates retreated.

"We just want to talk to you," I explained, my eyes narrowing. "We mean you no harm."

I held up my hands, and one of them flinched. My heart in my throat, I whirled, looking at my brother and cousin. The beings who created the Fated world wouldn't flinch. I saw the doubt in their own faces and, emboldened, turned back to the small creatures.

"Why are you helping King Hadeon?" I asked, inching closer.

This time, they held their ground, but there was no

mistaking the trembling beneath their robes. Why were they so scared? Perhaps this was the closest they'd come to their creations since bringing them into existence.

"Please," I pressed. "The Hadeons say you plan to demand Helle declare war on Hehven. We want to know if that's true."

Amare let out a soft gasp behind me, and I winced. I'd planned on filling her in before we did this, but it had turned out Dash had other plans.

I was close enough to one of the Fates now, I could see the rapid rise and fall of its chest. Knowing I wouldn't get this chance again, that I'd come so far, I dropped to my knees before it.

"We just want answers," I pleaded, my head bowed. "Please."

Waiting, I listened to the sound of the Fate's harried breathing. Before I could think better of it, I lifted my head and stared up at the being who held our lives in their hands.

I froze, staring up into the wide terror-filled eyes of a child, their pale skin almost translucent beneath their hood. A whimper tore from their lips and my breath caught in my throat.

"Who are you?" I whispered.

The child shook their head, their lips pressed tightly together. Leaning back, I looked at the three others who were turned towards us, watching. My stomach clenched, fear squeezing my lungs as I slowly, carefully reached forward.

Behind me, someone made a pained noise. I couldn't be sure if it was Amare or Dashuri, but as I took hold of the Fate's hood and gently pushed it back, it didn't matter.

I fell backwards, my hands covering my mouth as I stared up at a small girl, no older than ten, her dark eyes shimmering with tears.

"He'll kill my family," she whispered, her voice little more than a rasp.

"Who are you?" I choked out, looking between them.

The other three moved forward, taking their own hoods in their hands, and pushing them off. Two boys and two girls, all with pale skin and dark eyes.

"Please don't let him kill them," one of the boys said, tears already tracking down his hollow cheeks.

Footsteps sounded behind me as Amare swept forward, taking the small boy's hands in hers.

"You're safe now," she said, although her own voice trembled. "We'll do what we can to protect your families, too. Where are they?"

"Nefret," one of the girls said.

"Devland," one of the boys replied.

I held up a hand. "Wait. Where are those places?"

The little girl in front of me sniffed, wiping her nose with the sleeve of her robe. "Helle."

"You're Chaos?"

Bile rose in my throat as all four nodded. He'd taken the wings of children. A cold sweat coated my brow and I stood and turned away, my stomach heaving, as Amare spoke to them in a low voice. Dashuri was still standing where I'd left him, his eyes wide and his mouth in a firm line.

"Do you see now?" I said, stepping to his side. "This is what King Hadeon is capable of. He's mutilated children for Fate's sake. Do you still think Tiesa and Odio are safe?"

I pushed my fingers through my hair, wanting nothing more than to be out of this Fateforsaken cave.

"Pace?"

My mind reeling, I turned back to my brother. "What?"

"Where are the real Fates?"

I stared at him, the hundreds of questions I had mirrored in his own golden eyes. "I don't know."

Amare walked over to us, her blue eyes shimmering with tears. "He keeps them trapped down here. Someone brings food once a day and they drink out of the river. They said they didn't know how long they've been down here, but it sounds like it might be a couple of years."

My breathing quickened, my hands clenched at my sides, as I silently vowed that one day soon, I would ensure King Hadeon got everything he was owed.

"Does that mean they've been giving out orders from Hadeon all this time?" Dash said, a sheen of sweat gleaming on his brow.

"Yes," I said. "We've all been playing his game without realising it."

"But only for the last couple of years," Dash said, hope lining his words. "He wouldn't be able to keep up the pretence for long. The children would grow, and . . ."

I closed my eyes as he trailed off, realising the sickening answer to his own question. How many children had Hadeon sacrificed since he and his brother started this?

"I need to speak to Mother," I said.

Dash opened his mouth to protest, then sighed. "You're right. We're living in a world without Fate. There's no way to hide this."

"Take the boat," Amare said. "Dash, tell the Fated what's happened and send the boat back around for us."

I glanced over at where the four children were huddled, their sharp cheekbones and dark circles causing a tremor of rage beneath my skin. "Look after them," I said to Amare.

She nodded and I climbed into the boat, waiting until Dash was seated beside me before releasing the rope and allowing the current to sweep us away.

As the darkness enveloped us, I held my head in my hands. I'd suspected something was amiss, but I never truly suspected the Fates were gone. I winced. The Fates were gone. How long had it been? Had Hadeon killed them? Could you kill an immortal being?

When we emerged from the tunnel, I met Dashuri's eye and almost winced at what I saw there. He'd believed so strongly, and now that faith had been shattered beyond anything he could have imagined.

"You were right," he said quietly as we approached the waiting line of curious Fated. "All this time."

Gathering the rope, I tied it around the post, swallowing hard. "I didn't want to be, Brother. I truly didn't."

My heartbeat was thunder in my chest as I reached out a hand to Dashuri, the wary silence of the watching Fated stifling in the echoing chamber. Lifting my chin and raising my wings, I tried to appear like our world hadn't just fallen apart at the seams—like I wasn't about to fly to the queen of Hehven and tell her we'd all been living a lie—like half of my heart wasn't on the other side of The Crossing.

My brother mirrored my stance and with a final nod, I turned and strode towards the door, the Fated parting before me. I'd wanted answers, and now I had them. Blowing out a steady breath, I waited until the heavy stone door closed behind me before breaking into a run.

53
Sirain

The stone floor was ice cold against my cheek, a sharp piece of hay digging into my skin, hard enough to draw blood. I groaned, wondering for a moment whether I'd passed out or fallen asleep.

"Sirain?"

I blinked, trying to focus on the voice calling to me.

"Sirain? For Fate's sake. Say something!"

All I could manage was a groan, but it seemed to satisfy Kwellen as he uttered an impressive stream of curses.

"Sorry." I moaned as I pushed myself upright. "I'm not sure what happened."

"The king said he was going to clip your wings and announced my execution. Then you went all quiet."

Rubbing a hand over my face, I stretched my limbs until they popped. "How long ago was that?"

"You think there's a clock down here? I don't know. Twenty minutes? Half an hour? A Fated lifetime."

I grimaced, my head pounding in a way that made me think I'd smacked it against the stone when I'd fallen. "Okay. Relax. Anyone would think you had hours left to live."

Kwellen snorted and I blinked back the tears, but they'd already started to fall.

"I'm sorry," I whispered. "I tried not to get you involved. I—"

"Shut it," Kwellen barked. "This is entirely my fault. I was the one who marched up to the sneering smallwing giving lip to the teacher and demanded to be friends."

I barked a laugh, despite the pain tearing me in two. We'd been ten years old, and I remembered it like it was yesterday. Our teacher had threatened to beat Odio for chatting during her lesson and I'd threatened to take the stick she was wielding and . . . Well, I was a creative child. When she'd said that she'd beat me too, no matter who my father was, Kwellen had marched over and stood at my side, daring the teacher to take on all three of us. He'd only joined the class that day and despite having never said a word to me before, I'd been equally bemused and impressed by the long-haired boy with one arm.

A sob broke free, and I tried too late to smother it with my arm.

"Sirain . . . It'll be okay."

"No, it won't," I snapped, tears streaming freely down my cheeks.

After everything, the thought of the king taking my friend's life was too much to bear. I stormed over to the bars and gripped hold of them, pulling and kicking at them until a ragged scream tore from my throat.

"Sirain."

Kwellen's voice was a cool caress, and I hated it. I hated that he was so calm when it was his life that was coming to an end too soon.

Footsteps sounded on the stairs again and I whimpered, scrambling around my cell, feeling in the corners, and pushing desperately against the stone as though I might find a way out or something, anything, that might help us. I had no way of knowing what time it was, and whether the approaching guard was for me or Kwellen, but I wouldn't let it get that far. If I could find a weapon . . .

The footsteps came to a halt.

Perhaps if I hadn't been so desperate, I'd have heard two sets of footsteps, because as I reluctantly turned around, I found two cloaked figures before my cell.

"Sirain?"

My breath halted in my throat and in the cell next door, I heard the rustling of feathers against the floor as Kwellen scrambled to his feet.

One of the cloaked figures pushed back their hood and I almost fell to my knees.

"Odio?"

He grinned, lifting a ring of keys from beneath his cloak. "Ready to get out of here, Cousin?"

I stared, doubting my own eyes. "How?"

"Does it matter?" the second figure said, pushing back her hood just enough to reveal brown skin and large green eyes. "Let's go."

Book 3 Coming Soon

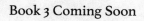

Pronunciation Guide & Origins

Name	Pronunciation	Meaning	Origin
Pace	PAY-ce (or PAH-chay)	Peace	Italy
Sirain	SIH-rain	Destroy	Philippines
Kwellen	KWELL-en	Torment	Netherlands
Dariel	DAH-ree-ell	Open	Old French
Odio	OH-dee-oh	Hate	Latin
Tiesa	tee-EH-sah	Truth	Latvia
Dragoste	DRA-ghost	Love	Romania
Hadeon	HAD-ee-on	Destroyer	Ukraine
Dashuri	da-SURE-ee	Love	Albania
Fin	FIN	End	France
Maluhia	ma-LU-hee-ah	Peaceful	Hawaii
Briga	BREE-gah	Argue	Portugal
Nemir	neh-MEER	Turmoil	Slovenia
Armastus	ar-MAS-tus	Love	Estonia
Amare	am-AH-ray	To love	Italy
Malin	MAL-in	Warrior	Old English
Amani	am-AHN-ee	Peace	Kenya

Cupids

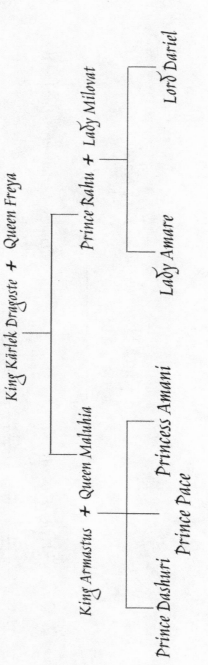

King Kärlek Dragoste + Queen Freya

Prince Rahu + Lady Milovat

Lady Amare

Lord Dariel

King Armastus + Queen Maluhia

Princess Amani

Prince Pace

Prince Dashuri

Chaos

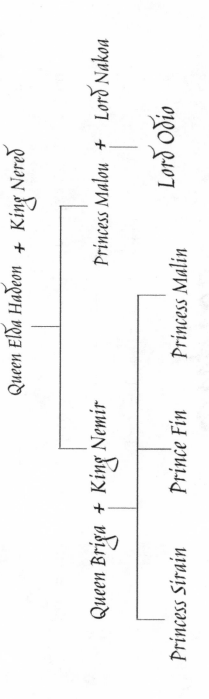

Queen Elda Hadeon + King Nered

Princess Malou + Lord Nakon

Lord Odio

Queen Briga + King Nemir

Princess Strain

Prince Fin

Princess Malin

ACKNOWLEDGMENTS

If you aren't annoyed with me enough to read on to this part, then thank you! I'm so glad you've stuck with Pace and Sirain to read the next part of their journey. I promise the end is coming soon. I can't promise it will be smooth, though . . .

Thank you to my anchors. My trident. My dream team. Miranda and Claire, I honestly don't know if I could do this without you both. Thank you for your patience, your imagination and your tolerance. You are literally the best.

Thank you to my Hands of Fate Street Team (HoFST), this book is dedicated to you. Thank you for your unwavering support and enthusiasm. Ali, Merrit, Danyel, Anshul, Meg, Lianne, Daisy, Michele, Chelsea, Hailee, Amanda, Lyra - Thank you. Let's do this one more time!

Thank you to my incredible proofreaders Gaelle and Natalie, not only for your eagle-eyes but your support and enthusiasm. I can't wait to show you what happens next! I would thank you, Lindsay, here too, but you always get so swept up in the story, you forget to look for errors! Thanks for being my number one fan. Love you.

Thank you to Emily Bowers for the incredible cover art and to Taire for making it into the stunning cover you see. Thank you to Tony for the beautiful portrait art throughout the book. It was a pleasure to work with you all - here's to more in the future!

CPSIA information can be obtained
at www.ICGtesting.com
Printed in the USA
BVHW040836270522
638301BV00011B/55/J